ANTONIUS
SON OF ROME

ANTONIUS

SON OF ROME

BROOK ALLEN

ISBN 978-1-7329585-0-0 (paperback)
Printed in the USA

To Carlton, who has supported me—body, soul, and wallet—
ever since I first had this crazy desire
to become a published author.

And in memory of my parents,
who always believed in my project.

REPUBLICAN ROME
CIRCA 71-50BC

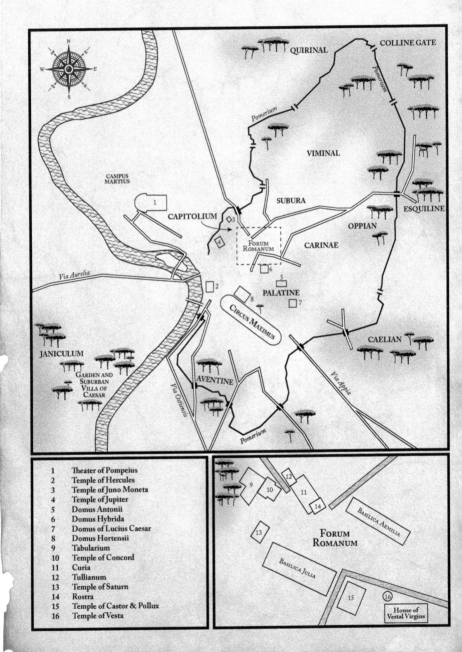

1. Theater of Pompeius
2. Temple of Hercules
3. Temple of Juno Moneta
4. Temple of Jupiter
5. Domus Antonii
6. Domus Hybrida
7. Domus of Lucius Caesar
8. Domus Hortensii
9. Tabularium
10. Temple of Concord
11. Curia
12. Tullianum
13. Temple of Saturn
14. Rostra
15. Temple of Castor & Pollux
16. Temple of Vesta

CHAPTER I
71 BC

FATHER WAS DEAD.

Eleven-year-old Marcus Antonius crouched against a column, hiding behind the peristyle shrubbery. Paralyzed in shock, his mind struggled to accept the news. A sun-dappled afternoon full of boyish laughter and games had ended suddenly, transforming into deep sadness and uncertainty. Unfamiliar feelings of loss, sorrow, and fear of the unknown made him breathe harder. He rocked slowly back and forth, tears burning his eyes.

He heard their voices again, and sat up, peering through a gap in the branches to where the adults were talking. Neither his mother, Julia Antonia, or Uncle Hybrida saw him.

Mamma sat motionless, staring at a wax tablet in her hands. Uncle fidgeted with the crimson stripe bordering his toga. He barked at a slave to bring them wine, then turned back to Mamma. "Your grief is mine, Julia. What can I do?"

"Nothing," she whispered.

"I always considered my brother to be among the best of men. Pity he bungled this mission. Sometimes there are sides to men one never sees until they enter politics and war. That's where true character arises."

The house slave reappeared, carrying a tray with two wine cups. "Ah," Hybrida sighed. "This'll dull the pain." Joining her on the old marble bench, he helped himself. After a long draw, he recalled wistfully, "Still, he was a good man in many ways, my brother."

Mamma took her cup, then tilted the vessel. Crimson liquid sprinkled onto the granite paving stones at her feet. From where he watched, Marcus swallowed hard. This was her first libation to Tata's spirit.

Marcus's eyes filled up again, so he squeezed them shut. He was fighting against a new, boiling stew of emotion. Silently, he prayed that Dis, God of the Underworld, would receive Tata.

"Yes, he was kind, but he had no mind for things that make men great," Mamma reasoned aloud. "He never even tried to teach his firstborn swordplay. He hired that former gladiator, Perseus, to train Marcus. Most fathers want some part of teaching their sons Roman ways, but not him."

Marcus frowned, wiping his face as grief turned into puzzlement. She shouldn't be saying that. It was immense fun learning to fight with a former arena champion.

"He spent far too much coin on such things," she went on, her voice rising in frustration.

Hybrida firmly grasped her elbow, halting her. "Shh—he loved you, Julia. He told me time and again. Say no more. You'll regret such words."

She removed her arm from his grasp and shook her head. "Leave me. I must gather my thoughts and tell the boys."

Tell the boys? Marcus looked about him, wondering where his younger brothers had gone. Then Uncle's voice caught his attention.

"You're distraught," Hybrida asserted. "I could speak with them myself if it's too painful."

Mamma shook her head. "No, it's my duty as their mother. But I'll need your assistance with the funeral. It can't be grand. We have next to nothing." She paused before adding, "You'll speak the eulogy, won't you?"

"Of course. His body should arrive within days, and perhaps the Julii—"

"No, I won't be beholden to Aurelia. Invite them to the banquet afterward, but I can't accept anything from that woman," she declared, shaking her head. "If these weren't such dreadful times. Only last winter I said, 'Either farm the land down in Misenum or sell it.' He never listened to sense."

Misenum? They had an old family home down there, far south of Rome. Marcus had only been there once, when he was barely old enough to remember. He couldn't recall Mamma and Tata arguing about the place. They were good at keeping disagreements private.

Uncle Hybrida swallowed another mouthful of wine, then cleared his throat. "There's something more."

Marcus frowned. The "something more" wasn't going to be something good.

"The Senate was enraged at his actions," Uncle Hybrida went on. "They have evidence he used force to requisition gold from the provinces he was supposed to oversee. Cicero complained he was nothing like our father, declaring him incompetent. The session ended with everyone demanding to know why he hadn't committed suicide. They declared his illness to be 'judgment from the gods.'"

Marcus's jaw sagged and his stomach lurched. The Senate wanted Tata to kill himself? Once more, his chest tightened, and here came the tears again.

Uncle Hybrida added, "And they've branded him with a new name, a derisive one. *Creticus*—'man of chalk.' Not just because he died in Crete."

"Meaning what, exactly?" Mamma questioned.

"That he was a nothing, not strong, I suppose; an entity easily erased from public record. Julia, the man was my brother. I thought I knew him, but what was he thinking? They say he treated with pirates, non-citizens no better than slaves. Sent by Rome to defeat them, he negotiates with them?" He shook his head sadly. "Despite honoring his spirit, I agree with the Senate. He made Rome appear weak, this family weaker still."

Marcus pondered the situation. With Tata gone, he was the oldest son and no longer a child. As heir, it would be his task to redeem the family's reputation from this disaster. But how? He was still too young to enter the Senate or become a military officer—though becoming a soldier had always been his dream.

Enough. If Uncle Hybrida and Mamma found him weeping like a girl, he'd feel ashamed.

Carefully, he scooted backward, away from the break in the branches. Eyes still wet with tears, he escaped into the colonnaded corridor. Once in his cubiculum, he flopped belly-down onto his sleeping couch, wiping his eyes and willing his weeping to end. Before he faced Mamma, he had to gain control over his emotions. When next she saw him, he didn't want her to see a boy, but a man.

After all, Marcus was growing. He was athletic and big-boned. Larger than other boys his age, wavy dark brown hair turned evenly over a broadening forehead. People were apt to say how his straight nose was like his grandfather's. Or how his brown eyes made girls stare. Yet it was his grin and laughter that always made Mamma smile.

Marcus rolled onto his back, his leather bulla tumbling onto the cushion next to his cheek. He'd worn the little good-luck charm since he was a baby. Mamma told him never to take it off. It protected him, she insisted. Heedless of her superstitions, he decided that if he was no longer a child, he didn't need good-luck charms.

Sitting up, he took a deep breath. His initial sorrow was over, and that was a good thing since he didn't want to shame himself with tears when returning his bulla to Mamma. On his way back to the courtyard, Marcus spied his three-year-old brother, Lucius, teetering dangerously at the edge of the family's fishpond. He vaulted nimbly over the hedge, grabbing Lucius by one arm. As he headed back toward Uncle Hybrida and Mamma, he lifted his little brother onto his shoulders.

"You'll need to be quiet," Marcus told him.

"Why?"

"Because Uncle Hybrida and Mamma are talking. They can't have little children interrupting. So don't say anything."

Fortunately, Lucius's response was obedience as Marcus rounded the corner of the peristyle garden.

Uncle Hybrida was leaning over Mamma now, his hands resting gently on her shoulders. His back was to his nephews, hiding them from her view.

"Listen to me, Julia," Uncle whispered. "You have three strong, healthy sons. Through them, you have the legacy of the Orator, which is a great one. Jupiter! The man was censor—the highest office one can attain. Rome will never forget his greatness. He was a good and moral man. I tell you, this will pass."

"Keep reminding me," she whispered.

Marcus watched sadly. From atop his shoulders, tiny Lucius remained surprisingly still and quiet. Even he sensed the weight of the family's misfortune.

"Did the Senate not consider that perhaps he *did* kill himself?" Mamma reasoned aloud. "It could've been an illness brought on by poison. There are other ways to die besides the sword."

Hybrida held out empty hands, slowly shaking his head. The acceptable suicide for a Roman general had always been by sword, so Marcus Antonius Creticus's memory was now subject to scorn.

Marcus chose that moment to make himself known. "Salve, Uncle."

Hybrida turned on his heel. Mamma craned her neck toward the voice.

Before she could speak, Marcus lifted Lucius from his shoulders and placed him next to his uncle. "Mamma, I overheard you and Uncle Hybrida talking."

"Then you know?"

He nodded, walking over to where she sat and removing the bulla from his neck. "Long ago, you gave this to me, saying it would protect me. But now Tata is gone, and I will have to be the one to take his place. I'm not just a boy any longer. So I give it back to you."

11

"You're too young—" she began, shaking her head.

Marcus silenced her gently by placing a finger upon her lips. "I am Tata's heir, and someday I'll do what I must to bring honor back to our domus." With that, he lifted the bulla and placed it around her neck.

Mamma looked up at Uncle Hybrida in wonder, then lifted the charm and gazed at it.

Uncle stepped forward and placed a big hand upon Marcus's shoulder. "Well said, boy," he murmured.

Mamma nodded, her breast rising and falling rapidly.

Tata had died in shame, but his son would rise in courage.

Marcus leaned his back against the fluted column, his body sliding down to the step above the black-and-white mosaic. "Gaius was with me until we stopped playing," he reported. "I don't know where he is now."

"Then we'll wait, won't we? In troubled times, one simply must breathe deeply and endure," Mamma whispered. She drew Lucius closer to her on her lap and pressed her lips to his head.

Troubled times?

Marcus had heard stories about how terrifying life was right before he was born. General Sulla, successor to the powerful autocrat Marius, had stormed Rome. Mamma always said he was just a puffed-up warlord. But he was a strong one, taking the city by force. Though he'd died around the time of Marcus's birth, the reprieve hadn't lasted long. Like a perfectly timed theatrical scene, Spartacus the gladiator entered and began a slave revolt that was ongoing. There was lots of talk about it in the baths, Forum markets, and here at the domus.

Spartacus had defeated Roman armies several times already. Indeed, he was trouble. But now Tata had been trouble too.

"Why did Tata try to make peace deals with pirates?" Marcus pried.

A boisterous noise interrupted before Mamma could answer. Unceremoniously bursting from the rear kitchen door, Gaius was bawling like a bear cub. Lucius covered his ears and screwed up his face.

Despite his sorrow, Marcus smiled, for he and Gaius were very close. Only three years separated them. Beneath his brother's dark, ruffled hair was a fleshy, freckled face that never failed in bringing good humor.

A one-eyed slave held him firmly by the arm.

"Let go of me, Cyclops!" Gaius exclaimed. "Take your filthy slave-hands away or—"

"That'll do, Gaius," Mamma ordered, calmly but firmly.

Gaius lowered his volume to a whimper, but he still squirmed, trying to escape the slave's hold.

Castor was the slave. Near Marcus's age, he was already a capable gardener. To the two older Antonii brothers, he was "Cyclops" because of his one blind eye. Plebs on the street always stared at him whenever he was out and about. Red, mottled scar tissue covered the empty socket where his eye had been. But to Mamma and the rest of the household, he was invaluable with the many plants in the peristyle courtyard.

Marcus liked him. Sometimes he challenged Castor to duels with wooden swords. The slave had no training with weaponry and was easy to beat, despite his size. A towering hulk of a boy, he would've been excellent gladiator material had he use of both eyes. Now, nearly grown, he was gentle as a kitten. Little did he know his partial blindness had probably saved his life.

"Domina, he was behind the kitchen, playing with a lizard," Castor explained.

"Well done," Mamma praised. "Now leave us. I'll speak to my sons alone."

Castor bowed his head respectfully, released Gaius, and disappeared.

"Sit with me," Marcus offered. His brother joined him on the stair, rubbing his arm moodily.

Mamma gently combed Lucius's hair with her fingers. He was still strangely hushed, sensing something serious and dark.

"My sons, I must tell you that your father has died and—"

"Tata dead? How, Mamma?" Gaius cried out in alarm.

Marcus glanced at his brother. Poor Gaius—he was heartbroken already.

She closed her eyes momentarily. Marcus swallowed hard. He could see his mother's strong determination battling her emotion. She was a handsome woman. With hair darker than most on her side of the family, she possessed the sparkling blue eyes that were characteristic of her line, the Julii. Her skin was as clear and translucent as alabaster, with strong features bespeaking her Patrician background.

"Let me finish," she whispered. Inhaling deeply, she forced herself to go on. "It must have been an illness. He didn't die in battle. In fact, I fear people in the city will say he was a coward—a fool bringing shame to Rome."

Gaius started to cry, so Marcus draped one arm gently across his shoulders.

"Consider this a lesson, my sons. Never, *ever* bring humiliation to your family. For now, we'll all pay for his—his mistakes. Disgrace is worse than death. It's an eternal shaming that men in the Senate never forget."

Frozen in place at her tone, Marcus inhaled sharply and caught his breath. Mamma had stopped before her despair led to tears. Now she fell silent, her hands busy smoothing Lucius's hair. She was a proud woman, and nobody would see her break. Not even her sons.

"Listen to me," she said. "The Senate gave your father a new cognomen. It's a shameful one, meaning he was weak. He is now Marcus Antonius *Creticus*. It's something we'll have to accept and get used to, for it's how he'll be remembered."

Man of chalk.

It was one thing for someone to die, but to destroy someone's memory by ruining their name? Such a slight marred the family dignitas—their reputation as distinguished Romans.

14

Marcus spoke before he could grasp what his words really meant. "Mamma, I swear by Father Jupiter that someday I'll restore honor back to our family."

Mamma stared hard at him, her eyes filling with tears. She rose abruptly.

He watched her hurry toward her cubiculum at the other end of the domus to grieve in private. Lucius immediately began to cry, and Gaius was still sniffling too. There was simply nothing more to do except reach out to his littlest brother and hold him.

Lucius sobbed onto Marcus's shoulder until his tunic was wet. The three of them sat there until Lucius fell asleep in his arms. Gaius's pent-up grief and anger eventually eased. He got up, stalking away without a word.

Still cradling Lucius, Marcus felt numb. He was the household heir, the oldest male in the domus, and yet he had nothing by which to remember Tata.

Nothing except shame.

The funerary preparations over the next few days were unlike any Marcus had experienced with other family or friends. Tata's body didn't arrive until the following week. And once it did, Mamma forbade him and his brothers to see it.

"Why?" Marcus demanded crossly. "If I'm never to see my father again, why can't I at least see him in death? I've seen other dead bodies at funerals. Why not his? And shouldn't we have a public viewing, even if some people shun us now?"

"We can't," she choked on the words, one hand flying to her mouth.

"But why? I want to know."

She turned away and left the room, refusing to talk about it.

Later, Marcus cornered Uncle Hybrida when he came to help plan the funeral. "I want to know why I can't see Tata," he demanded, man to man. "Mamma won't tell me why, but I'm the oldest son and heir. I want to know."

Uncle Hybrida balked a moment, but Marcus pleaded, "Please, Uncle, I'm old enough to understand. I have to be now, don't I?"

With a sigh, Uncle Hybrida spoke softly, "It's because of the natron, Marcus."

"Natron? What's that?"

"It's a preservative that keeps a corpse as whole as possible for long spans of time. But it dries a body up. Your father doesn't look like he did in life."

Marcus hesitated, puzzled. "Well—what's he look like now?"

Uncle Hybrida sighed, sitting down resignedly on the edge of the impluvium, the fountain tinkling behind him. "Your Mamma doesn't want you to know any of this because she cares about the memories you have of him, boy. She'd be furious with me right now if she knew we were talk—"

"She doesn't need to know," Marcus interrupted bluntly, glancing about to be sure nobody else was around. "Now tell me what he looks like."

Running one hand wearily through his hair, Uncle Hybrida explained. "His skin is dry as papyrus and darkened like leather. When flesh dries, it loses its natural appearance."

"How so?" Marcus wasn't exactly sure why, but he needed to know.

"Well, his lips have shrunken away from his teeth, for example."

Marcus blinked and chewed his lip nervously. "Where is he?"

"Your mother had me pay someone to store his body until the funeral. Marcus, just remember him as he was."

While lying in bed that night, tears coursed down Marcus's face. He hadn't cried since he'd first learned of Tata's death. Sadly, however, he suddenly realized he wasn't grieving for loss of life, but instead he was crying because he no longer knew how he felt about Tata. And now he'd never see him again.

CHAPTER II

A CHORUS OF LOCUSTS AWAKENED ON THE PALATINE HILL. Marcus tilted his head toward the sound, spinning the point of his wooden gladius on the ground in frustration. After lying awake too long last night, he was sleepy and irritable. And this morning Mamma had given him more bad news.

Perseus wouldn't be training him anymore. Mamma had met the former gladiator in the atrium and sent him away. She said nothing about the family's bereft state or even about Tata's death, only that they no longer needed him.

Now Marcus was depressed about two things: Tata's complicated death and the loss of his favorite activity—learning to fight. Recently, Perseus had said he showed great promise for his age and that he'd begin using a real gladius soon.

Since then, Marcus had fantasized about Tata's return. In his imagination, Tata was so amazed with his swordsmanship that he gave Marcus his sword—the one once belonging to Grandfather Orator.

Sadly, that would never happen now. Father's death and Perseus's dismissal shattered his boyish hopes. Instead of carrying on an illustrious family name, now he'd somehow have to restore it. He'd promised Mamma, and he was very serious about it. But how would he go about it, especially now that Perseus wouldn't be training him anymore? He had to learn about soldiering and fighting from someone. Who? Mamma had no plan, and her mind was on the funeral details.

Hearing voices in the atrium, Marcus set aside the wooden weapon, dashing to the other end of the domus to see who was here. It was Uncle Hybrida, arriving promptly to take him, along with Gaius, to the baths. The family steward, Syrianus, would accompany them. Mamma charged the old slave to scrub them to a polish, anoint their hair with fragrant oil, and prepare them suitably for Tata's last rites.

"Do as your uncle and Syrianus say," she reminded. "Today is important. Don't spend long at the baths. No games in the palaestra yard; nothing like that. Go now, wash, and be done with it."

Gloomily, Marcus followed Uncle Hybrida outside into the sun.

Leaving the domus behind, they followed the road through the Palatine Gate leading down into the crowded Forum Romanum along the Nova Via. Tiny shops lined every alley and cranny along the descent, where homes of the wealthy and politically prominent now spilled off the Palatine for want of more space.

High and vigilant in the southwest stood the regal Temple of Jupiter Capitolinus. Its altar was smoking with the day's most recent sacrifice. Painted statues rose among market stalls beside bustling streets, where masses of people flowed as steadily as the Tiber.

Foreigners in traditional costumes and august senators adorned in crimson-striped togas comingled, discussing politics, dinner plans, and trade. Litters bearing wealthy matrons clogged the road where slaves from Rome's finest residences jostled past, going about everyday business.

Marcus sniffed the air as they passed food vendors hawking sausages, wine, meats, and fresh cheeses. Delicious food scents blended with the smell of fresh paint around the Temple of Vesta complex. Public slaves were whitewashing Vesta's walls for the thousandth time to conceal obscene graffiti.

It wasn't a long walk to their destination, but weaving one's way through the multitudes always took time. Upon entering any public bath during male bathing hours, the chaos of the city abated into sounds of masculine laughter and splashing. Steam rose high in the air like an ethereal mist, escaping from the entrance and high-set windows. It gave the interior a mysterious, unearthly feel. Voices of countless men echoed in the tall, barrel-vaulted space.

Uncle Hybrida motioned the boys to remain close, nodding to a shelf in the apodyterium, where they'd leave their belongings. "Syrianus, stack everything there and ready the oil."

Marcus leaned against a wall, studying his uncle, who was unpinning his cloak.

Years back, Uncle Hybrida had served Marius's successor, Lucius Cornelius Sulla, during military operations in Greece. Allegedly, Hybrida had been cruel and unjust to the people he governed there. In fact, his name meant "bad dog." Marcus couldn't comprehend that, especially now, when Uncle had been so kind to his family.

Mamma had once said, "I believe Hybrida's high-handed taxing and violence on those poor foreigners was a funerary expiation for Septimia. She was the only woman he ever really loved. When he lost her, he lost his very heart."

Now Uncle Hybrida's only love was Antonia, the daughter who mirrored his dead wife. Unsurprisingly, he wasn't too popular in the Senate. He was yet another family example of how men paid dearly for their mistakes, through loss of dignitas.

Uncle had been close to Tata and spent a good deal of time at the domus. He could be gruff, that much was true. But cruel? Marcus just couldn't imagine that.

Uncle glanced over at him, scolding, "What are you gawking at, boy? Will your clothes strip off by themselves? Your Mamma won't complain to me we're late because of your dawdling."

Marcus flushed, hastily pulling off his tunic and following his uncle and brother toward the first pool, the lukewarm tepidarium.

As they passed two men, one gestured at him, commenting to his friend, "Look, Flaccus, that's Creticus's heir. I wonder if the son will grow up as yellow as his Tata. Maybe it's a good thing the Senate sent that fool against the pirates. Had he faced off with Spartacus, Rome would be doomed."

The other fellow guffawed loudly and added, "Better to be conquered by a slave than led by a coward, I say!"

Marcus hesitated momentarily, glaring at the men and pondering this mockery at his expense. Finally, he slid into the water next to Uncle Hybrida, self-conscious, angry, and hurt all at once. Syrianus poured scented oil onto his scalp, but he sat motionless, sorting out the men's comments in his mind.

"Start scrubbing—Mamma said hurry," Gaius fussed, massaging his own scalp vigorously.

Uncle Hybrida, however, noticed Marcus's expression. "Something wrong, boy?"

"What's it mean if a man calls you 'yellow'?"

Hybrida slammed his fist into the water with an enormous splash. Scowling, he demanded, "Who said that to you?"

Marcus shrugged, looking back over his shoulder. The two men had disappeared. By the look on Uncle's face, it was probably a good thing for them. "They're gone now," he replied with a shrug, scrubbing his oiled head.

Overcrowded as usual, Marcus sat on the edge of the hot caldarium pool, waiting for adequate space to open. At one point, an old man across the pool recognized him through the dense steam.

"You're Creticus's eldest, yes?"

Marcus sighed, looking askance with an eye-roll. How long would he have to endure this? Maybe if he just ignored the question...

"You're his heir, aren't you?" the elder pressed.

Gods, the man was a pest who wouldn't leave. Marcus nodded slightly, eyes downcast, by now well aware that being Antonian was no longer something of which to be proud.

The old fellow clapped him hard on the shoulders. "So sorry to hear about your Tata's poor fortune. I'll pray the gods are merciful enough to grant him a place among the dead."

Marcus's eyes widened in alarm. Did the gods refuse dishonored men a place in Elysium? A chill went down his spine.

Marcus stood by Mamma's side, dressed in a belted black tunic. She grasped his hand tightly as they listened to Hybrida's oration on his father's life. Glancing about, he noticed that attendance was pathetically low. He swallowed hard, fighting against another lump forming at the bottom of his throat.

"You mustn't cry," Mamma whispered, as though reading his mind. "Remember, you promised to be strong. It's not fitting for Romans to cry in public."

Swallowing hard, he forced the lump away, watching a sparrow glide from the top of the Curia Senate House toward the Palatine. Marcus Antonius the Younger would not disappoint. His eyes remained clear and dry.

After the eulogy, he led Mamma behind Tata's bier outside the city for the cremation. How clammy her hand was. Gaius followed, along with Mamma's body slave, Lydia, who carried Lucius. Behind were Uncle Hybrida, Cousin Antonia, and other family members with whom he wasn't well-acquainted.

There were three professional mourners and an expensive tibia player performing on nasal-sounding double flutes. Several household slaves wore funerary masks of the Antonii. Piercing the procession's solemnity, the tibia trilled from just behind them. It was so loud Marcus could hardly hear the cries of the three hired mourners.

Cremations always took place outside the city, in a dismal place—for death was impure. Gray with ash, chipped bone littered the grounds from previous torchings. Marcus bit his lip until it hurt. His stomach churned as acrid smoke from Tata's funerary pyre wafted through the small crowd of family, slaves, mourners, and friends risking public scorn in attendance. Everyone stood stone-still.

As the flames consumed his father's body, billows from the burning corpse turned the blue sky above them black. Marcus felt as though he and Mamma were crossing the Styx too.

Next came purification rituals, which he endured with gritted teeth, surrendering to more fumes from incense that made his eyes burn. The priest kept chanting strange Etruscan words over each family member. It seemed to go on forever.

All in all, it was a relief having the funeral over and retreating to the relative peace of Uncle Hybrida's domus.

Mamma asked Marcus to remain with his uncle in the atrium to receive guests, and he was more than happy to do so. Anything but standing about for more speeches or breathing in air polluted with death-filled fumes.

Uncle Hybrida's domus was aglow with polished marble floors, scrubbed to a shine. The household slaves had outdone themselves honoring Tata's memory. Black-ribboned cypress branches hung solemnly in swags over each entrance, tastefully signifying their loss.

Wax death masks and marble busts of long-dead Antonian ancestors were on display. Mamma had them moved to Hybrida's domus for the evening's banquet. Marcus examined each one, moving silently around the room. Two wax masks were missing and formed a gaping hole along the wall. Grandfather Orator died from beheading, so a magnificent basalt bust of the famous Roman took the place of his death mask. The second absent one was, of course, that of his father. Other ancestors had been more fortunate in their deaths, dying of old age. Marcus reached out, tentatively touching the wrinkled, peaceful-looking death-mask of his great-great grandfather.

"Uncle, why did they cut off Grandfather Orator's head?"

Uncle Hybrida sighed, walking over to stand before the shining basalt likeness of his own father. "I would to the gods I could be half the man my father was," he confessed softly. Then, turning to Marcus, he laughed drily. "You know, the irony is he was sent to

22

defeat pirates, just like your father. Only he was victorious, and the Senate honored him with a triumph. For a time, we flourished from his glory. But nothing lasts forever. And when Marius, a powerful general like Sulla, was heading home to Rome with legionary force, my father told the Senate not to allow him in."

"Why not?"

"Your grandfather recognized that Marius could destroy what was left of the Republic. He was a great Roman and wanted to protect and defend our government from men like Marius, who desired to rule alone," Uncle Hybrida explained.

"So Marius ordered him killed?" Marcus concluded.

"My father awakened us one night, and the whole family came together. Your mother and father had only just been married. She was so pale and fearful that night. You see, her own father was a close friend and advocate of your Grandfather Orator. He was in danger too."

"Did both my grandfathers die together?" Marcus asked, awed by this dark history that had started his family's downfall.

"No. Your grandfather Orator left us that night under cover of darkness. He fled south and hid inside a barn. Only, he chose the wrong barn. The ex-legionary who owned and farmed the land where he hid was a veteran of Marius. When his slaves found Orator, he was apprehended and executed. Both your grandfathers' heads were side by side in the Forum, stuck up on the spear-points of pila—soldiers' javelins."

"Gods. I never heard the story behind his death before."

"It's a tragic tale," Uncle Hybrida admitted, shaking his head remorsefully. "Your mother has been through much. Marius demanded the inheritance your father would have had if your grandfather hadn't been executed."

"The Senate turned their backs on him," Marcus pondered incredulously.

"They all had families of their own, boy. They were afraid to risk their own lives for his life and honor. So our family's riches became Marius's."

Marcus's eyes wandered about the room again, devouring the faces of his ancestors. But Hybrida's hand suddenly rested on his shoulder "Our guests are arriving," he announced gently, nodding toward the atrium door. "See to your manners, speak to each one, and show respect."

The first to enter the atrium was Lucius Julius Caesar, Mamma's older brother. She always boasted of his high senatorial standing in Rome. He had successfully served in a governing position in Asia Minor for several years. Mamma held him in high esteem, his persona very much like her father's, Lucius Caesar before him. A tall, striking man, his hair was thinning, making him appear older than he probably was. Uncle Lucius bore himself with a learned air, exuding scholarly authority. Marcus had seen him seldom due to his absence in Asia, so he barely knew this man who was aloof in his reserve. With him was his wife, Aelia.

He and Uncle Hybrida clasped arms. "Welcome, welcome to my domus."

Marcus inclined his head respectfully. "It's most kind of you to come, Uncle."

"If only our gathering was not due to loss," Uncle Lucius stated solemnly. Aunt Aelia greeted Marcus sweetly, kissing his cheeks and toying with his hair.

Hearing Uncle snort in disgust, Marcus glanced up. Whispering in his nephew's ear, Uncle Hybrida nodded toward his domus gate. "Take a look at them. I swear they all think their blood is purple as a Ptolemy's robe."

These last guests were other Julii, cousins on Mamma's side. Marcus recognized the two women. He'd sometimes seen them in Mamma's company, but he didn't know the man in the very back.

Uncle Hybrida was right; the lady in front bore herself like some Amazonian queen. Her austere beauty and dignity made her old and young all at once. Extending a hand, she rested it lightly on Hybrida's arm.

"Salve, Hybrida. I trust both you and your daughter are well?"

"Well as we can be at such a time, Aurelia."

She inspected Marcus next. "Ah. You have my condolences, young Marcus Antonius. Bear your grief nobly," she advised. She gestured to the young man behind her. "Greet your cousin, soon to join Crassus as a tribune in the slave revolt."

An officer? Marcus perked up in interest.

Strolling casually up behind her, the tribune was tall and lean, appearing to be in his thirties. At his side was the last lady, a wan but lovely creature.

Marcus nodded somberly. "Cousin." Feeling himself under scrutiny, he lifted his eyes.

"Cousin" stared back, his head cocked and eyes narrowed. Laughing abruptly, he embraced Marcus fiercely. "I'd call you 'little cousin,' but you're not so little anymore. Last time I saw you, you were barely walking. Let me reintroduce myself. I am Gaius Julius Caesar."

Hybrida's outdoor triclinium commanded breathtaking views of the Forum Romanum and Capitoline Hill. Perched on one of the steepest areas of the Palatine, evening breezes blew straight through the domus. Mamma said that Uncle had probably chained himself to worse debt by buying such a vista. The domus Antonii was located centrally on the Palatine, and its locale was modest in comparison to this stunning setting. Uncle Hybrida's expensive mosaics with colored tessurae and elegant fountains were designed to impress. And yet Mamma swore he hadn't any more coin than Marcus's family.

Tonight's banquet in his father's memory was the first time Marcus had attended a formal dinner among adults. Usually sent to another room along with his brothers, he felt important as he reclined between Mamma and Uncle Hybrida. Uncle even had him rise and stand beside him when he gave a libation in Tata's memory.

Only one other guest was present near his own age, Uncle Hybrida's daughter, Antonia. A few years older than himself, she sat at the end of the table in the place of least significance. Tall and quiet, with a shy disposition, she had auburn hair and a face full of freckles. Mamma often shook her head about "Poor Antonia—with hair like that, she looks like the daughter of a Gallic chieftain."

As slaves busily served the first courses, Uncle Lucius described time spent on his lands down in Puteoli. "It's been delightful seeing to my estates. Even with all the damnable slave revolt nonsense, I think if I'd not been born patrician, I would've loved being a humble farmer."

"Ha!" This from Aurelia. "You'd never dirty those carefully manicured hands."

He shot her a hard look. "If born a pleb, would I even be worried about soiling my hands, woman?"

Aelia gently intervened, asking Cornelia, Caesar's wife, "Who's caring for your sweet Julia Caesaris tonight?"

"She's home with her nurse. They're inseparable. The woman loves her like her own."

Uncle Lucius steered the conversation back to the revolt. "Spartacus raided the next villa to the south of ours—the overseers all killed in their sleep. Fortunately, the family was away, but they lost all their slaves to that brute. How fortunate we were. It could've been us."

Caesar asked Uncle Lucius, "Any news of Crassus's progress down south?"

"Not a word when I left, but I heard talk at the baths today. It's said he's scheming to cut the slaves off. But some doubters have no faith in him. They think Pompeius should come back from Spain and do the job."

"Didn't you just come from the front last month, Caesar?" Uncle Hybrida asked, draining his cup. "What's going on down there now?"

Caesar motioned for a serving slave to bring over a tray of stuffed olives. Taking several for himself, he placed a few on his wife's platter. "Cornelia, my love, eat something. Else, I'll look like a glutton." Then he returned his attention to the other men. "From what I've seen, these slaves are extremely well organized. Crassus will have to keep constant pressure on them to be effective."

"What's Spartacus like?" Aurelia ventured.

"A phenomenal leader," Caesar declared. "Think on this—he's rallied over one hundred thousand slaves to revolt and is still at large. That comprises a more than respectable army. And reliable reports suggest that disgruntled free men in the south are joining them in droves too. So it's not just slaves anymore. Quite a dangerous combination, I'd say."

"Gods above," Uncle Hybrida remarked, eyes widening. "Can you imagine the nightmare it'll be if they keep beating us?"

"Oh, come now, Hybrida," Uncle Lucius scoffed. "They're illiterate animals mostly, armed with cleavers and kitchen knives." Several guests laughed at his derisive tone. "Sooner or later, they'll lose heart and make a run for it. We'll catch this Spartacus by month's end, I'll wager."

Marcus saw everyone laughing except Caesar. "Wager what you wish," he warned. "I listen with admiration. You joke about an uneducated *slave* organizing an infantry one-hundred thousand strong. A *slave* who has fought well-equipped Roman armies and won again and again—a *slave* freeing other slaves, stealing weapons from free men. Cleavers and kitchen knives can kill any one of us in our beds just as well as gladii."

Marcus gazed at Caesar in admiration. If only this distant cousin would be willing to train a fatherless boy. He said, "He must be a born leader accomplishing all that, Cousin."

Caesar looked straight at him with fathomless dark blue eyes and smiled. "Right you are, boy. You know, I believe the gods give certain men gifts of leadership. Agreed, Mother?"

Aurelia met her son's eyes, nodding and smiling knowingly.

Mamma raised her cup. "Then I pray to the gods my own son possesses such gifts."

Grinning despite himself, Marcus felt his face flush red as they all toasted him.

Slaves set lamps atop great bronze stands. From where he reclined, Marcus looked out at the city aglow in torchlight.

Caesar unpinned his cloak, placing it over Cornelia's shoulders as the temperature cooled and Hybrida called for slaves to pour warm honeyed-wine for everyone.

Nobody said anything about the man who had died, the reason they'd all come together that night. Considering the circumstances, Marcus thought it was probably for the best.

CHAPTER III

WHEN FADIA ENTERED THE COURTYARD, MARCUS SMIRKED from behind his scroll. At last—an end to lessons.

Fadia was the youngest slave in the household, daughter to Mamma's body slave, Lydia. Possessing a mischievous face, high, delicate cheeks, and keen blue eyes, she was an appealing girl-child. Everyone acknowledged her cleverness. Even at her tender age, she knew every nook and cranny on the Palatine, every alley and street leading to and from the Forum Romanum. Thus she was the official errand girl of the domus.

Winded from running uphill, she knelt at Mamma's feet and pulled a purse from her belt to return remaining coin. Her stained slave tunic revealed wet strap marks where her basket fit tight against her tiny frame.

Marcus tossed his scroll to the floor with a resounding slap. "What's for dinner?" he demanded.

"Lamb stew with squash and leeks, Dominus," the girl answered, her sprightly face covered with sweat.

Mamma finished counting. "Excellent, child. Any news in the Forum?"

"Yes, Domina. Something happened in the south."

"What?"

Gaius piped up from where he was writing on a wax tablet. "Spartacus? Did we beat him?"

Fadia shook her head, looking at the floor. "No. Someone else. Cra—Cros—"

"Crassus," Marcus corrected. "Did Spartacus get away again?"

"No. Crassus trapped him."

"Then the war's almost won!" Marcus crowed, jumping up and grinning with excitement.

"Praise Mars, if it's true," Mamma murmured, eyes closed in relief. "Anything else, Fadia?"

"Yes. I met a servant named Timon from Caesar's domus."

"Ah, I know the one you mean."

"He told me to tell you Caesar would visit this evening."

"Really? Did Timon say why he was coming?"

"No, Domina."

"Very well, then." Turning to the boys, she said, "My sons, as you know my cousin Caesar will be an important guest. He's never been to our domus. We'll want to make an excellent impression."

Marcus caught Gaius's eye. Both boys were delighted with the promise of a new guest. Since Tata's funeral, Mamma had entertained very few of her friends. Usually, the only people visiting these days were the same boring relatives, like Uncle Hybrida, Antonia, Uncle Lucius, and Aelia. Marcus read glad anticipation on Mamma's face too.

"Fadia, pull out the fine silver," she instructed. "Polish it until it shimmers like stars. Caesar is a man of elevated tastes, and he shall not find us wanting."

"Yes, Domina."

"And you, my boys, will put away all these scrolls."

Hired Greek scholars were much in fashion for educating highborn Roman children. Unfortunately, the Antonii couldn't afford such luxury. So Mamma taught both Marcus and Gaius. Marcus was a quick study, just an unwilling student. Especially when so many fun and distracting things were afoot.

Marcus paced the atrium, waiting for Caesar's arrival. Mamma and Gaius were awaiting him in the triclinium. Ever since his father's memorial banquet, Marcus had been toying with an idea.

Finally, Caesar arrived, wearing a red military tunic, thickly belted with leather and studded military caligae—soldier's boots. Mars, the whole room resonated as he entered! On his shoulders rested a heavy military cloak clasped with a silver fibula on one side.

"Salve, Cousin!" Marcus exclaimed in welcome, as Syrianus shut the heavy door behind him.

"Young Marcus, how good to see you again." Caesar fondly ruffled Marcus's hair.

"We're all excited you're here, but I have a request. I need your help."

"Really? What can I do for you?"

"Mamma would never admit it, but we're not able to afford the gladiator who was training me to fight. We haven't much coin, so she has ended his lessons. Right now, I'm too young to defend our family honor. But if I'm not trained for military life, how will I ever improve our dignitas?"

"Ah—understood. Go on." Caesar smiled slightly.

"I was hoping, wondering if you could train me yourself. Since I no longer have a father, and all. You're already in the legions as an officer and I could learn so much from you."

There. He'd done it. Marcus's heart was thudding; surely Caesar heard it, while considering his request.

But Caesar's smiling face turned serious. "Unfortunately, I'm to return to the front soon, so I will have to leave Rome and wouldn't be here to help you," he answered.

Marcus's heart sank. There was just something about Caesar.

He longed to impress him as much as he'd once wanted to please his own father.

"Forgive my late arrival," Caesar sighed as Syrianus washed his feet with scented rose water. "I just left the Senate. Convincing our esteemed conscript fathers to do anything is sometimes heroic in itself." Reclining, he helped himself to some flatbread and oil with herbs. "Have you heard the latest?"

Marcus piped up, "We heard that Crassus has trapped Spartacus. Is it true?"

Caesar munched hungrily, one finger wandering over the edge of an intricately decorated silver wine cup. "Yes and no. He's been successful, but it's much too soon to hand him a victory wreath."

"Why's it taking so long?" Marcus asked, impatience bleeding through in his voice.

Caesar snorted, amused. "Warfare isn't something one rushes into, Marcus. And that's really a lesson our Senate needs reminding of also. Everyone wants a speedier end to the war. But siege-work and waiting on an army to engage sometimes takes weeks or even months. That's why I've been here, in Rome, as a messenger to inform the Senate of Crassus's activities, and to ask for their patience."

"I'm praising the gods that there's a Roman army between Spartacus and our city," Mamma said. "Though Crassus is untried as a general, my brother, Lucius, has much confidence in him."

"He's managing," Caesar agreed thoughtfully. "What surprised me was when Spartacus ventured south. I thought him too clever for that. He should've marched north into the Alps. That's what I would've done. He could've achieved freedom after giving us a good whipping and probably could have escaped for the present. He's let his advantage slip by. Now Crassus has him trapped with a series of barricades." He raised his eyebrows and shook his head. "For the most part, Spartacus has proven himself intelligent in the art of war, so if this is his only mistake, we may yet struggle to win."

"Oh, it's a dark day indeed when Rome is threatened by mere slaves," Mamma hissed under her breath.

"Julia, let me tell you something. The more I soldier, the more I learn to respect my enemy's strengths and skills. Spartacus has been a worthy adversary in every way. He's defeated us enough times that every senator in Rome is whimpering with tails tucked."

Mamma spoke softly, cold pride gleaming in her eyes. "Let's hope we finish him, and swiftly."

Gaius asked, "What would happen if Spartacus beat Crassus? Would he come here, free all the slaves, and kill us?"

Caesar reached over and placed a reassuring hand on his head. "That's not going to happen," he said with a wink. "If the Senate has their way, Gnaeus Pompeius may also join us in the effort when he returns from Spain. Truthfully," he added, "I expect Crassus's blockade to work before then. The slaves' supplies and stolen goods won't last forever. In time, they'll have to pitch a fight. And when they do—" He made a fist in front of both boys' faces, making them laugh.

Caesar snapped his fingers at a slave, asking for more garum, the popular fish sauce. "Julia, Cornelia and my mother are heading to Baiae. It's closer to where I'll be, so if I happen to receive any personal leave, I'll be able to visit. You've had a difficult year. Why not come along and bring the boys? I know you have a villa in nearby Misenum, but you'd be alone if you went there. Come to Baiae with my family until all this is over, and I'll provide a personal guard over the place."

Marcus's jaw dropped. Breathlessly, his eyes flitted back and forth from Mamma to Caesar.

Finally, she said, "We might be away for so long—"

"Please, Mamma," Marcus whispered urgently. At the least, it meant adventure and places he'd never been. And at the most, perhaps Caesar would work with him when he was able to be with the family. Even occasional training would be better than none at all.

"Gratias, but it's such an imposition. You already have Cornelia, your little Julia, and Aurelia to think about."

33

"The only imposition is the war," Caesar corrected firmly. "And I've invited your brother and his wife also. It'll be a nice, long family reunion, except without my presence most of the time."

Marcus squirmed. *Say yes!*

Mamma glanced over, seeing Marcus and Gaius pleading with their eyes. "Then I—*we* thank you dearly."

She couldn't say anymore, for the room exploded in noisy cheering. Thinking about it, Marcus realized he'd not even been outside Rome since he was three years old. He barely remembered it, and Gaius wouldn't have remembered at all since he was a baby at the time.

"It'll be a welcome change," Mamma admitted.

"Now there's other business I'll discuss with you, Julia, away from younger ears," Caesar said, reaching over to cuff Gaius's ear.

"May I stay?" Marcus asked hopefully.

"I need to speak to your mother alone," he replied. "In the meantime, you boys be helpful. We'll leave day after tomorrow. Julia, you and the younger ones will ride with Aurelia and Cornelia in the wagon. Marcus, how would you like to ride with me?"

Jaw dropping, Marcus tossed aside the lamb shank on which he'd been gnawing and wiped his hands quickly on a napkin. "On a horse? All the way to Baiae?"

He sat upright, face full of joy. Bless Fortuna!

Less than an hour later, Mamma appeared in the doorway of Marcus's cubiculum. He ended the knucklebones game he was playing with his brothers.

"Gaius, Lucius, go now," she ordered gently. "It's time for sleep." Reluctantly, they left.

Mamma sat on the end of Marcus's sleeping couch. He replaced the game pieces into a leather pouch.

She reached out, running her hand over his hair. "Let me share more happy news first. I know how much you've missed your time with Perseus. Marcus, we simply couldn't afford the man anymore. And teaching you to fight shouldn't be your mother's responsibility."

Marcus listened expectantly. He barely breathed and ground the game pieces together through the cloth pouch.

"Caesar has offered to begin physical training for you in Baiae. It'll be under his direction, but as you know, he'll probably not be there much."

Heart pounding, Marcus grinned brightly. Yes! Caesar would help him after all!

"Now, I expect you to be obedient. Caesar said that this phase of your instruction is to be more realistic than Perseus's sessions."

Rising up, Marcus flung both arms about her neck, kissing her face. "Gratias, Mamma." Little did she know that he'd influenced Caesar in this.

She chuckled softly, embracing him in return, "No, my son. Thank Caesar."

"Is that all?"

"No." She became more serious. "We must start locking up the slaves at night." Marcus complained, "Come, I seriously doubt Castor's going to take a hoe and murder us in our beds."

"It's a precaution." She leaned forward, placing both hands on his shoulders. "Son, have you any idea how many slaves live in Rome?"

He shrugged. "No."

"Caesar says hundreds of thousands. Perhaps more. It would be the death of us if they became as one to join Spartacus."

As Marcus considered her words, she added, "And I think you should be the one to administer their curfews. They need to see you bearing more responsibility."

Marcus wasn't pleased about this. He'd lived with these people all his life. Yet if Caesar was worried... "Very well, I'll see to it."

"Good. Let's pray we can trust Lydia and Syrianus, but we must be cautious until this war blows over."

"What about Fadia? She can't hurt us. She's just a little girl."

Mamma shook her head, lowering her voice even more. "Lock

her up. She's a child treasured by her mother. It'll ensure Lydia's loyalty."

That evening at sunset, Marcus escorted Fadia, Castor, and eight other slaves to their quarters at the far rear of the domus, near the kitchen. The long, dark corridor had tiny rooms on each side, sparsely covered with coarse leather flaps. Fadia had lived in one since she was born.

As Marcus prepared to shut the heavy bronze grate separating their quarters from the family wing, the girl was last into the dark passage. Her glistening blue eyes met Marcus's. He didn't feel right about this. Was it embarrassment, maybe? Or pity?

Whatever it was, he hardened himself, putting his full weight behind the door. The bolt slid into place with a loud rasping sound. Inside in the dark, he heard the slaves shuffle to their cubicles, grumbling. Marcus rarely entered their quarters but found himself imagining little Fadia in there all alone. She was always trustworthy. She'd never harm them. It bothered him that Mamma wouldn't allow her to stay inside.

For the next two days, the entire domus buzzed like a hive of bees; everyone packing for Baiae. And never was Marcus more elated than when Caesar gave him the reins to a tall, sleek chestnut mare.

"This is a cavalry horse," Caesar explained, "owned by the state. However, I've arranged to stable her at my villa in Baiae for the time being. That way you'll have her to use while you're training. We're in for a long trip. Are you up to it?"

Marcus's eyes were round as coins. He had some riding experience, but none since Tata's death.

Mamma stepped outside to find him sitting atop the tall, well-bred mare, complete with full military trappings. "I hope this is a gentle-spirited animal," she remarked to Caesar.

"Your son will ride safely to Baiae, I assure you," was his reply.

Marcus watched Mamma join Gaius and Lucius inside the

canvas-covered wagon with the other women and Caesar's little Julia Caesaris. It was a striking conveyance, brightly painted with flowers, and had upholstered cushions on the seats.

Aurelia poked her head out, smiling up at him. "You look happy as Bacchus with a clutch of grapes!" she exclaimed. "Julia, it looks as though he was born to ride."

"Don't fall off," Mamma called.

"Stop worrying," Marcus growled irritably. Gods!

Caesar mounted his own tall gray horse. He and Marcus led the way, along with a small detachment of legionary infantrymen under Caesar's command. The women's cart ground heavily along behind. Handpicked house slaves from both domiciles rode in another heavy, open-air baggage cart, following behind.

As they headed south along the Via Appia, Marcus surveyed the countryside surrounding them. What a beautiful, graceful land Italia was, with fertile fields, rolling hills, and rocky promontories. Umbrella pines lined the road, giving them a tunneled passage in the early morning light. Seasonal wildflowers in reds and purples raised their faces, wet with dew, while doves called from nests inside age-old tombs. Once, a hare sprang across the road, startling Caesar's horse.

Riding beyond the city was liberating, especially after they passed the necropolis housing Rome's dead. Here, in open country, farmland on both sides of the road spread open, inviting brisk canters ahead of everyone.

Previously when Marcus had ridden in Rome, it was either in the Field of Mars or Circus Maximus on non-race days with a borrowed horse. Tata sometimes gambled at the races and knew a few contacts who owned retired stock. On special occasions, he'd pay for his son to have lessons within a walled or fenced boundary. But out here in the open, Marcus experienced a sense of wonder and freedom. The road stretched unending before him.

Sometimes, he merely enjoyed the silence, listening to birds or songs of farmers and slaves chanting in the fields. At other times, he and Caesar talked.

Marcus loved that. Uncle Hybrida was a man of few words, and Uncle Lucius hardly gave him a thought, even if they were in the same room. It was too long since he'd enjoyed conversation with an older man. He found himself opening up to this charismatic cousin who sometimes made him laugh, consider things, or dream.

Whenever Caesar rode to the rear with his legionaries, Marcus often stayed in front. He imagined himself a victorious general, riding at the head of a triumph, the Antonii family honor forever restored. And whenever he took a canter along the road, he pretended he was Perseus astride winged Pegasus.

"So, boy," Caesar said after several days of riding, "how's your backside?"

"What?"

"Your ass, boy! You've just ridden six hours. If unused to horses, your buttocks should be screaming like the Furies."

Grinning, Marcus answered, "They're not screaming too badly right now."

Caesar laughed. "Oh, they will. Before I finish with you, your whole body will scream."

Unfazed, Marcus inquired eagerly, "Will I get to use a real gladius?"

"I have a man in my employ, a former top-ranking centurion. He'll instruct you like no other. His name is Lupus. You'll meet him once we arrive. And yes, you'll use real weaponry."

"Gratias."

"You want to be a soldier, then?"

"Yes. A general like Crassus."

"Well, working with Lupus will prepare you. Commanding and living on campaign isn't an easy life."

Marcus considered Caesar's words. In his imagination, living in a tent somewhere would be an adventure. He'd get to wear armor like Caesar's and sport a plumed helmet. Battles would be dangerous, of course. But if he learned to be a good enough fighter, nobody would kill him. Yet from Caesar's tone, it sounded like there was a lot more to soldiering than what he visualized.

"Did you know I was attached to your father as a legate only months before his death?" Caesar asked.

Marcus looked over at him in surprise. "No."

Caesar shrugged. "Well, I'm afraid he and I were never too well-acquainted. My time with him was brief. I was on his detail while awaiting an assignment to another post. He asked for me since your mother and I share blood. I had already gone when his troubles with the pirates began."

Not knowing how to respond, Marcus chewed his lip. Whenever someone brought up Tata, he never knew what to say.

Caesar must have felt the uneasy silence too. Smiling roguishly, he announced, "I'm going to speak Greek with you from now on. We Romans need good Greek to get by in this world. Our lingua Latina has yet to catch on in the provinces."

Marcus stared off to the side, watching a farmer shouting at his slaves. His Greek wasn't very good, so this worried him. Above all, he wanted to impress this man.

There was just an authoritative air about Caesar that everybody recognized and respected. Whenever he spoke, or even gestured, people paid attention. Legionaries accompanying them admired him. And whenever they approached a tavern at day's end, the establishment's owners always offered Caesar their best accommodations. Still, some of the places were flea infested. Everyone scratched, even the women.

Caesar stuck to his word, speaking Greek constantly. It amused Mamma, making her laugh whenever Marcus wanted his vocabulary enriched with Greek words for sore buttocks, fleas, and other phrases she informed him he didn't need to know.

His education expanded in other ways too. Caesar was always more than happy to discuss something Mamma never brought up—women.

"How old are you, Marcus?"

"Going on twelve."

"You're big for 'going on twelve.' Ever look at girls?"

"Sometimes."

"Women are beautiful, are they not?"

"Yes."

Caesar laughed aloud. "Ho! You do look, then?"

Marcus snorted. "Of course."

"What do you look at?"

Venus! What did he expect? "Umm—their faces."

"Ha!" Caesar laughed lustily. "Their *tits*. Come on, boy, you know you look at their tits."

Marcus joined his ribald laughter, agreeing in all honesty. "Yes, you're right, I look at their tits."

Caesar lowered his voice. "Do you like seeing them naked?"

Marcus grinned. "When they're not Mamma. I walked in on her once. She was really angry with me."

"I wager she was. What about your slaves?" Caesar leaned into him a little more. "They're your property, young Marcus. Do with them as you wish."

Marcus shook his head, wrinkling his nose. "Lydia is Mamma's body slave, so I would never think of her. She's too matronly. Fadia's her daughter and still so young. All the rest—well, there aren't many in our domus now, and Mamma's very careful who tends Gaius, Lucius, and me. The other female slaves are old and missing teeth. When I do decide to take a woman, it'll be a pretty one, not an old hag."

Caesar smiled and nodded. "You mentioned Fadia. Ever think how she'll look when she grows up?"

Marcus shrugged. "She's a cute little girl, I guess. That is, when she's not sweaty and dirty."

Caesar declared, "I agree. Women are never pleasing all grimy and dirty."

When they were south of Capua, Marcus walked his mare peacefully in front of the wagons. Not far behind him, he heard a clear voice. It sounded like a tender reed instrument. Reining in, he looked back.

It was Fadia. She was singing and turning about, making graceful interpretive gestures with her arms.

Smiling to himself, Marcus was genuinely surprised at her lovely voice and willowy movements. His recent conversation with Caesar came to mind.

Feeling grown-up and daring, he turned his horse back, spurring it into a canter. Seeing him coming, Fadia stepped off the road to let him pass. She blinked in surprise when he stopped at her side. The mare flared her nostrils, stamping. A puff of dust rose from the road.

Trying to avoid him, Fadia briskly walked on, head down. Marcus turned his horse again, following in silence beside her. Her singing and dancing had stopped, and she seemed uncomfortable in his company. Marcus caught her occasional sideways glances. Had she ever been on a horse?

"Salve, Fadia," he said.

"Salve, Dominus."

"What were you singing?"

She shrugged and continued walking. "Nothing. I was just making up music."

"Well, I thought it sounded rather nice."

She didn't reply. When he glanced sideways at her again, she was still staring down at the road. He kept riding next to her, saying nothing more until she finally asked, "Is there something you want?"

"No. I just heard you singing. You've been walking all day. Are you tired?"

Fadia raised her eyebrows in astonishment. "Tired? Why do you care?"

Her clipped response caught him off guard. "I just thought you might like to ride a while."

Fadia blinked and lowered her eyes again. It suddenly occurred to Marcus that perhaps she didn't like him very much. He'd been locking her up every night, after all.

Then in a split second, he saw her peering at him sideways again.

41

This was his chance, and he took it. "Come on, Fadia. My mare is gentle. It'll be fun."

She stopped.

He halted the horse.

She smiled shyly and whispered, "Yes, I'd like that."

Marcus dismounted and stood at her side. "I'll cup my hands. Just put your foot in and swing on."

Following directions, she reached upward, grasping one of the saddle horns as he lifted her frail weight. Once astride, she was obviously unsure what to do, her tunic bunched up around bare knees. Marcus swung up behind her, settling in close against her back. Fadia's olive-skinned thighs hung just in front of his legs.

"Knot your hands in her mane there," he instructed.

Reaching around her thin waist, he picked up the reins. The girl barely breathed, clutching handfuls of horsehair.

"What's his name?" she asked.

"*Her* name is Medusa."

"At least there aren't snakes on her head," Fadia exclaimed, glancing wide-eyed over her shoulder at him.

Marcus laughed. "That would be terrible, wouldn't it? We'd turn to stone. Now hang on!"

Before she could reply, he dug into the mare's sides with his heels. Fadia squealed as Medusa surged forward into a swift canter. They flew past the wagons, Mamma calling, "Marcus, what are you doing?"

He didn't look back, reveling in the moment. But he heard Caesar's throaty laughter. At that, Marcus gave Medusa her head. He smiled, hearing Fadia's joyful giggles.

Together, that day they were just two children having fun.

CHAPTER IV

⌐⌐

AFTER RIDING SO LONG, IT WAS REFRESHING TO WALK THE villa grounds alongside Mamma. A cool breeze blew, and Marcus drank in salty air from the Great Sea, which wasn't far away. Caesar's villa would be their temporary home.

The main house lay nestled between two rolling hillsides. A lofty terrace graced the front, rising from a granite-paved courtyard adjoining the stables. Stone staircases on both ends led to the atrium entrance. From there, one could view outbuildings that housed farming staff and the villa's slaves. Beyond, the landscape was lovely and serene, overlooking gentle farmland leading to the sea. Olive and almond groves surrounded the property, and vineyards flourished for Caesar's private use.

Mamma was downright emotional at seeing something for which she'd always dreamed. "What a fabulous latifundium," she exclaimed. "It's gold straight into Caesar's coffers. This is what I once hoped your father would do with Grandfather Orator's place in Misenum."

"Maybe he was afraid to spend the coin?" Marcus suggested.

"Pah," Mamma scoffed, bitterness from months of widowhood

bleeding through. "Afraid to spend? He was never afraid to spend when it came to gambling or being overly generous. If only he'd listened to me. We could have had a place like this."

Inside, the villa was just as impressive, with the largest atrium Marcus had ever seen. In the center stood Venus in her clamshell. She held little Cupid's hand, and water jetted out of his mouth into the pool, which sparkled in the warm sun.

Caesar's tablinum, an office where he conducted private affairs, was located to the back of the atrium. It was well furnished, decorated with a colorful fresco of Alexander the Great riding Bucephalus. Ornate bronze lamp stands and a marble desk gave the room an air of authority and importance.

Beyond the tablinum's walls were gardens that Aurelia had designed in the extensive peristyle courtyard. Her favorite roses grew in multicolored rows and patterns. On the edges of the beds were mature citrus trees, perfect for climbing.

Marcus's small guest cubiculum was more than adequate. Located on the upper level, it overlooked a fig orchard. Though sparsely furnished, it was large enough for his single trunk of personal belongings. Aurelia had even assigned him a house slave to empty his wastewater, clean his living space, and provide clean linens.

It was in the early morning of his second full day in Baiae that Marcus's life took a whole new turn. Before dawn, someone knocked loudly on his door.

"Get up, Marcus! You're training today!"

It was Caesar.

Marcus threw back his linen coverlet. He scrambled about in the pre-dawn light, yanking his travel tunic from a peg on the wall. Clumsily tugging it over his head, he hurried to the door.

Caesar was waiting outside in full armor. "I want to introduce you to your trainer, Vibius Lupus, before I leave this morning. A messenger came late last night. Crassus needs me on the front."

"Has something happened?"

Caesar shook his head. "Nothing of note, but it seems our good general has finished his wall to keep Spartacus at bay."

"Well, that's good news, isn't it? Doesn't it mean Crassus will win soon?"

Caesar smiled. "I'm sure he's hoping so."

The two of them walked through the colonnaded corridor and down the stairs, toward the back of the villa.

"Tell me about Vibius Lupus," Marcus said, excited to meet this man with whom he'd learn to wield a sword.

"He started out as one of 'Marius's Mules.' They were the toughened soldiers who served in Gaius Marius's army. He ended his career as a celebrated 'first spear' during the Social Wars."

"Gods, all that was before I was even born."

"Yes, I guess it was," Caesar acknowledged, patting Marcus on the shoulder. "The Social Wars are the reason we can safely enjoy some of this lovely bounty outside of Rome, you know. Lupus helped win the very war that brought all of Italia's tribes under Roman rule."

Marcus kept pace with Caesar out to the stables, where he spied another man leaning against a pillar. Upon seeing them, the fellow quickly stood upright in a posture of attention, saluting stiffly. Caesar responded with a curt nod.

"Vibius Lupus, this is my cousin Marcus Antonius. He is yours to train. Your orders are to teach him to fight with the pertinacity of a Spartan." Turning to Marcus, Caesar placed one hand firmly on his shoulder. "This training will not be childish games, boy. Work hard and endure, for no Roman achieves glory without blood. Consider Lupus your superior officer and follow orders. Understood?"

"Yes, Caesar."

"Good." Caesar clapped him once more on the back, then walked off to where one of his legionaries stood in the courtyard, holding his horse.

Marcus was face-to-face with his new trainer. From what Caesar said, he wasn't sure whether to be eager or afraid of whatever was coming. Even his body began to betray some foreboding, for suddenly his mouth went dry and his hands became sticky.

Lupus looked the very image of a centurion. Built like a bull, he was squat with flaring nostrils. Wiry gray hair, clipped short against his scalp, was thinning and revealed a white scar over his right ear. He smiled at his new student, but due to missing teeth, it was little more than a grimace.

Marcus was determined to prove his mettle. By Mars, he'd show Caesar he wasn't just any Spartan, but King Leonidas!

That first morning, Lupus showed him the best way to hold a real gladius, dulled and blunted to avoid serious injury. Heavier in his hand than any of Perseus's wooden swords, Marcus found himself bruised and sore after only a half day's practice. These new exercises were a far cry from the soldiering games back home. Mamma came out to watch, and he saw her cringe after he suffered several hard blows. Well, someday he'd prove himself.

He'd command legions.

He'd be Rome's greatest soldier.

On day two, the ordeal went from challenging to severe. Again, Marcus was up before Apollo lit the heavens. Lupus strapped a weighted pack of stones onto his back. As the centurion trotted alongside him on a donkey, Marcus ran six or seven miles without any water or rest. In short, he truly suffered for the first time in his life. He made it all the way back to the villa but collapsed in front of the barn, vomiting. Hands numb and tingly, he shook all over, drenched in sweat. Try as he might, he couldn't even squirm out of the pack weighing him down. Grumbling, Lupus finally came over and roughly jerked it off.

"You run slower than a lame tortoise and puke easier than a seasick sailor in a storm," the old centurion grunted. Then, sighing, Lupus sat down next to where he lay.

"May I go now?" Marcus moaned.

"Ha!" Lupus barked. "Go? If you can't run a decent pace, you're not fit to be in a legion. In fact, I'll bet any man in Spartacus's slave army could outrun you with five packs of stones on each of their backs."

Marcus glared at him, his stubbornness taking hold. No slave would ever best Marcus Antonius. Gritting his teeth, he rolled over and pushed himself up. Gods, he needed water. At least on that account, Lupus read his mind.

"Go over to the well and take a drink. Then come back and learn to work like a legionary. These stable slaves could use a rest. There are three stalls that need a good mucking. Get to it."

Marcus had never done any hard labor in his life, but he spent the rest of the afternoon shoveling shit out of stalls. Lupus perched on top of a gate, armed with a bucket of horse turds. If Marcus didn't move quickly enough to his satisfaction, or if he missed a pile, a brown missile whizzed past his head. Even though he dodged the excrement, it more often struck him. And so he developed a growing hatred for his new trainer.

Fed up with clods hitting his face, he finally whirled about. "Stop it! This isn't fair—you hitting me with shit."

Lupus snorted. "That's what any legionary thinks when an enemy bolt hits him while he's digging a latrine for his brothers."

And that was just the second day.

On the third, Lupus had him ride Medusa through homemade chutes. Inside each, short obstacles blocked his path, forcing the mare to jump. Marcus had fun and showed off, cockily clearing each obstacle with bravado.

Then Lupus waved him over.

"So you think you're a better rider than a Parthian archer, eh?" Lupus growled. Unexpectedly, he snatched the reins from Marcus's hands, knotting them and dropping the leather on top of Medusa's neck. "Stick your arms out."

"What?" Marcus was confused. He took the knotted reins again and lifted his arms halfway.

"Arms straight out, boy, and drop those reins."

Marcus blinked, obeying but feeling ridiculous.

"Now go through the chutes again. Arms out, no reins—and no falling off."

Dismayed, he had no choice. He spurred the mare, relying on his legwork and balance to prevent a tumble. But on the first time through, Medusa balked, tossing him straight over her head. Marcus heard Lupus curse under his breath as he landed hard, seeing flecks of light dance before his eyes. On the second try, the horse took every obstacle, but Marcus simply lost control, grabbing frantically at some mane before greeting the earth again. Stoically dragging himself back to his feet, he remounted. Lupus swore at him again. It all ended with a barrage of insulting remarks predicting his fate if unhorsed in a real battle.

Marcus randomly picked some hedges at which to stare with a steely gaze until Lupus finished his taunting. There was a smarting bruise forming on his back where he'd landed during one of his falls. Tense, he chewed his lip until it bled.

Lupus spat to one side. "Any intelligent Roman general would stick you in the front ranks to die before risking humiliation at the way you ride. And you expect to be an officer?"

That afternoon Lupus drilled Marcus at throwing pila—javelins used by infantry. He'd never done this before, so Lupus demonstrated, running and throwing at a far-off tree stump. His accuracy was astounding. The pilum landed squarely in the stump's center.

On day four, it was back to gladius work. And it was brutal.

"Forward!" Lupus barked savagely. "Get in fast, *faster*. Breathe deep and use that sword arm to punch at me. Better, but get back into position quicker and stay ready. Keep your feet apart for stability and balance. And stay behind that damned shield. Remember: take your eyes off me and you die. Now *move*, boy! Be lighter on those feet. Are they made of stone? Watch my face to see where my eyes move; watch my hands, the way my muscles tense on my weapon. Look for rhythm in my feet and body, for there's a dark rhythm to death you must see in your enemy. And today *I'm* your enemy."

Marcus tried desperately, focusing with all his being. Lupus was right about one thing. Consumed in defending himself and looking for offensive opportunities, he forgot to breathe. Until these lengthier training sessions, he'd never realized how important it was to take deep, regular breaths during a bout.

"No—*No!*" Lupus yelled. "Looking around needlessly means an arm severed or a stab in the belly. Is that how you want to die, with your noble guts hanging out for all to see and smell?"

Lupus laughed at that, thinking it was funny. It just served to make Marcus angrier. The old son of a bitch sounded like a hyena in a menagerie. Full of rage, he lunged toward Lupus, but it was a grave mistake. The centurion simply stepped aside, smacking him hard atop his helmet as he barged past. The loud clank made Marcus's ears ring. Disoriented and light-headed, he heard the hyena again.

"Thought you had me, didn't you? Think again. And forward, forward, always *forward*."

Forcing himself not to quit, Marcus reengaged. Gods, the man's defense was a like a wall. Would he ever find a weakness?

"Strike now," Lupus urged, still laughing in that irritating way. "If you're late with your weapon, I'll take you with mine." Lupus feinted sideways, his rawhide face shimmering with sweat. "How many times must I tell you—use that shield. It'll crush a man's skull, saving your little ass from sizzling in the Styx. Or you can come up underneath and gut an enemy straight through his balls."

Lupus cleared his throat and hawked a gob of phlegm to one side. "If someone attacks from behind, force them to change positions and move around quickly to deal with 'em. But be fast, or you'll never see tomorrow."

Marcus concentrated, still trying to figure out how to break through Lupus's guard. Holding his gladius steady, he kept his shield in front, parrying every blow. He was so busy defending himself he couldn't possibly use his shield as a weapon. Gods, he was hardly even able to get close enough to the man to fight back. He moved in dizzying circles, panting with his mouth open. There was no way he'd last much longer.

Breathe—

Marcus's wrist pulsed with pain. Lupus struck harder on purpose, moving forward aggressively with heavy, repeated blows until he simply had to duck and run.

"Get back here, you little coward. I'd pull out a scourge on any man running from the enemy! No Roman wants a scarred back, showing how he shit himself in battle."

Too tired to care, Marcus miserably stumbled back for more torment. Fortunately, it didn't last long. Lupus lifted one foot and shoved his shield hard, knocking him down. At that point, had the centurion come forward and slit his throat, it would've been a mercy.

But what happened next took them both by surprise.

"Stop! Just stop it!"

It was Mamma, desperately running toward them. She dropped beside Marcus, hands on his face, his hair...

Completely spent, Marcus welcomed the respite, but he felt embarrassed too.

"Look at him!" she shrieked at Lupus. "He's bruised and exhausted. Give him time to rest. He's only a boy, not some common soldier of yours." Then she rose up, striding toward the centurion fearlessly. "You're training the grandson of Rome's greatest censor, a man honored with a triumph. Train him; don't bully him."

Lupus bowed his head respectfully.

At first, Marcus thought he'd lighten up as a result of Mamma's words. But Caesar showed up briefly the next week, and the end product of her "discussion with Lupus" turned disastrous.

The torture became worse.

Marcus celebrated his twelfth year in Baiae.

His most useful gifts were timely. Increased stamina and endurance helped him withstand more physical duress. Any pain from heavy workouts conveniently morphed into a throbbing enmity for Lupus.

Oh, he was still respectful. He promised Caesar that he'd follow Lupus's orders and leadership. Begrudgingly, Marcus even learned to admire the old man's gift for tenacity and ruthlessness. Those were important skills too. What he found offensive was the man's utter disregard for his effort and improving skills.

Only several days after his birthday, Marcus's workout was especially severe. He ran as hard as he could, throwing himself against a dummy stuffed with straw. The objective was to knock the figure down using only weight and momentum. But Lupus held it firmly from behind, bolstering it upright. That made it harder.

Again and again, Marcus sprinted forward, hurtling himself against the effigy, pretending it was Lupus. Finally, when his legs were throbbing and unsteady, he sprang forward and cried out painfully. He'd pulled a muscle in his calf.

It wasn't going to stop him. In fact, he kept running, but Lupus called out, "You've gone and hurt your leg, haven't you?"

"It's nothing. I'll keep going."

Lupus shook his head. "No. There's no sense in making it worse if we want to continue tomorrow. Let's go to the stable, and I'll rub it down for you."

Marcus followed him inside the shaded barn, crumpling against a hay bale. Stretching back, he made himself comfortable. Lupus knelt in front, cradling his calf and deeply massaging it. It was hypocritical. How could Lupus, "god of pain and hate," bring healing?

Sighing, Marcus sank back farther into the hay, letting the centurion do his work. Eyes closed and relaxing, he could've fallen asleep when he suddenly perceived something else.

Lupus's hand gingerly moved upward, stroking lighter and dangerously close to his groin. Even at age twelve, he knew how some men, especially Greeks, preferred boys to women. Marcus's eyes snapped open, catching the old lecher grinning lasciviously and licking his lips. Instinctively, Marcus kicked his injured leg upward, catching Lupus squarely in the jaw. Then he launched to his feet, backing away, disgusted.

Lupus groaned, rubbing his sore chin. Marcus was so sickened that he said nothing, only snatched up his sandals and scurried away. He couldn't abide the man's presence. Just let him try that move again. He'd see what Marcus Antonius thought of it. He'd break his damned jaw next time. No lowborn pleb would ever touch him that way.

He considered telling Mamma, or even Caesar, but then decided otherwise. By telling, things could easily turn worse. It might even result in terminating his training, which he needed to achieve his goal. It was best to leave things as they were.

Marcus silently named Lupus the "Bastard," the first person he ever truly hated.

The next day he was at it again.

So far, Lupus worked him at sword point for an hour without stopping. Legs cramping, he tried to stay afoot by circling. He took in gulps of air, keeping both feet well apart.

The Bastard always enjoyed his fatigue. Whenever Lupus saw a weakness, he'd mercilessly take Marcus down.

Would this be what he'd face someday? Would some enemy beat him down a little at a time until he fell? No, he wouldn't let that happen.

There simply had to be some way past Lupus's defenses.

A stray drop of perspiration trickled into Marcus's eye, burning like a brand. His left arm wielded a shield, and he held his gladius in the other. He shook his head to rid himself of the sweat, blinking. That's when Lupus seized the opportunity. Somewhere in a single heartbeat, Marcus's legs flew out from under him. He landed hard on his back at Lupus's feet, his wind knocked clear to Asia Minor.

Lupus loomed above him like a wolf over its prey. Marcus felt his spittle land on his cheek. Being this close to the Bastard always sickened him, so he rolled over onto his stomach. In less than a blink, he felt Lupus's cool blade against the back of his neck. The Bastard's foot landed between his shoulder blades, pinning him down.

Lupus leaned down close to his ear. "Do you think some Gaul or Spaniard will politely step out of the way so you can sweat?" he sneered.

Unable to move, Marcus tasted blood filling his mouth. He'd bitten his tongue when he fell. With Lupus's weight holding him fast, he could barely breathe. The pressure made his sides ache. Tears of humiliation stung his eyes, rekindling his smoldering hate.

"Get up and fight, you little Antonian shit," Lupus spat, laughing when Marcus could do nothing but choke out a sob.

The centurion withdrew his foot, cocking it back like a scorpion's tail. Hastily, Marcus covered his head, anticipating a blow. Instead, Lupus's nail-studded boot took him in the ribs, hard. Marcus gasped, curling his legs into a fetal position and scraping them roughly on the hard ground.

Lupus bent over him again, voice whistling through the space in his yellowed teeth. "Caesar thinks you're a warrior, but all I see is a spoiled little son of a pirate-lover."

That did it.

Marcus still had his arm through the strap of his shield. He jammed it down, scraping the edge under loose gravel and dirt on the ground. Instinctively rolling, he simultaneously stood upright, hurling the load straight into Lupus's face. Gladius still in hand, he sprang forward, shoving Lupus with his shield, back, back, back—

The old man staggered, struggling to keep his footing and blinking both eyes to rid himself of grit. Marcus angled his shield to one side and aimed the gladius at his trainer's exposed chest.

"Marcus, *no!*" It was Gaius, shrieking from across the courtyard.

Dulled or not, the blade could be fatal if used the way he intended. And right now Marcus was a killing machine. Why, he'd enjoy the experience!

As if out of nowhere, Gaius careened into his side, knocking him down. The centurion was still blinking in distress, wiping dirt from his eyes.

Wind struck out of him yet again, Marcus lay as before, knees now bloody and wet tears of fury dampening his face.

Damn! Damn Lupus and damn Gaius for getting in the way when he almost had him.

"Gods, boy, that was excellent," Lupus exclaimed, squatting and holding his face in his hands. His voice intoned something Marcus had never heard expressed before—admiration.

Gaius knelt at his side, glaring at the old centurion, who finally revealed a hardened face caked with grime.

"Lupus, Marcus needs water. There's blood all over his mouth."

"I need water too, for my eyes," Lupus growled. "He blinded me."

Gaius went scrambling across the courtyard toward the well.

Marcus felt Lupus's unwelcome hand on his back. "Get away," he spat, reeling about and sending a fine spray of blood and saliva through the air. He ran his tongue across his teeth, which fortunately felt intact.

Lupus withdrew, sitting down next to him in the dirt. "You know, I almost quit with you. Until a moment ago you were nothing but a helpless, spoiled pup. Finally, I see a wolf in you." He chuckled, easing himself back on one elbow. He stared upward at the sky and rubbed more dirt from his eyes, adding, "You just gave me a glimpse of what Caesar thinks you have inside. So from now on, you'll work harder and longer with me till you leave this place."

At this, fresh tears burned Marcus's eyes. Miserably, he rolled away from Lupus and the strong odor of garlic emanating from him. The promised agony was the closest thing he'd ever get to a reward.

But Marcus got lucky.

Lupus canceled training the next day. Everyone at the villa heard about the incident, and even Uncle Lucius, who rarely gave Marcus more than a glance, clapped him on the back proudly.

Marcus slept in so late that Mamma came up to see if he was still alive. He ate a small meal down in the kitchens, then walked out onto the terrace. Relishing the sunshine, he leaned against the portico, gazing out over the hills.

That's when he heard it. A scraping noise was coming from the steps. Curious, he followed the sound to the other side of the terrace.

It was Fadia. There were lichens on the north side of the stone staircase, and she was hard at work paring them off. Her only tool was an old strigil. Sharpened to an edge, it had seen its share of public bathing. A large bucket of water sat at the bottom of the stairs next to a sack of lime. Marcus guessed she'd be scouring next.

"Salve, Fadia."

She looked up. "Salve, Dominus."

"It's a fine day, isn't it?"

Fadia shrugged. "As fine as a day can get, I guess."

"Well, I'm not wasting it. I'm going riding. Want to come?"

"I have to finish," she said, shaking her head.

"I'll find another slave to do it."

She stared at him with wide eyes, blinking.

He laughed. "Really, I will. After all, who's going to be paterfamilias of the Antonii once I'm of age?"

She just knelt there, looking up at him in amazement.

"So do you want to come? Didn't you have fun the last time you rode with me?"

She stood up without any more hesitation. "Yes, Dominus, I did. I'll come with you."

"Good. It'll be wonderful getting away for a while."

True to his word, Marcus ordered the stable boy, a slave of Gaius's age, to take over Fadia's scrubbing. Soon he and the girl were cantering down the road, away from the villa. They didn't need to talk because both were escaping. It was enough just feeling Medusa's steady, rolling gait. And there was adequate joy breathing fresh air, taking in fallow fields, and leaving everyday life behind.

While riding through the villa's almond orchards, white blossoms from the trees floated in the breeze, dancing about them like snowflakes. Fadia reached out, trying to catch them. At the edge of some woods, they happened upon a brook. It was small, but Medusa was blowing hard from the exercise, so Marcus stopped to allow the horse a drink.

"Look," Fadia exclaimed, jumping off before Marcus could react. Running forward, slightly away from the stream, she began picking some flowers. "Wild iris," she cried. Holding up her trophies, she began sticking them into the tight plaits of her nut-brown hair.

Marcus dismounted and sat upon a large stone next to the stream, grinding a stick into the streambed.

"How did you know what to call that flower?" he asked, for he knew what it was too.

"Castor taught me. I'm always kind to him. I never call him Cyclops."

Marcus shrugged. "He's taught me names of plants too," he responded. He wasn't going to apologize for calling Castor a funny name. He had one eye like Cyclops, after all.

"Everyone at the villa is glad you beat that old centurion, Dominus."

Marcus grinned, poking about with the stick until he flushed a fish from its hiding place. "Why? Don't people from the villa like him? He's very good with a sword. Caesar said he was one of Marius's Mules." With that, he turned around and looked at her.

She was staring at him, wide-eyed. The blue of those eyes matched the irises in her hair. For the first time, he fancied that someday she'd be very pretty.

"He doesn't look like a mule." She had taken him literally, and he started laughing at her.

"You're right. He doesn't look like a mule. He just acts like an ass!"

Fadia giggled at that, and her blue eyes sparkled. She rarely smiled. Probably because she was a slave. Marcus had never thought about it much, but being a slave and having utterly no rights had to be awful.

After too short a time smiling, Fadia became very solemn. "Dominus, that man does very bad things to slaves."

"What sorts of things?"

"He beats slaves that don't do his bidding fast enough or well enough. He hurts them and makes them bleed. And if they're women, sometimes he— he—"

"Rapes them?" Marcus finished for her.

Fadia nodded, head down.

Marcus tossed away his stick, wiping dirt from his hands onto his tunic. Her words didn't surprise him. Stretching his legs, he pushed farther back onto the rock. "Well, hopefully we'll win the revolt soon and get to go back to Rome. I'll miss learning to fight, but I won't miss old Bastard Lupus."

"I know my Mamma wants to leave," Fadia said. "I think she's tired of tending all those ladies." Then she smiled. "Your Mamma wants to go too. She wants to return to Rome and get married again."

Marcus's jaw dropped. "What? Where did you hear that?"

The girl clamped a hand over her mouth. "I'm so sorry, Dominus. Mamma says I always say the wrong things. Forgive me, please."

"I forgive you, but why did you say that? Did you hear my mother say something about another marriage?"

She sighed. "Yes. I was pulling weeds in the garden yesterday and heard her talking with your uncle. They didn't know I was there."

"Well, tell me what they said," he ordered impatiently.

"He showed her a letter from someone in Rome. I can't remember who, but it's one of your relatives— "

"Uncle Hybrida, probably. He writes sometimes."

"Anyway, your Mamma seemed very interested in meeting some man who's going to be consul."

Marcus's eyes grew wide. "Consul?" Jupiter Optimus Maximus!

Shaking her head, Fadia continued, "But your uncle doesn't like the idea. He wants to see her married again, but not to this man."

Marcus's mind reeled. Tata had been gone now for over a year, and Mamma was still a handsome woman indeed. But this news caught him unaware.

They rode back in silence. He had a lot on his mind. How should he approach Mamma, and what should he say? Admittedly, enough time had passed. Maybe the timing was right. She deserved happiness, didn't she?

Marcus knew he had no right to be selfish about it. He, Gaius, and Lucius would have to open themselves to another father.

CHAPTER V
70 BC

"YOU BESTED ME THIS TIME, BUT I'LL CATCH UP WITH YOU," Gaius said confidently.

Marcus smirked. "I doubt it."

With that, Gaius shoved him hard to one side, laughing. "We'll see, Marcus. Just you wait until I'm bigger."

Gaius had started a short beginner's routine with Lupus. But Marcus knew his brother would never be skilled at arms. Now that he'd developed ability, he saw how much Lupus had to simplify Gaius's sessions. It wasn't because he was smaller or younger. Marcus's beating heart was that of a soldier. His brother's heart was not. It was simple as that.

When Gaius shoved him again, even harder, Marcus tossed his practice gladius aside, and they wrestled in the grass.

That's when Lydia found them. "Dominus Marcus, your mother says to come quick. Caesar is home, and the revolt is over!" she cried, panting between words.

Marcus released Gaius from a headlock and got up. "I'll take the gladii back to the stable."

"I'll go on back and tell them you're coming," Gaius promised.

As they parted ways, Marcus headed toward the villa on a path leading through older gardens seldom tended. There were vine-covered benches and crumbling columns, left from who knew when. Had he been younger, it would've been a perfect place for hiding. Rounding an old retaining wall loaded with bird's nests, he stopped in his tracks.

Only paces away, Lupus stood by an old fountain full of algae-covered water. He was holding a squirming Fadia, who was struggling desperately, tunic soaked and dripping, Lupus was groping her everywhere.

"Come, girl. Sit with me a spell," he rumbled softly, as though coaxing a terrified horse.

"No!" she screamed.

Lupus ignored her cry, holding her in a threatening clutch. "A messenger came, did you know? The revolt's over. Everyone's celebrating. So let's celebrate together, just you and I."

Fadia struggled, squealing shrilly in desperation.

"How pretty you are, all wet and polished. Let's get you wetter—"

"Get away from her," Marcus snarled. He stepped forward into view. And, joy of joys, he still had the swords—albeit blunted ones. Oh, he was more than ready to finish Lupus off this time, with nobody to intervene. Nor did he care if the Bastard was unarmed. He had it coming.

Lupus released his grip on Fadia, and she splashed to the other side of the fountain to get away. "What are you doing here, boy?" he demanded.

"Get out of here and leave her alone," Marcus hissed.

Laughing hoarsely, Lupus reasoned, "She's just a slave. Consider her a spoil of war and join me. I'll teach you a thing or two about girls."

Marcus raised his chin defiantly, his tone low and controlled. "She's the property of my household, to which I'm heir. Get away from her." He took another step toward Lupus, pointing the tip of one of the gladii at his torso.

Lupus studied him a moment, jaw slack. Fadia watched nervously, eyes darting back and forth from Marcus to the centurion.

"Well, she's hardly worth the trouble," Lupus conceded. Still, base hunger burned in his eyes. With a final glance at Marcus to assure himself of no pursuit, he stalked off toward the stable.

Gaius ran up, passing the old Bastard. "Hurry, Marcus. Caesar's asking for you."

Marcus's original intent was to go to Fadia and comfort her. But with Gaius present, he hesitated. Instead, he met her eyes and gave her a quick nod. Though he felt rather ashamed, he left her in the filthy pool of water.

Caesar was waiting.

When Marcus entered the courtyard, everyone was celebrating. A group of Caesar's legionaries were whooping and cheering. On the veranda, Caesar embraced Cornelia and swung little Julia Caesaris up into the air, decorum be damned. "At last, it's over. We're going home," he exclaimed.

"This is welcome news, Cousin," Mamma called from where she stood.

"Can I ride a horse home with you and Marcus this time?" Gaius begged.

Uncle Lucius stepped up to clasp Caesar's hand. "It certainly took long enough, but Crassus finally has his victory."

Ordinarily, Marcus would've been thrilled and animated, but the encounter he'd just had with Fadia and Lupus dampened the moment.

Caesar responded to Uncle Lucius, "Actually, I was satisfied with most of Crassus's efforts. Unfortunately, he resorted to decimation at the end, quelling mutinous troops. Granted, certain situations demand it to keep order. Yet after killing four thousand of his own men, he seemed unfazed. It's ruined his reputation. People are calling him a butcher." He shook his head regretfully. "Oh, he did well enough for a man his age with no military experience. He's already stewing about not getting a triumph."

"Why no triumph?" Aunt Aelia asked in disappointment.

"The Senate would be hesitant at the very least to fete a general for defeating a slave army," Caesar chuckled. Then he added with a genuine smile, "Oh, it's good to be back among my own." With a slight frown, he glanced about. "But where's young Marcus? Hasn't Gaius found him yet?"

"He's down there," Gaius said, pointing to where Marcus stood watching in the courtyard.

Caesar cocked his head, calling out to him, "There you are! Old man Lupus must be making serious headway with you by now." Caesar paused, releasing Cornelia and Julia and glancing back at his men. Then, turning to a house slave standing attentively nearby, he ordered, "Find Lupus and order him here." He cried out to his legionaries, "How about some first blood?"

The soldiers all voiced approval. Everyone else stared at Caesar blankly.

"First blood," he explained, "is a little training tool I use sometimes among new legionaries. Since Marcus wants to be a military man, wouldn't it be an honor for his own family to be present should he shed his first blood today? Just watch. It's all in good sport."

Marcus felt every set of eyes land on him. How was he to respond since he knew nothing more than they of what "first blood" was all about? Mamma sought a place closer to Caesar, protesting quietly. Uncle Lucius caught her hand, stopping her. She was white as clean linen.

Caesar descended the terrace, stopping at the foot of the stairs, but Marcus ignored him. He was looking up beyond his family, where he saw little Fadia slip in. She stood quietly by herself in her soiled, wet tunic.

Footsteps from behind caused him to turn and look. It was Lupus. Marcus glared darkly at the centurion before feeling Caesar place a strong hand on his shoulder.

"Salve, Marcus. Today we rejoice. The revolt is over, and Spartacus is dead."

"Good news—yes," he stammered. His response lacked enthusiasm. He was still rehashing what Lupus almost did to Fadia. Right now hatred for the Bastard consumed him.

"I want to see this strapping young Spartan wield a sword," Caesar announced loudly.

The legionaries shouted with excitement, and Lupus stepped forward, sneering like a jackal.

Caesar reminded Marcus. "You're not an officer yet and won't be for some years. But young men always remember getting blooded. They remember every detail—where it happened, when it was, and with whom. You might have your first blood today, boy. Unless, of course, you fend off Lupus and shed his instead."

Marcus came back to himself, staring at Caesar. "How so?"

Caesar went on, turning to the centurion. "Lupus, since you've been training him, you may have the honor of being his opponent. Marcus, here are the rules. Real blades, but no shields. When someone's cut, the fight is over."

Marcus's heart raced. He was fighting Lupus—with real gladii.

Caesar continued the rules, warning, "And no stabbing at vitals. Remember, this is only a game."

Damn.

Caesar shouted at a legionary, "Flamius, lend Lupus your sword. Marcus, you may use mine." He drew his blade, handing it over hilt first.

The grip was smooth ivory with indentations where fingers were to fit. The blade shone in the late afternoon sun. Beautiful and deadly, Marcus balanced its weight in his hand. It was a different feel from the dull practice weapons to which he was accustomed. He liked it.

He looked up at the others, seeing Cornelia and Mamma standing together. As Caesar retreated to the terrace, Mamma left Cornelia's side, hurrying to her cousin. He heard her hiss, "Are you mad? He's not some gladiator—"

In the meantime, Lupus had moved to the center of the courtyard, waiting.

Marcus joined him, considering his chances. He'd gained height this year, so Lupus's short stature made their matches even these days, despite the weight difference. Old Bastard could move fast, and as his student, Marcus knew his strength. There was no shield with which to scrape dirt today. He'd have to move faster and be stronger.

They circled once, twice, three times. Marcus heard Caesar's legionaries placing wagers. It took no time at all for him to realize he wasn't the favorite. Then it began, and he thought of nothing besides what was happening in front of him.

Lupus swept in lightly, driving his weapon forward. Marcus deflected it. There was a clanging of metal against metal. The gladii rang and rasped before releasing. For once, he performed exactly as trained. He lunged at Lupus with force. The old man recovered, clumsily stepping to the side and repositioning. But his usual solid stance had crumbled. A look of mild surprise registered on his face, and he backed off a bit, breathing deep. Next, Marcus attacked backhanded in an arc, his left hand joining forces with his right to add more punch. It was a move unfamiliar to Lupus—something Perseus had taught Marcus several years before. Now that he was bigger, it was an added weapon in his armory.

Lupus withdrew again. Marcus watched carefully as they circled each other. The centurion was panting now, and Marcus's own heart hammered like a smith. For the first time, he had the advantage. He'd wear Lupus down. He inhaled deeply and evenly. Legs spread wide for balance, he stayed low like a young lion ready to pounce.

Repeatedly, he rushed forward, backhanding Lupus's weapon with his own, throwing all his weight into each blow. Lupus feinted back again, dodging away. But this time the Bastard regained balance quicker than anticipated, barreling forward. Marcus's blade flashed up, metal clanging as the blades joined. Lupus whirled about to defend himself, and Marcus saw his chance.

He sliced hard toward Lupus's undefended front, nicking him

in the belly. The blow shredded both his tunic and soft abdominal skin effortlessly, creating a scar the old man would carry until death.

"First blood! First blood!" Caesar's legionaries began chanting.

But the pain awakened Lupus's rage, and he charged, locking Marcus into a tight embrace with his left arm. With his sword arm, the centurion sliced his blade down across his shoulder. Marcus yelped, clinging to Lupus only long enough to breathe in his ear, "I got you first, Bastard. Never forget it."

He wrenched free, walking toward his family and stopping defiantly at the foot of the stairs. Searing fire pulsed across his left shoulder as warm blood trickled down his back. Chest heaving, he lowered Caesar's sword. A dark red smear—Lupus's blood—stained the front of his tunic. Shining spots floated in his vision. Marcus willed them away.

Caesar nodded in approval. "Well done, Marcus. Very well done. I'm most impressed." Then, looking toward Lupus, his mouth tightened. "And you overstepped your bounds, Vibius Lupus. I'll speak with you later. For now, you're dismissed."

Marcus wasn't listening. His eyes were on Fadia, who was watching from behind a column up on the terrace, eyes wide with relief.

You're safe now, he thought. *You're safe, and we're going home. He won't ever touch you again.*

Marcus adjusted his sling before opening the door. It was a cumbersome thing to wear. It was impossible to mount Medusa, hold a gladius, or even eat very well. He had to do everything left-handed.

He found Mamma sitting on her sleeping couch in the guest wing. She was talking to Lydia as slaves packed her belongings.

"Mamma, we need to talk."

She stood up and paced toward him, placing a gentle hand on his forehead. "Marcus, how are you, son? Any sign of fever?"

Everybody was worried his wound would turn septic. Admittedly, the night before he had been achy and feverish. He'd even passed on dinner.

"I'm fine," he said. "Except that I don't want what happened to come between our family and Caesar."

Mamma set her jaw. "What he did was inexcusable. I'll not stand by and watch Antonius Orator's grandson paraded through his skills like some cheap gladiator at the Circus."

"Mamma, hear me out. At first, I was upset about it too. But Caesar gave me the chance to prove myself. He did me a favor. In fact, he's done a great service by overseeing my training—"

She snorted derisively. "Well, he's done with you now. I intend to make certain he never has opportunity to do you any more 'favors.'"

Marcus sighed. "Mamma, we haven't the coin to hire someone in Rome to train me. You've said so yourself. I'm growing up, and I need to be able to continue what Lupus started here. Don't you want me to bring honor to our domus someday?"

She disregarded his points. "At least Caesar had that horrible beast of a man flogged and sent away. He deserved far worse than that, I think."

Ha. She didn't know the half of Lupus's horrible behavior. "You're not listening. Don't harden yourself against Caesar, Mamma. Please."

She studied him a moment and sighed. "I'll consider your words, Marcus. I'll grant you that much."

Reconciliation's seeds sown, Marcus breathed a sigh of satisfaction.

Marcus first noticed something strange as they neared Capua. A breeze from the northwest brought a distinctive odor that at first was merely peculiar. During the next two miles, however, it became stronger.

Then peculiarity turned to foul.

Gaius had gotten his wish and was riding under Caesar's watchful eye up ahead. Hopefully, this additional kindness would help soften Mamma's anger.

Since the smell was becoming so strong, Marcus chided his brother by shouting, "What's that smell, Gaius? Are you farting out your lentil soup?"

Gaius promptly turned about, making a face and lifting his buttocks from the saddle, shaking them crudely in Marcus's direction.

As they passed the outskirts of Capua, Marcus cantered up to Caesar.

"What's the awful smell?"

"It won't be the last time you experience it."

"But what is it?"

"It's death, boy. And once you've smelled it, you're not likely to forget it."

He was right about that. And it was getting much worse. Marcus squinted as they approached a rise in the road. On the horizon, heading up the hill, were rows of strange stick figures resembling scarecrows disappearing into the distance.

Caesar nodded toward the queerly shaped structures. "See those?"

"What are they?"

"Crucifixions."

Marcus frowned, puzzled. He'd heard people talk about such executions.

"It's a dreadful way to die," Caesar explained, "designed for slaves and prisoners who aren't Roman citizens. It's often used on insurrectionists and other criminals too."

As they proceeded uphill, the scarecrows became T-shaped wooden scaffolds, bodies hanging from every one. A long iron nail pierced each victim's wrists and feet, securing them into place. Additional ropes bound their arms adding support and fastening them, so their flesh wouldn't tear from their own weight.

But what halted their procession was the view from atop the hill. Before them, crosses lined the circuitous Via Appia snaking its path toward Rome. Each bore a condemned sufferer. The pathway of death didn't just end after a mile or so outside Capua but stretched unending into the horizon and out of sight. As they neared the first cross, the prisoner mumbled nonsense, jerking with weak cries of insanity. Ravens fluttered about him, intent on a feast.

Marcus stared, his eyes wide. It was the sort of horror that both terrified and fascinated in a macabre way.

"Hades, Marcus," Gaius gasped in a barely audible whisper. "He's still alive."

Marcus stopped his horse next to his brother's, both of them staring. Meanwhile, Caesar spurred his horse to intercept the wagon of women.

"Should we keep going?" Gaius asked.

Marcus shook his head, looking back and watching Caesar. "Let's wait and see what he says to the women."

Caesar soon returned carrying a silk cloth and gave it to Gaius.

"Tie this about your nose. The smell will get worse as we head north. If this continues, many will be dead, and we can expect putrefying remains."

Gaius took the rag, staring at it. "What's this? Perfume?"

"Yes, and be thankful for it. Marcus, you intend on being a soldier, so get used to this stink."

"Who are they? And why are there so many?" Marcus asked, still gaping down the road.

"They're the remains of Spartacus's army. Every slave or free man traveling along the Via Appia will take Crassus's message to heart. Nobody threatens Rome without paying for it with their lives; foremost of all, slaves."

The next several days were like riding in Charon's craft. The death scenes worsened the closer they came to Rome, like a surreal nightmare. Forced to travel slow as a snail due to the wagons, nobody could escape the moans of dying slaves. Many were still coherent, pleading for mercy.

Marcus was silent with horror. Farther north, they discovered Caesar was right. Most of the executed prisoners were already dead, their corpses scavenged by opportunistic birds and animals. Bloated with gases, the worst ones leached unspeakable, malodorous fluids. More than once Marcus quietly stopped, dismounting to retch helplessly along the road, as did some of the others, including Fadia. She did her best to stay in the baggage wagon covering her face, but at times she must have been cramped enough to feel a need to stretch her legs on the road.

The most dreadful moment was during the afternoon of the second day, traveling among slaves who still lived. Marcus heard high-pitched wails ahead. Nailed to a cross was a boy no older than Gaius. Fadia, walking by herself ahead of everyone, saw him first.

Unsure exactly why he wanted to protect her, Marcus cantered up to where she was. He unclipped his cloak with his one hand, pulling it off and offering it. "Wrap your face in this. It'll help with the smell, and you won't have to look anymore."

Fadia was staring straight up at the child, who cried piteously. The look on her face spoke volumes. Instead of accepting his gift, she jerked the cloak out of his hands and flung it into the dust. Then, running back to Caesar, she dropped to her knees, submissively extending her hands upward and pleading.

The tribune pulled his horse up short, nearly trampling her.

"Please, Dominus Caesar! Please, I beg you—he's only a small boy. How is he guilty of making war against you?"

Everyone froze at her display. The wheels of the wagons ground to a halt. The women poked their heads out, silk handkerchiefs at their noses.

"Help him!" Fadia wailed. "What if one of the young Domini was up there?"

"Get up, girl," Caesar spoke softly, but there was a steely tone underneath.

"Just him, please—can you not find it in your heart to let him go?"

"Move on, all of you," Caesar ordered.

Gaius needed little coaxing. His face was white, and under the perfumed silk tears streaked his face. Making a groaning sound, the wagon started moving again. Its side curtains drooped, and the women's faces vanished.

Fadia remained in a tiny heap on the roadside in front of Caesar's big gray, her frail shoulders shaking with sobs. Marcus sat dumbly, so wrapped up in his own emotions he could barely think. Part of him wanted to dismount and run to her. Another wanted to join her urgent pleas for the ill-fated boy.

"Marcus, get her out of the road and follow the others," Caesar ordered.

Marcus remained frozen, miserably surveying the scene.

"*Now*, Marcus. Get her off the road and moving!"

Shaken by Caesar's tone, he silently dismounted, walking to where Fadia knelt. The entire time the boy sobbed, begging for an end to his torment.

"Get up, Fadia," Marcus whispered. "Come now."

When she lifted her little sprite-like face, it was red and wet with tears. A string of mucus ran from her nose to her cheek. Grabbing Marcus with both hands, she astonished him with her strength. "Dominus—please, please. We must not leave without doing something."

Somehow, Marcus got her up and led her slowly down the road on foot, Medusa plodding behind. Fadia cried onto his sore shoulder. His sling became wet with her tears. Stricken by the awful scene, he looked back as Caesar resolutely drew his gladius and swiftly ended the child's pain. Tears stung as he struggled not to cry.

Fadia wriggled free from his offered solace, walking briskly ahead with her head down, still weeping.

Shocked beyond measure, Marcus reasoned that Caesar had done the boy a great mercy. He steeled himself, knowing that someday, as a soldier, he'd see things even worse than this. It kept him kept moving forward on the road, having learned how hard living was for both slave and free. In Baiae, he'd had but a taste of what his life would be like as a warrior. Now he saw it—and smelled it too.

As the family slowly picked their way along the road, surrounded by the overpowering odor of decay and swarms of buzzing flies, he contemplated his future.

Caesar was right. Being a soldier would not be easy.

CHAPTER VI

CHANGE CAME. IT BROUGHT JOY, DISILLUSIONMENT, AND the unexpected. Life as Marcus had known it since childhood was forever different in the domus Antonii after Baiae.

First, he suffered frequent nightmares about the trip home. Each was similar: walking a road alone, smelling an overpowering, sweeter-than-carrion stench, looking up, then seeing the crucifixions. Each time the ending was the same. He'd awaken sweating, panting, pulse racing. It was irritating because the source of his dreams was obvious. After suffering from them this long, shouldn't he be over it by now?

Once, he tried talking to Fadia about it while she was sweeping the peristyle colonnade. "Do you ever think of the trip home from Baiae?"

Her sweeping slowed. "All the time," she said sadly.

"Do you ever have trouble sleeping—because of what we saw?"

She stood up straight, looking him square in the eye. "No. I never have trouble sleeping because of something I cannot help. I'm a slave. There's nothing I can do about anything except try to live life as best I can."

Marcus frowned in puzzlement. Her tone was cold. "Are you angry with me?"

She shrugged. "You're Roman. I'm a slave. Spartacus lost, and Crassus killed the rest of his army and a little boy who had nothing to do with it. Because of these things, there is a sea of difference between us."

Marcus opened his mouth to protest but didn't know what to say. He almost told her the truth—how Caesar had sent the boy swiftly to Elysium, ending his suffering.

But he didn't.

Fadia turned away to finish sweeping and said nothing more.

Marcus had to admit they hadn't talked much since coming home. Caesar had to return Medusa. She was property of the state. So no more riding together. He missed the freedom he and Fadia had shared, ever so briefly. For a time, he thought they were friends. Saddened at her response and disinterest in communicating, he stalked off, disappointment and frustration churning his spirit.

The detachment from Fadia made the second change most timely. And it was further evidence that Mother was open to reconciliation with Caesar. For Caesar himself took the first step toward making amends. He sent Marcus a gladiator slave as a gift. Timon, Caesar's own steward, accompanied the brute, insisting that "Marcus Antonius accept this token; one capable of giving him further physical training."

Vindelicus—the gift—was an astounding specimen, to be sure. Tall as a colossus, he wore his long golden hair in a single braid down his back. And what fascinating facial hair! A long, well-tended mustache hung from both sides of his mouth, but no beard.

Intrigued by the foreigner, Marcus begged to keep him. "Please, Mother"—for he no longer called her "Mamma"—"let me have him. He can teach me more about fighting."

"Or he'll kill you," she retorted, shaking her head.

In the end, Marcus had his way, keeping Vindelicus. He wasn't sure what it would take for the gladiator to earn Mother's trust. But he and the big Gaul became inseparable. Together, they went to the baths, through the Forum on errands, and played games when Marcus got bored.

Sometimes for special occasions, Vindelicus braided his beard into tiny plaits around his chin. Marcus always thought that was funny. Deep scarring ran across the slave's neck and up the right side of his face. Another descended his left cheek. Whenever he chanced a smile, his face seemed as though it was happy on one side and sad on the other, like theatrical masks. Latin was difficult for him, and he often tripped on words, making everyone in the domus laugh. He was Vindelici, a tribe inhabiting high slopes all the way to a river called Danuvius.

But perhaps more importantly, once his shoulder completely healed, Vindelicus taught Marcus not only swordplay and wrestling, but even strange words in his own barbaric tongue.

For Marcus, it was profound relief to like his instructor instead of holding him in contempt. Within a month, Mother finally recognized their bond and allowed Vindelicus to sleep outside Marcus's cubiculum door.

"Someday," Marcus assured Vindelicus, "you'll attend me at banquets, walk behind my litter, and help me into my armor when I'm a general."

He had high hopes for himself and his Gaul.

The third change proved Fadia to be an excellent source of information.

After returning from the south, Mother attended all sorts of social engagements. None included Marcus or his brothers. Nowadays the three boys usually found themselves in the company of slaves. For Marcus, it wasn't so bad. He had Vindelicus. But Gaius and Lucius keenly felt her absence. Naturally, it was their big brother who confronted her.

"Mother, may I enter?" he called from her doorway.

Lydia was sliding in a final hairpin as Mother rose to greet him, arrayed like a goddess. "Of course, Marcus. What is it? Is something amiss?"

"Well, you keep going out. We never see you anymore." He

paused, carefully choosing his words. "Have you found a man who pleases you?"

She gave him a magnificent smile, stepped forward, and took his hands. "Yes, I have. Please forgive me my secret. I didn't want to make any premature announcements. He is last year's consul, Publius Cornelius Lentulus Sura. The Cornelii are a famous and powerful family, you know. Sulla was Cornelian."

Marcus frowned at her. Cautious, he spoke his mind. "But Sulla was a bad man, Mother. He marched his army against Rome."

Mother dismissed Lydia with a wave of her hand, inviting Marcus to her sleeping couch.

He sat down.

"Son, being of the Cornelii gens doesn't make Lentulus like Sulla. Do you want me to be happy?"

"Very much."

"Then trust me in this. I need your support. Lentulus brings me great joy, but your Uncle Lucius will not even give him the opportunity to prove himself. He's against joining our houses—"

"Joining? Then you're marrying him?"

She nodded. "Lentulus has asked for my hand. Now I don't need anyone's permission. I'm a propertied, mature, and widowed woman. But it would be nice having my family's approval. Uncle Lucius has refused it, so Lentulus turned to your Uncle Hybrida, who is his close friend. Naturally, it would be most important to me to have your consent." She gazed at him hopefully. "Will you support us, Marcus?"

Wide-eyed at having such a mature conversation with her, Marcus had half expected to hear this news, but he'd never even met Lentulus. Still, what could he possibly say?

Decision made, he reached out and took her hand. "You deserve a century of happiness to make up for the past year, Mother. If Lentulus pleases you, then I'll tell Gaius and Lucius that we should be excited. We're getting a new Tata."

In a rush of emotion, Mother threw her arms about him, burying her face in his neck. "Oh, Marcus, you've made me so happy today. So very happy."

At a simple family wedding at the domus Antonii, Marcus and his brothers watched as Mother and Publius Cornelius Lentulus Sura, recently Consul of Rome, were married. Strangely, he couldn't remember her ever being so jubilant and animated with his father when he was still alive. Now he suspected that her feelings for Marcus Antonius Creticus were never as deep as they were for Lentulus.

Not that he disliked Lentulus. His new stepfather was more than pleasant. Tall and stately, with long legs and silver-spun hair, Lentulus had a soft, steady voice that only boomed when barking directions at litter-bearers. He had big hands that made Mother's shoulders look slight when resting on them. But most of all, he had a frank face and engaging smile that drew one in, like a moth to fire.

Right before the wedding, he'd surprised the entire household by deciding to sell several of his properties. In a move that started tongues wagging on the Palatine, he elected to relocate his household into that of his bride's. Even Lucius knew that was unheard of, blurting out, "We get a new Tata in our old domus!"

At the wedding banquet, Lentulus stood up at the head table and pulled out an ornate box. The wood was fine, polished olive, well-oiled and trimmed with inlaid turquoise.

Marcus was intrigued.

Lentulus was giving Mother a wedding gift. He listened expectantly, sitting up on the dining couch in anticipation.

"What a glad day this is," Lentulus began, his smile warm. Reaching down, his hand clasped Mother's. "My heart is full, for not only have I an exceptionally stunning new wife, but three fine sons too. What man could ask for more?"

Marcus grinned, and Uncle Hybrida, lounging next to the bridegroom, called out, "Indeed, you're blessed by Fortuna."

Lentulus nodded. He released Mother's hand with a squeeze. "So tonight, in the presence of my new bride and family, I wish to honor my eldest stepson, Marcus Antonius."

Marcus's eyes widened. This was so unexpected.

"Come on up, boy," Uncle Hybrida urged, laughing.

Lentulus held out his hand invitingly.

Dazed, Marcus arose and walked forward to the head couch. His new stepfather placed a hand on his shoulder. "I desire to be as a father to you, Marcus. And as a memento of this glad day, here's a gift for my eldest son."

Heart beating wildly, Marcus watched as Lentulus held forth the sumptuous wooden box.

"My father once gave me one of these. Use it with care, and may it keep you safe."

Marcus accepted the gift. Upon closer inspection, delicate hinges fastened it shut. He gasped as he carefully lifted the lid. Inside was a magnificent pugio, the double-edged dagger all Roman noblemen valued. Its wooden hilt, also of olive, matched the chest in which it lay. The workmanship was stunning, its blade concealed in a fashioned leather sheath with polished bronze trim. This was his first real weapon, and Marcus was speechless. First, he gazed at Lentulus in appreciation, then over at Mother. Tears of joy glistened in her eyes.

All they had been through together, losing Tata, the dishonor ... And now this.

Setting the gift aside, he reached out, embracing Lentulus solemnly. "Gratias," he whispered. "Gratias."

"Use it wisely," Lentulus repeated in a low voice.

Marcus nodded, emotion extinguishing any more words.

Truly, Marcus had a father again.

In the months since Mother and Lentulus had married, he habitually strolled down to the Curia to meet Lentulus after Senate sessions ended for the day. Curiosity for senatorial business began to spark in Marcus's mind. Sometimes Lentulus would tell him about potential laws the conscript fathers discussed. But more often he complained about men too set in their ways who were never open to change. Lentulus wanted change in Rome—urgently. He believed the Republic was corrupt and dying.

Marcus had never thought much about politics. He knew he'd have to be a senator someday since only senators were appointed as generals. Still, politics were far less intriguing than the thought of going to war in full armor at the head of a legion. Soldiering and winning esteem for his family and Rome was still his dream.

Today, however, as he walked toward the Curia building, he saw the Senate doors suddenly burst open. A multitude of togate men exited together, bringing crowds in the Forum to a standstill. Obviously, something important had happened.

Breaking into a run, Marcus dodged kiosks of herbs and spice sellers, several snarling dogs, and a beggar who nearly tripped him. He sprinted past several houses and shops, taking a shortcut through an alley that emptied out near the Temple of Vesta complex. Moments later, he rounded the wall onto the Via Sacra. The huge group of senators silently walked down the street. Panting and craning his neck looking for Lentulus, Marcus noticed one thing. Not a single man was smiling.

At last, there he was. Lentulus was on the far side of the road. Marcus barged through, pushing a few senators out of the way. They glared at him, one cursing his rudeness. Finally, he was alongside his stepfather.

Lentulus was usually an amiable man, but not today. His face was dark with rage.

"What's wrong?" Marcus asked between breaths.

Before Lentulus could answer, they both heard a familiar voice. "Lentulus, wait!"

Marcus glanced back. It was Uncle Hybrida, bustling through the crowd of solemn-faced senators to catch up with them. Lentulus paused, waiting.

Uncle scowled as he breathlessly caught up with them. "I don't imagine you're looking forward to going home and telling Julia what happened. Why don't we take our time about it and stop for wine first? It always helps dull the pain."

Marcus cracked a smile. Uncle Hybrida did love wine.

It wasn't long until he found himself nursing a large cup of fine Falernian alongside the two men. Hybrida and Lentulus had been friends for years, before Mother ever met her new husband and former consul.

"Over sixty of us expelled," Lentulus complained heatedly. "I can understand a few per year—and for extreme corruption—but this is ridiculous. Self-righteous prigs."

"And the reasons were ludicrous too," Hybrida agreed, taking a long swallow from his cup. His cheeks were turning red.

"Doesn't expelled mean 'tossed out'?" Marcus asked, trying to make sense of the situation.

"Indeed," Uncle answered. "I'm afraid your Mamma won't be very pleased with either of us. Both of us were booted from the Senate today."

Lentulus snorted, rearranging the fold of his toga over one arm. "Debts," he spat. "Damned arrogant bastards—as though they've never borrowed a denarius in their entire lives. Didn't it sicken you, Hybrida, hearing the censors list all of your creditors in front of the entire assembly?"

As Hybrida nodded, morosely swallowing more wine, Marcus chewed his lip. The censors were the most powerful politicians in Rome, controlling the census and public morals.

Uncle Hybrida was right. Mother was not going to like this.

At all.

"And here you just sold all those urban properties of yours to try to become solvent," Uncle Hybrida pointed out. "Sometimes the gods are so damned unfair to us mortals. Ah, the irony—especially when we're amending our weaknesses."

Lentulus agreed. "I should've just kept my big domus on the Palatine and had Julia and the household move into it."

Hybrida snorted in agreement.

Marcus let them vent. They generously shared their wine with him, buying several more rounds for themselves and not forgetting to keep his cup full. They sat for several hours drinking, and when Lentulus had bolstered himself with enough grape to see it through, he and Marcus parted ways with Hybrida and headed back to the Via Sacra to climb the Palatine.

When they opened the domus gate and entered the house, Lentulus invited Mother into the tablinum alone. Marcus sat on the impluvium's raised edge, his back against a column, listening and chewing his lip. There was no difficulty hearing his mother's outrage through the closed door. Several times Lentulus shouted, but not in indignation. No, it was mostly so she'd hear him over her own vociferous arguing.

And to Lentulus's credit, his stepfather was promising that he'd make things right.

"Julia, calm yourself. I'll find a way back into the Senate and will do more than my part to change the way it governs. I swear it on the Vestals' hearth. I'm good friends with several influential men, and they'll help me."

"Who?" she demanded.

"Gaius Cethegus, for one—and Lucius Catilina."

"*Catilina?* Oh, Lentulus, that man's reputation won't improve yours."

And so it went on ...

Marcus hated hearing them squabble, but once Mother's initial resentment abated, life went on as normal. The biggest concern of Marcus's, the possible erosion of Mother's marriage, was unfounded. If anything, she and Lentulus drew closer than ever. For now, they shared a new objective: Lentulus's reentry into political life. They still laughed, kissed, and gazed at each other with that incomprehensible look, bespeaking love.

Love. It was becoming a concept of curiosity to Marcus.

Three weeks after Lentulus's ejection from the Senate, Marcus sat with Mother in the tablinum, impatiently ciphering. She had continued with his education and that of his brothers. They still couldn't afford a Greek tutor. It would only add to Lentulus's debts.

These days she had to corner Marcus into studying anything. It was becoming far too dull, sitting about, calculating some boring, bald philosopher's theorems on the size of the Great Sea. Today Mother took a more drastic measure to *make* him study. She threatened to cancel Lentulus's plan to take him to a gladiator match in the Forum.

"Either you finish your mathematics or you simply won't go," she said with a nonchalant wave of her hand. "Instead, you'll sit here, watching your stepfather, Gaius, and Lucius leave without you."

Irritated, Marcus worked feverishly, but his heart and mind were elsewhere. Gaius and Lucius were out in the gardens memorizing Homer. It wasn't often that he was completely alone with Mother, and despite his present frustration about possibly missing the match, something had been on his mind lately.

He interrupted the silence, "Mother, did you love my father?"

She stopped proofreading some of Gaius's writing on a wax tablet. "Oh, son, there are many things you needn't know."

"I want to know."

She sat back in her chair, and rubbed her eyes. "Your father was very handsome and kind. But as you know, he was not soldierly and not accustomed to war. Men in my family have always been just the opposite. At first, I think I may have loved him in a way. But because he rarely seized initiative—because he wasn't as capable as he could have been or should have been—I lost some of that love and respect I first had for him."

"What is it you love about Lentulus?"

She smiled and inhaled deeply. "I love the fact that we chose one another. Nobody told us to marry or forced us. He's loving and bold with his decisions, even if they aren't always the best ones. He's a risk-taker, and in politics that's a good trait. Together, we will do what we must to see him reinstated into the Senate, where he belongs. And he wants change in Rome. Oh, Marcus, he is my very heart. I do believe the world could end and I would still be complete if your stepfather was by my side."

Overwhelmed at her answer, Marcus momentarily pretended to get back to his work. But she was willing to chat, so he changed subjects and asked another pertinent question.

"Who was Fadia's father?"

"Oh, that was Quintus Fadius Gallus," she answered without pause. "He was a wealthy freedman who sometimes visited us years ago. He and your father had a very good relationship. Fadius was a very supportive client."

"If he was so fine a man, why didn't Tata allow him to have his daughter? Fadia could've been born free."

Mother shook her head. "Fadius sired a child on Lydia, Marcus. That means the baby was our property. A good friend like Fadius would never have asked your father for the child. It meant taking Fadia away from Lydia. Besides, as an additional slave, she was an asset in a time when coin was scarce."

"What happened to Fadius?"

"One day there was an accident in the Subura, where he was doing business. Some scaffolding above his litter gave way. It fell, breaking his arm through the skin in several places. Your father called for two physicians and even paid for his treatment. Fadius stayed here with us, but when his injury festered, he died within a week."

"How old was I when all this happened?"

Mother laughed in amusement. "Juno, Marcus, you're full of questions just to get out of your lessons, aren't you?" She sighed. "How old were you? I can't recall. Probably four or five. Lydia was early in her pregnancy when it happened."

As Marcus considered her words, her tone sobered. "Listen to me, son."

He met her eyes.

"I'm going to tell you something because you're of an age to understand. You're different from that slave girl, Marcus. You're of aristocratic birth and have a senatorial future ahead of you. Think about that. When we were in Baiae, Aurelia and some of the other women gossiped about your riding with Fadia. Remember, she's only a slave. Distance yourself from her."

Marcus stared back at his work. He and Fadia hadn't spoken since that day in the colonnade. Only this morning, he had passed her when walking to the kitchen. She hadn't even looked his way. After their last conversation, he figured she thought the same thing as Mother, that it was better they not be friends. They were too different.

He was Roman. She was only a slave. That saddened him.

Mother still hadn't come home. She'd been gone since late last night.

At breakfast, Marcus asked Lentulus, "Where is she?"

Lentulus helped himself to figs mixed with honeyed goat cheese. "Cornelia started having birth pangs, and Caesar sent for your mother. He probably thinks that since she had three healthy sons, her presence will be helpful. He's hoping for a son, you know."

Cornelia had given Caesar his daughter, Julia Caesaris, who was some years younger than Marcus. It had taken years for her to be with child again. He hoped everything would be all right. He was very glad Mother had gone. By now, her anger over what happened in Baiae had eased.

All day long, Marcus remained at home, waiting on her to return. Then afternoon turned into evening, and still he sat about, even studying some Greek and reading scrolls on philosophy just to pass the time.

But she didn't come home until the next morning.

"Is Cornelia all right? And the baby?" Marcus asked, meeting her in the atrium.

Mother shook her head mournfully. She took Marcus's hands. She'd been crying. Her eyes were red and puffy. "Cornelia tried so hard. Sometimes it's terribly difficult being a woman. Childbirth is one of those times. Someday, when you have a wife, remember that. She died this morning. As did the child."

Marcus frowned. "How is Caesar?"

"Devastated. I don't think I've ever seen him like this before. He truly loved her."

After the traditional visitation and mourning at Caesar's domus, Marcus attended the funeral with Lentulus and Mother. Caesar spoke Cornelia's eulogy. Twice while speaking, he stopped, overcome with sorrow. Steely in his resistance to tears, he forced himself to continue, despite obvious grief. It troubled Marcus, remembering how he had to swallow his own sorrow at Tata's funeral. Gods, it was inhuman how Romans considered it improper to grieve openly. And hiring and paying someone to do it for you? Those false and screeching bier-followers with fake hair that they ripped out? All that pretend crying and moaning?

It was stupid!

Wasn't it better to lament someone's death genuinely than to stage such a fake and hypocritical public farce? Marcus decided then and there that when he was older, he'd mourn if he pleased. He'd be his own man, regardless of convention.

As the days since Cornelia's death turned into months, Mother told Marcus that Caesar kept his loss very private. Instead of leaning on family, he threw himself into his work as quaestor, an office responsible for the state treasury and public records. Lentulus mentioned he sometimes saw him going to the Tabularium, Rome's newest public building. There, he researched and worked both day and night. Marcus mused that perhaps Caesar's upcoming assignment to Spain would serve as a merciful distraction. He'd be leaving within days.

Rome was a dangerous place and full of crime, so like any man of influence, Caesar kept hired bodyguards or paid gladiators to stand guard near his home's entrance. Marcus had seen them many times as he passed by his cousin's domus on his way to the Forum. Their presence discouraged unwanted riffraff or persons of ill repute.

Today, however, the place was empty. No clients, petitioners, or delegations from the Senate. Because of what happened in Baiae with Mother, Marcus hadn't seen Caesar except at a distance. Well, he wasn't going to allow the man to depart without at least expressing his condolences. And he wanted to thank Caesar for all he'd done for him.

Marcus was dripping as he strolled past the gate leading to the domus Julii. It was a dreary, wet Februarius. More cold air had blown in, trapped within the city's perimeters. An overhanging umbrella pine dumped icy rainwater on his cheek, making him shiver. He stopped before Caesar's heavy oak door and used the decorative bronze ring in the lion's mouth to rap loudly.

No answer.

He tried once more, and the peephole door finally slid open. Timon, Caesar's chief steward, peered out.

"Marcus Antonius to see Gaius Julius Caesar," he announced confidently.

"Sorry, young Dominus. He's not receiving guests."

Marcus gave Timon his most winning smile. "Please, I'm family, here to wish him well before he leaves for Spain."

Timon sighed, looking past him at the miserable weather. "Oh, come inside. We'll see what he says. But he's very busy and hasn't hosted anyone in months."

Still, Marcus was hopeful as the door opened, allowing him in from the rain. His footsteps echoed in the hall, rainwater dripping from his cloak onto the fine mosaic floors. Once the slave disappeared, he wandered the atrium, examining Caesar's ancestral busts and fine copies of Greek art, meant to impress guests.

Black draperies and swags of dying cedar still hung in the corridors. Marcus recalled his father's funeral. How long ago it felt since that day. Hearing footsteps, he turned about, optimistic.

It was Timon. "Forgive me, young Dominus, but Caesar sends his regrets. He cannot see you today. However, Lady Aurelia will greet you instead."

Disappointed, Marcus watched Timon disappear. Aurelia replaced the slave, floating down the hallway in a dark blue stola. She carried something in her arms that was light gray and sleek. It was a cat, with the most luminous eyes he'd ever seen.

"Young Marcus Antonius? What a delight. It's been too long since we last saw one another. Ah, look at you. Almost taller than I. What are you now—?"

"I recently turned thirteen."

"Your mother is blessed by Juno, having such a handsome boy." Aurelia smiled at him. "Please accept my son's regrets. An Egyptian delegation stopped by only two days ago. He's addressing their concerns about piracy problems in the Great Sea. Their King Ptolemy sent this cat for Julia Caesaris as a gift."

Marcus cocked his head at the animal. It was sleek and large-eared, adorned with a lavish collar embedded with gemstones. "She must be pleased."

"Oh, she is. I'm sorry my son can't see you. He's busy and fatigued these days. It's been a difficult time, you understand."

"Yes." Marcus nodded. "I was just passing by. But please give him my best. And tell him I'll sacrifice to Neptunus for safety on his journey."

She smiled at him sincerely. "You have a good heart, dear Marcus. Of course I'll tell him."

He hesitated but decided to ask anyway. "Will he be all right, Lady?"

Aurelia smiled wistfully. "In time. Cornelia was very dear to him, and he misses her terribly." Moisture glistened in her eyes.

Marcus had never seen royalty, but Aurelia possessed an air of what he imagined kingly nobility to be like. Mother didn't care for the woman much, and Marcus was beginning to see the reason. She and Aurelia were very much alike. Two unique lilies growing in the same field.

"Please tell Caesar I appreciate the help he's given me in training. And Vindelicus is simply amazing. I cannot thank him enough for such a gift."

Before Aurelia responded, the cat jumped from her arms, scampering away. Gently, the old lady reached out, placing her hand atop Marcus's shoulder. "Let me tell you something." Shifting her hand, she cupped his chin, tilting it up, and looking deeply into his eyes.

Marcus raised his eyebrows curiously.

"My son was most impressed with you in Baiae," she said, releasing his chin and patting his cheek fondly. "He told me how he'd want his own boy to be hearty and bold, just like you."

"Gratias, lady," Marcus responded, bowing his head.

Aurelia smiled warmly, but her voice became low and sad. "Someday he'll marry again."

Seeing her grief return, Marcus took his leave. "May he find happiness," he said. "And may there be joy ahead for this domus."

CHAPTER VII
69 BC

MARCUS RAN HARD.

Only one young man was challenging him now, and even he was fading. Nearly to the finish, Marcus heard Vindelicus's jovial laughter in the crowd. He dug his bare feet into the turf, gulping air, feeling a rush of energy from being in the lead.

"Go, Marcus! Faster!" Gaius cheered from atop Vindelicus's shoulders.

Pushing legs and lungs past their limits, he sprinted into the final stretch. He was sure to win at this pace.

Today was his chance to shine as the youngest runner in his group's heat. Ahead, a cluster of men stood yelling and shaking fists. As he finished the course, a deluge of bodies surged forward, laughing, embracing him, sweat on sweat. There were slaps on his back and buttocks, calls of approval, shouts, and masculine voices resounding.

Gaius latched on to him, jumping up and down, bursting with excitement. "You did it! You did it!" His words became a singsong chant, a younger brother's boyish exuberance.

Folding in two, Marcus gasped for air, hands on his knees. It was stifling in this press of bodies. Suddenly, the crowd around him parted at Vindelicus's daunting presence. The Gaul gently took his arm, directing him away from the press.

"Dominus, do not stop. Walk until breathing slows, yah?"

Gaius stayed at his side too. "Well done," he trilled. Then he turned back toward the mob of men, who were surreptitiously turning over wagered coins to one another. "My brother's the fastest man under twenty in Rome!" he bellowed.

"Shut up, Gaius," Marcus panted. "You're acting like an idiot." Then he addressed Vindelicus. "On to the baths. I'm done for today."

He was naked save for the wrapped cloth around his loins serving as an undergarment. Vindelicus carried his tunic and bath oil in a satchel strapped to one shoulder.

The three of them ambled off through the Forum. With each step, Marcus's tense muscles and competitive nature eased. As they passed some food stands, loitering slave girls giggled, pointed, and cast lascivious smiles in their direction.

"Look, Marcus, those girls are watching you."

Irritated, Marcus struck out with his fist, boxing his brother a good one on the ear. "Gods, Gaius—shut *up*, would you?"

Gaius continued, undaunted, "They were staring, and I think they liked what they were looking at." He laughed. Still eyeing the girls, he spun around, walking backward and grinning apishly. Unmindful where he was going, Gaius backed clumsily into a shopkeeper's rack of hanging carpets, nearly falling.

Marcus swore under his breath, shaking his head. He heard female laughter at his brother's antics, so he picked up his pace. By distancing himself, maybe he could lose Gaius in the crowd.

It happened more and more frequently. Marcus would be walking around on the Palatine and glance up to see some doe-eyed senator's daughter smiling at him, none too shyly. In the Forum, it was even more obvious. Slave and plebian girls slunk by, unabashed, brushing close on purpose. Now that he was fourteen, Marcus no longer found it bothersome, but entirely pleasurable. Unless, of course, his younger brother was with him.

Marcus dreamed about sex constantly and had already decided it was way past time to try it. The issue was how to go about it. Like any young man, he wanted his first experience to be exceptional.

Caesar had offered to help, but now he was in Spain. The most logical person to turn to was Lentulus, but he wasn't home much lately. He'd started courting senators to gain reentry into the Curia. Besides, as close as he and Mother were, Marcus was afraid he'd get her involved. Gods, he could only imagine how that might turn out. She'd probably insist on picking out the brothel herself, making sure it was a clean house. Or even worse, she'd want to find a marriage match for him.

A few months ago, he'd followed Hybrida to a lupanar, one of Rome's many brothels. Marcus had hidden behind a donkey cart laden with crates of geese as his uncle disappeared inside. As he watched the doorway for Hybrida, a scantily dressed prostitute had startled him from behind. She'd tugged him into an embrace, cooing, "A highborn dominus like you can pay a pretty coin, right?"

There had been no thrill, for Marcus's enthusiasm had turned to embarrassment. He had no coin on him whatsoever. What would she think, highborn without coin? Humiliated, he'd jerked free, running home with plenty of lust and zero satisfaction.

He pondered asking Uncle Hybrida to take him along next time. He'd probably do it—or maybe not. Uncle might tell Mother, just as easily as Lentulus. The mere thought of her becoming involved in his first sexual venture horrified him.

Frustrated, he entered the baths, Gaius still on his heels along with the Gaul. Vindelicus found their usual corner in the apodyterium, digging through the satchel and pulling out a cask of scented oil and a curved strigil for body-scraping. The boys stripped off their undergarments, stepping into the tepidarium.

Moments later, Gaius spied a friend and ran off. Marcus sighed with relief, seeing him chatting and splashing amiably with the other boy. With his brother gone, he allowed himself to slide underwater, relaxing, rubbing his arms, and stretching his legs. Vindelicus poured oil of sandalwood onto his head and massaged it into his scalp.

Feeling refreshed, Marcus fantasized it was a scantily clad slave woman doing the job instead of his big, lumbering giant.

"Look—I knew he'd be here."

A young man of about nineteen or twenty slid into the water next to him. Marcus saw that it was the competitor he'd beaten in the footrace. Other youths accompanying him submerged in another pool nearby.

"A fine race, Antonius," the newcomer congratulated, extending his arm.

Marcus accepted the friendly clasp. "Gratias, you also ran well."

"I'm Gaius Scribonius Curio. I've seen you a lot at the Field of Mars. You're quite an athlete."

Marcus smiled at the compliment. "One of my cousins has supported me in physical training."

"You have a very tall cousin," Curio snickered, looking up at Vindelicus standing dutifully behind Marcus.

Marcus laughed. "No. My kinsman's Gaius Julius Caesar, quaestor in Spain."

"Ah yes. I know who he is. Your mother's Julii, is she not?"

"Yes."

"And your father—"

"My father's dead." He let it go at that, and for a little while the conversation died. Vindelicus began scraping Marcus's neck and shoulders with the strigil, removing excess oil.

"Have you plans tonight?" Curio finally asked. "A friend and I are hosting a little dinner party."

"Really? Gratias, yes. I'd like that. Where is it?"

Curio leaned in closer, confidentially lowering his voice. "Actually, it's in the Subura. We have a...club of sorts there."

The Subura was the notorious slum district of Rome where the poorest of plebs lived in squalid insulae apartments. Buildings there were all jammed together, like amphorae in a merchant vessel. Once, Marcus had overheard Uncle Lucius compare it to a tinderbox, and plebs living there to flint. The district was a fire hazard, an engineer's nightmare. Tenement buildings were always catching fire, and poorly maintained flats often collapsed and killed occupants inside. Not to mention it was known for gambling houses, heinous crimes, and bloody murders.

Marcus had been in the Subura many times, following Hybrida or tagging along with Lentulus. There were always occasions to go there. It was the perfect place to buy cheap wine for slaves. Lentulus often had fullers in the Subura launder his toga. But one always went in broad daylight when it was safer. If Mother found out he was going to the Subura at night, he'd never make it out the atrium door.

Curtly, Marcus ordered Vindelicus to attend Gaius, wherever he was. Once his slave was out of the way, he asked Curio in amazement, "Your friend lives in the Subura?"

Curio smiled, unabashed. "No! He and I just rent a place there to entertain. That way we can host friends whenever and however we please." A raffish smile spread across his face.

Marcus's eyes widened, envisioning what sorts of entertainment would be in the Subura at night. Women in his imagination were stripping themselves of clothing when Curio broke his concentration.

"Will you come?"

"Yes. I'll bring Vindelicus as my...attendant." *And I'll have to get past my Mother*, Marcus added to himself. And that was about as easy as sneaking past Cerberus at the gates of Hades.

"Good," Curio replied. "I'll have my own body slave give him directions. I'll save a place for you on the couches and make sure there's a pretty girl to greet you."

Marcus's heart beat like a drum. Tonight. It would happen tonight.

After dark, Marcus donned a dark, hooded cloak before leaving his cubiculum. Vindelicus waited by the door, shifting uneasily. Marcus could sense his hesitancy about sneaking out without anyone's knowledge. Well, he'd have to get over it.

Now came the problem of getting past Mother, Lentulus, and the rest of the household unnoticed.

Fortunately, they were entertaining guests in the triclinium. Polite laughter resounded from the other end of the courtyard, along with clinking wine cups. The guest was probably another influential senator. Lately, Mother had joined Lentulus in his efforts to court favor. She'd even quit giving lessons, instead urging Marcus to go to the Circus or games in the Forum with Gaius. She and Lentulus remained at home, allowing for uninterrupted afternoons to plan dinner parties for guests without boys intruding. The best part was that Lentulus would wink, discreetly slipping Marcus a heavy purse of denarii with which to place bets.

Marcus snugly secured his pugio to his belt, low on one side, arranging his cloak a little haphazardly over his left shoulder. Next, he combed his thick hair forward and smoothed down his scant facial hair that was just beginning to coat his chin. Soon he'd have his first beard, and it would be time for his toga ceremony.

These days he was obsessed about appearance, and forefront in his mind was looking good tonight. Curio said there would be women there—wherever "there" was.

Silently, he stole outside with Vindelicus.

The Gaul wore a look of torment. "Dominus, please—"

"Quiet. Do you want them to hear? Come on, it's dark. We can sneak through the garden, over the wall."

Without further discussion, they hastened across the peristyle lawn, using thick willows surrounding the reflecting pool for cover. Afraid his slave was too tall, risking discovery, Marcus motioned Vindelicus down. Together, they crawled, finally arriving at the wall.

"Now help me up," Marcus whispered.

Vindelicus obeyed, Marcus using his broad back to step on, which was enough to hoist him halfway up. Heaving himself the rest of the way, he hugged the top to stay in the shadows. The drop to the other side was a lot farther than expected. He landed hard and nearly fell to his knees, gasping. Vindelicus plopped to his side moments later.

"All right, where to? You do know where to go?"

"Yah. I go there after the baths."

"Good. Let's go."

Vindelicus shook his shaggy head slowly. "Not good place, Dominus."

Marcus tilted his head back cockily, eyeing the slave in annoyance. "Did I ask for details?" Extending his arm toward the road, he indicated for Vindelicus to show the way. The big slave sighed, taking off through the dark, moonless night. Marcus followed close behind.

Once in the Subura, they took care, using elevated stepping stones above stinking streams of refuse. Many insulae were five or more stories high, blocking views and restricting light filtering into the street. It made Marcus jumpy whenever shadowy figures flitted by in the narrow passages, most streets being no wider than the breadth of a small cart.

Once, Marcus yelped as a hand groped him, probably for coin. Whirling about, he saw only darkness and stayed closer to Vindelicus. Several times the stepping stones were ill-placed, leading to mucky landings in the street. The sensation of warm, sticky sewage oozing between his toes repulsed him. He tugged his hood over his head and was just about to agree with Vindelicus that the whole business was a bad idea when the Gaul stopped abruptly. Just to the left, covered with graffiti, was a door.

The narrow street had widened slightly into a small plaza, sounds of a fountain trickling nearby. Were it not defaced, the entrance would have been rather attractive. Light danced beyond a yellow-tinted glass rondel decorating the portal. On the top hung a bronze phallic symbol. Marcus's pulse raced, hoping it wasn't just there for good luck.

Vindelicus rapped loudly, his back to the door, watching the dark street suspiciously. The acrid smell of stale urine hung dense in the still air. Nearby, a dog barked.

The door swung open, and a beautifully painted young woman appeared, smiling broadly. She wore a loose, bright green linen tunic draping dangerously low at the bodice. Marcus left the street, coming into the light, pushing Vindelicus aside.

"Salve. I'm Marcus Antonius. Gaius Scribonius Curio invited—"

"Say no more, Dominus. Welcome. Clodius and Curio are in the back."

It was a little odd. No official steward guiding him into the triclinium or announcing his arrival. Marcus headed in the direction indicated, pausing only when the girl snapped at Vindelicus, who was following dutifully.

"Not *you*. They want no slaves about. It's only for the young dominus. The likes of you wait behind the kitchen. And stay out of the food."

Marcus turned back, seeing grave concern on Vindelicus's face. "Just do what she tells you," he ordered.

"Dominus, please. This place is not good."

Marcus marched up to the Gaul, snarling through his teeth, hoping the pretty girl didn't hear. "Do as I say."

When he turned back around, the girl was smiling at him, and he sensed her eyes following him as he pursued the sound of laughter down the corridor.

He entered a room that wasn't really a triclinium at all, but just a large, dark chamber with lamps burning low. Chipped frescoes had been repainted red and covered with swags of wilting flowers, dangling so low he found himself nearly tangled in them. Although not a proper dining space, it was large enough to hold the customary trio of couches. And a tempting aroma of delicacies was proof that someone wasn't skimping on dinner.

"Antonius." It was Curio. He arose, coming over in greeting. There was wine on his breath. "Come, I saved you a place." He snatched Marcus by the hand, leading him to an empty spot on the couch. "Clodius, remember Marcus Antonius from the Campus Martius? He beat me today."

"Yes, yes. I saw the race. Welcome, Antonius. We're pleased for you to join us."

"Gratias for the invitation," Marcus responded.

Publius Clodius was twenty-something. Short of stature, he was still a striking young man, meticulously groomed, from his neatly trimmed black hair down to his elegant blue silk tunic.

"Don't I get an introduction?" cooed a soft feminine voice, sultry and slurred by wine.

"Of course, Sister," Clodius cajoled. "Antonius, allow me to present my sister, Clodia."

Venus! Marcus's eyes grew wide. He'd certainly heard of her. What male hadn't? She was a favorite discussion while at the baths. And walls all over Rome memorialized her many affairs.

Clodia reclined in a corner with a young man. Judging by his gaudy costume, he was probably a mime actor. Low birth or not, he was comely. Clodia herself had the same family look as her brother: shapely, with her petite form accentuated by a sheer Greek-style chiton.

As he reclined across from Curio, a slave untied Marcus's sandals. Immediately, his attention turned back toward Clodia, who was behaving shamelessly. She lay back against the young actor, who laughed drunkenly, dribbling wine into her mouth. Licking at it with her tongue, her suitor finally covered her mouth with his, seeming to devour her. Clodia twisted her body around, drawing her lover into the shadows, one creamy hand reaching out to extinguish the nearest lamp.

Marcus's blood pulsed wildly.

"Have some wine," Curio proffered, pouring a cup himself. "Here, we escape the seriousness of life. Older you get, the more escape you need, I think. Poor Clodius here will soon miss our company. He's headed east later this year."

"Armenia," Clodius mumbled through a mouthful of meat. "My brother-in-law Lucullus is there. I'll join him a spell. One has to start a career someplace."

"Antonius has a keen interest in the military, don't you?" Curio prompted.

"Yes. My cousin Gaius Julius—"

"Caesar, you mean? Has he been sponsoring you?" Clodius queried abruptly.

"Helping me some, yes. He's in Spain right now serving as—"

"Quaestor. I know." Clodius nodded to himself, reaching out with one hand to fondle the woman next to him. She moaned, laying back wantonly.

Marcus watched, feeling excitement begin to throb where it usually did whenever he thought about erotic things.

Someone brushed by his couch. Then he found himself face-to-face with the girl who first greeted him at the door. Smiling broadly, she showed straight white teeth and painted lips. Mesmerized, he watched her kneel close beside him, gently running a finger from his knee to his thigh. Then she tilted her head down, kissing him full on the lips. Marcus found her overwhelmingly distracting in a most pleasant way.

Curio said, "Clodius, I've been impressed with Antonius at the Campus Martius. He excels at sports. I seldom see youths his age with such talent."

Clodius guffawed. "No, Curio, you rarely ever notice talent at all in youths his age. At least not *military* talent." With that, he took a deep drink and began kissing the woman next to him, his hands on her face.

The girl who had joined Marcus was rubbing his legs in earnest now and began to recline against him. She paused, reaching toward a platter of fowl glazed in honey. She picked up the plateful, sticky in sauce, and offered it to him. Selecting a leg, he took a bite only to watch in amazement when she leaned toward him, alluringly licking the meat with her tongue and savoring a nibble. When he took a second bite and reached past her to rinse his fingers in a bowl of lemon water, she caught his hand, lifting it to her lips. Ever so gently, she began to suck the honey sauce off his fingers. Her full lips moved slowly, suggesting lurid pleasure. She smiled coyly when he reached for her. Then she offered her sauce-soaked lips to his mouth. He parted his own, tasting sweetness, and then pulled back, taking a sip of wine. It was lightly watered and heady.

Glancing at the corner, he saw Clodia in the shadows, rearranging her transparent garment. It hung loosely off one round ivory shoulder. The woman at his side was kissing his ear now. A rush of heat churned inside him, his heart pounding like horses' hooves at the Circus.

"Festus, we need music. It grows late," Curio said, yawning.

Whoever Festus was, he began playing loudly and wildly on a double-reeded tibia. Marcus saw Clodius get up, discreetly heading down the hall, carrying his wine cup. The woman who was with him on the couch followed.

"Are you enjoying yourself, Antonius?" Curio asked, not even glancing his way.

"Yes," Marcus said breathlessly. The girl was nibbling her way from his ear down to the lower part of his neck, all the while doing other things with her hands that distracted him from conversation and any other mental function.

"Feel free to use a room down the hall. That is, if you want privacy," Curio commented, casually flipping onto his back, both arms under his head and closing his eyes.

An entirely different appetite replaced Marcus's hunger for the honeyed fowl. Before he realized what was happening, the girl was above him, sheer linen dropping off one shoulder, revealing the round curve of her right breast. She smiled and tugged gently at his arm. He found himself following her. As her hips swayed in the flickering lamplight, he glimpsed bare skin through the sheer emerald linen she wore.

Curio laughed, shouting after him, "In case you wonder, her name's Metinara."

Metinara led him into a cubicle where a swath of worn material hung on the entrance for privacy. No lamps burned; it was completely dark. He reclined on a couch, soft with coverlets and cushions. Beside him, she invited him closer. He felt the soft curves of her body and heard her copper earrings tinkle as she threw her head back. Hungry for more, he kissed her neck.

Marcus tingled with anticipation. He'd never felt so alive.

Slipping his tunic over his head, he felt her hands moving toward his undergarment.

And after that, he forgot everything but Metinara.

For months, Marcus found himself pursuing a self-indulgent lifestyle. He spent every denarius Lentulus gave him on the private brothel in the Subura. Now that he was a shareholder in a den of prostitution, it bought him an assurance of women and wine whenever he craved diversion. Sometimes gambling rings paid a fee to operate from the "club." Those nights were especially wild and entertaining since more people came. Women included.

At first, Marcus successfully hid his new lifestyle from everyone in the domus. He and Vindelicus always scaled the wall so Syrianus wouldn't see them and inform Mother. The last thing Marcus wanted was maternal interference in his sex life.

But finally, one other person did discover their mysterious comings and goings at night. After only two weeks of visiting Clodius's lair, Marcus and Vindelicus nearly bumped into Fadia as they left to scale the wall. He and the slave girl never talked anymore. But dressed as they were in dark, hooded cloaks, it naturally aroused her curiosity.

"Salve, Dominus," she managed to say, lightly hopping out of the way as Vindelicus nearly bowled her over.

"Salve," Marcus replied, more tersely than intended.

Fadia mustn't have noticed. She giggled. "Where are you going, dressed as thugs?"

"To a party," Marcus lied. Oddly, he really didn't want her to know what he was doing.

Fadia studied him a moment. Gods! She knew he wasn't telling her the truth.

"Shall I let your mother and Dominus Lentulus know when you will be home?"

Damn, she was clever. His voice hardened. "Don't you utter a word. Do you understand me?"

Fadia looked down, her face flushed. Swallowing hard, she said, "Yes, Dominus."

With that, Marcus gestured to Vindelicus, and the two of them headed toward the garden wall, leaving her behind.

"You speak harsh to her, Dominus," Vindelicus said.

"She needn't know my business," Marcus replied, silencing him.

To her credit, Fadia was obedient. She told no one.

Vindelicus was loyal too, but Marcus knew he disliked the secrecy and sordid locale. The big Gaul swore time and again that a day was coming when a problem would arise. Marcus impatiently endured the fretting.

"What if we are attacked in the Subura?" he'd say. "It would not be good thing."

No, it wouldn't. But Marcus didn't care. For personal gratification and unbridled pleasure, it was a risk he was happy to take.

And then came the day of reckoning.

It wasn't yet dawn when Marcus awoke to a rooster crowing in the dark streets outside Clodius's place.

Strange, but he was completely alone. His head swam, and sitting upright only made things worse. Stomach lurching, he rolled sideways, vomiting onto the stone floor. With a groan, he collapsed again onto the lumpy, musty-smelling straw mattress. He needed to move, to leave. Shaking, mind reeling, he couldn't recall what had happened.

A few clay cups lay on the floor, an insect crawling inside one. Ever so slowly, Marcus arose, snatching his rumpled tunic from where it lay on the floor. He became dizzy again as he tugged it over his head. Bacchus, what happened last night?

He tried walking across the room and staggered into the doorframe. His whole body hurt. Even his buttocks felt like he'd ridden to Baiae without stopping. Then the world started spiraling once more, and he couldn't think.

Where was Vindelicus?

Every step was an effort as he stumbled into the small vestibule. It was only good fortune that took him to the right place. Vindelicus was waiting in the filthy space that served as a kitchen, sitting next to a refuse pile.

"Vind... Vindeli..."

The Gaul reached Marcus's elbow in two strides, and that was a good thing since Marcus could no longer make his feet move.

"Can you walk, Dominus?"

Marcus looked down, but his legs were immovable as paving stones. He felt wretched. Something dark and unnatural had happened last night. Something different. Drunkenness was something he stomached regularly, but this was no ordinary hangover. He felt himself sliding into semi-consciousness, barely able to breathe.

Unable to speak or move, he moaned as Vindelicus caught him, tossing him over one powerful shoulder like a sack of grain.

Undulating memories, hazy as dawn's mist, were muddled and indistinct. There had been women at dinner. Lots of wine, as always. Curio had been near, laughing, encouraging him to drink more. Then people were touching him, caressing him into a dreamlike state...

What strange drink had made him feel like such a mess this morning?

Vindelicus walked briskly. Marcus's head jostled against his back. It felt ready to split, and had a goddess sprung forth from it, he wouldn't have been surprised. He opened his eyes momentarily and saw the street's gutters bouncing in his vision.

"Dominus?" Vindelicus murmured.

Marcus heard him, but despite honest efforts, his tongue refused to work.

"Dominus, what should I do? Where should I take you?"

Marcus wished he could tell him. Closing his eyes hard, he thought as loudly as he could. *Home, Vindelicus, just take me home.*

Marcus felt Vindelicus turn and opened his eyes long enough to see that they were heading up the Nova Via toward the Palatine. His slave's chest was heaving from the uphill climb.

After a little more time had passed, everything suddenly stopped. Vindelicus's hold on him shifted, hands lifting then lowering him. Something cool, damp, and soft cushioned him now. Grass?

Marcus groaned, hearing bits and pieces of conversation between Vindelicus and someone else filtering through his head. It was much too mind-addling to determine the identity of the second party.

"What are you doing there?"

"Nothing." That was Vindelicus.

Parts of the conversation drifted. Marcus couldn't focus, and gall was burning his throat.

"Help you with what?" the other voice asked. "Aesculapius the healer! What happened to him?"

"Help me get him inside so nobody knows—please."

"Wait there."

Marcus felt a warm hand on his forehead. Heavy but gentle, meant to comfort, but Marcus wanted no man's touch. His stomach started rising to his mouth again. It took every ounce of willpower, but he managed to move away from Vindelicus.

He fainted for a time. Then, in what seemed like eons, something bristly and itchy slid under his arms. This time he endured the touching, helpless and unthinking. Next a noose tightened around his torso, pinching and stifling his breathing.

"I'm pulling him up now."

"Slow, Castor, please. You are good?"

Castor. That's who it was.

Marcus felt himself hanging limp as a puppet, his throbbing head knocking backward against the wall, sending a jolt of pain down his spine.

"Got him," Castor announced.

Soon he was in the grass again, his stomach still on the rampage. He tried just listening to them talk.

"Did you do something—"

"No," Vindelicus shot back defensively. "Boy goes out at night like this for almost a year now. I wish I am no part of it. It brings trouble."

"How did he get like this?"

"Do not know. First, it's fun, yah? How you say—adventure? Mostly women, but now he drinks. Last night, very, very bad."

"It won't be pretty when Domina finds out," Castor said bluntly.

"*Oh ho.* I no like to think it," Vindelicus moaned.

"Look. He's waking up."

"Mother," Marcus croaked. "Don't let..."

He stirred. His gibberish was barely comprehensible even to himself, much less anyone else. Sighing, he smacked his lips and opened his eyes. His mouth tasted foul. Coughing, he winced at the pink light of dawn.

Marcus heard Castor get up. The slave was chuckling mischievously. Then suddenly a gush of cold water splashed all over Marcus's face.

Gods above! Some of it ran straight into his nose. He gagged, raising quaking hands to his soaked face. Had he been able to move, he would've kicked Castor all the way to Greece.

What happened last night? Marcus took more water from Castor, taking a long draw to clear his head so he could think. It didn't have the desired effect. Moments later, he was moving on his hands and knees, crawling a short distance away to vomit again. Finished, he turned around in time to see his two slaves exchanging worried glances.

"Well—" he stammered, his belly at peace for the moment, "I'm perfectly well. I just need to sleep."

Stubbornly willing his legs to do their part, Marcus dragged himself upright. Despite the ground churning beneath him, he kept his eyes fixed on his cubiculum across the gardens. Thirteen steps or so were all he needed.

One. Two. Three. Four. He had to get inside. Five. Six—Gods, what happened? He still couldn't remember.

CHAPTER VIII

MARCUS WAS AS TALL AS LENTULUS NOW, AND HE WAS well aware of what a good-looking young man he was. Family, friends, the prostitutes he slept with, and even people on the street would make remarks. Especially women. They admired his muscular arms, broad shoulders, and solid chest.

At last, a thick, manly beard demanded a first shave, and that meant a toga ceremony was in order. In line with tradition, Lentulus took him to a barber in the Forum.

As Marcus tipped his head back, the barber told him to be especially still, the sharpened razor making clean streaks on his flesh. After each pass, the chubby little man wiped oil and facial hair onto his apron. During the shave, Lentulus loitered outside, looking for anyone he knew. Whenever he saw someone, he'd exclaim, "My stepson's becoming a man today. Come have a look!"

It was frustrating, lying as still as he could with a sharpened blade scraping his face, unable to respond to anyone's good wishes. People stuck their heads through the door, calling out, "Bona Fortuna, Antonius!"

Back home, the whole family helped him put on his pure white toga virilis, the toga of manhood. Gaius and Lucius rubbed white lumps of chalk onto the wool, whitening any areas the fullers missed. Lentulus stood at Marcus's side playing the paternal role while Mother and Lydia showed him how the folds of the garment should hang. Fadia held Mother's polished bronze mirror up high so he could see himself.

Pure white woolen sinuses hung in heavy folds about him. Like any young man wearing one for the first time, he was afraid to move. What if the drapes loosened and dropped off his shoulders? And how disastrous should he spill wine or food on it during the banquet in his honor. Togas required frequent attention from fullers to stay well-maintained. And Rome's fullers charged expensive rates to bleach them.

"They're dreadfully clumsy," Mother said, as though she'd been wearing one for years. "Keep your shoulders squared, and everything will stay put. That's what my father always said."

Lentulus laughed. "My father always said that the real reason we Romans have slaves is just so we can put on the damned things!"

Marcus laughed at that but stopped when he saw Fadia staring at him. Suddenly, memories of crosses along the Via Appia sucked all humor from Lentulus's joke.

Marcus stayed put in his cubiculum until the guests arrived. Then, prompted by Vindelicus, he paraded down the colonnade to the gardens while his guests cheered.

Fortunately, his toga remained in place.

Mother stepped forward, flanked by Gaius and Lucius, greeting him with fond kisses on both cheeks. She lifted a corona of roses, placing it atop his head. Lentulus was next, bringing forth a long bundle wrapped in fine silk. He presented it to Mother solemnly, and in turn she offered it to Marcus.

Eyes widening in rapt surprise, he pulled away the silk to reveal a gladius. Fashioned with an ivory handle in the shape of a Stymphalian Bird, a coin-sized garnet capped the hilt. Its scabbard was of hardened red leather and gilt bronze fittings, etched with a picture of Hercules in his lion-skin.

Stepping forward to kiss him, Lentulus said, "A Gallic man who does business in the Forum made it."

Mother and Lentulus sat on either side of Marcus during the feast. He was amazed. They must have spent an enormous amount of coin on the whole affair. To accommodate more guests, they'd even rented additional dining couches.

Later, Marcus stood with Mother and Lentulus in the atrium as the last of his guests departed. Mother eyed Curio in particular. He told Marcus a lewd joke on his way out the door.

Marcus guffawed. He had drunk quite a bit, but it was his toga ceremony, after all.

Once the guests were all gone, he turned to thank his parents, still holding his gladius proudly. "Gratias, Lentulus, Mother. It's been a wonderful day. We've never had such a party here. I'll never forget it."

Lentulus smiled warmly, embracing him. "No. Thank you, Marcus. Thank you for being a good son to your mother and forgiving my pitfalls as your stepfather."

Marcus looked at him, puzzled. "What do you mean? You're a very good stepfather, and you make Mother happy."

"Indeed," she agreed readily, slipping her arm through Lentulus's. He smiled, "Ah, well—I hope so."

Marcus grinned contentedly, nodding in appreciation.

"Marcus, my love, Lentulus and I have something to ask you."

"What?" He was fumbling with the gladius, trying to figure out how to attach it when wearing it.

"Here, let me show you," Lentulus offered. "You hang it on the right, you know." After demonstrating, he broached the subject. "Now listen, boy. Your mother and I know that in time you'll marry for position, but until then—well, have you a woman to satisfy you when you need one?"

Marcus met Lentulus's gaze, unwavering. "Not to worry, Lentulus. I've more than enough satisfaction when it comes to sex."

The look on Mother's face was hysterical. Brows raised to the heavens, her mouth had dropped wide open. Lentulus burst out laughing.

Boyhood had ended, but Marcus's nightmares continued with renewed vengeance. Yet lately the images had changed. The crosses were replaced by pools of blood. Marcus would wander aimlessly through a dark chamber, trying to figure out who was bleeding. Sometimes it was him. More often it was someone else, lying facedown on an ornate mosaic floor. Once, he awakened with a start as an unknown assailant wielded a gleaming pugio, stabbing someone repeatedly. It was impossible to see the victim's face, but the blade always dripped bright crimson.

Tonight's nightmare was altogether different and horrific. In it, Lentulus appeared, hands bound, his mouth frothing with pinkish foam. He moved his mouth as if to speak, but no words came out.

Marcus jerked awake in a sweat. Heart hammering, he found Vindelicus standing at the end of his sleeping couch, apprehension on his face.

"Dominus? You troubled?"

Marcus nodded, sucking in air and conscious that he probably didn't look well.

Vindelicus stepped forward, gently placing a hand on his shoulder. "You cry out loud many times. What is wrong?"

Marcus shook his head. "Nothing. Just dreams I have sometimes."

"Bad, yah?"

Marcus nodded breathlessly.

The Gaul squatted on his haunches next to the sleeping couch. Marcus knew he'd stay unless asked to go. Vindelicus loved him as a son. Never was there a more faithful friend than this tall, hairy warrior.

As his breathing slowed, Marcus laid back on one elbow. "Vindelicus, tell me again how you came to us." It was no bedtime story, but it would be a good distraction from the awful dream he'd just had.

Sadness clouded the Gaul's face. Nevertheless, he willingly retold his tale.

"A neighboring tribe of mine was bribed by Greek slavers. They attacked our village after sunset, and before I kill any of them, they hit my head with something hard and take me prisoner. When I awake, I hear screams and see men stealing our wives and mothers away. My own wife cried, holding our child. But what could I do? One of the men—he takes my child—my baby boy, and he stabs him with his javelin. He do that because a baby not worth nothing to slavers. Then they tie me to a cart with my brothers and men from my village. I never see my wife anymore."

"And after that, you were sold to become a gladiator, right?" Marcus recalled.

"Yah. I get these scars all over Italia." He held his arm out and rolled up his sleeve, displaying white lines on his shoulders and forearm.

"And then came Caesar?"

"Yah. He save my life, I think. I was getting old for a gladiator. I could not keep alive forever. He sees me in a fight and buys me. He says he wants me to train up a boy."

Marcus smiled.

Vindelicus finished his tale. "I give Caesar my word of honor as a warrior and was sent here. But I no have a boy anymore. I have a man now. And for the first time since being taken away, I am happy." The Gaul grinned, showing big yellowing teeth.

Vindelicus had the heart of a lion. Marcus was grateful for his kind, loyal strength.

Unable to fall asleep again, he asked, "Why do the gods plague us with nightmares?"

"Among my people, we used to tell of important dreams, good and bad. Sometimes they mean things," Vindelicus replied.

Marcus stared at him, aghast. Mean something? Gods, how could he possibly tell about these? No, cursed as they were, these nightmares would remain silent. He shook his head. "They're nothing," he whispered. "I just have them a lot." And now they led him to drench their horror in sex and drink—a cycle starting to whirl so uncontrollably fast he couldn't stop it. Marcus had lost focus, his dreams and goals becoming as unreachable as mirages in a desert.

He rolled over, stubbornly facing the wall. Some things he couldn't even share with Vindelicus. "Go back to sleep," he whispered.

Hearing the Gaul sigh deeply, Marcus felt him leave his side and listened to his retreating footsteps fade beyond the doorway.

The past night's debaucheries left Marcus nursing a headache as he wandered into the peristyle garden, squinting. Mother and Lentulus were lounging on cushions in the grass.

"Impressive, isn't he?" Mother was musing, trailing her hand in the fishpond and snapping off a water lily.

"Who?" Marcus asked, sliding down against a column across from them.

"Marcus? Well, aren't we the fortunate ones. I didn't think you lived here anymore," she jibed.

Lentulus snickered at her remark. "He's just a young man enjoying himself, Julia! Let him be."

"Well, then," she answered, "Gnaeus Pompeius is who I spoke about. To have eliminated piracy in only forty days. Lentulus and I would not even be having this conversation if Creticus had succeeded. His was the same mission from the Senate, you know."

"So it was," Lentulus murmured, picking seeds out of pomegranate pulp.

"If Pompeius keeps up like everyone thinks, what will stop him from taking the rest of the East?" Mother pondered.

"Taking the entire East would be a logical move." Lentulus remarked.

Marcus rubbed at his throbbing temples. Lately, Mother had been overly keen on politics. It seemed like whenever he was around her, it was all she talked about—who was doing what in the Senate, trying to figure out who'd be consul next year... It was tiresome.

"Yes, Pompeius will be the one to court when he returns. If anyone can get you back into the Senate, he can," she declared.

"Mother, can you talk about anything besides politics and whether Lentulus will ever get back into the Senate?" Marcus queried, sarcasm oozing forth.

She bristled. "If you're just coming out here to insult me, go back to the races or taverns you frequent. I want only the best for your stepfather."

Lentulus intervened. "I told you, love—Catilina has promised to help me."

Catilina again. Marcus hadn't been to many dinners at home lately, but he was aware that Catilina had been frequenting their triclinium.

Mother must have been reading his mind, for she sniped at Lentulus, "Catilina, Catilina, Catilina! We've not enjoyed a single dinner once in the past month without his company. Whenever we get an invitation to go out, even from family, you change plans, accepting one from him instead. Lentulus, his name is tainted—suspect among even liberal senators. And Aelia says some are gathering proof that he's treasonous. Should you really depend on his influence to clear your name?"

Marcus raised his eyebrows. Truth be told, he didn't know enough about Catilina to own an opinion about the man. However, treason against Rome was always punishable by death.

Lentulus hadn't responded, so prone was he to humoring Mother, even if she was in a bad temper. He was always so patient in letting her vent opinions. Not all men were so indulgent.

Mother bluntly concluded, "Well, I don't like him, and I don't trust him. There. I've said it."

Lentulus shrugged. "It's not necessary for you to like all my friends." He smiled, setting his pomegranate aside to reach for her hand. "There are plenty of things about our life together that you do like. Agreed, Marcus?"

Marcus smiled. "Agreed." He motioned to Lentulus to toss him the rest of the fruit. Upon catching it, he said, "Tell me more about Catilina's reputation."

Mother jumped in to answer. "Whenever he's here, Lentulus always sends me to retire with the women and children after dining. He never does that among other friends or family."

Lentulus responded to Marcus's question. "Your Mother's right that the Senate has a low opinion of Catilina and his radical ideas. As for sending her away with the women and children, when Catilina gets deep into his cups, he uses language I prefer her not to hear."

"Oh, please," Mother scoffed, sitting up suddenly. "Don't treat me like an innocent. I'm afraid of the influence he has on you."

"So you don't trust me?" Lentulus also sat up, frowning.

Oh gods. He was reaching his limit. Were they going to argue? Marcus wasn't sure his sore head could handle that. He tore into the last bit of pomegranate, pursuing the juicy seeds.

"Trust you? Of course I *trust* you," she insisted. "I just never want to lose the love we share to misguided ambition. We're a close-knit family—you, me, and the boys. You're a loving husband and father to them. I never want that to change. And I've seen life change for the worst too many times in the past."

Lentulus opened the palm of her hand and held it to his lips, kissing it. Then he arose and stretched. "You've nothing to worry about," he promised. "Now I've got some correspondence needing attention. Marcus, why don't you stay here and keep your Mother company a little longer? It's a beautiful day. Enjoy it."

As he left, heading to the tablinum, Marcus saw Mother gazing after him. "Is everything all right between you two?" he asked.

She nodded, her face full of concern. "Yes—I hope so. I think all is well between us, but he just won't tell me what's happening whenever he and Catilina are together."

"Men should be allowed their privacy, Mother. They're friends. Let them be."

"As long as that privacy doesn't endanger us, Marcus."

Marcus bit into a grape, its sweet juice filling his mouth. He'd made certain to attend this dinner, even giving up a night with Metinara for it. His eyes were riveted upon the family's most frequent dinner guest.

"Have you heard what they call him now? Pompeius *Magnus!*" Lucius Sergius Catilina drawled, like an actor in some melodramatic death scene. Though muscular and well-built, whenever he drank his face turned red as a rose.

Glancing at Mother, Marcus smirked in amusement. She was eying Catilina with intense dislike.

Marcus wanted to make a good first impression on Lentulus's friend. He commented, "But Pompeius's honors were justly earned."

Catilina snorted and shook his head. "You're young. Successes of other men will nauseate you someday too. Wait and see."

"Why?" Marcus challenged. "Especially if someone honors Rome in the process? Magnus did everything he said he would—and more."

Catilina chuckled. "In the Senate, Antonius, someone else's success is like … like a raunchy shit in the public latrines. You never notice how foul it is when it's yours, but everyone else does!"

Lentulus and Uncle Hybrida guffawed loudly, nodding their heads at the analogy. Marcus snickered and saw Mother avert her eyes. The men around her were carrying on as only men could.

Catilina guzzled through another cup, holding it up again for more and suppressing a belch. Marcus followed suit, grinning and emptying his cup as well. He waved to Syrianus, gesturing for less water in his share.

Mother moved closer to him, whispering, "Haven't you had your fill this night?"

Marcus ignored her.

"The Republic has died," Catilina droned on, a belch finding its way out after all. "My challenge to all Romans is simple. Rebuild and start anew."

"How?" Marcus asked. "In what way would you do that?"

"We would start by—"

"Son, would you escort me to my cubiculum?" Mother arose in one lithe movement.

Marcus glared at her in irritation, but she ignored it.

"Please?" She closed her eyes momentarily, lightly touching her temples as though in pain.

Marcus cocked a critical eyebrow at her dramatics. "Very well. If I must." To Catilina, he added, "Excuse me, Lucius Sergius. I'll return shortly."

He offered his hand to her none too gently, escorting her toward the peristyle corridor.

Outside, she pulled away, walking briskly toward her bedchamber.

Marcus growled, "Seems you're suddenly cured. Aesculapius be praised."

Mother paused, turning back. "I can't abide having that man under my roof anymore. If he's here tomorrow, I'll dine elsewhere."

Marcus shook his head, watching her go. He was just about to return to the triclinium when she scolded, "And when did you start drinking so much? I saw you asking Syrianus for less water in your wine."

He rolled his eyes.

"Whatever has come over you?" she hissed, approaching like a bitch with raised hackles. "You rarely join us for dinner anymore. Or if you do, it's only a short time before you hurry off. Then there's your choice of friends, which frightens me. Do you really want to risk your reputation with the likes of Curio and Clodius? You hardly see your family anymore."

Marcus bristled at the reprimand but guarded his tongue.

"I couldn't believe you tonight. Guzzling like a common legionary!" she went on. "You had five full cups before the third course."

"No, four. You miscounted," he corrected.

"*Four*, then. Does it matter? You just took the toga virilis last year and you act like a spoiled adolescent. You're a man of seventeen years. Act the part."

That didn't even warrant a response. Marcus turned on his heel, starting back toward the triclinium.

"Wait. Please, Marcus." Her tone changed, making him curious. He stopped.

"I need your help," she entreated, edging close enough to speak confidentially.

Marcus remained detached, willing to listen but little more than that. Especially after such a tongue-lashing.

"I know you're interested in Catilina's ideas," she began. "I watch you; I understand your growing fascination in these matters. But, Marcus, he's dangerous."

"Go on," he said.

"My greatest fear is your stepfather being swayed too much by his agenda, not to mention his scandalous ways. Nothing good can come of it. I need to know what Catilina is trying to accomplish in all these meetings with him. Lentulus won't tell me."

Marcus crossed his arms. "Ah. You want me to spy on Lentulus for you?"

"Not spy. Just listen whenever they're together. It would be more natural for you to be present—"

"That's spying. Gods, Mother, how could you? I thought you loved the man. He's given you much—given to all of us."

Coming closer, she took his hand. "Exactly, Marcus. I love him and couldn't bear losing him."

When he didn't respond immediately, she desperately went on. "You know these are dangerous times. What if someone in the Senate prosecutes Catilina? What if there's proof he's a traitor—and Lentulus is involved?"

"Just because Lentulus is Catilina's friend and confidant doesn't mean he'll risk life and limb for him. Trust him like a wife should. Stay out of his business." Marcus jerked his hand free of her hold, his closing words firm and final. "Go ask Hybrida or someone else to do your dirty work, if you insist on it, because I won't."

CHAPTER IX
64-63 BC

CROWDS OF MEN JOSTLED FOR SPACE AT THE GAMING tables. Curio and Marcus were hosting a night of iactus, every Roman's favorite dice game. Word got out, then someone told some merchants down at the Tiber docks. By nightfall, nearly a hundred men of varied status had crowded into the Suburan club. Each was laden with coin enough to drink and play the night away.

Marcus sat at a table facing three merchants. Eyes closed, he shook his dice around in a little wooden cup, hoping for better luck. Lentulus had given him a good start of three hundred with which to enjoy himself earlier in the week. The night started well. He'd gained five hundred denarii, totaling a purse of eight hundred. But in the last few rounds, he'd lost almost everything. Now he was down to a sad little hundred.

One more loss meant forfeiting the entire night.

He threw his dice on the table, hearing them clatter and bounce to a stop. Slowly, he opened his eyes, afraid of what he'd see.

One two, two threes, a four, and a five.

Gods. How awful. So far he'd claimed a coin token and two dogs.

He was harboring hopes of regaining some of his losses. But the coveted Venus—five sixes—was playing hard to get.

Opposite him sat the three players who'd won nearly all his coin. They were grinning like a pack of hyenas. None of them had as many tokens as he, but they each had a lot more coin. When it came to playing iactus, silver and gold meant lasting power. For Marcus, the evening would soon be over unless things turned around in three more throws.

Curio lounged at his elbow with a cup of wine in hand. Taking a swig, he suggested, "Promise something to Fortuna. Maybe she'll help."

Marcus snorted. He harbored little faith in Fortuna. For luck, he plopped his dice back into the cup and breathed on them. At his toss, the dice clattered out a second time.

One six, two fives, and two ones. Damn.

"Well, at least you're on your way now," Curio whispered near his ear. Marcus edged away from him. Curio had a nasty habit of invading his space in a way that reminded him of Lupus.

Marcus picked up all the dice except the single six. A gain of four more sixes would win the game, but the odds of that happening in two rolls were slim.

He glanced over at the hyenas as he shook his cup. The oldest had a girl sitting on his knee. Her mouth was at his ear, and whatever she was saying had him smiling. One of the other two farted loudly, and his friend burst out laughing.

Suddenly, another man strolled up to his other side. Marcus eyed him. Dressed expensively but gaudily, bald, hook-nosed, short, and squat. He gave Marcus a courteous nod. Marcus's response was a cough, gagging on the newcomer's heavy perfume.

He rolled for the third time. Two fours, one three, and another six. He needed that Venus, so he kept the second six, gathering up the other three dice.

One more roll...

Chewing his lip, he tossed a final time.

It was downright painful. Marcus groaned. Two ones, a five, and two sixes. He'd missed the Venus by only one six. That hurt worse than not having any.

Disgusted, he shook his head, preparing to leave the table with nothing but an empty purse. But the perfumed stranger next to him spoke up, his Latin tinged with a Greek accent. "Gentlemen, I'm making this young man a gift of three hundred denarii."

Marcus stared at the newcomer in amazement. The offered gift was kind, but Marcus didn't know him. Kindness was something for which Rome wasn't known. Curio was swift to move closer and whisper an explanation in his ear, "He's Callias, a big creditor with a shop down in the Forum and an expensive domus on the Esquiline. He used to handle all of Clodius's business."

Marcus asked, "And yours too?"

"Used to. Right now I've got debt running out of my arse like diarrhea."

Marcus snorted at Curio's crudeness, then responded to Callias. "Thank you, sir. But what's your rate? I can't afford much tonight."

"No worries," Callias replied. "It's a gift. May it earn your future business."

Most men had creditors. Marcus knew Lentulus dealt with someone, but he wasn't sure who. Some were shady characters. "Gratias, then. I'll visit you next time I need coin."

Sadly, Callias's gift didn't impress fickle Fortuna. The only thing Marcus ended up with was his good looks. At least Metinara and her friend, Serapia, saw value in that.

Marcus left the table. He and the two women disappeared into one of the brothel's cubicula to reverse his losses.

Vindelicus gave Marcus the usual leg up onto the wall. He was drunk and weary from gambling and sex. Clumsily, he leaped down into the peristyle garden. This was the fourth night in a row with no coin in his pockets and a growing debt. Soon after their first meeting, Marcus had started an account with Callias the Greek in the Forum. However, things weren't looking good. Curio cornered him and said the club was in trouble. Clodius, still in the provinces, had written, refusing to send any more money to support the place. Unless Marcus forked out more coin, they'd have to shut down. Oh, they could open to the public, of course. But the whole point was having a *private* club. It was a matter of pride. It was theirs, exclusive—except by invitation.

Marcus suggested to Curio they take turns on rent payments. Curio agreed, but only grudgingly. It was the only solution. Otherwise, there'd be no more Metinara, Serapia, Mallia, Flavia ...

As he headed to his cubiculum, his ill humor faded, recalling tonight's revels through a wine-induced haze. Curio hadn't shown up until late, so Marcus had had the place to himself. Sweet Venus! The things he and Serapia had done tonight. Ho, he should have been born an acrobat.

With a yawn, he opened his cubiculum door. Vindelicus grunted good-night wishes, bedding down just outside, as usual. Head spinning and sleepy, Marcus sat down on his sleeping couch. His belt and pugio clanked noisily to the floor when he jerked them off. He collapsed backward onto his pillow and dissolved into relaxation, his cheek sinking into soft goose down. His eyes were half-shut when the voice spoke, nearly causing him to fall out of bed.

"It's late, Marcus. Almost dawn."

Leaping to his feet and losing balance in the dark, he staggered clear across the room. Unable to stop his clumsy momentum, he plowed into the wall for support. His right hand collided with a tall lamp stand on its tripod. Grabbing at it, he barely prevented it falling to the floor.

"Mother?" he gasped, heart racing.

And it wasn't just Mother. Both she and Lentulus stepped out of the shadows near the door. He'd walked right past them.

"We thought you might be interested in hearing what happened to Fadia tonight."

Marcus pressed his eyes shut, shaking his head, dazedly trying to focus. This was unreal. "Fadia? What?"

Mother sat on his bed, making herself at home. Lentulus remained next to the door.

"Fadia was out near the Subura. She was attacked by a thief."

"Tonight?"

"Yes. The beast tore her tunic halfway off. She awakened the entire household banging on the door, trying to get back inside."

Marcus was speechless. He'd barely noticed the slave girl since discovering the Subura. Things had become so awkward between them that he just found it easier avoiding her. Gods, anything to erase the memory of that terrible return trip from Baiae.

Marcus blinked back to the present. His head felt fuzzy, a harbinger for feeling worse later. "Why was she out near the Subura?"

Lentulus finally spoke, eyebrows raised in curiosity. "We were rather hoping you'd help us with that one."

Marcus frowned, his eyes darting from one to the other. "How's that?"

"Because she was following you," Lentulus said, crossing his arms.

Mother explained, "That's how we learned that you've been visiting the Subura yourself regularly. I can't much blame her curiosity. I'm rather curious about where you've been going as well."

Puffing his cheeks out, Marcus sighed heavily, walking back to his bed. He sat down, trying to keep his voice calm. "I'm a grown man. I needn't answer to anyone concerning my whereabouts."

The tone of Mother's response was just as controlled. "Is that what you think? Then let me ask you a question. How many full-grown men climb walls to come and go from their domus? Your father always used the atrium door, and so does Lentulus, regardless of where he's headed."

Marcus's headache was coming on now. And he had absolutely no response.

Mother forged on. "When it comes to embarrassing this family, you'll answer not only to me, but to Lentulus as well. He seeks reentry into the Senate. Therefore his reputation must remain spotless. As for me, I happen to enjoy my social life and don't want it compromised by your pleasure-seeking behavior. And let's not forget your brothers. They'll have political and military careers eventually. So do you see? Your behavior affects all of us."

Marcus clenched his jaw. "Someday I'll have a career too."

"Oh, really?" she queried sarcastically. "When? After you come home drunk again tomorrow?"

Marcus reached up with one hand, rubbing between his eyes. His head was throbbing now. He clenched his teeth, breathing irritably. "I don't feel like arguing with you tonight."

It was Lentulus's turn. "Good. Truly, we've no desire to argue either. Today your mother and I decided something on your behalf since you've been out so much lately."

Marcus frowned. Where were they going with this? He was in no shape to spar with them, and something about this didn't sound good. "Decided what?" he managed.

Mother brushed a wrinkle from the linen coverlet on his bed. "Caesar wrote to me from Spain, asking about you. He'll be returning any day, seeking new officers. Naturally, he thought of you, but he had the courtesy to ask Lentulus and me first since you're still a young...man, as you say." She pulled a folded piece of parchment from her robes and handed it to him.

Marcus stared at the letter. If it was from Caesar, it was too dark to read now. He stared at it, desperately blinking Bacchus from his eyes.

"We know many prominent families whose sons are your age," Lentulus said. "Most of them have already accepted positions as junior staff officers."

Mother smiled, taking her time and yawning. "And we've declined Caesar's offer."

Marcus froze, gripped with shock and hurt.

Mother rose, moving to the other side of the sleeping couch, standing next to Lentulus. "We feel you could better represent Rome once you give up consuming habits, which might threaten your career."

Marcus lurched clumsily to his feet. Though he wanted to slug Lentulus and shove Mother from his room, his drunken state had immobilized him.

"Get out of here!" he raged, his voice cracking. In his present condition, it was all he could think of. "Get out and stop interfering with my life!"

Lentulus turned on his heel and left immediately, but Mother stayed. Calm and cool as ever, despite his angst, she remarked, "I must tell Fadia to wash that tunic of yours. It reeks of some prostitute's cheap perfume. Sleep well, Marcus."

Once she shut the door, he looked down at his hands, still holding the letter from Caesar. They shook. Was it wine or anger causing it? Probably both. He felt as if some quack physician had bled him weak.

Serapia had vanished from his mind, replaced by tormenting truth. He had lost an incredible opportunity.

Three weeks later, Marcus moved forward with hopeful resolve. He had decided to maneuver without Mother, Lentulus, and their scheming. With a freshly shaved chin, he snatched his finest cloak and hastily exited the domus.

Purposefully striding down to the Forum Romanum with Vindelicus in tow, he paused long enough at a food stall to buy steamed meat from a street vendor. From there, he turned down the Via Sacra toward the Rostra, munching on the savory wrap. He stopped abruptly, spying the very person he sought.

Marcus grinned broadly.

Hopes rising, he handed over the remains of his meal to Vindelicus, who eagerly gulped down the rest. Marcus wiped his mouth and shouldered his way through the crowd. Vindelicus followed at his heels, licking grease from his long mustache.

Temporary wooden scaffolding was going up quickly around

the Rostra. Soon games thrown by the recently elected aedile, Gaius Julius Caesar, would commence.

"Cousin!" Marcus hurried toward his kinsman, arm raised in greeting.

Caesar turned about. He was much leaner, his forehead higher due to a dramatically receding hairline. He had combed all his remaining hair forward. Caesar stared at Marcus long and hard, then suddenly laughed, shaking his head in disbelief. "Is this really Marcus Antonius?"

Marcus held his arms wide, embracing Caesar like a bear. This man he had always respected, admired, and wanted to please was now slightly shorter than he. "Remember, you've been gone since I was thirteen."

Caesar laughed heartily. "Well, the gods have blessed you with strength and stature. Let me look at you."

Marcus couldn't help comparing himself with Caesar, and it was especially pleasing. How muscled his own arms and shoulders were in comparison. It was obvious; he was perfectly suited to be in a legion. "How was Spain?" he asked eagerly.

Caesar laughed aloud, addressing two togate men beside him. "How refreshing when someone takes interest in one's work. Antonius, let me introduce you to two very important friends. Meet Marcus Licinius Crassus and Marcus Tullius Cicero."

Inclining his head politely, Marcus clasped the hand of the wealthiest man in Rome. "Salve, sir." The same General Crassus who had finally defeated Spartacus and was responsible for leaving the harrowing trail of crosses all the way to Rome.

"It's a pleasure meeting any young man interested in current events," Crassus responded.

Cicero nodded in turn. A serious man, his face looked as though it would crack if he smiled. "Salutations, Antonius." Returning his attentions to Caesar, Cicero said, "Forgive me, but I must decline the rest of the tour and return home. I've works in progress needing more attention than construction sites. Rest assured, however, I'll attend your games with expectation and enthusiasm." With a polite nod, he latched on to a sinus of his toga and walked away.

Once beyond earshot, Caesar leaned close to Crassus. "I doubt he's ever displayed enthusiasm in his entire life unless it was for one of his own speeches."

Crassus tossed his head back, laughing.

One arm draping over Marcus's shoulder, Caesar explained, "We were touring the makeshift amphitheater. They're finishing it today. Crassus kindly granted me a generous loan, guaranteeing that my games as aedile will be memorable to the people."

Crassus clapped Caesar on the back. "Friends help each other, right, Caesar?"

"As you say."

"I imagine it's been a good long time since you've seen your cousin," Crassus observed. "Let me leave you two and I'll see you at the games."

Crassus blended into a mass of other senators outside the Curia, leaving Marcus and Caesar as alone as two people could be in the middle of the Forum Romanum at noon.

"How are you, Marcus? I see you still have Vindelicus."

Marcus glanced back at the burly Gaul standing humbly in the native breeches he always wore. "He's the best thing you ever did for me."

"Good. How's your swordplay?"

"I still beat Gaius and sometimes participate in competitions in the Campus Martius."

"Excellent."

"I want to hear more about Spain. But first I must ask you something."

They moved to an olive tree east of the Curia, where ample shade beckoned.

"Mother told me you wrote her concerning an officer's position. I want to join you. Please, will you appoint me?"

Caesar's smile faded somewhat.

"Marcus, Lentulus wrote me on behalf of himself and your

mother. He told me the offer was ill-timed." He paused. "It was your mother writing in her own hand explaining why."

Of course it was. "Oh, please," he scoffed. "Would I be the first Roman officer wanting a woman or cup of wine now and then?"

"That's not the point," Caesar explained. "It's when such behavior is unbridled that it becomes unacceptable. I don't host Bacchantes, I lead hardened soldiers."

"I'll stop, change, do anything. You know I want this."

Caesar sat down on a bundle of straw, soon to be strewn in the amphitheater. "I know you can be a soldier," he began. "I believe you would follow my commands, ride into battle without question. What I'm unsure of, along with your parents, is whether you're ready to lead as an example to other men. As an officer, you must inspire legionaries to follow you to death. Can you motivate a man to put his life into your hands like that?"

Marcus blinked, looking away. He was unsure how to answer.

Caesar continued, "When I was in Spain, I saw a statue of Alexander the Great. Only the gods know how long it stood in the temple where I happened on it. Admiring it, I felt ashamed. What had I done in comparison to a man who conquered the known world when he was younger than I? Encountering his image became my defining moment. I knew I must succeed as a leader, militarily and politically. Now I drive myself to achieve whatever future is mine for the taking."

"How do you mean?"

Caesar sighed, shrugging. "Olympus never allows us to see more than a glimmer of the glory in store, but I believe I was born to attain greatness. Now I ride a tide of events, determining what that glory will be. You must seek to do the same."

Marcus stared down at a long string of ants filing one behind the other, disappointment sucking away his hopes. "And just when will I ever have a 'defining moment,' as you call it?"

Caesar stood up again and clapped him on the back. "When you find yourself. Then, and only then."

Marcus attended Caesar's extravagant games with his brothers. Lentulus joined them several nights in a row, but Marcus ignored him, infuriated with his stepfather for siding with Mother against him.

On the final day of spectacles, Lentulus pulled him aside in the atrium as they were leaving for the evening entertainment. "Marcus, let's talk. I'm truly sorry about your missed opportunity. However, there will be others."

Marcus set his jaw, speaking with cool demeanor, "You are paterfamilias—the head of our household, Lentulus. You could've countered her."

"Come along, boy. Don't you know how fond I am of you? So is your mother. Though you can't see it now, she loves you more than her own life. Other chances will come. Wait and see." He paused before speaking again, keeping his voice low. "Listen, I need your help."

Marcus stiffened, still resentful. If Lentulus wanted something, he'd damn well be paying for it.

"For a gift of silver, might I borrow your Gaul tomorrow afternoon?"

Silver? That meant interest-free rent for the Subura brothel. It would be worth swallowing a little pride for that. Curio would be pleased. Marcus made himself soften. "You need Vindelicus? Why?"

"Well, I have good news. I'm officially a senator again. Several colleagues have already approached me concerning a law they're trying to pass. They face much opposition, so we're meeting tomorrow afternoon. They suggested bringing a bodyguard. You know how awful the streets are these days. I promise to return your brute safe and sound."

Marcus felt a twinge of guilt. He hadn't been at the domus enough lately to hear Lentulus's news. Sighing, he pushed the feeling aside. His stepfather would still have to pay up because ruining an opportunity like the one Caesar offered had lasting consequences. It would take some time for Marcus to get past that.

"I'm glad you're back in the Senate," Marcus stated. "If it would help, you may keep Vindelicus for the whole day—for another bag of coin, of course."

Lentulus scrutinized Marcus a moment before agreeing. "Of course. Very well, I'll return Vindelicus tomorrow night. Many thanks, Marcus."

Marcus watched him go uncertainly. What sort of law was Lentulus helping pass that required safety from a bodyguard? He chewed his lip, unsettled. Something didn't feel right.

Since Lentulus wasn't with them, Marcus seized the opportunity to take his brothers to the Subura after the games. Gaius found the women to his liking, and twelve-year-old Lucius got more than an eyeful. When they returned home, faces flushed with wine, Vindelicus was waiting in the atrium.

Marcus ribbed Gaius, "If I were you, I'd stick to whores. No commitments that way. But, Jupiter! Stop eating so much, or you'll grow so fat no woman will want you."

Gaius held out his hands, grinning. "Does it really matter? If I do get fat, there's more of me for a woman to love."

Marcus shook his head. "You're crazy, Gaius. No girl wants a fat man."

Lucius punched Marcus in the arm, grinning. "Thanks for letting me go, Marcus."

"Dominus," Vindelicus interrupted, stepping forward.

Marcus turned to him, still amused at the thought of his youngest brother with a girl. "What? Why so serious, Vindelicus?" He laughed at the Gaul. "Looks like you just swallowed hemlock!"

"Dominus, I speak with you in private—now."

Gaius joked, "He looks too solemn. He needs a romp with a girl at your lupanar."

Marcus smiled at the humor but locked eyes with Vindelicus. Indeed, something was wrong. As he followed the Gaul down the corridor, Gaius called after him, "Promise to take us back soon, Marcus."

He turned back, warning, "Just remember, Mallia and Serapia care nothing for fat men. You don't want to lose them to Lucius!"

Lucius howled with laughter.

Vindelicus opened Marcus's cubiculum door for him, following him in and shutting it securely. Without a word, the slave dropped to his knees, trembling like a sacrificial goat.

"Gods, Vindelicus. What is it?"

"Dominus, I serve you good, yah?"

"Of course."

"You trust me—you believe what I say when I talk?"

Marcus sat down on his sleeping couch, frowning. Pulling a wreath of wilting flowers from his head, he tossed it aside. "Something happened today when you were with Lentulus?"

The Gaul nodded, grimly staring down at the black-and-white floor tiles.

"What?" Marcus asked.

Vindelicus hesitated, still as stone.

"Tell me," Marcus growled.

"Believe what I say." His voice dropped even lower. "Dominus Lentulus is part of something very bad. It is—how you say when someone makes war against your government?"

"Insurrection? Revolution?"

"Revolution." Vindelicus nodded in certainty. "He is leader of this revolution in the city."

A chill went down Marcus's spine, danger quickening his senses. "Where did he go today?"

"A tavern on the Esquiline."

"With who?"

"Catilina and your uncle."

"Uncle? Which one?"

"Hybrida, the soldier one."

"Then they weren't really meeting about some law?"

"No, Dominus. No law. They plan a revolt."

"When will it be?"

"They work on it now. Not for some time." Vindelicus bowed his head fearfully.

Marcus sat in shock.

Vindelicus continued, "Dominus Lentulus is leader for Catilina's plans here in Rome. Uncle will try to be consul with Catilina."

"That makes sense. I've heard that Cicero is standing for consul too. They must be trying to seize partial, if not total, control."

"Dominus Lentulus thinks me stupid, that I hardly talk and know Latin," the big Gaul added with a snort and dour smile.

Marcus smiled. "My stepfather's more a fool than anyone knows, then. What to do? If I go to him and beg him to reconsider all this, he could punish you for telling me. For that, I'd never forgive myself."

Mother had been right all along. Lentulus could bring death on himself and destroy the whole family in the process. Gods! He could destroy Rome. Marcus should have helped her, after all. Perhaps together they could have prevented things going this far.

He wandered over to a table and basin of water. Scooping up a handful, he splashed his face, shaking the excess off and trying to sober up. The Gaul watched, leaning against the wall in silent consternation.

"I need to find someone to help us," Marcus said.

"Mamma's brother, the consul?"

Marcus shook his head emphatically. "Lucius Julius? No. He's a difficult sort. Has been ever since Mother remarried. He despises Lentulus and rarely deals with any of us now." With a sigh, he made his decision. "I'm thinking Caesar would be the best choice."

"I hear Catilina say his name today."

Marcus stared at him in concern. "What was said?"

"Catilina maybe try to gain his support too."

Jupiter! How many were involved? "Ho. Then I must try to get to him first." He chewed his lip, trying to think.

Vindelicus nodded in encouragement. "Go to Caesar. Maybe go to Lentulus, no matter what he does to me, but do not tell Mamma."

Marcus shook his head slowly in agreement. No. Of all people, she mustn't know.

CHAPTER X
63 BC

MARCUS AND VINDELICUS WAITED INSIDE CAESAR'S spacious atrium. Every footstep echoed in the silent, cavernous chamber.

Marcus paced, rehearsing what he'd say. Several senators were ahead of him, and he and Vindelicus stood about anxiously. The older he got, the more Marcus scoffed at the state religion. Yet today he found himself praying silently to Jupiter that Catilina hadn't beaten him here.

Timon exited the tablinum, followed by several senators who saw themselves out. "Caesar will see you now, Dominus Antonius."

"Come, Vindelicus," Marcus invited.

Caesar sat behind a simple cedar desk, writing rapidly on a wax tablet. As they approached, he snapped it shut. "Marcus. Forgive me for being so long, but obligations weigh heavily today." Seeing Vindelicus, he smiled pleasantly. "I see you brought a friend."

"Yes. He's here because he first conveyed to me information I must share with you. Caesar, we must speak privately. May we close the door?"

Caesar raised his brows but nodded approval. Vindelicus immediately saw to the task.

"This sounds serious," Caesar said.

"Yes."

"Please sit down."

Marcus related the Gaul's story. "I wanted to see you before Catilina did. I beg you to support our family and dissuade Lentulus from taking on this danger."

There was momentary silence before Caesar finally asked, "What do you think of the conspiracy?"

"Truthfully, I don't know the particulars. But insurrection against the Republic? That thought horrifies me. It would be treason against Rome and nothing less."

Fine lines alongside Caesar's mouth tightened. "But what if the Republic of which you speak is no longer reality? Then what are they rising against?"

"You're like them? You believe the Republic is dead?"

Caesar snorted. "Marcus, this business Catilina is plotting may only be the beginning of Rome's 'revolution.' There are powerful men all over this city who strongly desire radical revision of our country's government. And yes, I'm one of them. Some of us—Populares—support the people's cause. Every man in the Senate knows of Catilina's constant scheming. Men like Cicero would like to see him burned alive. But I admit Lentulus's involvement surprises me."

"Catilina dines often at our domus, feeding him ideas," Marcus said. "He makes it sound so desperate: 'Save our city from worse than death,' like it should be Lentulus's patriotic duty or something. Mother's been worried sick about it, but until Vindelicus overheard their conversation, I was never concerned. I just can't stand by and let Lentulus do this. It's madness. It would destroy Mother and dishonor our family again, not to mention what it could do to the city."

Caesar tapped his fingers on the desk, making a rhythmic, drumming sound. "Our first problem is legal. Vindelicus is your only witness, and he's a slave. Therefore his words aren't lawful evidence—unless he's tortured. Our second problem is that Lentulus is a grown man, older than I. He wouldn't tolerate either of us dictating to him what his political proclivities should be. So unfortunately there's nothing to do except wait. I promise you this much, if anything transpires publicly involving him, I'll speak on his behalf."

That was it?

Someone knocked softly on the door.

Caesar called out, "Enter."

A vision of red silk glided into the room. Marcus had only seen her from afar, but he knew instantly that this was Pompeia, Caesar's new wife. He arose politely upon her entry.

Pompeia gazed at Marcus a little too long as she crossed the spacious marble floor. Her painted green eyes examined him head to toe, making him shift uncomfortably in her husband's presence.

"Wife, have you met my young kinsman Marcus Antonius?"

"No, but I've heard of him." She responded, tongue licking over her upper lip suggestively. "He's friends with Clodius and Curio."

Marcus cocked an eyebrow. Oh shit. What had she heard?

As if reading his thoughts, Pompeia's moist lip curled coyly, showing off little white teeth, perfect as pearls. She turned to her husband, inquiring, "Might I take a litter to the Forum and find something for Crassus's party tomorrow night?"

Caesar's eyes bore into hers darkly, his displeasure obvious. "No. You've exceeded your allowance this month already. I won't be bankrupt due to my wife's overspending."

Marcus noted a fleeting look of anger and defiance in her eyes. She showed them all her back, exiting without another word, not bothering to shut the door.

Caesar ignored her, continuing where they left off. "Remember, we don't know if or when this whole affair will come to light. I'll keep your words in confidence. If anything transpires, we'll alert each other."

The interview ended with too many unanswered questions. Had

Catilina already persuaded Caesar to join him? Was he trustworthy? Was it a mistake coming here?

Caesar left the chamber without another word. Marcus felt no different than when he first arrived, and it was unsettling receiving no peace of mind about the situation.

Ever since October, when Marcus learned of Lentulus's involvement with Catilina's plotting, he was constantly on guard. He listened and sought for any signs of further activity.

Nothing happened.

There was something to celebrate, however. Uncle Hybrida beat Catilina for the consulship, which Marcus greeted with relief and joy. It was the first time since Grandfather Orator that an Antonian sat in the curule chair. From what Marcus heard around the Forum, so many people either detested or feared Catilina that Uncle was simply the more popular vote. And it felt wonderful to cast a vote for family.

Cicero was the other consul elected. The two men would share the office for the year. That would be interesting, for they were total opposites.

At the same time, Lentulus stood for praetor and won. Now both men were back in the saddle of power and prestige.

Then came the Saturnalia season.

Celebrations had already begun prematurely, as they always did during this most popular time. Saturnalia was a time of year when chosen household slaves assumed the attire of their favorite or least favorite owner. In turn, masters were supposed to dress as slaves. Most households still participated in the tradition, but some senators disparaged it now. The Spartacan revolt was over but not forgotten.

Saturnalia was also a season of gift-giving. Marcus, his mother, and brothers had joined in the spirit by visiting friends' and relatives' homes to drink, eat, and chat for a spell. Now they were returning from Caesar's domus, having gifted Julia Caesaris with a pet bird.

Castor had a way with animals as well as plants. In the brief time they'd kept the parrot at home, the gardener taught it to speak. One heard the same phrase repeated all day long throughout the domus: "Lentulus is praetor! Lentulus is praetor!"

It was hilarious. Marcus sincerely hoped Caesar had voted for his stepfather.

Rowdy crowds packed the Forum. Lightheartedly, he watched the activity around him. Public slaves, owned by the city, were busy hanging boughs of pine and other greenery on temple columns, statuary, and even the Rostra.

The Antonii brothers decided to try out their costumes for Saturnalia's festival day. Naturally, Marcus swapped identities with Vindelicus. The big slave wore one of his master's looser tunics in a bright shade of blue. Marcus even loaned him his pugio to wear under his heavy, dark blue cloak.

Dressed in Vindelicus's calf-length breeches, Marcus took great lengths to look like his slave. He even wore a blond wig, braided in two long plaits that hung over his shoulders.

As he led the way onto the Nova Via toward home, Marcus glanced back, making sure the litter-bearers were keeping pace. Mother had closed the curtains for privacy. Gaius and Lucius, dressed up like Syrianus and Castor, flanked either side. Despite it still being daylight, nobody could be too careful these days in crime-ridden Rome.

Just as they were halfway along the Nova Via, Marcus thought he heard someone calling. The crowds were so dense that he paid little mind until he very clearly heard it again.

"Dominus Marcus! Dominus Marcus!"

Up ahead, at the foot of the Palatine where the road began to ascend, stood Fadia. Clearly, she'd been running. Face flushed, she was waving wildly. A chill December wind was whipping her hair.

Hordes of people were moving forward all around them, and progress was slow. But Fadia didn't wait. As Marcus continued through the press, she impatiently dodged and pushed her way through the burgeoning crowd.

Why was she so anxious?

She hurried up breathlessly. "Dominus Lentulus wants you home."

Marcus shrugged. "We're coming home."

"He wants you back *now*," she pressed. "It's important."

Marcus glanced over at Vindelicus. The Gaul heard, frowning in concern. Marcus turned back to Fadia. "Did he say why?"

She shook her head. "He just wants you home—now."

"Vindelicus, stay here with Mother. Try to get home quickly." Tearing his wig off, Marcus tossed it. Briefly, his eyes met Fadia's. There was no time for explanations. He bolted off at a swift run, literally shoving through masses of people. Some old pleb shouted a curse at him.

Just ahead was the Palatine Gate. And not far beyond that— home.

He had to get to Lentulus.

Marcus charged up to the domus door, panting. He banged loudly with both fists, and when Syrianus opened to him, he shoved the slave aside. Looking first in the tablinum, he found no one. The place was empty and eerily silent.

No sign of Lentulus.

Next, he tried his parents' cubiculum. The door was slightly ajar. Nobody there.

Where was he?

Then he heard a shuffling of parchment somewhere outside. Sticking his head out the doorway, he looked toward the triclinium.

Lentulus was standing in front of a brazier used for warmth during cold winter months. He was burning scrolls, dumping the ash and grinding charred bits into soot with his feet.

Marcus made it down the corridor to him in a matter of heartbeats.

"Is your mother here yet?" Lentulus demanded, more curtly than usual.

"No, but she will be soon."

"Good. There's some trouble in the city, so I'm going to send all of you down to Misenum until things resolve."

Marcus set his jaw. "We're not going anywhere."

Lentulus cocked an eyebrow. "Don't argue, Marcus. There's no time for that. I'll tell you everything once your Mother—"

"I know all about your part in Catilina's conspiracy," Marcus declared.

Lentulus raised his eyebrows, genuinely surprised.

Marcus charged on. "How's he doing it? Did he leave the city these past months to raise legions?"

"Not legions, exactly."

"What, then?"

Lentulus hesitated, muttering, "I haven't time for this—"

Marcus ground his teeth in fury, raising his voice. "I'm heir of this household and have every right to know your intentions!" As the last portion of Lentulus's scroll flamed up beyond repair, Marcus's eyes grew wide. "Were those your orders from him?" he gasped, pointing at the smoking papyrus.

Lentulus sighed, brushing ash from his tunic. He turned to face Marcus, man to man. "Very well. You may as well know. Catilina is relying on me to execute his plans here. He's raising an army of slaves, disgruntled freedmen, and Gauls. They're marching on Rome. I sent him the message that we're ready."

"Oh, Lentulus, why have you done this?" Marcus cried.

"Slaves have been known to make excellent soldiers, as we learned eight years ago with Spartacus. Once Catilina begins his siege on the city, I'll inform other supporters here. They'll torch the town, creating plebian panic, and assist Catilina in killing aristocracy not yielding to us."

Marcus's jaw dropped. Torching the city? Butchering nobles? A sick feeling churned in his gut. "Then what will you do? Report outside the city walls to join in the slaughter? Will you kill us if we refuse to join you?"

"No. Catilina charged me with the most important task of all. I'm killing Cicero, the man opposed to Catilina from the beginning."

Stunned, Marcus stared at him wordlessly. Cicero was a powerful influence in the Senate, as well as consul, along with Uncle Hybrida. Sure, he operated among the more conservative faction, but had Roman politics become so torn asunder that murder was the only recourse? If his own stepfather was about to commit treason against the state, what if the Senate declared the rest of the family guilty by association?

"Marcus," Lentulus said in a low voice, seeking to persuade, "listen to reason. It'll be safest if you're all out of the city and down at your father's estate in Misenum until everything's over. Once things stabilize, I'll send for you."

Maybe he was right, but Mother deserved the truth. Standing straight, Marcus took a step forward, hissing into Lentulus's face. "Mother will be here any moment, and I rather doubt she'll want a holiday in Misenum once you tell her what's happening. Tell her at least part of the truth. She loves you, Lentulus. She trusts you."

"Marcus, don't be difficult!" Lentulus barked.

Marcus faced him defiantly. *"Difficult?"* he shouted. "You think I'm the one being *difficult?* I'm not the one starting a revolution under my family's roof."

They both heard commotion in the atrium. The family had arrived. Marcus stalked out of the triclinium, heading toward the front of the house, Lentulus calling after him in exasperation.

"What are you doing, boy?"

"Mother!" Marcus called loudly. "Lentulus has something important to discuss with you." Whipping back around, he snarled at Lentulus, "And stop calling me 'boy'!"

He was furious, partly with Lentulus, but mostly with himself. So many times he considered bringing up the matter with his stepfather. Vindelicus had urged him to do so, in fact had begged him, especially after meeting with Caesar.

But Caesar had said to wait.

Something inside Marcus, fear for Vindelicus or the fear of confrontation, kept suppressing it. Truthfully, he hoped it would all just blow over, fall through, not even come to fruition. Hearing and noticing nothing in the past two months had convinced him that nothing would even happen. Never had he been so mistaken.

Mother stood in the atrium accompanied by the others, looking confused. Lydia came up to her mistress, taking her hand. It was terrible seeing the anxiety on Mother's face. "Lentulus?" she murmured.

"Listen to me, Julia," he began, trailing in on Marcus's heels. "Don't be frightened, but we must get you and the boys out of Rome."

"Why? What's wrong?" she asked, her brows knitted together in consternation.

"There may be trouble here for a few weeks—"

"Gods, Lentulus," Marcus interrupted impatiently. "Try telling her the truth."

Mother glanced from Marcus to her husband in confusion and alarm.

Lentulus took both her hands, looking tormented. Mother's face went white as travertine marble, for he only got one word out.

"Catilina."

Thus began the longest night in Marcus's memory.

Everyone congregated in the triclinium. Marcus sprawled atop the dining couch, poking a silver spoon deep into a pear as far as it would go. He pulled it out, then jabbed it in again and again. His mind worked furiously.

Would there be cries of "fire" consuming the Palatine and the rest of Rome? Or would Catilina's army of non-citizens just barge in, killing before asking questions? And what if someone loyal to the Senate intercepted Lentulus's message to Catilina, leading enraged magistrates straight to the domus Antonii?

And Lentulus wanted them to leave? What if they did? If they left the city on one of the main roads, they'd still risk running into the rebel army. What would that be like? They might kill the whole family, confusing the Antonii with aristocracy they wanted extinguished.

Anyway, that hardly mattered. Mother refused to leave.

Marcus left the pear in a pool of juice, turning about to study her with sad fascination. He saw Lentulus occasionally kiss her face. She wept, burying her face in his tunic.

Such behavior seemed incomprehensible. It was as though Lentulus had done no wrong. She still loved him—still grieved over the possibility of losing him. Though Marcus had encountered sex in a hundred positions, he'd not yet loved. To him, her response to this crisis was astonishing and illogical. She loved Lentulus beyond his faults, beyond danger, anger, even herself. How could mere emotions have such sway over someone?

Surprised at himself, he pitied her, regretting their differences of late. Inside, he knew the love she harbored for him. He shared it. They'd grown apart since he'd become a man. She could never accept his lifestyle. Nor could she understand the dependency he had for wine.

It was his escape.

He looked elsewhere, allowing them privacy. Even the house slaves loitered, aware of the peril. His eyes followed many of them moving about respectfully in silence. Castor sat alone at attention next to the small garden fountain, pruning shears at his side. He was so loyal and steadfast he'd probably try defending everyone with them.

Fadia and Lydia huddled together on one of the triclinium stairs, their backs against a column. He'd barely noticed the girl since joining Clodius's club. She'd certainly matured. Little of his childhood friend remained. Marcus smiled to himself, cocking an eyebrow and taking in her charms for the first time. Her worn slave tunic was lower in the neckline than he remembered, accentuating shapely curves of soft, firm breasts moving gently as she breathed.

Her hair was charmingly tousled, even when braided. Small strands escaped, stubbornly refusing to stay in place. Somehow Marcus had missed how enticing she'd become, supple in all the right places. It was as though a butterfly had suddenly burst from its cocoon, spreading its wings before him.

Vindelicus sat motionless at Marcus's feet. Like everyone else, he was hushed, subdued. This maddening silence was nothing less than suffocating.

Marcus discreetly sent a house slave for a cup of wine. He needed it. Lately, he was trying to consume less, though it was harder than he wanted to admit. Another nightmare had visited three nights ago, making him long for escape again. This time pale, white-faced people as sparse as skeletons lifted bony hands toward him, begging for mercy. They spoke in an unintelligible tongue, but Marcus still knew they were dying.

Just thinking of the dream made his body scream for Falernian, Chian, anything. Right now he'd settle for an amphora of sour legionary posca. But no. He'd only allow himself one cup tonight. He needed his mind clear.

His brothers were head to head, whispering, mischievous grins on their faces. Gaius was probably telling a dirty story. Soon Mother would have no children, only three young men.

The last thing Marcus remembered was watching his brothers as he sipped wine. Toward dawn, he jolted awake, still lying on the triclinium couch. A thunderous banging resonated from the atrium. It stopped momentarily, then resumed.

Marcus arose, heading resolutely toward the noise. Gaius and Lucius tagged along behind, whispering worriedly. House slaves stood stone-still, eyes round with alarm. Several scurried to the atrium along with Marcus and his brothers, all looking terrified. Lydia and Fadia were embracing in fear. Everyone watched the huge door, vibrating from the savage banging.

Mother and Lentulus appeared from their cubiculum. Lentulus wore his broad-striped senatorial toga praetexta. He turned to Mother, kissing her fully on the mouth. In their own private world, they briefly joined in a loving embrace. Lentulus had to remove her arms from about his neck, then he left her without looking back.

A powerfully trained oratorical voice called from beyond the door, "Open in the name of the Senate and people of Rome!"

Lentulus strode to the center of the atrium and said calmly, "Syrianus, open the door."

The aging slave's mouth dropped, his bewhiskered jaw shaking tremulously.

Lentulus repeated the order. "Open the door, slave."

Trembling, old Syrianus stood as though cemented to the mosaic tiles. He shook his head, fearfully looking down in shame. Terrified, the poor man couldn't move.

Heart pounding, Marcus moved to his stepfather's side. "They might mean violence," he whispered, swallowing hard.

Lentulus nodded, veins in his throat bulging with stress. "Go back to your mother, Marcus. Send another slave up since our steward lacks the nerve."

Jaw set and teeth grinding, Marcus stepped forward himself, reaching for the heavy iron bolt. He placed both hands on it firmly, pushing his own fear to the back of his mind. Then, looking back at Lentulus, he said, "You gave me my gladius, Lentulus. I don't share your politics, but you're my paterfamilias, and I'll stand by you."

Lentulus's mouth parted in speechless emotion.

Marcus turned back to the door, focusing on the task at hand. He acted, shoving the heavy bolt to one side.

He never pulled the door open. Once the bolt lurched clear, people on the other side propelled it violently. Marcus careened backward, the door itself lifting him through the air. Hard floor tiles knocked his breath away as he fell, rolling sideways.

It seemed that all of Rome poured inside into their atrium. There had to be at least a hundred cramming in, and more outside. Voices agitated, fists raised, the noise rose to a deafening thunder. Most of the horde were common plebs, but in front strode a large group of togate senators. Their leader was a man Marcus remembered meeting briefly once before.

Cicero.

Stern and impassive, the consul raised his hand in a grand gesture, silencing the mob before speaking. "Publius Cornelius Lentulus Sura, we demand your presence in the Curia. We order you answer to the conscript fathers on charges of high treason to the state. What have you to say for yourself?"

"That I will most certainly accompany you, answering whatever concerns the Senate and people have. As you see by my attire, Marcus Tullius, I was coming to today's session to sit as praetor since the Senate and people called me to that office." Admirable courage and control emulated through Lentulus's response.

Marcus pulled himself to his feet, hearing Cicero order the crowd back. His power over them was impressive. Once they began dispersing, in marched Cicero's lictors, bearing fasces to escort their consul and Lentulus to the Forum Romanum.

Marcus desperately shoved two of the lictors out of his path to make it to his stepfather's side. One of them intervened, pressing the blade of his ax to Marcus's throat. Marcus froze, panting. Traditionally, fasces were weapons for show, but the blade was sharp, pressing into his flesh.

Upon seeing him, Cicero sneered in mockery, "Go back to your lessons, boy. If you're the son of Creticus, you'll need them."

Marcus glared at him wordlessly, furious at the unsolicited insult.

But Lentulus reached out and grabbed his arm, addressing him firmly. He said only one thing, "Marcus—take care of your mother."

Everything moved quickly then. Cicero and his lictors marched Lentulus outside, surrounded by the jeering mob. Marcus tried to follow, but someone grabbed his wrist.

It was Vindelicus, holding him back. Together, they watched helplessly until Lentulus completely disappeared into the crowd.

CHAPTER XI

LYDIA CAREFULLY ARRANGED THE FOLDS ON MARCUS'S toga. Pride sparkled in Mother's eyes where she sat in silence, watching.

Marcus was numb. If he failed today, only two others would speak up on Lentulus's behalf—Hybrida and Caesar.

Mother came over, wrapping him in an embrace. "Wouldn't it help if I went? I could plead with him, Marcus. He might listen."

"None of us are in Uncle Lucius's inner circle any longer, and I won't have you begging, Mother. Lentulus wouldn't want that."

"Then take Vindelicus. There's too much terror in the city and—"

"No. He's staying here to watch over the domus. I'll be careful."

It was a short walk to Uncle Lucius's domus. Over on the east end of the Palatine, it was much larger, a grand home boasting all the wealth Marcus's family didn't have.

He found the atrium door open. It was awkward coming into a household where he'd never been a welcome guest. Thinking back, he doubted he'd crossed this threshold more than twice in his entire lifetime.

Clients stood about, impatiently awaiting Lucius Julius Caesar to either summon them or come out to answer petitions. Marcus looked beyond the crowd of patrons into the peristyle court. Aunt Aelia was out meandering in the colonnade with another woman—probably her body slave. He worked his way into an anonymous group waiting to see his uncle, deciding it was best to remain unseen. Quietly addressing a merchant of some sort, he asked, "Have you seen Lucius Caesar today? Where is he?"

"In his tablinum. He's been there with a delegation of senators since dawn. Something must have happened."

How correct the man was.

Uncle Lucius's tablinum was a corner room. Marcus pressed through the crowd toward his destination. A large slave blocked the door. He was probably Uncle's bodyguard. The fellow stood motionless at his post, muscular and burly, with a neck like an ox. Marcus forced an amiable smile at the fellow.

"Salve. I must speak with my uncle."

Of course the idiot didn't recognize him any more than he could recite Homer. Shaking his head, the slave responded, "Dominus is busy. You wait like the others."

Marcus assessed him. Tall as himself, just bulkier. Powerful, but probably slow. Yes, he could do this.

Reaching up, Marcus banged loudly on the door. Immediately, the bodyguard snatched his wrist from behind, but Marcus had used his left hand on purpose. Swiftly, he rammed his right elbow deep into the man's soft gut. Then, whipping around, he smacked his balled fist into the fellow's nose. The bodyguard staggered backward, looking bewildered, nose broken and bleeding, his breath knocked clear to Scythia.

Marcus would have to thank Vindelicus for teaching him that one. Ah, well, desperate measures for desperate times. He opened the door and strolled right in, shutting it securely behind him.

Sure enough, Uncle Lucius was talking quietly to some senators, and Marcus's sudden entrance elicited quite a stir, the men stopping in mid-sentence to stare at him darkly.

The door opened again beside him, and Uncle Lucius's

bodyguard tottered through, one arm wrapped protectively around a sore midsection, his nose dripping blood.

Marcus inclined his head respectfully, ignoring the slave. He addressed his uncle and the crowd of senators. "Please forgive my entrance, Uncle. However, I must complain about your servant's manners. He tried preventing one of your cherished nephews from visiting."

Uncle Lucius's jaw was set in a forbidding, hostile expression.

Marcus kept going while he had the momentum. "How regrettable to interrupt what appears to be an important meeting, but I must speak with you concerning an urgent matter."

He recognized a few faces. One man was a senator he'd met at a theatrical performance. Another had paid his respects when Father died. Now they all stared at him like he carried a plague. Boldly, he moved farther into the room, back straight, reminding himself that his pedigree was as superior as theirs. Now Uncle Lucius had no choice but to introduce him, though Marcus heard the distaste in his uncle's tone.

"Friends, in case you don't already know, this is Marcus Antonius—Lentulus Sura's stepson."

Pompous ass! Not even acknowledging his nephew.

Marcus implored, "Uncle, please. A moment of your time?" So far he'd done well, keeping his voice soft and even.

"As you see, Antonius, I have guests just leaving and clients outside. I've no time to see you today."

One senator, a grizzled fellow, spoke up, "Lucius Julius, we'll advise Cicero of your imminent arrival. I trust you won't tarry long."

"Indeed not," Uncle Lucius snapped, holding Marcus in an icy stare.

The door opened and shut again as they all left. The bodyguard remained, and Marcus glared at him haughtily. "Outside, slave. I'll speak with my kinsman in private."

Receiving a slight nod from his master, he skulked out, glaring at Marcus, blood still oozing from his broken nose.

Alone with Uncle Lucius at last, the hardest part lay ahead.

Marcus wasted no time. "Uncle, I know there's evidence to convict Lentulus. I've not come today arguing that. However, I'm here to ask that you plead for exile instead of execution."

He saw Uncle listening, so he continued. "You needn't speak in his defense or espouse Catilina's revolution. Just consider your sister, who would be widowed a second time. Have pity on her if you can't find any for him. Ask the Senate to send him to an island someplace. Anywhere. Please, please do not concede to execution."

A great silence descended as Uncle Lucius considered his words. Beyond the door, clients' conversations continued in the atrium, sounding distant, far-flung.

Uncle Lucius studied Marcus a time before speaking. "I wonder, what could you possibly offer me in return for such an act of mercy, Marcus Antonius?"

Marcus blinked in disbelief. This was a side of Uncle Lucius he'd never imagined. The bastard was demanding a bribe. Well, what would he want?

An answer came surprisingly quickly. It's what he remembered Uncle loving more than senatorial privilege itself. "Father's farm down in Misenum. If you want it, consider it yours."

Uncle Lucius smiled, tilting his head back, assessing Marcus coolly. "Creticus's farm?"

"Yes."

"Does it bear grape?"

"I should think so."

"How much is it worth?"

Marcus shrugged, frustrated. "I've no idea."

He twisted his lips in dissatisfaction. "Is it in ill repair?"

"It may need some work, but it's in a desirable location."

"No."

Marcus hated doing it, but he resorted to pleading. "Uncle, please, it will all be yours. It's what I'm able to offer. It's a fine property overlooking the sea."

"No. I think not. No property of your humiliated father could possibly compensate for the political risk I'd take standing up for Lentulus's miserable life."

Marcus couldn't believe his ears. Bitterly, he swallowed the verbal retaliation welling up. "I ask once more," he repeated, keeping his voice level, "intercede on my family's behalf. You're a great and steadfast influence in the Senate and highly respected."

Uncle Lucius ignored him, moving toward the door.

Frustrated in his failure, Marcus growled, "I only ask for you to try to spare his life. That's all." Taking two quick steps, he planted himself in front of the door, blocking it. Uncle's face was hard as granite.

In a voice hushed and icy, Uncle Lucius declared, "I warned her not to marry that fool. I *warned* her. My duty is to Rome and the Republic. Lentulus is guilty of treason against our government. And as for you, this whole city knows how you drink, carousing with whores, sneaking about, making your family look like nothing more than Suburan plebs. Your willingness to bribe me proves that Creticus's corruption runs in your veins."

Desperate, Marcus humbled himself even more. "I admit my faults gladly, begging forgiveness. Now we both know Lentulus has strange political leanings. I agree with you on that. There we share some common ground. But he's a good husband, a fine stepfather to me and my brothers in every way."

"Stand aside, boy. Though it pains me, your family is no longer welcome in my domus."

Defeated, Marcus clenched his fists, furious enough to beat his uncle's sneering face to pulp.

Uncle Lucius opened the door wide, striding out in his usual aloof fashion. Marcus's voice raged behind him, his temper taking on a will of its own, breaking all his hard-fought composure. "I won't forget this, Uncle! Never will I forget!"

Hosts of clients crowding the atrium watched in stunned silence.

Crowds in the Forum were more daunting than ever. Plebs weren't stupid, just curious and fickle. They'd gotten wind of revolution and were everywhere, milling about, talking feverishly among themselves. Shops were closing, and there was general unrest. Really, there was no way to get through all the people except to push and shove. And they often pushed back.

Boys and men straddled statuary, sat atop walls, all vying for a better view. Thousands of eyes focused upon the Curia building. Finally making it to the Via Sacra, Marcus did the only thing left to do. He sent messages to both Uncle Hybrida and Caesar asking them to do everything in their power to spare Lentulus.

Finally, he sought an ideal place where he could watch the Curia like everyone else. Taking a running start, he swung a leg up onto the Rostra. Shoving his clumsy toga to one side, he settled onto some brickwork between two rams from unfortunate enemy ships. It wasn't a comfortable spot, but at least it offered a close view.

He was there a long while when he suddenly heard a familiar voice beneath him. "Dominus! Dominus Marcus Antonius!"

It was Fadia.

Lightly jumping down, he stood before her. Flushed and breathless, she drew close so they could talk. For a fleeting moment, Marcus recalled the first time he'd felt her up against him, when they were galloping down the road on a horse toward Baiae.

Fadia spoke loudly due to all the chatter around them. "Dominus, I have a message and didn't know when you'd come home. I searched everywhere for you—even went to your Uncle Lucius's domus and—"

"You found me," he interrupted. "I was waiting for the session to end. Caesar's in there, along with Uncle Hybrida. If nobody else speaks for Lentulus, surely one of them will." He glanced back toward the Curia again, checking for activity.

Suddenly, she took his hand. He glanced down at the physical contact with mild surprise.

"More men than Lentulus have been arrested. One is Gaius Cethegus. Vindelicus said a group of slaves from his household and yours is attempting a rescue to get Lentulus and others out of the city. It's said that Cethegus was storing arms for the revolution at his domus."

"What?"

"A rescue," she repeated. "Your slaves love Dominus Lentulus. This is their way of showing it. Vindelicus is with them. He told me to tell you, so I am." Finished with her message, she released his hand.

Marcus shook his head in disbelief mixed with panic. "They can't do this. Their motives may be good, but if captured, Cicero will trace them back to our household. That would mean Vindelicus would have to die and the rest of us could be held suspect."

Fadia nodded, understanding. There was wisdom far beyond her fifteen years behind those blue eyes. "Let's pray they're not caught," she replied.

He nodded, upset, and most of all, helpless.

"How's Mother holding up?"

"Worried. She wonders about your meeting with your uncle. She's starving for news. What should I tell her? Will you be—"

A loud roar erupted from the populace, drowning out her question. Marcus pulled her back from a swelling wave of plebs rushing back. The boys who had been on top of the Rostra with him began jumping down, shouting and gesturing. Fearful that they were in the middle of a mob, he guided Fadia toward a small row of olive trees.

Plebs jumped, screaming for blood, but it wasn't clear for whose blood they thirsted. Fists in the air, jeering, stamping in riotous pandemonium; several citizens were pounding on the Curia's tall bronze-plated doors. Slowly, they swung open, one pleb speaking to the lictor at the entrance.

Marcus started walking. "Come, Fadia," he ordered.

She followed him, looking about fearfully.

The crowd was growing. Now it was so large it spread to the base of the Palatine. High up on their verandas, Patrician families were apprehensively watching. They were the only ones who were safe.

Together, Marcus and Fadia wove in and out of the masses. He led her toward the Nova Via's abrupt ascent to the Palatine. Then suddenly he lost her. He stopped dead still, eyes combing the masses.

"Fadia?" Gods, where was she? "Fadia?"

She had stumbled, falling amid throngs of people charging and pushing past them. He saw her now, breathlessly trying to rise, yet stampeding plebs shoved her back down in the press. Trying to make his way back through the thick horde, Marcus felt like a fish swimming upstream. But he reached her, shoving at anyone in his path. Swiftly, he lifted her up in his arms. She was light as a baby bird.

As he set her back on her feet, he warned, "Take my hand and don't let go. We can't risk being separated again."

She obeyed without hesitation, and they proceeded.

Plebs started whooping again in cacophonous thunder, causing Marcus to pause at the Palatine Gate. Looking back down through the entrance, he saw a senator exiting the Curia. In command of the crowd, he moved behind a large, protective assembly of lictors. People parted ways for them. The lictors took the lead.

Marcus recognized him. It was that loud talker, Cicero. Where were they going?

He didn't have to wait long for an answer. A chill crept up his spine. Cicero and his lictors were leading the massive crowd straight toward them—up the Palatine.

"Quickly, Fadia! We've a good start on them, but they have crowds pushing forward in their favor. We need to get home before they get up here." He didn't share his worst fear. He'd heard how mobs often trampled people to death in the Forum.

Marcus kept on the outskirts of the moving mass, allowing room enough to escape if things became violent. Occasionally, he looked back, wary of where Cicero was and what he was doing.

Damn! There was so much congestion. People were pushing through the Palatine Gate in panic. An old blind man who habitually begged at the gate on a regular basis fell under the press. Marcus could hear screams over the rest of the discord as the poor wretch disappeared under hundreds of tramping feet, never rising again.

As they slipped through the gate, tight against its stonework,

Marcus gripped Fadia's hand, pulling her closer to his side. Only moments ahead of Cicero's party, armed men suddenly materialized, as if out of nowhere.

There were more cries behind, and Marcus glanced back. Cicero was just passing through the gate and halted his assembly, lifting his hand in authority.

Marcus paused, panting. He didn't know what to make of the armed men. Who were they? Were they the armed slaves of whom Fadia spoke? But no. Instead, the group of thugs saluted Cicero, holding aloft bloody gladii. Cicero embraced one of them in grand gesture, the crowd responding noisily with mixed opinions. Then, just as abruptly, the consul returned to his lictors, leading everyone back down through the gate toward the Curia again.

Marcus chewed his lip. Oh, how he wanted to be wrong. But his heart was heavy. Cicero extolling the thugs could mean only one thing—the rescue attempt had failed. Something dark had happened.

"Let's go," he breathed.

For the second half of the day, Marcus made sure every entrance to the domus Antonii remained securely bolted.

For now, he stayed with Mother. With Lydia at her side, she sat on her sleeping couch with a cup of wine, sipping at intervals.

Marcus sat at her feet, his back against the couch, nervously waiting. And for what? He wasn't even sure. Awaiting confirmation of a failed rescue attempt? Of Lentulus's death? If the gods were real—and Marcus was more and more skeptical of that—only they knew.

Mother interrupted his fretting. "You only told me that Lucius wouldn't support Lentulus. Tell me what happened."

Marcus sighed. He hadn't wanted her to know. "He refused to speak for Lentulus. I tried."

"Surely, more passed between you? He didn't just refuse?"

Marcus hesitated.

"He's my brother, Marcus. I have a right to know, especially if he refused to help us."

Sadly, she had a point. Maybe she needed to know what sort of stubborn ass her brother really was. "Well, at one point, he suggested I bribe him with something."

Mother lifted tear-filled eyes to look down at him. "What?"

He nodded wearily. She was right. He'd tell her everything she wanted to know. Maybe that would repay Uncle Lucius in kind. He'd no longer have a sister. "Yes. I offered him our land in Misenum. I thought he was going to accept, but then he turned me down."

Her eyes widened in incredulity. "And he thinks Lentulus is less honorable?" she murmured. Her hand strayed down to his face, stroking it fondly. "You did all you could, Marcus. You should never have had to humiliate yourself in such a way."

Marcus shrugged dismissively. "Doesn't matter now." Rising, he helped himself to some of the wine.

"I overheard the slaves," Mother said. "They're trying to rescue Lentulus and get him out of the city."

It was best to change the subject. "I wonder where Gaius and Lucius are?"

"In the Forum, I should think—watching the mob like everyone else."

Marcus nodded, absently. He hoped they were safe. Both were reckless young men, much like him.

At that moment, someone hammered at the door again.

Marcus bolted to the atrium. Slaves halted in the corridors, fearful and watching. Their eyes were wide with foreboding.

The hammering started again. "It's Castor! Please let me in!"

Marcus was still uncertain and peered through the peephole to confirm a mob wasn't using his slave to trick him into opening the door. What he saw made him gasp. Stunned to his core, he hauled it open wide.

Fadia, who had followed him, cried out.

In limped Castor, shivering, wet, and foul-smelling. He was hauling a makeshift litter bearing a large form wrapped in a cloak.

The one-eyed slave set down the contrivance gently, facing Marcus in disgrace. Submissively dropping to his knees before his young master, he wept so hard he shook.

Marcus placed one hand gently on his head but spoke sternly, trying to mask how shaken he was. "Speak, Castor. What happened?"

"I beg your forgiveness." Castor sobbed, lifting both hands in entreaty. His voice cracked in sorrow. "We only wanted to help."

Marcus turned away from Castor and approached the motionless figure on the pallet. Carefully, he lifted the woolen cloak covering Vindelicus's pale face. His hand moved faster, roughly jerking away the rest.

Fadia cried out, "No!"

Vindelicus was stiff and waxen. The wound was straight through his ribcage; his ripped tunic soaked in blood.

Castor explained, "Someone in our party betrayed our plan to Cicero. We all fled. I stumbled in the panic and fell. Hearing Cicero's men coming, I crawled into a sewage shaft. Vindelicus was still running with the others."

Marcus dropped to his knees next to his slave, tears in his eyes.

Castor went on, "I stayed in the sewer a long time. When I came out, I started back here, and that's when a few others found me. They said Vindelicus fought like a lion. It took eight men to bring him down."

Marcus sobbed. A sudden croaking sound came from deep in his throat. He placed his hands on Vindelicus's cold arm, wishing he could will it to move.

Mother had heard the commotion and hurried out of her cubiculum. Slowing at the horrific scene, she addressed slaves who'd gathered in the atrium, gently but firmly. "Come, come, all of you. Let him grieve privately. Fadia, fetch water and scented oil. Tend to the body. Lydia, stay with me."

Marcus stayed where he was on his knees next to Vindelicus's corpse. His left hand traced a curiously patterned tattoo on the Gaul's muscular arm that had always fascinated him.

He heard footsteps as Fadia hurried to do Mother's bidding.

She carried a tray of steaming water, a cask of fragrant oil, and clean linen.

Marcus sensed her presence, then felt her hand alight on his shoulder. He lifted his head, and they were face-to-face. Her hand moved from his shoulder to rest on top of his, gently prying his fingers from the dead slave's arm.

He let her.

"Be still," she breathed. Moistening a corner of the linen with cool water, she ever so gently brought it up to his eyes. He pulled back at first, causing her to hesitate. Reaching out once more, she tenderly wiped away his tears, and he closed his eyes at the feel of the cloth—warm, moist, comforting.

Fadia's voice was full of peace. "Today, before he left, Vindelicus told me to tell you to be careful. What kindness he had," she whispered, her own emotions revealed. Reopening his eyes, he watched her wring out the cloth. Her hand shook ever so slightly before dipping it into the clean water again. After wiping his face once more, she moved to Vindelicus's side, carefully removing bloodstained garments and cleansing the wound in his chest.

Marcus just sat and watched, beyond words. His tears were in the very water cleansing Vindelicus, preparing him for his journey.

Fadia glanced up at him again, and his eyes bore into hers with intensity. Once this nightmare was over, he'd have to reward her for her goodness. Slowly, he reached over Vindelicus's still form to grasp her hand. His words were solemn and sure. "I've not lost a slave today, but a beloved friend. I'll pay for his funeral myself and honor him like the warrior he was, showing respect and kindness, as you now show me. Gratias, Fadia."

CHAPTER XII

GAIUS ANTONIUS HYBRIDA TO MARCUS Antonius:

Nephew, I write quickly from my curule chair in the Senate.

Cicero has trumped up a ridiculous story about Bona Dea rites at his domus, hosted by his wife, Terentia. He claims that during the rituals she heard the goddess speak through flames on the altar, insisting Rome execute "the traitors." Cicero has many advocates, ready to act on this superstitious nonsense. Caesar spoke, advising the Senate to deliberate carefully and not deny the accused a trial.

Regrettably, Cicero challenged his words and received backing from everyone present. Caesar stood again, insisting the Senate spare the prisoners' families from bloodshed. Fortunately, they have agreed. I must add that there was mention of denying Lentulus burial. Also, your friend Publius Clodius may have been in on the plot.

You must inform your dear mother that there
will be no trial. Lentulus is to die tomorrow inside the
Tullianum, along with the other conspirators.

Marcus held Mother's hand in comfort. His own breath was visible in the chill air. As slaves bore their litter through the mist-filled Forum Romanum, he shivered. No matter what one wore, it felt cold.

Hired gladiators flanked them for safety's sake, on loan from Caesar's domus. They were big brutes, surrounding the litter as it coursed its way down toward the Curia.

Marcus was amazed. Mother had borne the news calmly. Even now she was composed, reclining on the other end of the litter. Her palla, the modest veil Roman matrons wore, covered most of her face.

Through a break in the litter's silk curtains, he watched the crowds. It was eerie. Plebian faces held looks of curiosity, hope, fear, respect. They didn't yet know that Lentulus and the other conspirators stood condemned—without a trial.

Yes, he was guilty.

Yes, he was a fool.

But this was Rome. This city was supposed to be an unparalleled civilization of justice, was it not? These men deserved a damned trial!

"You all right, Mother?" Marcus whispered, still gazing outside.

"Yes," was the soft reply. Her tired eyes stared straight ahead, resigned and defeated.

"Look—there he is." Parting the litter curtains farther, Marcus pointed.

Out from the mist emerged a large group of lictors flanking Cicero, moving along the Nova Via toward the Curia. On his right was Lentulus. No longer in his toga praetexta, he wore a simple white tunic.

Marcus clenched his jaw in disgust, grinding his teeth. Cicero made it look as though Lentulus was a goat heading to sacrifice.

Rapping on the side of the litter, he ordered, "Bring us up closer to the Curia."

As the slaves repositioned, Marcus kept watch as his stepfather approached.

"Shall I call out to him, Mother? Tell me quickly; they're about to pass us."

Anguish contorted her face. She was so pale, breathing deep, her eyes red from crying and lack of sleep. It was the last time she would ever see her husband alive. Her gaze followed Lentulus until he disappeared into the crowd.

"Let him remember me as I was, before all of this," she said. "I don't want him to see my eyes full of tears."

How unfair life had been to her. Marcus cursed silently. If Dis, Father of the Dead, was real, he hoped the dark god would grant Lentulus dignity until the end. Not adept at praying, he invoked a quick plea, begging the gods to receive Lentulus—even if denied burial.

Cicero's procession passed. Mother was silent. Marcus eyed her. She was tranquil, pausing every few moments to wipe away tears with her fingers. He drew the curtains again, assuring their privacy.

More movement outside caught his attention. The four other prisoners were passing by. Cethegus was last. Cicero reappeared, pacing back toward the other four, seeing them to their fates.

Then Marcus froze, his blood churning hot with outrage. None other than Publius Clodius hurried to Cicero's side. Turning this way and that, Clodius eyed the mob, then clapped Cicero fondly on the back, like they'd been friends for life. Armed, and accompanied by others carrying cudgels, it was instantly obvious that Clodius, now returned from the East, had ingratiated himself with Cicero. By acting as the consul's security, he was attempting to prove his innocence in the conspiracy. Clodius paused to redirect hired gladiators in pressing the mob back. Cicero smiled as he spoke to him. Whatever he said, they both laughed.

Marcus felt physically ill. He swore to himself that all monetary backing for Clodius's brothel would cease. It was time to move on. Never would he back anyone supporting Cicero.

The prisoners' destination was the Tullianum, Rome's notorious underground prison for political prisoners and executions. Plebs had a dismal riddle Marcus had heard since he was a boy: "Where's the one place in Rome where a man goes in but never comes out?" The answer was the carcer—the Tullianum prison.

Sick of feeling helpless, Marcus made a sudden, impulsive decision. "I'm going to stand with Lentulus. He shouldn't have to die alone."

Mother snatched his wrist. "No, Marcus—"

"Someone from the family should be there! I'm head of the family now. I'll go."

"Marcus, they won't allow you down there!"

"Maybe not, but I'm going to try." He sprang out of the litter and wrestled his way through the crowd, pausing only when he saw Cicero's lictors guarding the building housing Rome's prison and place of execution.

Built of thick tufa stone, Marcus knew he could only enter the Tullianum if allowed to do so. Several senators mingled near the entrance, deep in conversation. One of them was Caesar.

Caesar would help him.

With no time to waste, Marcus interrupted their conversation. "Caesar, can you get me inside? I want to be with Lentulus."

Caesar frowned, pulling him aside. "Do you really want that? You know how it'll happen."

"Yes. But he's my stepfather. I may not stand for his political views, yet I can't allow him to die alone."

Caesar hesitated only a moment, then swiftly motioned Marcus to follow, hustling him past the lictors and inside the windowless walls of the prison.

He'd never been inside. It was small and crowded with Cicero, Clodius, Cethegus, Lentulus, and the other doomed men. Then there were Cicero's lictors and several disreputable-looking bruisers who were probably the executioners. And in the center of the room was a large, dark hole in the floor. One of the executioners was adjusting a ladder into its gaping mouth.

"What's the meaning of this?" Cicero demanded of Caesar, seeing him enter with Marcus in tow.

"You won, didn't you?" Caesar snarled. "They're going to die, so let them do so with as much civility as a man can have in this place. He's only here to support his stepfather. Grant them that much."

Marcus moved over until he was in the torchlight next to the wall. "I'm here, Lentulus."

Lentulus was pale, but he managed a nod in Marcus's direction. Face haggard from lack of sleep, he was grizzled under unshaven stubble. His eyes were bloodshot and sorrowful. Marcus met his gaze, willing him strength and fortitude.

The lictors descended into the lower level, climbing down the ladder one by one, fasces resting on their shoulders. Cicero and his senator witnesses followed. Afterward, it was time for the prisoners to begin their descent.

Lentulus turned toward Marcus a final time. With eyes full of desolate resignation, he said, "Take care of her."

Marcus nodded and tears stung his eyes. This man had been the father he'd lost.

Once the others disappeared into the bowels of the prison, he moved to the edge of the hole where the ladder remained. As he looked down, he heard Cicero order someone to remove it. That bastard didn't want any supportive stepsons climbing down to witness the execution.

A foul stench rose up from below. It was a combination of urine, feces, mold, and death. Marcus swallowed bile rising to his throat and spat to one side, determined not to shame his stepfather. Crouching near the hole, he listened. It was impossible to see down there. There was dim torch light, but all he could discern were shadows.

At first, there was only silence. Then he heard a man cry out in panic, "No—No! Not this—kill me by the sword!"

Marcus clenched his jaw so hard it ached.

Someone else groaned, and he heard shuffling.

Neither voice sounded like Lentulus.

Give him strength, Dis. Don't let it hurt much. Welcome him...

Cicero interrupted Marcus's prayer. Each prisoner would receive his sentence, but since Lentulus was the leader of the revolt in Rome, his came first.

"Publius Cornelius Lentulus Sura, I, Marcus Tullius Cicero, in the name of the Senate and people of Rome, hereby condemn you to death. You stand guilty of leading Catilina's insurrection within the city of Rome. Together with members of the Gallic Allobroges tribe and others, you plotted to kill senators of Rome, including myself. Today, inside this carcer, you will be strangled until death."

Silence again. Marcus swallowed hard. It was horrific enough just listening—he hoped beyond himself that Lentulus could bear up. He pictured the noose going around his stepfather's neck. Only a few more breaths on this side of the Styx. "Courage, Lentulus! Courage!" Marcus called down into the hole.

Out came a choking, gurgling sound. More shuffling and the guttural gag of someone trying to gasp and unable to reach air. It lasted and lasted... Marcus squeezed his eyes shut, praying for Lentulus's heart to stop and end his suffering. But still it kept on, with a rasping, airy whine that pitched downward until a few final strangled gasps went silent. In the sudden quiet, Marcus heard the dripping of water. Then several men began weeping—probably the other prisoners. After that, a heavy thud.

Lentulus had fallen.

Marcus was hardly breathing himself. Eyes still shut, all he saw was his nightmare of Lentulus foaming at the mouth.

Tears drenching his face, he bolted out of the carcer toward the direction of Mother's litter.

It wasn't there. Where was she? Uncaring of who saw him in such an emotional state, he paced, waiting and hoping she'd come back. Just when he considered walking back home alone, there was more movement from the Tullianum.

It was Cicero and his cronies, reappearing before the crowd, accompanied by other senators of rank. Clodius was back with his thugs, pushing plebs aside so the consul could approach the Rostra. Even Uncle Hybrida was at his side as co-Consul. Poor Uncle. Marcus felt sorry for him. He'd just lost a close friend.

A public slave carried over some wooden stairs, and Cicero mounted them to the top of the Rostra, arms high in a victorious posture. His retinue followed. The crowds fell silent to listen.

For a man known for rhetoric and lengthy orations, his words were surprisingly brief. "The conspirators' lives have ended," he proclaimed.

Smiling broadly, Cicero clasped the arms of fellow senators standing near him. The rabble took his lead, breaking into wild cheering, as though he'd just conquered a major province.

Marcus turned his back on the appalling display, slowly heading toward the Palatine. The plebs kept roaring their adoration of Cicero, chanting that he was their "Pater Patriae"—the father of their country.

No. Marcus Antonius would not stand by watching Cicero receive glory and honor for putting to death a husband and stepfather without a trial.

"Gods, Mother! Where were you?" Marcus exclaimed in concern. "With all that's happened, I've been mad with worry. I looked for you after—"

Mother stood in total composure, holding up one hand to calm him. "I went to secure burial for Lentulus."

Marcus nearly dropped his jaw. "You went to *Cicero*?"

"I went to his domus. We both know he wasn't there. I dealt with Terentia, his wife."

"Terentia? I've heard she's a feral bitch."

"I'd heard the same thing," Mother admitted. "But she's not. She's kind, strong, compassionate, and understanding. She assured me that Lentulus would receive burial. And she thinks her husband overstepped his bounds."

"Ho! That he did," Marcus affirmed fiercely.

"Now I'm going to bed. I'm beyond weary and have no more tears left."

"Before you go..." Marcus hesitated. She'd been through so much. He hated to upset her or cause any more grief.

"What?" she asked.

"I just wanted you to know that Lentulus was fearless to the end."

"Was it terrible?"

"It was quick." That was a lie. He just wanted her to have peace and closure.

"I don't feel he's gone yet," Mother whispered. "It still seems like he'll walk back through the door with Hybrida, full of wine, life, and good humor. For that, my son, was who Lentulus really was, after all."

Marcus placed his arms around her there in the atrium, trying to comfort her. She'd feel his absence later. They all would. They clung to one another in anguish. Marcus placed one hand on her head and held it to his shoulder like that of a babe.

He really was paterfamilias now.

As the deceased's closest male relative, Marcus would deliver the eulogy at Lentulus's funeral. The body lay in the center of the platform on its funerary bier, draped in black and adorned with pine boughs.

Mentally exhausted from the past days, Marcus's head throbbed. The dry air and bright sun of winter worsened the burning in his red eyes. Mother hadn't been the only one crying.

The entire family stood before him, slaves included. Marcus noticed Caesar and Aurelia standing several rows back with lovely Julia Caesaris. Uncle Hybrida stood next to Mother, accompanied by his red-haired daughter, Antonia.

Right where Marcus now stood on the Rostra, Grandfather Orator had once received accolades of praise from the people at his triumph. Thinking of his grandfather here long ago gave him confidence. Dressed in a black toga, he gazed down soberly at Mother. Then he lifted the largest sinus of his garment to reverently cover his head.

Every eye in the Forum was upon him.

"My family, people of Rome, I ask you to pause today, remembering a man of the Cornelii. He died bravely, despite condemnation, showing great dignitas, gained from holding magistracies as praetor and consul. But most of all he enjoyed life with friends and family. There was love in his life for my mother. And he had sons. I was one of them. But he also had core beliefs; one of which was that our Republic is dead."

Marcus stopped. A stiff, cold wind from the river blew the mantle of his toga off his head, ruffling his hair. Though it wasn't his original intent, he changed course in his oration.

"The Republic *is* dead, good Romans." Becoming impassioned, his voice rose, echoing amid the stone-and-brick architecture. "It is dead, for we have allowed men to die without due process of a trial. We've allowed one man to dictate the law without letting wisdom from our Fathers aid us."

Slowly and deliberately, he turned his eyes to Lentulus's shrouded corpse. Sinking to one knee, he tenderly placed a hand atop it.

"Today I bury my stepfather, Publius Cornelius Lentulus Sura. I request nothing from you but silence. Let us have no sound but our own weeping, for today we won't just bury him, but we'll bury the remains of our Republic."

Marcus Antonius's first speech in the Forum ended. As requested, dead silence ensued. Several magistrates, who had first shown their backs to him, turned and watched, impressed by his fervor. A small group of plebs broke into cheers as he descended the stairs. Briskly walking to Mother, he offered her his arm, leading her to the waiting litter swathed in black. He himself would walk behind Lentulus's funeral bier, along with his brothers. Several professional mourners began wailing. Detesting their artificial rants, Marcus signaled hired musicians to play dirges.

Then, readjusting his black toga, he walked slowly behind the litter between Gaius and Lucius, steeling himself to light his stepfather's pyre outside of Rome's walls.

This was his second funeral today. Vindelicus's ashes still smoldered.

Marcus craved sleep.

Ever since Lentulus's arrest, his closest friend had been insomnia. Whenever he did fall asleep, in raced more nightmares. And on the heels of the dreams was depression. To cure the misery, he escaped.

Gambling, whoring, and drinking—they were his release, his only freedom.

Since the funeral, Mother had isolated herself in her cubiculum. Marcus didn't want to intrude on her mourning. That was something private. But he craved solace himself. Just a few days ago, he visited a high-end brothel. After the sex, in which he found little satisfaction, he came upon a tavern selling decent wine on the cheap. There, he gambled the night away, accruing more debt.

And he drank himself into a stupor.

Tonight, he felt empty and numb. Despair was like a vice pinning him into a black void with no hope in sight. With the family name besmirched again, he no longer believed he had a purpose, much less a future. He sat motionless against a fluted column across from Vindelicus's empty cot. Weary, his head drooped, and he closed his burning eyes. Once more, sleep would not come. Two thin trails of tears streamed down his face. Romans were supposed to control their feelings, especially in public. But now Marcus's heart released into an outpouring of tears and sobbing. He wept for Lentulus, for Vindelicus. He cried for loss, unrestored honor, and unattainable joy.

Then someone touched him.

Opening his eyes, a small light danced in the darkness. Its brightness blinded him until he made it out to be a lamp.

It was Fadia, kneeling before him in silence. She placed the lamp on the stair and caressed his face. Venus! She was beautiful—alluring. Creamy skin and high, firm breasts. Eyes of matchless blue twinkled, and her skin gleamed gold in the flickering lamplight. Marcus blinked, inhaling a familiar scent. She'd stolen some of Mother's costly perfume. Oh, what an entrancing vision—a goddess of love, awakening his senses with her fingers.

Her touch lingered on his neck, toying with the ends of his dark hair, and she inhaled sharply when his hand swiftly caught her wrist. He'd surprised her, his fatigue turning into sudden passion. Fadia yielded, and he scarcely breathed, kissing her hungrily. Skin prickling alive with desire, his lips coaxed a small cry from the girl.

As he stood, she followed. He embraced her, his muscular, hard form rigid against her softness. Timidly, her hands came up, encircling his neck in surrender.

While they kissed, he considered something remarkable. She was the first woman offering herself to him without expecting monetary payment. And here she was, showing him tenderness as he'd never known.

Completely taken aback, Marcus totally lost himself to love. She pressed her body closer, hungry and yearning for more. He moved one hand to her shoulder, grazing her skin teasingly with his thumb and loosening her tunica. When she assisted, breaking their kiss, Fadia slowly lowered her garment to reveal her breasts. She took his hand, backing into his cubiculum, leading him to the sleeping couch.

There, she opened herself in perfect submission. Never had sex been like this. Shyly, delicately, she drew him near, touching, gentle, without any haste. There was no demand, no high price except her own sacrifice to Venus. And that? She ceded it willingly.

They spoke with fingers and lips in a harmony that transcended understanding. This was a gift. And afterward Fadia held him and comforted him like a child.

Marcus lay in her arms, completely at rest and full of wonder. He didn't know what had just happened, but whatever this was, he'd never let it go.

CHAPTER XIII
62-61 BC

FOR THE FIRST TIME IN A LONG WHILE, MARCUS HEARD Mother laugh. It was sweet music.

She sat on the dining couch holding a squirming baby. As she bounced the little one on her knees, it reminded Marcus of happier times, when Lucius was little.

He ambled over and fondled a lock of the infant's wavy auburn hair.

Mother introduced the child. "Marcus, meet one of your distant cousins, Octavian."

She held out the bundle for him to hold. Marcus accepted the little lad, cradling the baby. He addressed the boy's mother. "We heard of your joy, right before our own tragedy, Atia. Felicitas."

As he held Octavian, he noticed the baby's underarms and neck covered with a raised pink rash. Leary of disease, he walked over to Atia, returning him to her. "He has a rash—"

"The physician assures me it's not contagious."

"I wish him only good health," Marcus said.

"He's a disagreeable child," Atia admitted. "Nothing like his sister. Wailing, waking the whole domus at night—I tell you, Julia, he'll wake the spirits of the dead."

Mother forced a laugh, but the thought of waking dead spirits didn't elicit amusement the way Atia had intended. Black swags still hung from doorways and rafters throughout the domus Antonii.

Marcus was relieved when Mother changed the subject. "Has a priest read his horoscope yet?"

Atia nodded her head in awe. "It's bizarre. Such a sickly disposition, yet portents have been particularly auspicious. I think every priest, astrologer, and fortune-teller in Rome has visited *us*. One even predicted that Octavian would rule the world."

Marcus snorted. What a pitiful leader this little runt would make!

Atia gazed over at him. "What plans have you for yourself, Marcus? I remember your mother once said how anxious you were to join my Uncle Gaius Julius on the battlefield."

Marcus thought quickly before answering. "Caesar? It would be an honor to serve under his command. My time will come," he added hastily.

"Well, let's hope Hybrida brings honor to Rome," Atia said. "I heard he was friends once with Catilina. It must be hard on him, facing off with a former friend. Civil war is such a terrible thing."

Cicero had charged Uncle Hybrida with commanding the very army that would challenge Catilina. At least Uncle had military experience. He'd left a week ago, asking Marcus to join him, but Mother had begged him not to go. "I don't want your name associated with the conspiracy. You must begin your career in an unblemished and noble way."

It wasn't worth upsetting her, but Marcus had been disappointed. He'd just told Atia that his day would come, but only the gods knew when that would be.

"Would you care to join us for our midday meal, Atia?" asked Mother, once again changing subjects.

"No, we must go. The physician is coming sometime today to tend Octavian."

"Be well, then," Mother said. "Come back soon. I miss the invitations I used to have. Hopefully, things will improve with time."

Reaching out, Atia squeezed her hand. "Dear Julia, of course they will."

Marcus rarely ever saw Atia, so before today she'd always struck him as being indifferent to his family. However, as she leaned over, babe in arms, warmly kissing Mother on both cheeks, he thought that perhaps he'd misjudged her.

"Our steward, Syrianus, will see you to your litter," Marcus said, gesturing to the waiting slave.

She nodded politely, taking her leave.

Marcus watched her, carrying little Octavian. There was still something about that side of Mother's family that was unnerving. Maybe it was their eyes. Different from other Julii, they were pale blue, cold and staring.

When Atia was out of earshot, Mother scolded him. "Marcus, you should've seen her out yourself. She's family, after all."

"It was your company I wanted," he answered with a winning smile. He motioned to a slave, who brought forth their meal. Marcus reclined on a couch opposite her. "How are you?" He had waited weeks to ask again.

Grief had dampened her usually strong and vibrant personality. She'd remained distant since Lentulus's funeral. In the privacy of the domus, she was quiet and resigned. It worried Marcus how she bottled sorrow inside. In fact, he feared she'd try joining Lentulus to relieve her pain. Out of respect, he gave her space, allowing her to mourn in her own way. But he maintained a wary vigil too. Lydia and Syrianus always informed him whenever she was especially distraught.

"Marcus, though you lamented Vindelicus and Lentulus deeply, my grief is entirely separate from yours."

"That may be true, but you're lonely. You miss your social life, especially when other women reject you and wish to distance themselves from a branded rebel's widow. Mother, you've barely forty years. Perhaps in time—"

"No." She spoke emphatically, looking directly at him with a stern face to make her point. "That part of me is finished. I look forward to a quieter, gentler life. No man could possibly fulfill me the way Lentulus did."

Marcus nodded in silence. He'd never force the matter.

Mother picked up a citron, tearing at the peel. "You've no idea what it's like losing one you love. You've lusted—a great deal from what I hear—but have never loved."

He grinned mischievously. This time she was wrong. "I do love, Mother. In fact, that's why I wanted to talk with you."

Her eyes widened, urging him on.

"Do you want to guess who?" he asked with a smirk.

"Most certainly not. Just tell me."

Marcus laughed. "Very well, then. It's Fadia."

Mother froze, and her face hardened. A long moment passed before she spoke, and her words had a frosty edge. "I was made aware by house slaves that she's been in and out of your cubiculum. Remember something, that it's wiser for you to simply lust over her. Don't love her."

He sighed at her predictable response. "Because she's a slave."

Mother eyed him, discarding a large portion of citron peel on the table. "My son, you too often forget yourself, in public and in private life."

"My life is my own," he countered firmly, plopping an olive into his mouth.

She shook her head in frustration. "What good can come of such love? As I said, *lust* after her all you want, but keep it within these walls and out of your heart."

"Fadia's been part of this family since birth. What's wrong with loving her?"

Mother sighed impatiently. "Be sensible. Don't you wish to marry into an influential family, bringing your own household dignitas and imperium? You must consider continuing your lineage, Marcus."

He said nothing. There was plenty of time to sire children.

"And take care how you deal with her," Mother added. "She could be manipulating you."

At that, Marcus scoffed. "I seem to remember Uncle Lucius disagreeing with your relationship with Lentulus. Yet you were never happier than when you married someone you wanted."

"Don't you dare compare poor Lentulus with a slave!" Mother snapped, raising her voice. "He was Cornelii, and you know that's practically royalty here in Rome. Besides, he held imperium in the Senate, despite what Lucius ever thought of him."

Marcus held up both hands in surrender. "Very well. I stand corrected. I only wanted to point out that—"

"You're a son of Rome, Marcus Antonius, of ancient bloodlines going back farther than Tarquinius Collatinus, a founder of the Republic. Whatever made you desire less than the best for yourself? When Hybrida returns, why don't I get him to invite us to dinner and have some senators present with their wives and eligible daughters? People may not wish to grace our triclinium yet, but your uncle will be most welcome in the Senate after defeating Catilina."

"No, thank you, Mother. I'm in no rush to marry."

"It does worry me, how people in the Forum gossip about you. Your gambling, the company you keep—like that dreadful Curio."

"I've not even seen Curio since Lentulus died," Marcus stated defensively. Curio had been avoiding him—he owed Marcus coin.

He swept nutshells onto the floor and got up. It was no surprise that his feelings for Fadia triggered such a response. But he didn't want a lecture.

Regrettably, it was a shorter meal than he'd intended. "Here I am, feeling blessed by the gods, as you were when you found Lentulus," he said to her. "Now I finally have someone to love. And within confines of this house, dissuading me from spending nights in brothels. I thought that would please you at least. Considering all that's happened, because of what we've suffered, I'd hoped you'd share in my happiness. I see I'm mistaken."

There was nothing more to say. The rocky fault that was between them before Lentulus died heaved open again as wide as the sea.

Unfortunately, Mother's treatment of Fadia changed course. She delegated the girl to lower household tasks. She emptied bed-pots and scrubbed floors. It spurred Marcus into action. Three days a week, he sent her to a well-respected seamstress in the Forum to learn to sew.

Fadia took to the new trade like a fish to the sea. Soon she was cutting and creating her own patterns and designs. She fashioned several tunics for Marcus that were well-made and comfortable.

But it didn't matter what she made or if it was for him. He was simply happiest when they were together, especially in the peace and privacy of his cubiculum. With only a single lamp lighting his way, he took great satisfaction in driving Fadia to the heights of passion. And in turn, she took great delight in learning the art of Eros.

He only knew he loved her—more than his own life. Certain he'd give his last breath for her, he'd savor these days. Mother was right. Someday he'd have to marry.

Following another night of lovemaking, Marcus arose well before dawn to tend to the long-avoided business of severing ties with Curio and the Subura. Their friendship had cooled, even before Lentulus's death. Curio owed him over a year's worth of rent for the place, and Marcus needed repayment. He needed to give Callias an installment on his account.

Marcus cinched his belt tight, running his fingers through his thick, tousled hair. In his bed, Fadia was still sleeping. When he trailed a finger up her leg toward her thigh, she rolled over, stretching like a cat. He grinned. Her long brown hair spread over the smooth linens.

How was it that he already missed her flesh against his? Hot, blood-racing desire filled him again.

She peered at him through half-closed eyes.

Marcus chuckled. "Spying on me, are you?"

She wiggled her nose in reply, dreamily shaking her head.

"I'll return before midmorning," he promised.

"It's not even daybreak. Where are you going?"

"To see Curio. But don't worry. My reason for going is to sever ties."

"Curio's no good for you," she murmured.

Marcus cocked an eyebrow. "Now don't go sounding like Mother, please."

Reaching over, he brushed loose strands of hair from her face and lowered his mouth to hers. She responded hungrily, like always, arching her back toward him with abandon. Pulling away to look down at her, he smiled and whispered, "I almost feel like changing plans."

"Then do." She rolled toward him, exposing her creamy nakedness.

"Damn Curio." He rose abruptly, heading for the door. "By the way, I left something on the chair for you."

"Another love letter?" Fadia giggled with a yawn, covering herself again to stay warm.

"Lazy girl," Marcus teased. "Get up and look for yourself."

A few days before, he'd left her a very sweet love letter inside a wax tablet. Impassioned, he'd wanted to express his feelings for her in wax but had completely overlooked the fact that Fadia was illiterate.

After returning from the Circus, she'd been waiting all day, dying to find out what he'd written. Even now, his loins stirred with hunger, recalling how he'd read it to her in bed, making love in exactly the way he fantasized, through his own words in wax.

Now Fadia kept that tablet safely under their sleeping couch. None of the words made sense to her. Yet several times he'd caught her gazing at the raised edges of wax that his stylus had carved.

"Marcus, teach me to read," Fadia said suddenly, as though reading his mind. Her words stopped him in his tracks.

Oh gods, no—he hated reading. Mother had coerced him to read one too many scrolls crammed with philosophy. Nor did he fancy himself a teacher. Considering what to say, he paused a little too long.

Fadia persisted, "Don't you want me to be clever like your mother?"

He laughed. "Of course I do. I'll have Syrianus teach you. It'll give him something fun to do."

She propped herself up with an elbow, exposing delicate dimples with her teasing smile. "Kiss me again."

"Only once more, then I must go," he obliged.

Out the door and on his way, Marcus imagined what his seamstress-slave would think of the expensive, fiery yellow silk and pearl-drop earrings he'd left for her. Imagining the soft, undulating material barely concealing her breasts, he nearly turned around.

Dawn's first light was anointing the walls at the domus Scribonii when Marcus arrived.

A client of old man Scribonius was just ahead of him, speaking to the steward. The doorway was already open, so at least some family members were up and about. Marcus nodded curtly to the steward as he passed, and the man barely looked his way.

The domus was large with a grand, open plan. A house slave stood attentively against a wall, posted to see to clients' needs.

"I'm here to see Curio. Could you point the way to his room? He's expecting me." That part was a lie.

The slave nodded toward a wing on the south side of the domus. Marcus immediately took off down the corridor, glancing inside rooms. Most were unused, probably for guests. But there was one door cocked open just ahead. Inside, a taper burned in a large bronze lamp next to a sleeping couch, on which Curio lay naked.

Marcus barged right in. "We need to talk," he said tersely. He shut the door firmly behind him.

Curio rolled over toward the voice. Marcus saw him tense up when he saw who was calling.

"What do you want, Antonius?" he asked in obvious displeasure.

"You damned well know what I want."

"No. Enlighten me."

Marcus snorted. "You owe me over a year's rent on the Subura property. You promised we'd share the payments, but you've not offered up a cool copper since late last summer, despite numerous reminders."

Curio propped himself up with one elbow.

Marcus impatiently gestured with his hands. "Just pay me your part. That's all. After that, I'm done with the place."

Curio's response was to mutter something Marcus didn't catch. He was probably hungover.

Marcus said pointedly, "Curio, for what we've been paying for that pit, we could be seducing whores in some Eastern palace. Now kindly go to wherever it is you keep your coin and pay up."

"I paid your share for months when you first started coming."

Marcus rolled his eyes. "I was fourteen, and you know it. I had no means to pay for anything back then."

An uneasy silence followed. Curio was staring at him in a strange way. The desirous look on his face raised Marcus's hackles. Rising lazily, Curio swaggered toward him until they were face-to-face. Marcus shrank back from his body warmth. It repulsed him. Ill at ease at such an invasion of space, he stepped back again—directly into the wall. He was going nowhere in a hurry.

Curio leaned in, his voice soft and seductive. "Ah, I remember when you were fourteen. Have you never understood the real reason I asked you to the Subura?"

Marcus had always gone to Curio's place for his own selfish gratification, never once considering why Curio had first approached him. He thought it was to foster friendship, but to say that they were close friends was stretching the truth. When it came to carnal needs, he'd always assumed Curio preferred women, same as him. Now he perceived something else—something that made him think way back to Baiae.

Without warning, Curio reached over, stroking Marcus's face where early morning stubble shadowed it. "You were so beautiful in those days, Antonius. You still are, you know. You love Greek

174

theater, Greek art, even Greek cooking. Can you not return my love in the Greek way?" Removing his hand, he placed it on Marcus's upper thigh.

Marcus no longer saw Curio, but Lupus, licking his lips and ogling him. Humiliation consumed him again, the lost coin no longer mattering. Batting Curio's hand away, he rammed forward. Curio grunted and careened backward onto the sleeping couch. He barely pulled himself up on his elbows before Marcus attacked him like a lion.

"I may love Greek things, Curio, but I only have tastes for women when it comes to sex. Surely, you must know that."

Marcus battered Curio's face with his fist mercilessly, blood spattering onto the bedding.

"Oh, I remember…nights…when you never complained!" Curio exclaimed between blows.

What? Marcus's fist froze in mid-air, the skin on his scalp crawling. His mind worked furiously, thinking back. There were nights he couldn't remember at Curio's. He'd always had his fill of wine. Entire amphorae were available whenever he wanted it. Had the bastard added something besides water to his cup?

Gods, there was that time Vindelicus had to carry him home. He recalled nothing about that other than being hungover and sore. And he hurt *everywhere.*

Curio laughed aloud, despite his buffeted face. "You know you enjoyed it!"

Snarling like an animal, Marcus punched Curio's face twice more. Then somehow Curio managed to barrel sideways, gaining enough momentum to roll both of them off the sleeping couch, locked together like wrestlers. Marcus never had the satisfaction of killing Lupus, so maybe he'd kill Curio instead.

But Curio landed on top, pinning him down. He tried kicking his way back into a position of advantage but wound up whacking his ankle on the edge of the sleeping couch instead. Wincing, he groaned, trying to rise up, but Curio flipped him over, gaining the upper hand. Quickly, he bounded atop Marcus's back, twisting and anchoring his wrists behind him.

And it was at that very moment that the Fates sent Gaius Scribonius the Elder to casually walk through his son's door. Indeed, the scene was blatantly scandalous. Curio was not only naked but pinning Marcus Antonius on the floor in front of the sleeping couch in a universally submissive position.

When Curio saw his father, he jumped up immediately, releasing Marcus. He bowed his bleeding head, respectfully awaiting chastisement.

"What in the name of the gods..." old man Scribonius breathed in horror.

Curio seemed to revert back into childhood, his sire's chastisement making him cower like a whipped pup. "Father, listen. You know my weaknesses. Don't be overly angry, I beg you." Sinking to one knee, he extended a hand, like a slave begging for mercy. "I confess, Antonius has always wanted me, and I him. I've been the object of his love for years."

Marcus staggered to his feet, trembling with rage. He blurted out the only defense he could. "Liar!" he shrieked. Then desperately he addressed Gaius Scribonius. "Sir, what you saw coming through this door is not what you think it was."

Curio's father came forward, eyeing them both, stunned and pale. One eye twitched erratically. Saying nothing to either of them, his fist shot out, catching Curio solidly in the jaw.

The blow propelled him backward onto the stone floor. He moaned, more blood dripping from his mouth. Gaius Scribonius turned next to Marcus, fist still clenched.

"It's not what you think," Marcus insisted. "I only came here to demand payment on a debt he owes me. Your son is both a thief and a liar."

Gaius Scribonius breathed angrily. "Get out of my domus, Marcus Antonius. Get out and never come back."

Marcus clamped his jaw until it ached, hissing through his teeth, "We're not lovers!" Gods! Now they weren't even friends!

Gaius Scribonius yelled at him, "Get out! Set one foot in here again and I'll drag you bound before the censors!"

Marcus shifted his gaze to Curio's bloody countenance in utter abhorrence. Walking away with as much self-respect as he could muster, he made it out the door, limping on a bruised, throbbing ankle. Repulsed to the point of nausea, he ground his teeth in rage. Such violation of his person and dignitas, inflicted by a supposed friend.

Slaves were busy with duties as he passed through the house. In the atrium, client groups awaiting old man Scribonius looked his way curiously. Had they not heard arguing in the younger Curio's cubiculum, they were deaf.

Marcus strode past them all, eyes fixed straight ahead. He didn't stop until he arrived at the baths, sitting half the day awaiting the men's hours. The second half he spent soaking and scraping clean until he was raw from it.

CHAPTER XIV

BY EARLY EVENING, MARCUS HAD FINALLY ARRIVED HOME from his bizarre escapade at Curio's.

As he went to the door, he was surprised when it swung open. Nor was he expecting what happened next. Mother appeared in front of him, and without warning, she slapped his face. The sound resonated like a whip cracking. Staggering back from the force of it, Marcus blinked in bewilderment. He was about to ask why she'd hit him when she advanced two more steps and slapped him again, even harder.

They were both outside the domus now, the doorway jammed with curious bystanders. Gaius, Lucius, Lydia, Fadia, and about three or four other house slaves besides Syrianus were all watching the show.

Marcus raised one hand to his face and rubbed his jaw. If she tried it again, by the gods, he'd defend himself! Mother stood before him in a heated rage, panting like a feral bitch.

"Syrianus," she barked. "Hand it over!"

Syrianus scampered forward with a scroll, offering it to her. Mother snatched it up. Her hands were trembling. Marcus had never seen her like this before. "What in Hades is wrong?" he managed, warily taking a sidestep as she brandished the scroll at him.

Then she addressed everyone at once.

"Marcus doesn't seem to know what this scroll contains. Well, it'll be all over Rome only too soon. All of you should hear first-hand what it says, straight from the source:

> *"Gaius Scribonius Curio the Elder to Julia Antonia:*
>
> *Our heirs have committed indecent acts performed only by Greeks and lowborn theater performers, unacceptable to true Romans. I have disciplined my own son, as head of my household. I forbid him ever to see your son Marcus Antonius again, to speak of him, or have dealings with him in any way, on pain of death. I utter this oath as paterfamilias of my gens. If your son ever approaches mine, I swear by Minerva, who is fair, I will have justice against the domus Antonii and those who live within. I have chosen to make this imprudence public, hopefully changing the course of my own son's path. It appears that Marcus Antonius is no better than his father or Publius Cornelius Lentulus Sura, the madman you married.*
>
> *This outrageous homosexual behavior must not happen again.*
>
> *Written with the heartfelt zeal of a true Roman."*

Mother dropped the scroll at Marcus's feet. He stared at it, face flushed with humiliation and outrage.

Finally finding his voice, he spoke through his teeth. "Old Gaius Scribonius walked in on Curio and me when we were fighting over money he owes me. I have not been intimate with him—"

He stopped when he realized the host of family and slaves were all still watching from the doorway.

"Go on, Marcus," Mother challenged. "I'm listening."

Angrily, he replied, "Well, it would've been nice had I been able to explain myself in the first place. Instead, I was attacked by a harpy."

"Oh, you've not yet seen the harpy abiding in me, my son! When will you ever learn that whatever you do has consequences for us all?"

"If you were listening—" He stopped, regaining composure. Addressing everyone in the atrium, he shouted, "All of you, leave us! This is not for your ears. This is a private matter, and whatever Gaius Scribonius wrote should've remained so until the paterfamilias of this household saw the message. And the paterfamilias is me. So be gone—all of you!"

The slaves retreated immediately with Syrianus. Mother smiled smugly when Marcus addressed Fadia, who was still standing her ground. "You too, Fadia."

Once she had gone, Marcus related his side of the story to his mother and brothers. Gaius and Lucius shrugged the whole matter off, convinced by his explanation.

Mother was another story. And once the gossip got out in Rome...

Damn, it was aggravating. How could she or anyone in the city ever know the truth of what had really taken place that morning in Curio's bedchamber?

For want of any other solution, Marcus handled his humiliation the same way he'd handled most of his life's stresses. For a month or more, he stayed away from the domus, drinking and accruing more debt at gaming.

Today he was trying to shed last night's hangover with Lucius at the Circus, watching teams train.

"Marcus, Lucius! I have news!"

He turned about to see Gaius's bulky form charging up the Circus Maximus's wooden stairs. He plopped down heavily beside his older brother, winded and agitated with excitement.

Lucius, seated at Marcus's right, reached across, offering Gaius a wineskin.

"Falernian, Gaius. Have some."

Accepting the skin, Gaius took a draw, wiping his mouth with one hand, chest heaving. "I just came from the Forum," he announced breathlessly. "Pompeius disbanded his army and is back from the East."

Marcus screwed up his face impatiently. "Old news," he scoffed. "Is that all it takes to enthuse you, Brother?" He refocused on chestnut mares just below. Spirited, nervous, just put to harness, they shied from the chariot, squealing and dancing.

"No. There's more," Gaius persisted. "Uncle Hybrida's army defeated Catilina's."

Marcus came to attention.

"Tell us everything," Lucius begged.

"Bloodier than expected. None of Catilina's men surrendered. They all died fighting for their cause."

Marcus snatched the wineskin from Gaius, swigging deeply. "Then may the gods grant them rest and honor," he replied grimly, swallowing hard. "They died like soldiers." With that, he turned back to the horses.

"But listen," Gaius insisted. "Uncle Hybrida didn't take the field. His second-in-command, Marcus Petreius, won for him. I can't understand it. Petreius isn't even noble, just the son of a centurion. Why would Uncle concede his command—especially to him?"

Wrinkling his brow, Marcus admitted, "That is strange. Hybrida always wanted a top command."

"Criers in the Forum said he was ill, but it makes no sense. He'd have to be at Dis's door before giving up his command to someone else. Maybe this will explain it." Reaching into his belt, he pulled out a canister containing a scroll. "This was just delivered to the domus. It's from Uncle Hybrida—to you."

Marcus popped the lid and tilted the cylinder so that the papyrus slid into his hands. It was a long sheet, so he stood up, moving away from his brothers' eyes to read alone:

Gaius Antonius Hybrida in Pistoria to his nephew Marcus Antonius in Rome:

I write this letter with shame. Dishonor follows me like an evil spirit. I have no relief. It's as though Lentulus himself haunts me.

Privy as I was to Catilina's plans, why did I not die a traitor inside the Tullianum with the others? I knew of the plot, attending meetings in secret alongside the accused.

All my life I dreamed of high command, Marcus. I have wanted men to hail me as a hero. Now it will never happen. The guilt I bear, due to cowardice in circumstances surrounding your stepfather's death, has driven me to pay for my crime. Cicero knew of my guilt. He bribed me into this mission for two reasons. Firstly, he's a coward himself and didn't have stomach enough to go to war. Second, he knew I'd have to annihilate a former friend: Catilina. He had the Senate punish me in his own way since I didn't die with the others.

Therefore I myself have opted to pay for my crimes. Today when sacrificing, I promised the gods another man would earn the victory. I'll always remember how another rode in my place, earning my soldiers' praise. That's my penance: to forfeit that which I wanted above all else.

Upon receipt of this message, you'll hear of my victory, but now you know the reason I was inside my tent feigning illness. Forgive me, Nephew. I felt compelled to confess because your stepfather was my loyal friend.

I should have died at his side.

Marcus stared at the letter, his heart heavy as stone. Feeling his brothers' curious eyes upon him, he quickly rerolled the papyrus.

"What's it say?" Lucius demanded.

"Nothing," Marcus muttered. "He was ill. That's all."

There was a slight pause of uncertainty before Lucius shrugged the business off by saying, "We should tell Mother."

Marcus rolled his eyes. Nodding toward the mares, he changed subjects, "What do you think of them, Gaius?"

"Promising, but I prefer seeing horses run before placing wagers."

"Oh, come on," Lucius snickered, taking a pull on the wineskin. "They're Greens—they always win."

Marcus smiled, clapping Lucius on the shoulder. "Tomorrow at the races, I'm putting an eighth of a talent on them. Hopefully, Fortuna will finally allow me to win back what I lost to Curio and more." He snatched the wineskin and took another long draw.

Gaius frowned in consternation. "Take care, Marcus. Don't forget what happened last week. You forfeited thirty thousand denarii. Surely, your debt runs deep."

Glaring at him coldly, Marcus snapped, "No worries, *Mother*, I won't forget."

Lucius whistled, shaking his head. "He's pissed now, Gaius."

Annoyed, Marcus tossed the near-empty wineskin back to Lucius, heading toward the stairs. A low, sonorous belch forced its way out.

"Where are you going?" Gaius called.

"Anyplace where I can have a little peace without family meddling in my affairs," he muttered back heatedly.

Wooden scaffolding under him creaked plaintively with each step as Marcus unhappily contemplated his situation. He and Mother were hardly on speaking terms since old man Scribonius's letter. He couldn't possibly confront her with his financial problems. Callias the creditor was his only answer, despite his high interest rates and dubious reputation.

Cheap, scantily clad prostitutes who frequented the Circus archways approached him hopefully, calling out propositions and specialties. Uncertain where to go just to be alone, he waved them off.

Several plebians ogling the women saw him. One called out loudly, "Hey, man-lover! I heard Curio's always on top!"

The women joined in the raucous laughter.

He should have gone to war with Uncle Hybrida. Instead of Uncle selecting some unknown, lowborn son of a centurion, he might have selected his own nephew to take the glory.

Marcus sighed. He really did have ambitions down deep, but fear of failure always raised its ugly head. Father had failed. Lentulus had failed. Even his own mother didn't believe in him anymore.

Casting long shadows, the sun stretched its rays all the way past the long, grassy spina in the middle of the racetrack. Soon it would be nightfall. Circus slaves were setting up braziers under the archways to warm themselves.

Passing one already blazing with flames, Marcus paused long enough to drop Hybrida's letter into the fire. As the papyrus crackled, he whispered a desperate prayer in case the gods really listened. "If there's any hope for me at all, let the failures of my line burn with his letter."

As he walked off, he shook his head sadly. He didn't really believe any god would intercede on his behalf. Well, at least there was cheap wine at gambling houses in the Subura. Tonight, he'd go drown in it.

Marcus pushed the door open more noisily than intended. It banged against the wall, ricocheting back on squeaking hinges.

The clamor awakened Fadia.

Throwing back the coverlet, he stared down at her. She was gazing up at him, her blue eyes starry and shining in the dim lamplight. Usually, he found her naked and waiting for some lovemaking. But tonight she wore a gown that seemed to explode with gold. The golden pearl-drop earrings he'd given her lay against her neck. And she was wearing the yellow silk. It cascaded in graceful folds down her trim form, clinging to her body alluringly.

Climbing atop her, he kissed her slowly, brushing hair from her face. With one hand, he deftly flipped open the fibula holding one shoulder of the gown together. He smiled, pulling the silk aside to lean in and kiss her trembling flesh.

Fadia arched her back, sighing languorously. "Kiss my neck," she murmured.

As he went to obey, the jingle of her necklace caught his attention. Foggy though his mind was with wine, he remembered he hadn't given her that—only earrings. It was a splendid piece, worked into an intricate design. Adorned by perfectly placed pearls and green stones in shapes much like those in her earrings.

"Where did you get this?" he asked.

Her eyes grew wide. "I—I borrowed it."

"From who?" Who would give her such a thing to use? Then the truth came to him before she could answer. "Did you take this from Mother's strongbox?"

Fadia sat up, one firm little breast still exposed from the loosened shoulder fabric. "I only borrowed it for tonight. I'm going to put it back first thing tomorrow."

"How did you get into her strongbox?"

"I know where Mamma keeps the key. Please don't be angry. I swear I'll return it tomorrow. She'll never even know. I just wanted to look beautiful for you."

His concern lifted at that. "You are. You are so beautiful. And you made this today?" He fondled her through the silk as she breathed in desire.

"Yes, it didn't take me long. I was supposed to work some embroidery for your mother to wear to the Bona Dea festival, but I was too excited. I never get to make things for myself. I couldn't help it. I had to finish it before you came back tonight. I'll work on your mother's stola today."

He leaned in, kissing her mouth deeply and pinning her arms onto the sleeping couch, running his tongue down the side of her neck. Taking Mother's gold necklace in his teeth, he snarled playfully like a beast, shaking it in his mouth until she laughed at him.

"I love you, Dominus Marcus," she confessed.

Grinning, he let the necklace drop from his mouth and studied her, so vulnerable and innocent. "I love you too," he whispered. "I think we've loved each other since we rode together the first time."

She smiled sweetly. "I think we tried not to love one another for too long a time."

His heart rejoiced. Strange how in this one little person he was genuinely happy. If only he'd recognized their love years ago. He felt cheated of joy he could have had much, much sooner.

CHAPTER XV

THE MOMENT MARCUS STEPPED BACK INTO THE DOMUS, he knew something was wrong. Household slaves stood around cowering like abused dogs. Gaius and Lucius were both there, solemn-faced, and old Syrianus stood by the door, visibly shaken.

"Tell, him Syrianus," Gaius prompted.

"Domina found Fadia wearing one of her necklaces and had her whipped."

Marcus grabbed hold of the slave's shoulders. "Is she all right?"

Syrianus nodded, trembling. "She's in the slave quarters. Domina left orders to leave her there until the two of you could speak."

"Take me to her."

They hastened toward the back of the house. Gaius and Lucius followed behind. Marcus cursed himself for not taking the necklace back to Mother's cubiculum himself.

"I take it Mother's still at the Bona Dea rites?"

"Yes, Dominus."

The heavy iron door Marcus had once shut on Fadia during the Spartacan Revolt so long ago stood wide open. A host of slaves congested the tunnel near her small chamber, making it a tight squeeze.

"Out, all of you!" Marcus bellowed. It was damp and smelled moldy in the passage. He hoped she was all right.

Lucius remained in the doorway, keeping the curious slaves out of the way. Gaius was still on Marcus's heels, both brothers stopping when it became too dark to see.

"I need light!" Marcus yelled.

Someone lit a torch and passed it to Gaius, who held it aloft. A leather flap was all that covered Fadia's portal. "Bring the torch closer, Gaius."

Gaius lit the way as they entered her tiny space.

She lay motionless on her stomach. There was greasy sulfur salve smeared across her back. It reeked like rotting eggs.

Gaius offered an explanation. "Syrianus said that Mother allowed some of the slave women to tend her wounds."

"Well, wasn't that generous of her," Marcus muttered disgustedly. Outraged, he dropped to his knees beside her.

Gaius moved in, holding the torch high so he could see the extent of her injuries.

Bloody lash marks marred Fadia's back, all the way up to the nape of her neck. Gently lifting some of her hair from the affected area, he felt sticky blood. It was drying, caking in her hair. He was sickened and infuriated. Mother did this? He knew she disagreed with his love for the girl but hadn't realized the depth of her loathing. Surely, a mere misunderstanding over a necklace shouldn't have ended like this.

He shook his head in pity. "Oh, Fadia. Fadia, what were you thinking? You should never have taken it."

Afraid of hurting her more, he touched her face gently, then sat down next to her, cradling her head in his lap.

Gaius lodged the torch into a bracket on the wall. "I'll leave you, Marcus," he whispered, exiting the room.

Marcus barely heard him. "Oh, my girl..."

She parted her lips slightly, semi-conscious and whimpering, just now realizing who held her.

For a long while, his mind raced back and forth, considering options. This was serious. He loved Fadia and wouldn't risk Mother abusing her further.

She had a useful trade—seamstress work. But Marcus couldn't afford to rent a place for her outside the domus. Not with the mounting debt he had. He kept coming back to one solution. It would utterly infuriate Mother, but it would keep his beloved at home and, hopefully, safer.

"Fadia, I'm going to free you," he promised softly. "And after that, I'm going to marry you. And it won't matter to me what people think or say. Mother can move out of the damned domus for all I care."

He reached out, taking a rough woolen coverlet off her pallet. Tenderly enveloping her small frame within it, he whispered, "Let's take you to our bed. It's damp and cold in here. Once we get you settled, I'll send for a physician."

Twice a year, Roman noblewomen gathered at the domus of a chief magistrate to perform secret rites for the good of the city. On the night of the Bona Dea—the festival of the Good Goddess—male inhabitants of a hostess's household vacated the premises. They even had to take along their male slaves, male animals, and any male busts or death masks. Plebs loved standing outside near a hosting magistrate's domus, watching an ox-drawn wagon full of marble likenesses grind to the nearest place it could sit until the festivities ended.

As much as Marcus was at odds with Mother, he also knew how much she looked forward to attending the Bona Dea.

Since Lentulus's death, she'd had no invitations to banquets, nights at the theater with friends, or gossip with other women. Rome's high-ranking society shunned her as the wife of a traitor.

Only a handful of extended family members had been kind enough to include her in a few social gatherings.

Caesar was currently praetor and had also recently become the pontifex maximus, Rome's highest religious official. Therefore his wife, Pompeia, hosted the Bona Dea, though everyone knew that Aurelia would be the one in charge. She was exceedingly devout to the state religion, as was Mother.

Naturally, Aurelia had invited her.

Marcus hadn't seen Mother this excited since Lentulus first asked her to marry him. For weeks, she planned what she'd wear, how her hair would look, what earrings might go with her stola ...

It was all rather tiresome to Marcus, but he let her have her fun, so long as she stayed out of his way. Since the Curio scandal, they'd pretty much lived separate lives.

But that night, when Mother finally returned from the Bona Dea, Marcus was waiting in the tablinum. He sat behind Lentulus's desk, drumming his fingers on the cool marble. As he anticipated the confrontation, he ground his teeth. Gaius had asked to be there, and Marcus consented. He'd even told his brother ahead of time what he had planned for Fadia.

When Mother entered the atrium, Marcus commanded from his seat, "Get in here and sit down. We've some talking to do."

Mother cocked an eyebrow and regarded him coolly but came into the tablinum. However, she ignored the invitation to sit, standing before him with her chin held high.

Marcus arose, walking around the desk so they were face-to-face. "You will *never* touch her again."

Gaius moved near them to keep the peace. Mother remained defiant and unafraid. "That girl is trouble," she spat. "She's nothing but a thieving little slut."

Marcus grabbed both her shoulders, shaking her hard until she cried out. Gaius intervened, latching hold of Marcus's wrists. Mother staggered backward, rattled and trying to remain composed.

"Say anything more about her and I'll lock you inside your cubiculum like a child until next winter," Marcus vowed.

"Like it or not, I'll say this much—even Fadia isn't as troublesome as you're becoming, Marcus." Her eyes flashed in the lamplight.

He frowned darkly. Her words didn't correlate with the matter at hand. At least the matter with Fadia, which he was most concerned about. "What are you talking about?"

"You've many titles, my son. All of Rome is acquainted with them: drunkard, homosexual, gambler—"

Marcus stiffened, clenching his teeth.

"Leave her be," Gaius insisted, placing a firm hand on Marcus's shoulder, steadying him.

Mother went on, unfazed. "Look what you've become. Look at yourself! I saw your friend Publius Clodius tonight. He showed up at Caesar's, dressed as a *woman* and defiling our sacred rites. Did you have something to do with that? Did you promote sacrilege?"

Marcus snorted. "I've not given Clodius a thought since he showed up with Cicero the day Lentulus died."

"And how can I believe that?" she demanded. "You deny being Curio's lover, but I happen to know at least one thing you can't deny."

Marcus glared at her. "What?"

"You have a creditor in the Forum, around those filthy stalls near the Subura. Having one wouldn't necessarily concern me; Lentulus had one. But businesses in that part of the city aren't trustworthy. Your debt will grow instead of shrink with high interest from someone so dishonest."

"How did you know I had a creditor? How?" Marcus demanded, taking a menacing step toward her.

Gaius, reading his brother's body-language, interceded again. "Easy, Brother."

Mother answered Marcus's question boldly. "You've caused me such concern that I had you followed. That's how I know. And don't go asking who followed you. You'll never know. How much do you owe? You could put all of us in danger dealing with scum in the Subura."

"Not your business," Marcus answered coldly. This encounter wasn't turning out the way he'd planned. He'd intended on holding her accountable for what she'd done to poor Fadia. Instead, he found himself on the defensive. Heading toward the door, he warned her, "Never go near Fadia again, Mother. You hear me?"

"She's a slave, Marcus," Mother hissed. "Only a slave!"

Ha! This was his chance at a small victory. "Not for long. When she heals, I'm taking her to the Forum to see a praetor. I'm freeing her."

Mother sighed, shaking her head. "Another brilliant idea. Then I'll free Lydia, and Gaius and Lucius can go free Syrianus and Castor. Then all the other household slaves will be standing in line, wondering who gets to be next. By the time you're through with us, Rome will have another Spartacan revolt, adding to your list of successes."

"You watch your tongue, woman. You watch your tongue."

Marcus kept his word.

Noisy plebs in the Forum were oblivious to his and Fadia's joy. As they approached the Via Sacra, pressing crowds were as suffocating as ever. Sellers hawked dyed cloth, shouting prices in singsong chants and waving samples before passersby. Beggars lifted hopeful hands, crying for alms.

Marcus paid little heed. Nothing would worry him today. No dark omens shadowed his mood. Today was his—and Fadia's. To celebrate, he'd bought her an expensive tunic of green silk, along with a new pearl necklace that rested on her throat.

Fadia's back bore permanent scars but like a phoenix rising from ash, she had prevailed. Today she'd become a freedwoman and Marcus's wife. And though she and Mother hadn't been in one another's presence since her whipping, he deeply hoped both women would someday come to accept each other.

Near the Curia as they passed, Marcus glanced darkly at the Tullianum. Just past the horrible prison, a smaller stretch of road led to the massive Tabularium. Relatively new, this house of public records was located on the west end of the Forum. Majestic archways graced its porticos, keeping both plebian and aristocrat cool in the hottest part of late summer.

The place crawled with people. In a stall before them sat a long desk of heavy mahogany, edged with inlaid ivory in a meander design. Long queues of citizens awaited various services, documents, or legal requests. A frantically busy staff of public slaves attended each need. At times, impatient clientele hurled curses at them, dissatisfied with their long wait.

Upon arriving, Fadia paused while Marcus went behind the desk, asserting his highborn status. After flashing a silver denarius at one of the slaves, the fellow led them to a more private area.

There, he accepted the coin, speaking to Marcus confidentially, "Wait here, young Dominus."

As they stood patiently under the enormous arches, Gaius and Lucius arrived in the family litter, as planned. Soon after, a togate man came out of the Tabularium, striding toward them. He carried a heavy volume of long-lasting vellum. Waving his hand, he beckoned Marcus and Fadia over to a smaller desk, away from the noisy populace.

Marcus had arranged for one of the year's praetors, Quintus Caecilius Metellus Nepos Junior, to preside over Fadia's manumission.

"Salve, Metellus. Gratias for the favor of your presence today."

Maintaining an air of cool professionalism, the praetor inquired, "Is this the slave?"

"Yes. She's to be manumitted," Marcus answered, his hand protectively clasping Fadia's atop the table.

"Have you a witness?"

"Two. My brothers here." Gaius and Lucius both stepped forward. "I need to have this documented officially for public record," Marcus told him. It would be important for him and all of Rome to know that Fadia was a free woman prior to becoming his wife.

"As you wish, but I'll require your seal," Metellus said, beginning to write.

Marcus fingered his father's signet ring. It was rich, heavy gold with a jasper intaglio of Hercules's son Anteon, legendary founder of the gens Antonii. The sole personal item returned to the family along with Father's remains, Marcus treasured it. It had belonged to his line for well over a hundred years. As melted wax dripped onto the vellum, he pressed in the seal.

"The slave must also make her mark; then your witnesses may sign," Metellus instructed.

"I can write my name," Fadia proudly announced.

Marcus had made good on his promise, having Syrianus give her occasional reading and writing lessons. She was the first to admit her lack of proficiency. However, she could read names of shops in the streets. Not long ago, Marcus recalled how she recited filthy graffiti about Cicero on the Curia's back walls. Now *that* was worthwhile reading.

Marcus watched Fadia eagerly pick up the reed stylus. She dipped it into the ink slowly, lightly tapping excess over the inkwell. Then she methodically scribed the name she had chosen as a free woman. Once done, she beamed with satisfaction. Her work revealed:

ANTONIA FADIA

Lifting the single page, Metellus called for a passing scribe, who accepted the document, tilting the vellum and blowing on it to dry the ink. Next, he raised a baton symbolizing senatorial authority, lightly tapped her head with it, and said, "Antonia Fadia, you're free."

The rest of the day would be a celebration.

"Fadia, I planned something special," Marcus announced. He offered her his arm, escorting her to the entryway. In the street closest to the Tabularium, the family litter awaited, accompanied by its bearers. She had never been inside it. Countless times Marcus remembered her walking behind it, accompanying Mother to the Forum or the family tombs.

Tears of joy filled her eyes. "Where are we going?"

"To the races, but—"

"The races? At the Circus?"

"Yes, of course at the Circus."

Fadia clapped her hands together with excitement. "Then I'm dreaming, and please, Morpheus, never let me awaken."

"I have freed you, my love. And now I declare you to be my wife."

"That's all there is to it?"

"Yes. Most people have ceremonies, but it's never required in Roman law. I'm afraid it's too awkward for us to celebrate that way—at least right now. But I assure you, we'll celebrate tonight in private."

"I'm still afraid. Your mother will not welcome me in the domus as one of you."

Scooting over to her side of the litter, Marcus gently cupped her chin and kissed her.

Fadia sighed. Her cheeks flushed pink; whether in embarrassment or nervousness he couldn't tell. "I don't ever want to disappoint you, Marcus. She's going to be so angry—with us both."

He snorted and shrugged. "Sometimes I think Mother stays angry with me. We both have to get used to that, *Wife*."

Fadia smiled sweetly. "Hearing you say that gives me joy."

As they reclined inside the litter, Marcus pulled the curtains to, leaning back opposite her, still holding her small hand in his. Gaius and Lucius shouted from outside that they'd meet them at the races. Fadia stretched out like a lioness.

She was his wife now.

And he had to tell Mother.

The magistrates outdid themselves at the Circus. They surprised everyone by serving fresh bread, garum, goat's cheese, and wine to the entire crowd. Marcus couldn't imagine how much it all must have cost. It had to have been astronomical. Probably the same amount as he owed Callias.

When he and Fadia returned to the domus, the sun had nearly set. Gaius and Lucius had both found eager prostitutes outside the Circus Maximus and probably wouldn't be home before dawn. There would never be an ideal time to tell Mother their news. This would have to suffice.

"Where's Mother?" Marcus asked Syrianus as the old man opened the door.

"In the peristyle courtyard, playing her cithara."

Mother loved music. She and Aurelia had become much closer since Lentulus died. The two women often played together, filling the entire household with sweet sounds.

"I don't want to be there when you tell her," Fadia whispered.

"You have to. If you're my wife, you need to be present. We both know it won't be easy, but she has to see us unified, or she'll never accept it."

He led her into the courtyard. Next to several lit braziers and lamps, Mother sat on a bench with her instrument, quietly playing a melancholy melody.

"Salve, Mother," he greeted softly, approaching and sitting with Fadia on a bench opposite her.

Mother examined Fadia from head to toe. "I suppose I should be glad that's not my necklace," she remarked tersely, eyeing the girl's pearls.

"Please, let's speak in peace," Marcus implored. "Neither Fadia nor I want further argument with you."

"Then what do you want?"

"To tell you two things. First, Fadia is now Antonia Fadia. She's free."

"So? You did what you said you were going to do," Mother murmured with a slight shrug. "Very well. What else have you to say?"

Something you won't want to hear, but you must, he thought. "Fadia and I are married. We are not celebrating publicly, but we have agreed together to step out in a marriage commitment. We hope, in time, you'll accept us and allow her to call you 'Mother.' That is our wish."

Setting the cithara aside, Mother sat very still, staring down at the stones in the garden path. "Ever since you were small, playing out here with your brothers, I always dreamed that your wedding day would be an occasion of banqueting, good fortune, and rejoicing. You should be courting Caesar or Pompeius for a chance to prove yourself in the field, to impress some senator who has a daughter near marriageable age. That's what was supposed to have happened, Marcus."

"Well, Mother, you made that quite impossible with your decision on my behalf, didn't you?"

She chose not to answer that question but asked another. "Suppose for a moment that you did find a position. Let's say you left Rome and—may the gods forbid it—died in battle. What then will become of this 'wife' you've married? She has nowhere to go, no father's domus where she might return. And I certainly wouldn't keep her here."

Marcus felt Fadia's hand go clammy. She was looking down at her feet, trying not to cry.

"If anything happened to me, I would expect you to be kind to her and care for her," Marcus stated resolutely.

Unexpectedly, Fadia spoke up. "That wouldn't be necessary. I have a trade. I can make clothes. In fact, I shall prove myself capable of earning coin."

Marcus shook his head, "Fadia, I don't want you to—"

"Please, Marcus. It's something I want to do. I want to prove that I have ability. I'll earn respect in this domus, as my own mother has done."

Marcus was at a loss, but when he glanced at Mother, for the first time she was staring at Fadia with a brow raised in what appeared to be a seed of regard. "We'll see about that," she said. Then, meeting his eyes again, she added, "I shall do my best to stay out of your way, Marcus—yours and your *wife's*."

"You know that's not what we want."

"You bent me, and now you've broken me. And we are done with this conversation." Standing up proudly, she picked up her cithara and carried it away, a solitary figure walking toward her cubiculum.

"She hates me," Fadia whimpered. "She'd beat me again if she had the chance."

"She hates you now," he admitted. "But did you see the way she looked at you just then, when you said you'd start earning coin?"

Fadia shook her head, looking puzzled.

Marcus placed his hands on both sides of her face. "I saw the beginning of hope. Give her time. We both must give her time."

Four days after confronting Mother, Marcus and Fadia sat together at breakfast. Lydia scurried in, glancing behind her warily.

"What's wrong, Mamma?" Fadia asked.

"None of the other slaves must know I am here," she said, still looking about fretfully. Then, with tears in her eyes, she burst out, "I don't even know what to call you now."

"Call her 'Fadia,'" Marcus interjected. He'd noticed the slaves avoiding her. Naturally, they were resentful of her new status. He hadn't considered how Fadia's new role would play out in the domus social order.

"And what should the others call her? They want to know," Lydia said.

"They may call me Fadia too," Fadia offered.

"No. That won't do," Marcus said, shaking his head. "You're married to me now. You are their domina, and that is how it must be."

Fadia said desperately, "Then they might hate me as much as your mother does."

"They still have to remember their place," he reminded firmly. "You have my answer on this, Lydia."

Lydia sank to her knees in obeisance. "Then you need to know something, Dominus."

"Go on."

"They are saying things about Fadia. They say she is the 'little whore of the household.' They don't think she should have been freed or that you should have married her."

"And what do you think, Mamma?" Fadia asked before Marcus could respond.

"I believe you have forgotten who you are. It is one thing to be free. For that, I praise Olympus, and I thank you, Dominus," she said to Marcus. "But to marry him? That was a mistake. For him and for you."

Marcus felt himself go cold. "Then I will tell all the slaves this: if any of them says or does anything to insult either myself or my *wife*, they shall risk the same whipping she received, threefold. And should they raise a hand against her, they will pay for that with their lives. I'll assemble them all and tell them as much."

Shaken, Lydia wiped her eyes and stood up. "Yes, Dominus." She hurried back down the corridor out of sight.

"Marcus, you upset—"

"Listen to me. The only thing that has changed is your status. Not theirs. They are still our slaves. You must also accept that. I'm afraid this is the price of your freedom—saying farewell to an old life for a better one."

In his mind, he seriously hoped it would be so.

CHAPTER XVII

THEY CALLED HIM ORION.

The Nubian anxiously paced the makeshift arena's perimeters, wielding a gladius. Skin well-oiled and black as mahogany, he was condemned because he had murdered his wealthy master, whom he had served as a body slave.

Today he was Marcus's pick for the second match.

But the day didn't start well. Of all people, Publius Clodius had to plop down in the stands just a few tiers in front of him. It seemed that whenever Clodius showed up, portents never read well.

"Who did you place your purse on, Antonius?" Clodius called out to him.

Marcus pointed a finger toward Orion. "The Nubian there."

Clodius snorted. "Gods, he has no chance if they send out anyone with skill. I'll bet he has no clue how to handle a gladius."

Marcus shrugged dismissively. "I got the inside on this match. He's fighting a beast, not a man."

Clodius became interested. "A lion?"

"Not sure."

"Ha. It's fun when they surprise us!"

Marcus hoped his tip from an arena slave would prove worthwhile. He had a lot of gold sitting on Orion down there.

A heavy gate screeched open on the opposite end of the wooden amphitheater. Noise in the stands fell to a hush as a huge brown bear ambled out into the sun, bawling. The animal's backside was bloody. Keepers had prodded it through its cage with a spear to aggravate it. Now the creature padded out in the bright sunlight, disoriented. Plebs cheered and called out wildly as it stopped and stood upright, sniffing the air.

Orion stopped pacing, sizing up his opponent. Someone in the stands threw a stone at the bear but missed. That started a hailstorm of other objects raining into the arena. Rocks, pieces of fruit, bones, even shards of pottery pelted both the bear and the hapless African.

"Come on, my ebony friend, I need a win today," Marcus breathed, scooting forward on the bench in anticipation. His palms were sweaty; his insides churned. Winning this match could stall Callias, who'd been pushing for higher and more frequent payments.

Agitated, the bear clawed thin air, batting at falling objects, sometimes whirling about, bluff charging if struck, then stopping abruptly again. Orion remained motionless at the other end of the arena.

Oh gods. Were his legs shaking?

Marcus observed a game sponsor speaking quietly to a nearby arena slave. Lifting his spear, the slave edged as close to Orion as possible, still safely outside the arena. He jabbed the condemned man hard enough to draw blood on the back of his muscular shoulders. The African winced and hopped sideways.

But his movement caught the bear's attention. It lifted its nose, sniffing the air. The suspense was audible as the crowd's noise rumbled into ominous murmurs. Descending back onto all fours, the bear took several strides toward Orion. The condemned man glanced about, moving sideways cautiously. He was desperate to seek an escape.

Clodius turned around again. "This could get interesting."

Just as he spoke, the bear charged. Orion leaped sideways, his gladius outstretched and positioned toward the animal. Marcus groaned. The African was completely off balance with his weapon. He'd fall, especially if just one swipe of that bear's paw—

It happened.

Once the bear's foot hit the blade, it bellowed in pain. Staggering to one side, Orion collapsed backward into the arena's wooden wall panels.

Plebs nearest the action leaped up in the stands, shaking fists, cheering or jeering, depending on where their wagers lay. However, Marcus missed Orion's last moments when a beringed hand grasped his shoulder.

Oh shit. Callias.

Fortunately, he didn't often see the greasy little Rhodian, but whenever he did, he regretted the night he accepted the man's offer to cover his iactus stakes.

"I hope you put your money on the bear," the creditor hissed in his ear. When Marcus turned to respond, Callias's single gold-capped tooth gleamed amidst other yellowing ones.

Making a face, Marcus cared little if he saw it or not. Callias was the last person he wanted to see, especially after losing aureii on that inept murderer lying dead in the arena.

Yanking free of his grasp, Marcus waved him off. "We'll speak later."

"No, Antonius. You'll speak with me now."

"Do you think I'm stupid enough to bring gold here, with all these thieves around us?"

"All men bring something to the games, young friend. Otherwise, there would be no betting, no buying the whore Fortuna in the heat of day. There'd be no reason for me to do business here." The tooth glittered again.

Marcus's irritation grew when he saw Clodius glance back at him again, laughing aloud and shaking his head.

Callias pressed in close. Sour, hot breath against his ear was enough to turn Marcus's stomach. "Pay me a fifth of your debt by month's end, or I'll triple your interest."

Marcus stood up at that, facing off with him. "Triple? That's illegal—it's robbery."

Callias smiled again, moist lips curling about the gold tooth. "Illegal? No more so than your betting. Remember, in court Cicero would find you as guilty as your stepfather. In fact, he'd enjoy doing so, I'll warrant."

A chill crept down Marcus's spine. "We have an agreement—in writing," he reminded angrily.

"Ah yes. So we do. Did you know I've a knack at altering documents to assure prompt payments? And if my business doesn't suit, I encourage you to visit the censors with a complaint. Think they'll respond warmly in concern?"

Marcus chewed his lip, cornered in public with Clodius looming nearby, listening to every word. Damn, it was humiliating.

Callias laughed. "I'll look forward to month's end, then. Or I'll have close friends ensure my portion arrives when expected."

Marcus glared at him darkly. "Is that a threat?"

Callias turned to go, casting a cold stare over his shoulder. "No, Antonius. A guarantee."

Callias's dire warning cast a dark pall over Marcus's heart, and only one thing lightened it.

His greatest pleasure would surprise a great many people, including Mother. It was neither wine nor gambling. It wasn't winning a wrestling match or laughing at ribald jokes at taverns.

It was simply watching Fadia and seeing life anew through her eyes.

Since freeing her, he'd seen a beautiful bird whose cage door suddenly opened, sending it to the skies. Despite the bad name she endured in the domus and Mother's disdain, she still managed to make everything celebratory. Whether it was walking hand in hand under shaded umbrella pines, traveling by litter to the Circus, or hearing musicians play, her sense of innocent wonder astounded him.

And her favorite pastime was watching a drama.

Tonight, it was an Athenian tragedy. Marcus paid a Greek slave woman to sit by her during the performance, whispering a rough translation in her ear. Watching her from his own seat among the men, it warmed him seeing her so captivated.

Oh, life could have been so fulfilling if it wasn't for his ever-growing rift with Mother. It pained him more than anyone knew, even Fadia.

Lately, Gaius had become Mother's favorite. And to Marcus's chagrin, he found himself jealous of her affection toward his brother. He, on the other hand, received nothing but cold stares and sharp words.

Nor could he hope to trust Lucius with confidences, as he had less discretion than a Forum crier when it came to keeping something quiet. And most of the time he took whatever he knew straight to Mother.

As for friends, there used to be Curio, but it turned out that he was never a true friend at all. Clodius? Not since the day Marcus saw him marching toward the Tullianum with Cicero. Oh, Marcus could gamble and drink with the likes of him, but trust him? Never.

Only one person knew his inner turmoil, put up with him, and loved him regardless.

Fadia.

She bombarded him with questions after the play.

"How dreadful that poor king tore out his own eyes," she exclaimed, adjusting her pillow as she reclined in the litter. "I'll have nightmares tonight after seeing that."

"Sophocles's tragedies are dark. Better in the theater here, where it's fantasy rather than finding me sleeping with Mother." He laughed at his sick joke.

"Oh, Marcus, how disgusting." Still, she laughed, hitting him playfully with a cushion. "Do you know I overheard someone at the baths saying that incest happens all the time in Egypt? Brothers marrying sisters, fathers marrying daughters—I could never live with myself if I carried on like that. The closest relations we Romans marry are cousins, though some people even frown on that. Is it true about the Egyptians?"

"Apparently so."

The next morning, they were back in the litter again, this time heading to one of Fadia's clients to deliver an order.

Over the past months of their marriage, she had taken her words to Mother very seriously. Determined to have a successful trade, she had opened a small sales stall at the foot of the Palatine. After paying Castor to help paint and prepare the space, she hung her work up to display. Wealthy merchant women adored her bright colors and embroidered patterns. She sold enough finery in the first month to begin buying better materials, including silk. Now even a few senators' wives bought her unique needlework.

Marcus had never been so proud of her. He didn't care what some people thought of him. Oh, he heard how people gossiped about Marcus Antonius, grandson of the great Orator. How could he marry a lowborn slave, then allow her to work in the Forum? What sort of person was he, doing such things?

Sadly, he had nothing of which to be proud.

Leaning back in the litter, he finally surrendered to the subject he'd been dreading. It was the one thing between them they were both aware of yet hated to face.

"Fadia, I must tell you something."

Fadia studied him, her expression serious at his tone. She picked nervously at threads in the pillow under her arm.

Marcus sat up and took her hand. "You're the one stable thing in my life, the only person who loves me as I am."

She looked down at the cushion.

"You have your trade in sewing. Yet I have nothing. Sometime, somehow... I have to make something of myself."

"You could still become an officer. You could ask Caesar—"

"And if he says no again?"

"Then Pompeius. He's a powerful man too. You mustn't be afraid to try."

Marcus stared past the silk curtains out into the Forum as the bearers carried them up the Esquiline toward their destination.

"I haven't any confidence. I hope admitting that doesn't make you ashamed of me."

"You drink too much, Marcus. That's what worries everyone. I know it's your means of escape, but you must conquer it. I could summon the physician who healed my back," she suggested. "Perhaps he can help you."

He shook his head emphatically. That was ridiculous. "I'm not wounded or bleeding," he scoffed.

"Yes, you are," she insisted. "Just wounded and bleeding *inside.*"

Her concern touched him. "Gods, how is it that you know my very heart?"

She giggled. "Maybe because I sleep with my head on your chest. I know what each heartbeat says."

As the litter stopped, he leaned in to kiss her. They'd arrived at her client's domus.

Fadia picked up the neatly packed stola for delivery. "I'll not be long," she promised, hopping out of the litter.

Iophon, Fadia's newly purchased bodyguard, shadowed her, standing nearby as she spoke to a slave in the doorway. Soon the portal opened, and she disappeared inside.

It was a fine domus her client owned. Its high walls were bright yellow with a thick stripe of white around the top edge. It belonged to a wealthy merchant whose wife often commissioned Fadia. It was the third time this month Marcus had come with her to this residence. He lay back, closing his eyes.

An ominous peel of thunder rumbled in the distance. Hopefully, she'd hurry so they could return home before the storm arrived. A cool breeze filtered through the litter's curtains. Dogs barked in nearby streets. Somewhere, a woman argued with a street vendor.

Sleep was nearly upon him when he heard a heavy thud, rapid

footsteps, and what sounded like a scuffle. He ignored it all—until Fadia screamed.

In a heartbeat, he was out of the litter, glancing about. He saw Iophon lying on his side, blood running from his head. A powerfully muscled man held Fadia by her throat against a wall. He was kissing her and pushing his tunic up.

In two strides, Marcus was behind her attacker, drawing his pugio out of its sheath with a hiss. With no second thoughts, he plunged his weapon straight into the man's back, fairly surprised at the sensation. It wasn't much different than skewering a large piece of meat at dinner. He moved so quickly the attacker's hand slid from Fadia's neck, allowing her to break free. Collapsing to his knees, the man had a look of disbelief etched on his face. Marcus jerked his pugio out, blood gushing from the wound, staining the thug's tunic. Wiping his blade on the attacker, he slid it back into its scabbard.

Fadia panicked, darting sideways, quick as a deer. Marcus snatched her wrist, stopping her in mid-stride. "Don't run; you're safe now!"

Momentarily, she resisted, out of her mind with terror. Marcus held her firmly but patiently until all struggling stopped. Her tear-filled eyes were wide and her breathing ragged.

Behind them was a soft moan. Iophon was alive.

Still holding Fadia close, Marcus glanced at the slave. Pushing up to his knees, Iophon touched his head tentatively, feeling his own blood. From the doorway to the patron's house, Marcus saw two slaves peering through the peephole, whispering nervously. They'd need to leave quickly before the whole household got involved.

"Can you get up?" he shouted at Iophon.

The slave grunted hoarsely in reply, staggering to his feet, dazed. He'd be useless the rest of the day.

"Fadia, get in the litter—you too, Iophon," Marcus ordered.

The slave gawked at him as though he hadn't heard correctly.

"You heard me right—get in. You're in no condition to walk." Spying Fadia's sewing satchel, he addressed her next, "Give him some cloth to staunch that blood. Mother will castrate him if he soils her litter!"

Fadia got in first, followed by a hesitant Iophon. Marcus surveyed the bearers. They were edgy, awaiting orders. It was late afternoon, and anyone passing would notice a man lying outside, bleeding from his back.

Marcus glanced back at the peephole. The trap had shut. Those slaves were probably off telling their Domina all about it.

Returning to the assailant, Marcus knelt beside the toppled man, turning him over. Blood already soaked the paving stones. His chest heaved as he struggled to draw breath. Marcus felt like whipping out his pugio to give the bastard a few more jabs with it.

Finding voice, the brute spoke in a croak. "Marcus Antonius?"

"What?" Marcus attempted to wipe blood off his hand, shaken that the attacker knew him.

"A message from Callias—" The man coughed, bloody spittle spraying the air. "No more waiting. He wants large regular payments, or next time he'll pierce your very heart."

The attacker started convulsing with audible gurgling. Bloody froth formed at his mouth. Grabbing Marcus's wrist with one hand, he met death with a long exhale.

Iophon parted the litter's curtains, calling, "That man followed us, Dominus. I remember seeing him when we left the domus."

"Did you know him?" Fadia cried.

"No," Marcus answered honestly. "But I know where he came from."

"Where? Who was he? Why did he attack me?"

Ignoring her, Marcus barked at the litter-bearers. "Get moving! I'll walk."

Carefully concealing his pugio under his cloak, he hurried behind the litter. The slaves lifted it in unison. Striding alongside, Marcus glanced back furtively, seeing two plebian youths already circling the corpse, ready to strip it of valuables.

Inside, Fadia wanted answers. "Tell me who he was," she demanded, parting the curtain to make eye-contact with him.

"Shh—lower your voice. Be calm and quiet and close the curtain."

Pursing her lips, she obeyed but kept talking. "Tell me who he was," she repeated.

"He was sent from a man I know."

"Who? Your creditor? Is Callias your creditor?"

He owed her that much. She had obviously overheard the thug's words. "Yes. Callias is my creditor."

Fadia fell quiet for a time. Marcus glanced about nervously. He could see Iophon peering about from within the litter too, watching for trouble on the other side of the street. A noise from behind made him whirl about defensively, hand on his pugio. His breath caught in relief. It was only a beggar. Relieved, he reminded himself that he'd be out of this soon enough.

"How much do you owe?" Fadia asked.

"That's no worry of yours."

"I'm your wife, I want to know."

"Well, sorry. You don't need to know."

"Is it a lot?"

Ignoring her question, he looked back again. Skittish as a colt all the way to the Palatine, he started at any normal sound of business in the streets. Even a butcher's shrill whistle raised his hackles. Those damned litter-bearers couldn't move fast enough.

Once in front of the domus Antonii, Marcus made sure his blade was well-hidden under his cloak. After assisting Fadia out, Iophon followed, and the three of them walked into the atrium in edgy silence. Inside, Mother was just exiting her cubiculum.

Superb timing.

Marcus spoke low, "Iophon, go to the slave quarters, and please go the other way, away from Mother. Hurry and she won't notice you." The slave nodded, walking in the other direction, head turned slightly to conceal his injury.

Marcus turned to Fadia, but she flippantly headed off, showing him her back, perturbed he wouldn't disclose his debt.

Within seconds, Mother stood before him. "Marcus? How unnerved you look. Is everything well, my son?"

Sweating like a slave in a silver mine, he tried looking calm, but she'd already seen through it. "Everything's fine. I decided to walk back, nothing more." If he ever did enter politics, he'd have to get a lot better at lying.

She tilted her head back and eyed him shrewdly. "Fadia looked anything but 'fine' when she passed. Did you have a lover's tiff?"

He glared at her. "Let it go." Walking away, a thought emerged. He stopped. "Mother, how much do you think the villa in Misenum is worth?"

"You're thinking of selling it?"

"Just answer the question."

"I have no idea, but if you advertised, I imagine you'd get a good price for it. Perhaps even good enough to cover a *large debt*," she said with emphasis. "Misenum is still highly fashionable. If it helps ease your plight, do it. We never go there."

Fadia avoided Marcus the rest of the day. It wasn't until later that night that he finally entered his cubiculum.

She sat on the sleeping couch with a polished bronze mirror propped on her pillow, brushing her long hair. Judging by her silent treatment all afternoon, she was still angry with him.

Wearily, he pulled off his tunic, tossing it haphazardly into one corner. "If I were in a legion, they'd say I was blooded today," he commented.

Nothing.

He continued the heroic tactics. "I should at least get a 'gratias, Marcus' for saving your life."

"Gratias, then," she said shortly.

"Ah, that makes it all better," he chortled sarcastically. Hidden from her view, he rolled his eyes. She remained silent. "Come on, girl. All married people have some secrets from each other."

"It doesn't matter," she replied coolly.

Really? He shook his head, running one hand through his hair. "What will it take to make you forgive me?"

"Tell me how much you owe." At that, she turned about to meet his eyes. She had changed tunics, wearing only a thin silk shift, transparent as water.

Venus, how she could make him want her.

"It's that important to you?" He sat down on the sleeping couch, reaching for her brush.

"Yes."

He brushed her extraordinary hair. Taking long, slow strokes, he was careful not to catch a knot. With his other hand, he reached up, slipping fingers through its cascades. Long, silky, soft ...

Lifting her locks to one side, he nuzzled her neck with his lips, whispering into her ear. "If I tell you, promise not to tell anyone?"

She leaned back against him. Marcus dropped the brush, wrapping both arms around her.

"What if I tell someone to save your life?" she whispered back, turning her neck slightly, making it easy for him to kiss her.

After the kiss, he replied, "The amount is so much that my life is worthless in comparison."

"Tell me," she breathed into his mouth, covering it with hers.

Kissing her hungrily, he moved lower, burying his face in her neck. Lifting his head briefly, he whispered in her ear. "Over two hundred talents."[1]

Her response was a swift intake of air. He pulled back, gazing at her. Her eyes were round pools of azure in the dim lamplight. Pausing only a moment, she pulled him slowly down atop her. With one hand, he reached sideways to pinch out the flame on the lamp next to the bed.

While making love, he moved to assuage his need with the usual

---

[1] By the time his debt was at its worst, it may have been as much as 250 talents. Biblical scholar Joel Drinkard (2005) estimates that one talent in the 1st century AD was the equivalent of $576,000. Multiply that by Antony's debt, and it becomes a cool $144 million. Eleanor Goltz Huzar, in her biography of Antony's life (1978), describes his debt to be one and a half million denarii, with four or five times the purchasing worth of our money today. It was an extravagant sum.

urgency of physical desire, but inside his head the stabbing replayed itself over and over.

Finally, he had killed. It was out of necessity, protecting a loved one; therefore he had no regrets. Still, as he moved against Fadia, feeling his usual pleasure in their union, the words of a dead man remained very much alive in his mind.

He needed to pay up, or someone would pierce his heart.

CHAPTER XVII
59 BC

IN MARCUS'S OPINION, COUSIN GAIUS JULIUS CAESAR HAD been mighty busy in the past year. He was now Rome's newly elected consul.

Not only had he risen politically, but shortly after Clodius's scandalous attempt to enter the Bona Dea, he had divorced Pompeia. There was talk that she and Clodius had been lovers, and Caesar wouldn't tolerate any gossip about it. He openly declared that his wife "must be above suspicion" and promptly cast her aside.

So he married a third time. His new bride was Calpurnia, daughter to the wealthy and well-respected senator Lucius Calpurnius Piso.

Tonight, he was opening his home to a hugely attended dinner party. Marcus was especially happy to attend, for the invitation included Fadia. This would be her first foray into high society, and though excited at the opportunity, she was understandably nervous.

As Marcus approached the atrium, followed by Fadia, Mother, and his brothers, Caesar stood in the entry welcoming guests. "Antonius, welcome. Calpurnia insisted all your family attend," he said cordially, nodding at the others.

Marcus clasped his hand. "We appreciated the invitation, Caesar."

"And this is your wife?"

"Indeed," Marcus said, smiling. "I present Antonia Fadia."

Fadia nodded deeply. "It is such an honor, sir. I thank you graciously for including me."

Caesar, ever the charmer of women, gave her a grand smile. "I can see why Marcus finds you so lovely. Do make yourself at home."

"We congratulate you on your consulship," Mother said. "You'll do great things for Rome."

"It should be an eventful year, and afterward."

"Yes. I've heard you hope to go to Gaul," Marcus said. "Please consider me when you select staff."

"When the time comes, I shall," Caesar assured him.

And then the evening soured. As Mother, Gaius, and Lucius went into the domus to mingle, Marcus saw Uncle Lucius Julius standing nearby, eyeing him. They hadn't spoken since that fateful day before Lentulus's execution. Intense dislike burned in the older man's steely gaze.

Caesar followed Marcus's eyes, noting Uncle Lucius's animosity. "I see you may need to speak with your uncle. I'll leave you to it while I welcome more guests."

Wonderful. Now Marcus found himself face-to-face with a man he despised.

Enmity like hot coals burned between them. Stiffly, he began by introducing Fadia. "Uncle, I present to you Antonia Fadia, my wife."

"Ah, yes. The slave."

Fadia never ceased to surprise Marcus. She was quick to fend for herself, calmly and matter-of-factly. "I am no slave. I'm a free woman, with a trade that brings in honest coin."

"Hmph," Uncle Lucius snorted, looking down his considerable nose at her. "Your husband will need extra silver to pay his innumerable debts. Right, Nephew? And, tell me—do you intend to be in command of your behavior tonight?"

"I begged pardon for it once. You ignored that request, along with another I made that day," Marcus responded icily.

"Then we're still at odds."

"At odds?" Marcus snarled, unaware how his voice was escalating. "The only *odd* thing was your flat refusal to speak out on behalf of my stepfather!" Some imperious heads turned his way. Fadia placed a hand gently on his arm, stilling him.

Uncle Lucius glanced about uncomfortably. "Already your manners lack civility appropriate for polite society," he whispered in disgust. That said, he moved away.

The evening got even worse before getting better.

Extra dining couches spilled outside into the open air, accommodating the large numbers of guests. Slaves busily tended glowing braziers placed here and there, keeping everyone sufficiently warm.

Marcus watched Calpurnia lead Mother to the head couch beside Aurelia and Atia. He, Fadia, and his brothers, on the other hand, wound up well away from the Julii, seated next to none other than Cicero!

Marcus wasn't sure if the slight was because Fadia was there or if Caesar was subtly suggesting he make amends with the former consul. Well, if so, that might be the way Caesar played politics, but Cicero's crimes against his family were far too grievous to forgive.

Nonetheless, Cicero engaged him. "Young Marcus Antonius, good health to you. I take it this is your...wife?" The elder statesman toyed with a mushroom, twirling it around in a bowl of garum, idly studying Fadia.

Marcus would sooner kiss the Gorgon before wishing this bastard good health! "Yes, Marcus Tullius," he muttered begrudgingly. It was all he could manage.

"Is it possible to forget the stormy circumstances between our families?" Cicero queried.

"No, it is not," Marcus responded, cold as a corpse.

"I see. Then we'll spend a dismal evening here, I fear."

"Sharing a couch with you was *not* my idea." Marcus accepted two cups of wine, one for himself and the other for Fadia.

"Perhaps Caesar desires our reconciliation?"

"Ho!" he barked unpleasantly. "Unless Caesar can raise the dead and bring Lentulus back, patching things up between us is impossible!" This was beyond irritating, and Marcus's voice had risen again. Several nearby senators regarded him distastefully.

At that, Cicero kept his peace.

Marcus and Fadia ate their delicacies in tense silence. He used every ounce of self-control to rein himself in from drinking too much. Excellent courses of sesame cheeses served with assorted breads, squid in celery sauce, roast peahen, and vegetables mixed with garlic were all lost on him. Gaius and Lucius, noticing their brother's discontent, mindfully kept their own counsel, chatting amiably to guests nearest them.

At the head table, a Greek bard accompanied himself on a traditional lyre of tortoiseshell, launching into the familiar tale of Odysseus. Marcus noticed Mother's rapt attention to the musician. Next to her, he was surprised to see Caesar's new bride, Calpurnia, smiling and watching him. She motioned to a slave to bring her shoes. Then, leaving her place, she walked straight to where Marcus, Fadia, and his brothers were sitting.

Discreetly, Calpurnia leaned in, whispering to Marcus, "There are only two couples on the couch there." She gestured, indicating a quieter area with fewer guests.

Immediately, Marcus and Fadia arose, joining Caesar's wife. As they settled, two attentive slaves tended their mistress, offering fruit. Calpurnia waved them away. "Welcome to my domus, Marcus Antonius." She extended her hand warmly.

"It's a pleasure to meet Caesar's wife." She wasn't beautiful like Cornelia or Pompeia had been. Her nose was a little long, lips a trifle too thin, but her sunny smile was completely disarming.

"And this must be your wife?"

"I am Antonia Fadia." Fadia nodded graciously.

Calpurnia turned her attentions to Marcus. "I was watching you at your table. I could tell you weren't enjoying our party."

Marcus cocked his head, studying her. They'd only just met, but already he was beginning to comprehend what he liked about this unique woman. In only the few words they'd shared, he could see that she was genuine. Unlike her husband and most of Rome, she wasn't after personal or political gain. She was just Calpurnia.

"Forgive me, lady. I'm rather rude at times, finding it difficult to conceal distaste for people I dislike."

Calpurnia laughed in pure delight. "Why, I think an honest nature is a wonderful trait. Most men tend to sidestep inquiries about true feelings."

"Not my husband!" Fadia laughed.

"Guilty as charged," Marcus admitted. "Unfortunately, no 'sidestepping' is necessary to admit my very strong dislike for two of your guests."

"Hmmm, one is Cicero, I have no doubt. I watched you through dinner. You were practically in Fadia's arms, shrinking away from him."

It was Marcus's turn to laugh. "Really? Well, being in Fadia's arms is no bad place! But was I that obvious?"

Both women laughed and then paused, glancing toward the singer, as the ballad reached an apex in recitation of Odysseus's wrestle with Scylla and Charybdis.

"Who's the other guest you dislike?" Calpurnia pried.

Marcus nodded toward the head table. "The man sitting on the end, my Uncle Lucius Julius."

Her glistening hazel eyes flitted between Cicero and Lucius Julius, appraising them. "You dislike scholarly types?"

"No, it's not that. Though both he and Cicero could probably teach me volumes about rhetoric or literature."

"Then I'm relieved! If you disliked scholarly people, you wouldn't like me. I love reading, studying philosophy, and writing poetry."

"I'm learning to read," Fadia said shyly. "I'd like to read more books and learn more things."

"I'll send you my volumes of Homer. Read the *Iliad*, first. Then turn to the *Odyssey*. The story will be in sequence that way," she advised.

Marcus's discontent eased. It pleased him to see Calpurnia attentive to Fadia. Everyone else mostly ignored her.

Did Caesar know what a splendid woman he'd married? Her father, Piso, was among several men expected to stand for consul next year. No doubt this marriage was nothing but a political alliance. Caesar's goal after his term ended was to campaign in Gaul. If Piso was consul next, then marriage to his daughter guaranteed any legislation needed to further his own imperium.

What began as a disastrous evening turned into something memorably pleasant. Marcus watched Calpurnia rise to greet other guests, weaving her way back to her husband's table.

He admired this unexpected new friend. Here was a person he felt he could really trust.

Halfway through Caesar's consulship, Marcus was spending another hot afternoon at the baths. Barely a summer breeze blew.

He dried off, his linen towel soaked in sweat. He often engaged other young men in good-natured competition in the small palaestra there. Winning an overall reputation of "champion" wrestler gave him inner satisfaction. It was a spark of needed hope that Fortuna would yet nod favorably in his direction.

But Fortuna was taking her sweet time! He'd approached both Pompeius and Caesar about staff positions. Neither made any promises.

Wearily, he motioned Syrianus to pick up his things, heading toward the apodyterium to dress.

"Antonius!"

Marcus stopped, recognizing the voice instantly.

It was Publius Clodius. They had come to an odd sort of unspoken understanding of late. Neither mentioned their past conflicts. Clodius never brought up the Subura, the money Marcus lost on it, or his gambling. In turn, Marcus never brought up Clodius's humiliation at the Bona Dea or his affiliation with Cicero in the Forum during the Catilina Conspiracy.

Marcus assessed Clodius's attire. He was downright dignified in his toga, with all its elegant folds. "Where've you been? The Curia?"

"I'm going there next. Did you win again?"

Marcus sighed. "It was nothing, really. Just wrestling a few men of leisure like myself. Sadly, none of them has any real training. Not even Brutus."

"Marcus Junius?"

Marcus nodded. "With his lineage, he should have the strength of a lion, but instead he reminds me of my Uncle Lucius Julius. I think he'd just prefer carrying scrolls around and whimpering about the 'end of the Republic.' But he's probably four years older than me with no commission in sight either. Makes me feel a little better!"

Clodius clapped him on the shoulder. "Personally, I dislike that philosophic little prig. Always complaining about some sort of baggage. Too much like his caregiver, Cato, for my tastes." Clodius paused a moment, then ventured, "I heard you sold your father's land recently."

Marcus stopped at a stone basin, splashing water on his face. "Yes. A farm down in Misenum. It was in a good location. Farmable, and on a hill not far from the sea."

Clodius pushed closer to a nerve. "So. I take it your problems are solved? Or should I say solvent?" He sniggered at his attempt at humor.

Marcus wasn't having it. He changed the subject. "What is it you want, looking for the likes of me, all dressed up to rub shoulders with the influential and famous?"

Clodius smiled charmingly. "Can I count on your vote when I stand for tribune this December?"

"Tribune? Of the plebs? *You?*" Marcus whistled, waving Syrianus on inside. Smirking, he added, "I thought magistrates were supposed to have dignitas."

"I'm serious, Antonius."

Marcus laughed. After Clodius's escapades at the Bona Dea,

it was hard taking him seriously. Lifting his head from another splash in the basin, Marcus wiped excess water away. He sighed, studying this man who some now claimed to be the most influential revolutionary in Rome since Catilina. Clodius was short and stocky but still a fine-looking fellow, graced with chiseled features and curling black hair.

Marcus crossed his arms, leaning back against a brightly painted column. "All right. Tell me what you stand for. Impress me."

"Well, the plebs have it hard," he began. "They need someone taking a stand for them. I'm damned tired of seeing babes starving in our streets. How much better for them if they had free grain?"

"Excellent, but where does free grain come from? It never rains down from the skies."

"A technicality that may change if Caesar enters Gaul."

"Only if torching isn't needed to take it. What else?"

"I'll ensure that the incoming consuls, Gabinius and Calpurnius Piso, get their entitled provinces. Gabinius shows great interest in the East. That should also assist with free grain."

"And?"

"There's the issue of collegia, our guilds. Having plebs bonded together in unity could give them more clout against stiff-necked optimates."

Optimates were the conservative faction in the Senate.

Marcus pushed away from the column, continuing toward the apodyterium with Clodius in tow. "Sorry, Clodius," he said. "I'm afraid you've failed. To win my vote, you must appeal to my needs too."

"Oh, I almost forgot!" Clodius exclaimed. "There's a little bill I'm considering, exiling all those who have condemned Roman citizens to death without popular sanction or trial."

Marcus halted in his tracks. Now Clodius was going to *oppose* Cicero?

Turning slowly, he saw the shorter man smiling at him complacently, extending his hand. "Now might I depend on your vote this winter, Marcus Antonius?"

Marcus stepped forward and clasped Clodius's wrist firmly. "Give me your word to take Cicero down, and you'll have the votes of my brothers too!"

There was nothing Marcus would rather see than Cicero's demise.

Marcus rolled over, draping his arm over—nothing. He opened his eyes. Fadia wasn't there. Blinking, he looked around the room. The door was ajar.

Opening it wide enough to let himself out, he stole outside, making his way to the atrium fountain feeding into the impluvium pool.

There she was.

Fadia was leaning over, cupping her hands, catching cool water and lifting it to her face.

"Can't sleep?" Marcus asked.

She stared up at him.

Gods, she was pale. Or was it just the darkness? "Are you ill?"

"Maybe something I ate?"

Somewhere beyond the walls of the domus, a rooster crowed. Shaking water from her hands, she sank down miserably on the edge of the pool, staring straight ahead.

Marcus sat down next to her, gently rubbing her back.

Suddenly, she leaped up, bolting toward the rose garden. Once there, she vomited. Shoulders heaving, and none too gracefully, she heaved up dinner. Every bit of it.

"How can I help?" Marcus asked.

"You can't. Please go back to bed," she pleaded. She was crying now.

"How about some honeyed wine? Mother used to give it to me when I was sick."

"No," was her pathetic reply.

"Dry bread? Just something—"

"No! No, I don't want anything!" she cried out impatiently. "Go back to bed."

She didn't usually have an intolerant or testy side. This tone was something new.

"Then come back with me. I'll hold you."

"No, Marcus. I want to be alone!" she nearly shouted.

His jaw dropped. It was as though she'd slapped him.

And for the next ten to twelve days, she was dismissive of his every approach.

If he touched her or went to kiss her at night, she'd recoil and begin to cry. Several times he went to the small room she used for sewing, but initiating any conversation was impossible. She became more and more distant.

What had he done? Gods, he'd not slept with another woman since the night they'd first made love! He wished he could go and ask Mother for advice, but since she despised Fadia, that wasn't even an option.

In his heart, Marcus was beginning to grieve. Fadia was as cold as rain in December.

Weary of weeks without Fadia's usual warmth, Marcus waited for the results of his sacrifice outside the tiny Temple of Hercules. Clodius and other acquaintances were springing into careers, but his life was going nowhere. His biggest fear was that Fadia no longer loved him because she was disappointed in him.

Shifting uncomfortably, he stared at the smoking altar. If Hercules really had powers of godhead, he hoped the Strong One would be merciful to his supposed descendent. Marcus was not a religious man, but here he was sacrificing the finest piglet in the Forum Boarium!

The animal squealed loudly when the public slave led it away to sacrifice. Afterward, he'd have it roasted and donate the meat to some poor family living in the district. These stock and poultry markets were filthy. It couldn't hurt, introducing himself to people here with generosity.

Lately, he had successfully curbed his desire for drink, only allowing himself a certain amount of wine per day. He was hoping this newfound sobriety would make Fadia notice and soften toward him.

Oh, something was terribly wrong between them. Sometimes he overheard her crying when she thought he was asleep. With such odd fluctuations in her mood lately, he had given up on confronting her. Either he was going about it all wrong, or she no longer loved him.

Being without that was something he wasn't certain he could handle.

He remembered how Mother had been ever patient and forbearing with Lentulus. Truthfully, she had been an impressive model for him in those days. He decided acting in the like manner could only aid him with his own love. He'd have to be patient with her, even though celibacy was not to his liking!

Marcus was a man with vast reserves of energy, and without wine or sex, he succumbed to his other great temptation.

He began gambling non-stop.

Sometimes he attended the races, and at night, without Fadia's attentions, it was back to unmentionable places in the Subura, where he tested Fortuna at iactus. More than once, prostitutes temptingly offered themselves.

If only Fadia could see—he even walked away from them.

However, the talents he'd gained from Father's land went immediately to Callias. They had become a mere splash in an endless ocean of debt, sure to drown him unless he was able to swim his way out.

And with all this recent gambling, his debt continued to grow.

At last, the skinny little priest walked down the stairs toward him, his hands bloodied. "Son of the Antonii, your offering was found to be adequate and the hero-god has spoken."

He placed his bloodstained, dripping hand onto Marcus's

forehead, proclaiming words of knowledge: "The great one whose labors took him on countless travels proclaims you will also have many journeys. He divines you will have two loves, one bringing you greater joy than the other, but also bringing loss and death. You'll rise to greater honor than your ancestors, and your life will soon change course. That is what the god says."

The priest removed his hand, and Marcus felt residual blood sticking to his face. Well, the words were mostly promising, but his lack of confidence in himself, joined with his unbelief in the spiritual, left a void of doubt where hope should have been.

He paid the priest and left coin for several extra pigs to feed a few more families. As he walked back toward the Palatine, he heard the priest's voice in the back of his mind: "You'll rise to greater honor than your ancestors..."

CHAPTER XVIII
59-58 BC

"MARCUS, I WANT TO GO WALKING. WILL YOU COME?"

Fadia wanted his company? "Of course. Where are we going?"

"I'll explain when we get there."

Down the Palatine, across the Nova Via, and now up the Esquiline. They went as far as the Temple of Juno Lucina, goddess of childbirth. Fadia stopped in front of the building, its façade covered with women's offerings.

Marcus watched her kneel before the little exterior shrine as though a devout follower. Full realization dawned on him. After she finished her quick petition, Fadia motioned him over to a wall in the temple's shade.

She spoke matter-of-factly. "I'm with child. It will be born around the time of the elections this winter. Soon I'll need to find a good midwife."

Stunned, Marcus was at a loss for words. "You—oh, Fadia." A mix of emotions stirred—shock, frustration at not knowing sooner, anticipating unseen responsibility—this was something he knew nothing whatsoever about. But underneath everything was great joy that part of him was inside her. Heart bursting with emotion, he pulled her into a jubilant embrace. "My girl!"

He lifted her, spinning in the crowded street, laughing.

This explained everything—her withdrawn state, her unwillingness to interact or make love.

"Don't worry. I'll take care of you."

"Marcus, I'm so afraid."

All initial bliss vanished in a rush. "What? Why do you say that? This babe is of our love."

Uneasily, he reached down, gently seeking to place his hand on her abdomen. She stepped back, evading his touch, putting space between them.

"I know a time is coming when you must leave Rome. Then where will I be? How will your mother react when she finds out? Would she harm our baby? I don't know that I could stand living under a roof so full of hatred."

"Fadia," Marcus cried. "Stop this and get hold of yourself. Nobody will harm you or our baby. Least of all Mother."

She began to cry, crumbling against him. He held her steady, rocking her back and forth, oblivious to the countless plebs carrying on with daily life all around them.

He'd heard how pregnant women were sisters to the Furies. "Nothing will happen to you," he assured with his calmest voice. Certainly, his words would settle her.

"I'm afraid to have this child, so afraid."

"Why?"

"I saw a physician. He said that because it's my first and I'm small, it could be difficult. He thinks the child will be very big. You are very big." She pressed against him, shaking. His tunic was damp from her tears.

Long ago, Mother had told him to remember how difficult it was for women to have a child. All he could do was try to soothe her. "Hush, now. Try to be joyful, the way a young mother should be. We'll leave the rest to fate."

Fadia kept shaking her head, weeping.

He led her just inside the temple doorway. Sheltered there, they sat against the frame of the entrance until evening, shadows falling over the place in angular patterns. He held her the entire time, and when she finally quieted, relaxing against him, they silently walked home.

The stark reality of their situation started sinking in, curbing his initial excitement. Oh, the baby would not have a bad life, but Marcus's mounting debt prevented him from supporting Fadia and his child the way he'd prefer. And there was the issue that, though they were married and their issue would be legitimate, its lineage was still only half-noble. As their child grew into adulthood, that could prove detrimental socially.

He cursed himself. He was a fool, a wastrel, and a gambler. Still, Marcus would never admit that their marriage had been a mistake. As happy as they had been, how could it be wrong? Now he'd have to start paying back Callias's debt in earnest. *If* he could pay it back, as monstrous as it was.

The passage home in the dark was long and distressing. They'd wasted too much time lingering at the temple, when traversing Rome's streets was safer in broad daylight. Marcus fingered the hilt of his pugio, praying to Mars it would remain unused this night of nights.

The next morning dawned in pink radiance. As he rose, it occurred to him that his head ached from lack of sleep, not drink. Fadia still slept deeply, motionless beside him.

He found Mother conversing with Castor in the peristyle garden. The domus pear trees were producing a hearty crop this year. Castor had sliced one apart for Mother to sample. As Marcus came outside, she glanced up, a pleased smile dancing on her face, making her look young.

"Marcus, they're sweet like honey. Your father wasn't much of a general, but the man certainly knew fruit trees."

The slave offered him a slice, but he shook his head. "Castor, leave us. Mother, sit down, I have news."

She studied him, all pleasantness fading from her face. Before retreating, Castor offered her a moist rag, and she wiped her sticky fingers on it. Then she followed Marcus to a nearby bench. She sat down, but he paced before her anxiously, chewing his lip.

"There's no easy way of saying this, so I'll just speak it outright. Fadia's with child. She's seen a physician who thinks her time will be around the elections this winter."

"I'm surprised it hasn't happened before now," Mother replied calmly.

Marcus was astonished. Awaiting her usual chastisement, none came.

She spoke again before he did. "Is that all?"

He laughed dryly, awaiting an anticipated and most unpleasant lecture. "I was about to ask you the same question."

"What is it you expect me to say? You're married to a former slave when most men your age already have a career and a wife of noble birth. Contrary to what you may think, Marcus, I deeply regret the hostility between us. I wish with all my heart things were different."

"I love her; you know that."

Tears filled her eyes. She looked away, sighing deeply. "It always comes down to that girl."

Frustrated, his voice rose. "Why do you hate her so? She borrowed a necklace without asking. Gods! Can you not let bygones fly? It'd be different if Fadia were Lucius Julius or Cicero. They destroyed our family honor when they had Lentulus executed without trial. Fadia isn't heartless or destructive like them. Yet you harbor more hatred for her than the men who had your husband killed unjustly."

Mother wordlessly wiped a tear from her face.

For a time, they were both silent. Marcus sat down next to her on the stone bench. He wondered who was more stubborn between the two of them. When the silence became too long, he clumsily reached out, taking her hand in his. "Do you ever wonder if Lentulus sees us wherever he is?"

"Only the gods know."

"If he sees us, wherever the dead are, I wager it grieves him knowing we argue so with one another," he rationalized.

She nodded in agreement, smiling faintly. "He never liked arguing."

"No."

"He was a man who loved giving and being loved because of it. How strange he was a revolutionary."

"He'd be disappointed in me," Marcus said softly. He felt her fingers lace through his. It was so long since they'd conversed pleasantly together; he had a hard time finishing his thought. "Do you know what his last words were to me?"

"No."

"He said, 'Take care of your mother.'" He shook his head ashamedly. "I've not done a good job of that."

Her slender fingers tightened around his.

"You may start now. Perhaps we can maneuver about the way you and Clodius do, avoiding things on which we disagree." With her other hand, she reached out, turning his face gently toward hers. She smiled. "I'll try if you do, and if you like, I'll acquire a good midwife. Winter's a harsh time of year to have a baby."

It was the dead stray dog that shook Marcus to his core.

The animal had had its heart ripped out, and Syrianus found its limp body nailed to a hitching post outside the domus Antonii.

Marcus swore the old gatekeeper to silence, only involving one other person: Iophon. He charged the two slaves to keep a silent watch outside the house, looking for anything unusual.

"What should I be looking for?" Iophon asked.

"I really don't know. Strangers loitering, more dead animals— anything odd."

Callias wanted another sizeable chunk of payment, which Marcus didn't have. He began assembling personal belongings of worth, pawning them, and sending Iophon to the creditor with vouchers for the gold.

Upon the fourth delivery of aureii, the big slave returned home shaking his head. "He wants a minimum of five talents—and very soon."

Whenever Marcus went out, he took both Castor and Iophon along as bodyguards. And most importantly, he never left the domus without his pugio tucked away and hidden under his cloak.

"Why do Iophon and Castor follow you all the time?" Fadia asked.

"They're helping me move items from a warehouse to pawn for Callias's payments."

It was nothing more than a blatant lie, but in her naivety it pacified her.

Strangely, at this same time the two women in Marcus's life suddenly eased their animosity toward one another. By her actions, Mother finally acknowledged that Fadia and her son's happiness went hand in hand. Marcus knew she probably clung to the hope that someday he'd cast Fadia aside, divorcing her for a different wife and a career. But at least she joined them at dinner now.

Gaius and Lucius had always liked Fadia, even when she was a slave. They accepted her almost as though she were a sister, including her in conversation, especially if she discussed things interesting them. All the while, Mother tolerated the added company with ladylike forbearing, remaining aloof but pleasant.

Fadia always waited for Mother to speak and address her first, but gradually the two women relaxed in each other's company. Right now their common ground was Fadia's pregnancy.

As the months passed, she grew swollen like a wine-filled goatskin. Almost daily, Marcus placed his hands on her stomach, feeling their child kicking with life. The whole thing was fascinating.

In early December, the physician visited a final time. The child was due any day, and Mother fulfilled her promise to Marcus, finding a midwife. Just past child-bearing years herself, the woman had excellent credentials, having assisted both senatorial and wealthy merchant women. Intelligent and friendly, she bonded with Fadia during her brief visit, assuaging the girl's fears and assuring all would go well.

Every preparation was complete. Now it was a waiting game.

For Marcus, this period was his introduction to responsibility. And the imminent birth was the least of those burdens.

By early December, he'd sold most of his own valuables. Then Mother came to him, suggesting he sell Lentulus's family litter. Indeed, it brought a fair price. Next, they sold four of the serving slaves, the kitchen staff taking over duties in the triclinium at mealtimes. If they kept this pace going, the domus would be empty by the time the babe was born.

A solemn, mournful atmosphere prevailed on the day Marcus auctioned off some marble statuary belonging to the family for decades. One was a Hercules. Father had been particularly fond of it.

He returned from its sale in a foul temper. "The spirits of our ancestors are probably begging the gods for my punishment."

"Why? What happened?" Mother asked, her face paling at the look of him.

"Just *guess* who won the bids on the Hercules."

She shook her head.

"Cicero," he spat venomously. "Old bastard probably cares nothing for its beauty but bought it just to humiliate me."

"Nonsense, Marcus—everyone knows how much he loves art. You should have seen his peristyle court the day Lentulus died. I thought I'd ascended to Olympus. I've never seen such a collection of gods and goddesses. Now that he owns the Hercules, he'll be forced to recognize what good taste we have."

When the tribunal elections took place, Publius Clodius won his magistracy. Marcus, Gaius, and Lucius had all voted for him, hopeful the win would bring some retribution to Cicero for Lentulus's illegal execution.

To celebrate that hope, Marcus held a dinner party for the family.

"Clodius is having a big party tonight, too," Gaius commented, taking a generous portion of sliced pork onto his platter. "He should have invited you, Marcus."

Mother jumped in with a quick response. "If Clodius is hosting, then we all know the sort who will be there. Marcus, you're best removed from such entertainment. You'd be too tempted to indulge in whatever distractions he's hired."

When the slave approached Fadia, the woman placed extra meat on her platter.

Marcus laughed, ribbing Gaius, who always ate more than his fair share. "Her appetite has increased threefold. I swear she eats more than me."

"Well, since I'm the one giving you the child, I deserve something," Fadia responded.

The three brothers all laughed at her.

She shook her head in frustration. "Everyone keeps telling me my time is near," she said, licking a fruity sauce from her index finger. "Well, December elections have come and gone, but here I sit. Just look at me."

Mother smiled wryly. "Walk." she suggested. "I remember I thought Lucius would never come into this world. He was late arriving at his birth, and to this day he's late to every party and event to which he's invited."

"But I know how to make an entrance!" Lucius exclaimed with bravado, lifting his hands self-importantly, to their amusement.

Everyone was laughing, smiling. At last, Marcus saw Fadia and Mother experiencing feelings of happiness and common ground. These were the people he loved, and it warmed him to see Mother enjoying Fadia's company.

"Walk the paths around the Palatine," Mother urged her. "It does wonders. You'll have the child before the week is out."

Marcus chewed his lip.

He just couldn't sell Lentulus's old marble desk. Mother would probably insist, but he couldn't find the strength to do it. Composed of solid Egyptian granite, the surface gleamed so smooth he saw his own face. It was a fine piece, capable of bringing a rich price, but it bore too many memories.

No, he wouldn't do it.

Old Greek scrolls lay encased in a cedar box Lentulus owned long before his marriage to Mother. Supposedly, they were original Euripidean manuscripts. Mother wouldn't miss them. Marcus imagined the fine collector's price they'd bring.

He felt rather than heard Iophon's presence at the door.

Clumsily toying with the peculiar latch encasing the scrolls, he gave orders as he worked. "Once Syrianus takes your post, take these to Caesar's domus and give them to Calpurnia. Her father has a vast library down by Herculaneum, and he may be able to assess their worth. I'll give you a note for her explaining my request." He shook his head, hating himself. If these really were originals, it was probably a terrible insult to Lentulus's memory to sell them.

"Dominus, the same man in the black and white cloak is back again, asking to see you."

Marcus said nothing, still fiddling with the latch.

Iophon went on, "He said to tell you he is a friend with important advice."

Giving up on the delicate lock, Marcus sat back, puffing his cheeks out in a sigh. He shook his head sadly. "Tell him to return to Callias, reminding him I'm paying up, best I can—and on a regular basis too. Tell him that if it's really coin he wants, he's getting it, slowly but surely."

Deep down, Marcus wondered whether Callias even wanted payment now. Maybe he was just more interested in getting even and getting rid of him. With a debt this size, one impossible to repay unless he was an Egyptian pharaoh, it would undoubtedly be more satisfying to simply murder him. He was constantly watching his back.

Iophon was still loitering in the doorway. He could never take

Vindelicus's place, but he was a good, loyal man, owning a calm, gentle spirit, much like the Gaul's had been.

"Speak openly, Iophon. I can tell you want to."

"Dominus, perhaps … perhaps you should leave Rome for a time."

"I've considered it, but not with Fadia about to give birth. Afterward, I think I probably shall."

"These men you deal with, they are dangerous."

Marcus nodded, looking at Iophon sternly. "Yes, and I don't wish to alarm the rest of my family. So you and Syrianus are bound to your oath. Say nothing."

"Yes, but…your mother and brothers … are they safe, Dominus?"

Marcus wrinkled his brow. "Remember the man who attacked us at Fadia's client's domus? He warned that I would suffer next, did he not?" Marcus pointed out. "Let's take him at his word, praying Callias won't harm anyone else."

He cursed himself again. Debt was a sword of Damocles hanging over him. There was no way to pay it all back. Iophon was right. Marcus had to get a commission or something soon, enabling him to leave.

Iophon hovered in the doorway. Obviously, there was something more.

"What else?" Marcus asked testily.

"You should tell your mother."

He laughed bitterly. "Ho! Tell her what? She's assisted me in selling most of our household wares, slaves, and whatnot. I think she knows a bit of what's going on." He was getting flustered. "This is not your business. Go do as I say."

CHAPTER XIX

"WHERE'S FADIA?" MARCUS INQUIRED.

Mother, Gaius, and Lucius had gathered in the winter triclinium, enjoying warm honeyed wine and fresh bread as an early morning meal.

Lucius shrugged, chewing hungrily.

"Lately, she's been walking with Iophon in the mornings," Mother said.

"She's not with him now," Marcus said.

He blinked drowsiness from his eyes, trying to think. He'd stayed up late with his brothers, drinking and playing iactus. He'd just seen Iophon in the atrium, laughing with Syrianus as they changed their shifts.

Was she with Lydia?

He paced back to Mother's cubiculum doorway toward the front of the domus, seeing the slave woman just inside through the open door, changing linens on her mistress's sleeping couch. She looked up. "Dominus?"

"Have you seen your daughter this morning?"

"No, Dominus."

Marcus was concerned now. He headed into the atrium next. "Syrianus, have you seen Fadia?"

The old slave looked up absently, plumping his pillow and readying himself for sleep in his niche. "Yes, Dominus. She went for a walk right before dawn."

"Who accompanied her?"

"She was alone, Dominus."

"Alone?" Marcus was incredulous. His voice escalated in fury, "You let her go alone?"

Hearing his master raise his voice in such a threatening way, Syrianus groveled humbly on both knees. "Mercy, Dominus, I did not know—"

"Your mind is *gone*, Syrianus!" Marcus kicked the slave roughly.

Mother, Gaius, and Lucius hurried into the atrium to see what the row was about.

Mother was first to react. "Marcus, what's wrong that you'd treat Syrianus so?"

"His mind is going. He let Fadia go out by herself."

She laughed. "It's *your* mind going, not his. Fadia has every right to take walks to speed her time along. What upsets you about that?"

Mother never got her answer. Bolting out the door, Marcus was in the street before she could say another word.

Marcus saw his own breath in the frigid air. He didn't know where to go. There was no way of knowing which way she had gone.

Cursing softly, he realized he'd run outside unarmed. Hearing footsteps, he whirled around and was relieved to see his brothers. Gods, he should have brought his pugio!

"Marcus, what's wrong?" Gaius demanded, panting.

"She shouldn't be out here—not by herself," Marcus answered, frantic.

"Why not?" Lucius sniggered. "She's pretty, but not that fine. Especially now, big as a cow!"

Marcus glared at Lucius but ignored the remark. More dangerous things were afoot.

He ordered, "Gaius, head east toward the path skirting the Palatine. Lucius, go north toward the Forum. I'll look south, nearest the Circus." He was already moving down the road, shouting back at them, "If you find her, bring her home!"

Lucius followed Gaius at first, muttering in irritation. But Gaius rounded on him, "Gods, Lucius—just go your way. He's upset."

"He's always upset," Lucius spat, angrily.

Marcus glanced back only once, relieved to see them finally part ways and do his bidding. Continuously looking about, especially in secluded areas or alleyways, he paused at every intersection or path, willing himself to see her.

By now, morning's first sunbeams had anointed trees and rooftops. Slaves were busy with daily chores outside residences. Two donkey carts hauling building supplies rolled by, trying to leave town before the roads closed to them. The clattering wheels set some dogs to barking. Behind trees to his left, a nurse hushed a crying child while a clean-shaven senator exited the same house. A host of clients followed closely behind, talking amongst themselves.

Marcus kept moving, peeping between the walls of houses. Soon he came within sight of the Hortensius domus, a big, stately old place owning some of the Palatine's finest views. Directly over the Circus, the property included magnificent gardens stretching out to its southeast corner. Beyond that were paths leading through more properties on the hill's east side, dominated by a stand of majestic umbrella pines. Marcus veered off in that direction. It looked like a nice place for a stroll.

And praise Juno—there she was.

Fadia was sitting with her back against one of the big pines, looking off into the distance, beyond the Circus Maximus. Glancing his way, she saw Marcus and smiled. "No wonder highborn people love living up here on the Palatine. It's so beautiful and peaceful."

Marcus panted, "Gods, you've given me a fright. You've no idea how glad I am to see you. In future, kindly let me know if you want to walk. I'll go with you myself. Or at least take Iophon with you next time."

Mildly puzzled at his alarm, she said, "Iophon usually comes. But this morning I woke up early and wanted to go alone. Your mother said walking works."

"Yes? Well, what'll happen if your pains begin out here, away from the domus with nobody to help you?"

"I'm sorry. I didn't mean to worry you. You know, it's strange taking advice from your mother. There was a time when I really hated her. I'll have her mark on my back forever. Now it's as though my anger against her is finally at rest."

"I'm glad you trust her now."

"Trust?" Fadia asked, laughing. "Oh, I didn't say that."

Marcus smiled. Carefully, he eased down beside her. Pulling his cloak off, he tossed it over the two of them, snuggling closer. "Look over there." He pointed in the chill air. "Even the fountains have icicles hanging from them."

"I know. It's lovely, I think."

For a while, they held hands underneath his cloak, just sitting there overlooking the massive Circus Maximus. A waking winter sun showcased oversized postings advertising competing teams: Reds, Greens, Whites, and Blues. Roosters crowed, and they could hear whinnies of horses impatiently awaiting grain. Because the air was so frozen and still, it amplified the voices of priestesses chanting from inside the Temple of Juno Moneta. What a wonder they could hear them all the way from the Capitoline.

Finally, Marcus squeezed Fadia's hand. "Come, we should get back. We can't have our child getting cold."

Fadia looked over at him with soft eyes. Reaching up, she stroked his face. "You are too good to me. I must have done something very fine in my short life to have earned your love."

Taking her hand, Marcus kissed it. "You are my very heart. Now let's go. I'll help you up."

She'd become so ponderous in her pregnancy. He took her by both hands, pulling her up to him. He wrapped his cloak about her tightly, the chill air on his bare arms making him shiver. It didn't matter. They'd be home soon.

There was nothing but the rhythmic sound of their feet on the path as they walked arm in arm. So when Marcus heard the scuttle of someone else's footfalls from behind, he let go of Fadia and whirled around.

In the two heartbeats before it happened, he felt helpless without his pugio. Something heavy and hard crashed into his skull and dropped him to the earth like a sack of barley.

Everything turned into a slow nightmare, just like the dark dreams he'd always had. Only now that he was living one, it seemed unreal. As he fluttered back into consciousness, he heard a woman's guttural cries. It was Fadia.

Oh gods, get up—get up!

These screams weren't high-pitched like a woman in fright. No. They were low, as though in agony.

Forcing his eyes to open, Marcus slowly tried to lift himself. His head throbbed, and he saw shining sparks before his eyes. With one hand, he reached up to discover warm stickiness.

Blood—

Pushing with his legs, he tried getting up again but dropped back, dizzy and nauseous, his head aching. Hearing a thud, he twisted around enough to see the real horror unfolding.

Fadia was lying on the ground. Kneeling above her, a man in a black-and-white cloak was pummeling her with his fists. Then he stood and started kicking her repeatedly. His aim was deliberate and sure—straight at her abdomen. And the bastard was smiling and enjoying himself.

No! Fadia! Our child!

Marcus tried to cry out. He wanted to stop the demon and lure him away. But he was still only half-conscious from his knock on the head. His efforts produced only a desperate grunt.

At least it was enough to turn the attacker around. He stepped away from Fadia, still grinning like a jackal. Yellow teeth parting, a cloud of breath appeared when he spoke. "Marcus Antonius," he pointed his finger down, gesturing at his handiwork, "*this* is your message from Callias."

Finished with his statement, the evil apparition picked up the cudgel he'd used to knock Marcus senseless. Chuckling and taking one more look at Fadia's still form, he appraised his handiwork approvingly, then disappeared through rows of hedges.

It took several tries for Marcus to finally stagger to his feet. He nearly fell twice. Clumsily, he stumbled over to Fadia, dropping to his knees beside her.

She lay on one side, face buried under her thick hair. He gently pulled her over onto her back. She gasped repeatedly, trying to breathe. Tears stained her cheeks, but she couldn't make much sound. Marcus grasped her hand.

There was blood all over her face. Sick son of a bitch wanted to kill her with his hands, not a weapon.

He had to get her back home. If Hercules was really his ancestor, he needed him now.

Praying he wouldn't drop Fadia and compound their situation, he reached beneath her. Planting his legs firmly, he lifted. Somehow, despite a pounding head and blood trickling into his eyes, he managed to keep his balance. Breathlessly taking one uneasy step after another as quickly as possible, he held her close. Fadia shivered, taking sharp, painful-sounding breaths.

Despite her thick garments, something felt wrong under her backside. Oh, Juno—he felt a warm, sticky wetness drenching his bare arm.

Surely, this was all just another nightmare. He'd awaken any moment.

Marcus yelled for Iophon. He kicked the heavy atrium door open, and it banged against the wall with a resounding crash.

Mother rushed into the atrium with Lydia. The poor slave woman spied her daughter and cried out, "Her time—is it now?"

"She's bleeding. *Iophon!*" Marcus shrieked.

Iophon emerged from the back of the house with Syrianus, both slaves chewing breakfast. Iophon saw Fadia's sorry state and bolted toward the front of the domus.

"Fetch a physician," Marcus ordered him. "And don't go unarmed."

Panting, he carried Fadia to his cubiculum before Iophon was even out the door. Gently, he laid her on the sleeping couch. Mother followed with Lydia, who brought a steaming basin of water along with clean linen. She began loosening her daughter's garments.

Mother turned to Marcus, taking his arm and speaking gently but firmly. "You're hurt too. You've a lump the size of a fig on your head." She tore off a piece of linen from what Lydia brought in. "Hold still—" She reached for his bleeding head.

He grabbed her wrist, shaking his head. "Tend to Fadia, not me."

"What happened out there? Were you in a fight?"

"We were attacked—"

"Calm yourself. You're shaking."

Breathing hard, Marcus stared at his hands. She was right. He was quaking like a leaf.

"He beat her...kicked her...and enjoyed it, Mother! I saw him smiling and laughing as though he were playing a game at the baths."

She took one of his shuddering hands, trying to reassure him. "We're going to clean her now," she explained calmly. "If you insist on staying, step aside, for she needs attention from womankind."

Mother and Lydia pulled away Fadia's garments until she was naked. Marcus stepped closer, trying not to get in their way but wanting to be near. He was desperate to help.

Blood kept coming from between her legs. It wasn't the bright red sort, like when one cuts a finger. This blood was dark, evil-looking, the kind drawing death. Never in his life had he seen so much. It didn't gush as from a wound but flowed steadily without stopping.

Fadia began shaking uncontrollably. She clawed the bed sheets, reached blindly for her mother, who dropped what she was doing and grasped her daughter's hand, weeping.

Marcus stepped forward, taking her other hand, his spirits falling as things became even worse. She started convulsing. Her eyes rolled back into her head, and her whole body began to jolt.

Chewing his lip, Marcus helplessly entwined his fingers with hers, whispering endearments of encouragement and trying to steady her juddering. Lydia held her on the other side until it passed.

But the bleeding continued.

When the physician finally arrived, he hastened in without a word, probing Fadia's bloodstained lower abdomen. Bruising was manifesting itself. Red areas on her belly and around her groin were turning into bluish blotches.

The physician's face was sober. Moving to Fadia's head, he placed his fingers on one side of her neck. Withdrawing, he rinsed his hands in the basin. Behind him, Lydia brought over a warm wool blanket, covering her swollen nakedness.

"Are you the husband?" the physician asked Marcus, flicking water off his fingers.

"Yes," Marcus whispered.

"Her injuries are probably very deep inside."

Marcus frowned, glancing at Mother, who stood near the door.

"Look here." The physician turned back to Fadia. He lifted the lower portion of the blanket, shaking his head. "See all the swelling and how her blood runs dark? That color means it comes from deep within. Unless it stops, she'll die. It's a heavy bleed. Who knows what she's like inside? As for the child—if she was beaten as hard as it appears, it's probably dead already." He shook his head, sighing. "I predict no delivery and that it's likely she'll die."

His words staggered Marcus. He turned toward the doorway. This was too much to take in, and he craved air untainted with the coppery smell of his wife's blood.

"Stay with her," Mother ordered the physician. "Do what you can to stop the bleeding. If the child dies, try to save the girl."

Marcus broke out into a cold sweat, full of guilt. In reality, *he* had done this.

Barely making it outside, he sagged against a column, tears filling his eyes. His shoulders quaked with sobs. This was all because of him.

Mother knelt beside him, taking one of his big hands in hers and rubbing it steadily. "Shh, Marcus, my dearest son, listen to me. Her bleeding is heavy. She's lost much blood. You must prepare yourself."

Beyond words, he could only shake his head. An enormous lump in his throat prevented any sound escaping.

"Who did this to her? There's more you're not telling me, isn't there?"

Slowly, he lifted his face, stained with tears. "This is my fault, Mother," he whispered.

"*Your* fault? No, don't go blaming yourself. Rome is a violent place. We both know that."

He shook his head. She didn't understand. "Mother, this happened because of me."

Baffled, she said, "What do you mean?"

She leaned forward in concern, but Marcus put up a rigid hand to stop her. Biting his lip, trying to keep his emotions in check, he shook his head from side to side. It was useless. Another sob choked his explanation.

Mother took his face in both her hands. "Tell me."

"One of my creditor's swine did this to her. Mother, I am— this whole household—is in debt. It's deeper than Hades—it's unfathomable. I've tried paying it back honestly, but—"

"I need to know how much," she whispered.

Marcus shook his head. He never wanted her to know.

She took a surprisingly firm hold on his wrists. "How much?" she repeated, louder this time.

Never would she forgive him, but did it really matter now? His life would be nothing without Fadia.

"Over two hundred," he murmured, almost unintelligibly.

"Two hundred?"

He stared ahead at nothing. "Greek talents."

Dropping his wrists, Mother sank back onto her haunches, stunned, "Two hundred—*Greek talents*?"

He simply nodded, sick at heart.

Mother sat frozen, hardly noticing when he got up, stiffly returning to the cubiculum.

The cold, terrible day slowly advanced into evening.

Resting his head on the same pillow cushioning hers, Marcus felt Fadia tremble. He raised his eyes hopefully.

At the end of the bed, the physician removed more soiled linens, soaked black with blood.

Eyes open but fading, Fadia tilted her head toward Marcus, staring as though she saw straight through him.

Lifting her small, pale hand, he kissed it softly, breathing her name. "Fadia."

"Cold." Her whisper was barely audible.

Marcus swiveled to the side, opening a chest on the floor full of linens and blankets. Pulling one out, he rose and draped it over her. He pressed Fadia's limp left hand between his two, rubbing it, trying to warm her. She felt like ice.

Behind him, the physician spoke, "There's nothing more to be done. Her bleeding continues. I placed clean linen beneath her. Now I'll give you privacy."

Desperately, Marcus looked over his shoulder at the man, who held out helpless hands before leaving the room.

They were alone. Marcus gently pushed her hair back from her forehead.

"Marcus." She opened her eyes again.

"Yes. I'm here."

"What happened? Who did this to us?"

"Oh gods—forgive me, my girl." He brought her hand to his lips to kiss but began crying over it instead. Her fingers gave the tenderest of caresses, brushing his face like goose down as he admitted, "This was because of me—my debt."

"All will be well, my love. I'm not angry with you. Look at your head. You're hurt too." She gave him a ghost of a smile, trying hard to look at him and focus. "Please don't cry. I'm just sorry about the baby."

He shook his head sorrowfully, tears still dripping down his cheeks. Surely, he'd not cried this much in infancy.

"You will love again someday," she promised.

"Not without you."

She gave a slight nod. "Someday—not soon. Someday."

"Don't talk this way. You mustn't."

"Shh, I must. Be strong for me."

He stared at her, shaking his head. "I'll die without you, Fadia."

She placed her finger over his lips. "You must not. Live, Marcus. Live life and promise not to harm yourself. You are a good man, and I have loved you so." She smiled weakly.

"My only happiness is you. Don't go, please. I can't—"

Only the subtlest tremor signaled death. The fingers that had just touched his lips went limp. Fadia's once lively blue eyes became still and dull. A tiny sigh escaped her parted lips. She didn't move again.

Marcus kept rubbing her hand. He lay his head on her pillow, fresh tears anointing her face. Unmoving, he stayed there until he felt her warmth fade.

His heart felt like stone.

Dazed, he lifted his head, studying her still form. He gently closed her staring eyes with the lightest brush of his fingertips. Rising stiffly, he pulled the woolen blanket solemnly over her face. Stricken, he looked down at her, blinking in disbelief.

This morning, he'd awakened anticipating that he'd be a father before the week was out. Now he would never see their baby. Gods, he'd never see Fadia again.

As Marcus shifted on his feet, his foot brushed something beneath the sleeping couch. Absently looking down, he saw the corner of a dusty wax tablet. Recognizing it, he picked it up, finding inside the love letter he'd scribed back when Fadia was illiterate.

Swallowing painfully, he bit his lip against memory and grief. As more irrepressible tears burned, he placed the tablet under the coverlet into her bruised hands.

Indeed, Callias had succeeded in ripping out his heart.

Marcus strode purposefully toward the wall where his gladius hung from a peg. Enraged and shaking, he cried out furiously, his fist smacking against the plaster.

After a time, he breathed more steadily, focusing on what had to come next. Wiping his face, he reached up, fingers pausing on the leather belt of the sword Lentulus had given him. Much heavier than his pugio, he lifted it from the peg, fitting the scabbard strap over his left shoulder. Its weight hung heavily at his right. He looked back at the still, small body on the couch, briefly returning to Fadia's side.

Placing one hand on her shrouded head, he closed his eyes reverently, granting himself one final touch. Then, without a word to anyone, he departed.

CHAPTER XX

ALL WAS DARK. IT WAS WELL AFTER THE SIXTH HOUR THAT night, when nobody stirred except whores, thieves, and men with scores to settle.

Marcus waited, leaning against the walls of a sandal-maker's shop. He'd been waiting for hours. More blood would flow tonight. But this time it would be the blood of someone who deserved to die.

He straightened, hearing voices. His heart began to race.

Four men exited the domus Callias on the Esquiline, one of the finest in the district. Marcus observed their path down the hill, then silently stole out of the shadows, keeping a careful distance. He paused, letting them pass under torchlight near an upper-class tavern.

Damn. Callias wasn't with them. He was hoping he would be. But Callias seldom went out at night. He had too many enemies.

Still, one man stood out. Forever etched on Marcus's memory, he was the largest of the four and wore a curiously patterned black-and-white cloak.

Fingering the hilt of his gladius, Marcus moved in closer, drawing his hood lower over his face. He stumbled on a raised stone in the pavement. It caught his sandal, making an unexpected slapping sound.

Quickly, he flattened himself into a tight space between buildings, holding his breath.

One of the men looked back. Fortunately, he must have seen nothing, for he turned back to his friends, sharing a joke, accompanied by raucous laughter.

Near the bottom of the Esquiline, they veered off toward the Subura. Marcus breathed some relief as they led him past Clodius and Curio's old brothel. At least he knew the area. He glanced at the wavy glass rondel on the door, but there were no signs of lamplight. All was dark.

Just beyond, the street widened amid shops surrounding a well.

Marcus chewed his lip. This added space allowed more room to maneuver with four assailants. Plus it made sense to fight in familiar surroundings.

Long ago, old "Bastard" Lupus had given him instruction on how to take on more than two men at a time, but only in theory. Several years later, under Vindelicus's tutelage, the Gaul had challenged Castor, Gaius, and Lucius to "attack" Marcus all at once, staging a mock brawl. It was hardly realistic. Castor had no clue how to handle a blade, and his brothers thought the whole business a laughter-filled game.

Tonight he was taking on four men at once, and he didn't care what happened as long as he killed the one with the black-and-white cloak.

Silently as possible, Marcus drew his virgin gladius. With his back against a shop wall, he cried out, "Salvete!" All four men turned at once. Marcus pointed his gladius at the man with the distinctive cloak. "You're dead."

Cloaked Man smiled like a cur with bared teeth, stepping forward readily. His lip curled into a sneer. "Is this your suicide, Antonius? Taking us on will get you killed."

It wasn't worth responding. Marcus simply positioned his gladius in hand and held his ground. There was no sense in conversation. He was here for one thing only.

Cloaked Man's speed in smoothly drawing his pugio was impressive, and the other three weren't far behind.

Marcus waited, heart pounding. Cloaked Man lunged at him, and their blades scraped. As expected, the others all joined in. Unmoving, Marcus focused on keeping his back against the wine shop's entrance. He needed to have all of them in full view in front of him.

Old Bastard Lupus had warned him never to allow an enemy in from behind. If they were all visible, he might be able to last.

One of them, with a scar down his nose, darted too near.

Marcus punched his gladius forth like lightning, taking him down with a howl.

Now there were three.

Patiently staying his ground, he forced them into the offensive.

Cloaked Man suggested to one of his men, "Go round his other side. He can't keep this up forever—can you, Antonius?"

Marcus ignored him, eyes constantly darting from one man to another.

"Did she bleed hard? Did she die?" Cloaked Man barked like a dog.

Marcus ground his teeth. The mockery enraged him, but he channeled his hatred into the fight. One man skirted to his left, his stance unbalanced. Still, he attacked swiftly, trying to get in close with his pugio. Instinctively stabbing, Marcus took him square in the chest, but in doing so, he opened his right side to the other two.

Cloaked Man took full advantage. Marcus gasped in pain, taking a slice in his shoulder. Turning to fend off the blow, he felt a swooshing rush of air as the second assailant's blade narrowly missed his neck.

Shoulder throbbing, he blinked in shock, his heart beating erratically. Blood crept down his back like warm fingers. Marcus backed away toward the wall, retreating just enough to gather his wits.

Only two more. Both had their legs spread in a firm stance. These men were clearly capable of withstanding a good fight.

Rome was a city that never slept, and hearing the scuffle, a crowd of curious plebs had gathered. They stood well out of harm's way, some holding oil lamps, others torches. It actually made fighting easier, their light illuminating the blackness.

"Together, from both sides," Cloaked Man instructed his partner. The other man, with dark, reddish hair, nodded.

Marcus thought he was probably Gallic.

With little pause, they rushed him simultaneously. Intuitively using his right leg, Marcus tripped the Gaul, jabbing his weapon downward into his flesh. Then, turning clumsily, he maneuvered into the open square, now facing Cloaked Man alone. Red Hair's shrieks were reassuring. At least he was down and out of the fight.

Now Fadia's murderer was against the wall.

Plebs were noisily pitching bets, wagering who'd win, and shouting encouragement to both men. Things turned ugly when several bystanders thought it might be fun to hurl rocks and garbage at them.

Something hard smacked Marcus's back, making it sting. Cloaked Man took a few hits himself. When an onion pelted the side of his face, the impact was Marcus's opportunity. His opponent's attention strayed as he blinked and shook his head.

Charging forward ruthlessly, Marcus's thrust was so powerful it pinned Cloaked Man against the wall of the wine shop. His plunging gladius skewered Fadia's killer, his only response a sagging jaw, shaking limbs, and bloody bubbles gurgling from his mouth.

Meanwhile in the crowd, some pleb was displeased with the outcome. When Marcus turned, wearily facing the assembly of gawking faces, a well-aimed stone struck him square on the bridge of his nose, smashing the cartilage. It knocked him senseless, and for the second time that day, he dropped heavily to the ground, unconscious.

Somewhere, in the brink of wakefulness, Marcus floated, not knowing how long he lay in the street. Blood ran into his eyes, and his shoulder was paralyzed in pain.

The first thing he recalled was women's voices. One sounded vaguely familiar.

"Is he dead?"

"No. He lives," answered Familiar One.

"Who is he?"

"An old friend."

"You *know* him?"

"Shut up and help me."

Footsteps and movement, a shuffling near his head, then hands were tugging on his arms. Someone was dragging him. He groaned at the strain on his wounded shoulder. They didn't seem to notice, or else they didn't care.

After a while, he became vaguely aware of his head knocking against something rough and hard. Grinding wheels were rumbling, jostling him. Each jolt added to the agony.

Marcus had no memory after that until he awakened to pounding. The sudden noise stirred him back to semi-consciousness. He tried opening his eyes, but now he was blind. Drying blood had glued his eyelids shut.

"Who's there? Who's that? A prostitute? We don't want your kind here, woman. Go back to the Subura."

That was Syrianus.

"Is this the domus Antonii, yes or no?"

"It is. What do want with us?"

"Look for yourself. I brought your dominus home—Marcus Antonius."

Marcus heard the viewing portal slam shut. Excited voices sounded from inside, along with running feet. Then the main door opened.

"Who are you?"

That was Gaius.

"Name's Metinara," was the answer. "Your brother's in the cart."

Someone treaded cautiously, circling where Marcus lay. Then suddenly they hopped onto the cart, causing his head to jar painfully against the baseboard. A low moan escaped his lips.

"He's injured!" Gaius exclaimed. "All bloody—help me get him inside."

Gentler, familiar hands held him now. Marcus felt himself lifted by his brothers and Castor. It took all three of them to haul him into the house.

Metinara followed, and as they lay him against the impluvium to wash his face, he heard her speaking to Mother.

"What happened?" Mother screamed.

"Got roughed up in a fight," Metinara said. "Took four of them down, he did, and would still be standing too if some ass in the crowd hadn't slung a stone in his face. Saw the whole thing from my window."

"Lydia, go fetch something for her—a piece I never wear. Gaius, finish washing him and bring him to my chamber. He'll sleep in my bed."

Her terse order cleared Marcus's sore head, returning him to wretched reality, making him regret being alive. Fresh tears mingled with the blood caked around his eyes.

There was a reason he had to rest in Mother's bed. Fadia lay dead on his sleeping couch.

Days of mourning and funerary rituals blurred together.

Marcus remained in a numb state since Fadia's death. He'd only been able to grieve formally for the past several days, as his own recovery was slow in coming. He had no desire to live.

Mother stubbornly force-fed him, his emotions plummeting

to new lows that were hellish and consuming. Then came a raging fever from the wound in his arm.

It took him weeks to recover.

Now sound enough to walk about, he made another daily venture down the Via Appia. These visits were solemn observances that Mother and his brothers didn't dare dissuade. Not far from the Antonii tomb, evening had descended in a silent pall. A pair of ravens flew overhead, calling out coarsely.

Marcus felt as cold and hard as Fadia's little tufa stele, on which he placed his hands.

Gaius had purchased the slab, hiring a stonecutter to chisel an image of a young woman sewing cloth. Marcus had wept in grief and gratitude when his brother first brought him to the place and presented it to him. Inside, they'd placed Fadia's little clay urn, a few small holes in the top allowing ritual libations.

Closing his eyes, Marcus drew his cloak over his head in reverence. If he could turn back time, it wouldn't be rough stone in his hands, but instead the smooth curve of her face.

"We were robbed of knowing if our child was a son or daughter," he whispered. "You would have loved being a mother. I know it in my heart." Letting his forehead drop against the little monument, his fingers deftly traced the inscription with memorized precision. Marcus had composed the short epitaph himself:

Dis Manibus
Antonia Fadia was a fine woman.
Seeing beyond a bolt of frayed cloth
She believed a worthy garment could be made of it.
Fadia died loved and free.

As he'd been in habit of doing these past days since her spirit fled, Marcus murmured the words repeatedly, lips pressed to the cold stone. Finally, he pulled out a small flask of wine from a satchel. Unstopping it, he poured some through the top of the stele.

Hearing voices, he sighed. He'd come back tomorrow. Other

mourners visiting tombs of their departed were heading home. He turned to follow them but received a surprise as he stepped onto the road.

Standing under some trees, awaiting him, was Gaius Julius Caesar. Adorned in his crimson-bordered toga, his lictors surrounded him, bearing their fasces. People passing along the road all stared, giving Caesar's party a wide berth.

"Antonius?"

It occurred to Marcus that Caesar barely recognized him. He had ceased shaving to mourn, and his nose and face were still swollen. No longer caring about his appearance, he refused Iophon's efforts to groom him.

"Cousin." His response was barely a whisper.

"Jupiter! It's almost dark, yet you risk another incident with that damned creditor by coming out here alone?" Caesar was incredulous, shaking his head. "Come with me. My lictors will offer us protection."

Having no choice, he joined Caesar's entourage.

"Mother sent you?" Marcus assumed as they began walking toward the city walls.

"She didn't 'send' me. I asked her where I could find you," Caesar replied, shaking his head. "Two hundred talents... Granted, I've been in deep debt myself before, but that's excessive."

Passing a little tavern along the road, Caesar halted the lictors, ushering Marcus to a table and calling for wine in an authoritative voice.

For a time, they sat in silence. Caesar ended the calm after Marcus drank his third cup. "Your best course of action is leaving. Let Callias, or whatever his name is, lose his target. He'll be forced to focus on new ones. To avoid causing your mother any more trouble or shame, and to prevent you from racking up more astronomical sums of gold, here is what *I've* decided to do about you."

Marcus looked up, staring at him blankly. He half hoped Caesar would offer to take him to Gaul. But then, why would he? Look how Marcus Antonius had ended.

"You'll journey to Greece to study rhetoric and military tactics,"

Caesar announced. "I'll fund your journey. However, you'll need to arrange your studies with the stipend I provide. You'll be on your own, eat modest meals, and live independently. During this time, you're to make something of yourself other than a nuisance."

"My family might still be in danger," Marcus argued. "I won't leave them knowing their lives could be at risk, as was Fadia's."

"True," Caesar acknowledged. "So I'll also see to the protection of your mother and brothers. Leave that to me. Consider it done."

"I'm going to kill Callias. I will—"

"You'll do no such thing, for you'll be in Greece. And besides, you owe him a fortune."

"Take me with you to Gaul," Marcus pleaded.

Caesar shook his head. "You've yet to find yourself. And until you do, you're of no use to me. Go study rhetoric and military tactics. Throw yourself into worthwhile learning. Otherwise, your life will be dismally short."

Marcus set his cup down heavily. He stared at the splintered wood of the table. "Did Mother put you up to this? Did she plead with you to help me?"

Caesar lifted his head imperiously. "Of course she spoke with me. Does that surprise you? However, she could never coerce me into anything I wouldn't do willingly. We're family, and I do have a fondness for blood ties. But I warn you, I'll humor you only this once."

"Humor me?" Marcus snorted in disgust.

Caesar studied him for a moment. "What a sad, sorry sight you are. You know, I've no son—a fact haunting me more and more often these days. Years ago in Baiae, I saw something in you, watching you fight. It made me wish *you* were my son. I saw courage worthy of a Roman."

Lost in his depression and incapable of responding, Marcus sat morosely, listening to Caesar's lecture continue.

"My generosity today is a final attempt in encouraging you to bring some sort of honor and dignitas back to yourself and your family. For if you waste yourself in Athens and overspend the stipend I give, expect nothing more. I'll turn from you and never look back."

Caesar stood up, signaling it was time to go. "I'll sacrifice to Neptunus on your behalf tomorrow. It'll be a long time before we see one another again. You'll be off to Greece, and I'll be leaving for Gallia Comata soon. Come. Let me see you home."

Marcus reluctantly stood up, and together they walked back through Rome to the Palatine. Neither spoke.

Torchlight illuminated the city, and plebs huddled around cooking fires. A lot of heads turned upon hearing the lictors tramping. Caesar nodded at the people courteously, sometimes lifting his hand in greeting. They loved that; many called to him. He was becoming their champion.

At last, they arrived at the domus Antonii.

Caesar turned to Marcus, placing a stern hand on his shoulder. "Be well, Antonius. Don't be foolish. Recover from your losses and pray we meet again when you're more certain of yourself and your future."

CHAPTER XXI
58-57 BC

ATHENS WAS FULL OF STRANGERS AND FAR FROM ROME.

Mother had begged Marcus to take Iophon along, but he had refused. He wanted no companionship, for one already journeyed with him. Albeit a dark one. Grief was his name, and he stalked Marcus everywhere.

For once, he did follow advice—that of Caesar. After walking the six miles or so from Piraeus's port, his first destination was the Agora. Athens's lively and crowded marketplace was bustling with eastern traders and merchants. Towering temples to Ares and Hephaestus remained centerpieces in the lifeblood of Pericles's famed city. More of a foreign feel pervaded than in the Forum back home—diverse languages and people wearing different types of dress.

Marcus's goal was to first find a scholar and then some lodging. After inquiring at several market stalls, and realizing how deficient he was in Greek, a cloth merchant gestured toward the imposing Stoa of Attalos. "Inside the colonnades are scholars for hire. You can't miss them."

Marcus walked along the shaded colonnade. Indeed, there were plenty, and he didn't know how to begin. How did one find someone trustworthy from whom to learn? Mother had always been his teacher.

One young philosopher-type approached him, speaking in rapid Greek. It was hard understanding his words, but obviously he was trying to sell his expertise and knowledge. Marcus tried his own halting Greek, asking the fellow to repeat himself, but the young academic scoffed in disgust and walked away.

Marcus stared after him, incensed.

"You need a teacher who speaks Latin, don't you?" a deep voice commented behind him.

Marcus turned. He beheld a balding old man with a hunched back who carried a staff for balance. He had bright, twinkling eyes, and his Latin was perfect.

"Ah, finally I can understand someone," Marcus exclaimed in relief.

"But if I taught you, it would be in Greek," the old wise man warned. "You must learn Greek, Roman. It is still the world's language, no matter the countries your people have conquered."

Humbled, Marcus set his vexation aside. "I speak a little, but I didn't know how little until now. Do you teach rhetoric too?"

The scholar nodded. "And military history and tactics, for by the looks of you, you'd be needing that as well."

Old, but perceptive. "I haven't a fortune. Only a modest stipend. I must use it carefully."

"We can decide on a fee later. I am Rhesus of Athens. And you are?"

"Marcus Antonius, grandson to Antonius Orator."

Rhesus raised his brows. "Orator? Now there was a great man of courage. He should not have died at the hands of Marius. Have you a place to stay, Marcus Antonius?"

"Not yet. Do you have somewhere in mind?"

"I own a small property on the outskirts of town that I sometimes rent to students. It happens to be available. If you hire me as your tutor, I'll offer it reasonably."

So the day ended in good fortune. Rhesus of Athens was a kind, honest man. By nightfall, Marcus had rented his tiny, one-room dwelling near the remains of the destroyed Long Walls encircling the city. There was no furniture inside for such a fair price, so Marcus had to get creative, using his traveling trunk as a desk whenever he needed one. In the corner, he folded his bedroll, spreading it over a pallet at night. The place really wasn't bad. It had new roof tiles and a small window. For his needs, it was adequate.

The following week, studies began. Rhesus's sessions typically ended by early afternoon, and afterward Marcus went straight to the nearby gymnasium Rhesus had recommended. Typical workout regimens in Rome focused on military skills. But here in Greece, fitness itself was an art form. Running, swimming, even long-jumping became part of his routine.

It was at the gymnasium that Marcus made his first friend in Greece. He became acquainted with one of the trainers, Eumenius, who was a competent, respectful young man, critically appraising clients' skills in a candid, unassuming way.

They were well-paired in exercise. Marcus was always superior at swordplay, while the lithe, agile Greek outran him and usually bested him at distance swimming. An impressive athlete, to be sure, Eumenius's greatest gift was equestrian arts. He worked with a local horse trader, and the animals seemed drawn to him as if by magic.

Eumenius was likeable because he never pried. He never asked about Marcus's life in Rome and accepted him at face value.

Nearly a dozen young men and youths studied under Rhesus of Athens. Some were Romans, others wealthy Athenians, Macedonians, and Ephesians. Marcus was his eldest pupil, and he sometimes felt like the odd fish in the pond. However, the old Greek was a sensitive man who read him well. Possessing a keen gift for discerning individual temperaments and personalities, Rhesus fostered a relaxed relationship with him.

For his first two weeks of study, he paired Marcus with another Roman student, Decimus Sentius, to study military history. Specifically, they studied Alexander the Great's progress into India. Rhesus wanted specifics: How many transport carts did Alexander need? What sort of pack animals would be best over the terrain leading to India? What sort of peoples would he meet along the way, and would they welcome him or be hostile?

Marcus surprised himself. This part of education was useful and helpful. New hope began to dawn in his spirit that perhaps someday he'd make decisions similar to those Alexander had.

A month into his studies, Rhesus plopped down on a small folding chair beneath an olive tree outside the Temple of Ares. There wasn't a better spot in the world to discuss warfare. Marcus's favorite lessons were on military tactics. During each session Rhesus posed a situation to him, as though he were leading a battle. It was a brilliant mental exercise.

"All right, Antonius. You're on flat, hard ground. No trees, good visibility. You've got five thousand infantry and two hundred cavalry. Your enemy has double the infantry, but no cavalry. How do you win?"

"What season am I in?"

Rhesus snorted. "Let's say late spring—just like today's weather."

Marcus paused, then answered, "If I don't have any reinforcements in sight, I make certain my men get reprieves while fighting. Among us Romans, our layered formations afford that with the right training. I'd make damned sure my men had it. Next, I'd probably wear the enemy down and use my cavalry to hit one of their flanks once they've weakened."

"You could," Rhesus agreed. "But two hundred cavalry isn't many against those numbers, despite being on horseback. And remember, you never want to send horse in too deep. It's a death-trap if an enemy outflanks them due to distance or sheer numbers."

Marcus considered a response. "Then I could keep my cavalry in reserve, especially if I have enough infantry to relieve my men on the front periodically."

"More than reasonable. In warfare, relief and rest can be weapons as worthy as gladii. Remember that."

At the end of the session that day, several of the students drew Marcus aside. Young Sentius spoke for them all. "We're going to a local tavern. They have cheap wine. Want to join us?"

Marcus smiled. Wine never hurt anything. Now that he'd formed a routine in his daily lessons and exercise, it might be good to join some others for some harmless drinking.

And drink they did. It had been years since Marcus binged on this much wine. As the sun set, so did his inhibitions. His head was spinning when several young prostitutes joined in the men's fun. Before he could think, he had one of the girls inside a small cubiculum, instincts taking over. It had been ages since he'd had sex. The physician and midwife had discouraged it in the final months of Fadia's pregnancy, and sex had been the last thing on his mind since her death.

As always, he found welcome physical release. But afterward, he felt disconsolate and empty. His chosen whore was probably Fadia's age, but that was all they had in common. She had been enthusiastic, but there had been no emotional bond between them, and that outweighed the pleasure. Here was just a willing girl, and it was only a quick act of lust.

What he'd had with Fadia was something of inestimable worth, something more treasured than gold or glory. One simply couldn't place a price on true love.

Julia Antonia in Rome to her son Marcus Antonius in Athens:

May Fortuna smile upon you. I sacrifice daily for your health and well-being.

First, I have news of our Cousin Caesar. Word is he defeated fierce barbarians called the Helvetii. Some senators are accusing him of provoking the Gauls into war. Personally, I disagree. Gallic peoples invaded Roman territory once already. Though it was long ago, what's wrong with preventative measures? Considering our past, we Romans have every right to strike first, protecting our own lands.

Now to happier subjects. Tribune Publius Clodius called on me this morning, prompting me to write this letter. He has successfully passed legislation sending into exile anyone guilty of putting another citizen to death without trial. He worked the Forum crowds into such frenzy against Cicero over Lentulus's execution that plebs razed the man's house. Marcus, he wanted me to write straightaway, informing you that Cicero is on his way to exile in Macedonia.

Your brothers send their best. Study hard, my son. Never waste knowledge.

An unexpected mid-summer thunderstorm drenched the Agora with a rumbling downpour. It didn't often rain in summer, so nobody was prepared, people dodging one another for cover.

Marcus ducked beneath the awning of a food-stand he often frequented. With sessions over for the day, he thought he'd go ahead and eat something now since the rain was too heavy for much else. Perhaps later things would dry out ...

In line to purchase stewed meat and vegetables, he idly watched people scurrying through the deluge. Suddenly, a man in front of him bumped into him as he turned around.

Marcus was ready with a sharp word until he looked up and froze in disbelief.

Uncle Hybrida?

Uncle was just as unprepared to see Marcus, and they both stared at each other before breaking out into joyful laughter and embracing.

Marcus hugged him like a bear. What a welcome sight. Seeing

a familiar face in Athens's most chaotic and crowded space was unbelievable. It was simply overwhelming to be consorting with family again.

"What are you doing here?" Marcus exclaimed. "I can't believe it's you!"

"I'm on my way home," Uncle replied.

"From Macedonia? Already?"

"Yes, bit of a story there," he hedged.

"How long are you in Athens?"

"I was going to find a boat in a few days."

"Well, you'll stay with me for a week at least, won't you?"

Uncle Hybrida smiled, but it was a sad, defeated smile. "Of course, Nephew. Gods, it's good to see you."

Marcus studied Uncle Hybrida. He had aged greatly. A large bald spot now crowned his head, previously covered with wavy, dark hair, much like his own. Most alarming was how he walked— like an old man. And his face bore more wrinkles than before. The years weren't being kind to Uncle.

"And what are you doing in Athens?" he asked Marcus.

Marcus turned toward the food counter, ordering his usual steamed vegetables and mutton. "Studying. I've been here for almost five months now." He plopped down some coin for the vendor, snatching up the warm, wrapped meal.

"Good for you," Uncle Hybrida murmured approvingly.

Sunlight was beginning to break through the remaining storm clouds. "It's a bit of a walk to my little domus," Marcus commented, noticing how stiffly his uncle moved. "We can eat as we go."

"Bear me out and I'll make it. My arthritis pains me a lot these days."

Along the way, Marcus purchased a large cask of wine to celebrate his unexpected visitor. Later that evening, sitting atop his pallet, he waited for Uncle Hybrida to finish reading Mother's letter.

Uncle held it up to the lamplight. Marcus saw the older man's eyes moisten with tears. Hastily, he brushed them away. It was probably guilt again—over Lentulus and the Catilina conspiracy.

Uncle Hybrida believed he should have died too. In the back of his mind, Marcus wondered why he hadn't turned himself in. Or died by the sword. Was it cowardice? Perhaps he was more like Father than anyone in the family cared to admit. That thought led Marcus to reach over and refill his cup. Remaining respectfully silent, he stroked his beard, which had grown thick while mourning Fadia. Lazily, he stretched his legs out onto the pallet.

"I so miss your stepfather," Hybrida said suddenly, his voice husky with emotion.

Marcus nodded. "Lentulus was a good-natured man. Just misguided. All of them were."

"I used to think you sympathized with Catilina," Hybrida remarked, setting the scroll aside.

Marcus poured more lightly watered wine into his cup. "I agree the Republic is dead. It was Catilina's methods I disliked. All Rome now knows his plan was to extinguish our entire social class, rebuilding it from scratch. Had he succeeded, just who would've lived or died? In what way would restructuring have taken place? My gut tells me there would simply have been a new aristocracy, and Catilina would have led it. It would've been no different than things are now. Just a different set of players."

"Ah, well." Uncle became strangely quiet.

"I was young then but could never have espoused such hypocrisy." Marcus paused, expecting some response. But Hybrida sat in morose contemplation. "Why such a long face, Uncle?" Marcus finally asked. "I thought Mother's letter was great news. Old Cicero the Chickpea forced into exile, Caesar pushing northward—"

Hybrida's finger wagged. "Now that should set the Senate into debate."

"And I don't get it. Because he prevents war from happening before it does? Mother's right. Think about our history. Gauls have threatened us more than once. It's high time they were dealt with—subdued, conquered, call it what you will." He took another long draw on his cup. Wine kept him numb, placating his companion—

grief. He had started drinking heavily again whenever he wasn't studying or at the gymnasium.

Hybrida arose from the only chair in the cramped room, shuffling to the window. It was the domus's only source of ventilation. Leaning into the moonlight, his thinning hair moved in a quivering breeze.

"Earlier today you asked what I was doing here." Hybrida's words came hesitantly.

Glancing up from his cup, Marcus stared at his uncle's back; the brown fabric of his tunic was darkened with sweat.

"I lost Macedonia," he confessed sadly. "The Senate has recalled me."

At that, Marcus took an extra-long draw from his cup. Failure seemed synonymous with the name "Antonius." He sighed heavily.

"I'll be charged with 'illegal acquisition of money abroad.'"

"Are you guilty?" Marcus asked directly.

Hybrida snorted. "No less guilty than any other man sitting in the Curia. We're all *guilty*, Marcus," he emphasized. "Some of us cheat, swindle, and steal our way into power to bring 'honor' to our names. Others, like that cousin of yours, slaughter their way through hapless nations to establish imperium."

Hybrida spoke again, slowly lowering himself back into the chair. His topic was completely different. "I believe it's the gods' will that we found one another, Marcus," he began. "There is a matter of which I wish to speak—one of great importance to me."

Marcus cocked an eyebrow curiously.

"As you know, I've only one daughter, my Antonia. You may remember she married years ago, but Geta died of food poisoning shortly before Cicero's consulship. Due to my own ineptitude and failures as a father, she hasn't remarried. So my line has no heir. I want you to consider marrying her when you return home. She's still young enough to bear sons and is timid as a mouse. She'd obey you in anything. I know you're still saddened over your own loss, but we must all live out the days the gods grant us."

Marcus sat tongue-tied, both with wine and the burden Hybrida had just laid before him. Still heavy with grief, it was hard even imagining another marriage right now. That, and the fact that he hardly knew Antonia. However, knowing someone well was certainly no requirement for betrothal. Thinking back, he could barely recall what she looked like other than remembering deep auburn hair. She'd been attractive, but that was all he remembered.

But who was he to criticize anyone's appearance? His own nose had been shattered the night Fadia died. It hooked downward now, giving his profile an odd, flat sort of look depending on the angle.

He had to reply appropriately, so he managed, "I've no promising future, and I'm in deep debt to a violent man in Rome. That's the real reason I'm in Athens. I fear I'd only disappoint you. I have absolutely nothing to offer Antonia." What more could he say? He couldn't possibly love her. Love was dead.

"Just consider it, please. I want to see her safely married again. She's been lonely without me these years, yet so dutiful about keeping up my household." Hybrida rubbed his eyes wearily.

Marcus reached to pinch out the nearest lamp, the two men settling in for the night.

"If you turn her down," Hybrida explained, "I must turn to your brothers. I doubt I'll find anyone else since I'm disgraced now. No man of consequence will have her while I face trial. I can't allow my own misfortune to affect her life. As family, we must consider one another's honor and uphold it."

In the darkness, nephew and uncle rested side by side. It being such a hot night, it was difficult finding sleep. Marcus lay awake, quietly tolerating his uncle's noisy snoring.

How long would he have to stay in Athens until it was safe to return home? He had no desire to wed Antonia, but if he didn't do it, then Gaius or Lucius would be asked. Everyone would once more look down on him for refusing his poor cousin. Hybrida had approached him first, for he was the oldest. Gods, he'd look blacker than Pluto's ass for refusing. Caesar's expectations were for him to make wiser choices and make something of himself. Marcus lay awake a long time that night, pondering what to do.

The searing summer night was still except for Hybrida's strident exhales and the scraping sounds of a rat, gnawing somewhere inside the walls.

Marcus Antonius in Athens to his Mother, Julia Antonia, in Rome:

Salve. I read your last letter with pleasure, learning of Clodius's success against Cicero. I'm also pleased to keep abreast of Caesar's exploits in Gallia Comata.

Uncle Hybrida spent several weeks with me. He graciously paid half of my rent. His ship left Piraeus harbor yesterday, sailing for Rome. He's riddled with misfortune, for the Senate recalled him. He'll stand trial upon returning.

Uncle Hybrida spoke to me about Antonia. He wants me to consider marrying her. I have no feelings for her and would prefer to refuse, but due to family obligation, I feel I must accept. I don't know if you'll welcome this news or be angry with me. However, before he left, I gave my word to marry her when I return to Rome.

I trust Caesar has kept his word and that you, Gaius, and Lucius are safe. May Fortuna shine her face upon our domus. As always, if you are well, then I am well.

Marcus never minded his time with Rhesus of Athens.

The old Greek sometimes told stories of Sulla's ruthless attack, when Rhesus was a budding philosopher. "Sulla himself invited me to dine," Rhesus would boast, "asking for my declamation on 'Dionysian promises of eternity.'"

Tall and wiry, Rhesus would have been even taller if it weren't for his hunchback. Marcus never heard him complain, but undoubtedly it caused him misery. He sauntered about, always leaning on his long staff to keep his balance and ease his way.

Any student of his would agree that he was a conscientious man who often worked with learners one-on-one. And Marcus got his share of private lessons—especially at rhetoric.

Today he and Rhesus were borrowing the magnificent space of Athens's Theater of Dionysus. Rhesus had a few friends in the Athenian ecclesia who allowed him to use it occasionally. What better place than this to refine one's oratory skills?

"You don't appear to fear public speaking, Antonius," Rhesus observed as Marcus removed his cloak and strode to the front of the orchestra. "Have you done it before?"

"Just once."

"When?"

"At my stepfather's funeral."

Rhesus put his hand over his heart. "Ah. Your mourning is mine."

"My mourning has ended. His death was some years ago."

"In your youth?"

Marcus puffed his cheeks out, sighing and thinking back. "I was nineteen."

"Well, let's hear your discourse," Rhesus said. "Remember, there are always words jumbling about in your head. When speaking publicly, you must arrange them wisely and artfully."

He hobbled away, his staff clicking resonantly on the pavement, striking a regular rhythm as he instructed. "No argument possesses power if you present it too quickly, without necessary 'swordplay.' Be like a gladiator with your words, not a soldier. Never go for the kill too early. Tease the listeners and draw them in. Now let me hear you."

Drawing himself up, Marcus inhaled. Mother had once said Grandfather Orator believed that whenever a man spoke publicly, words should pour from his heart, not his head. Fine. *Grandfather, place your words in my mouth ...*

Marcus stood in the sun, framed by the scaenae frons, a backdrop added by some wealthy Roman benefactor. Unrolling a scroll, he began: "Hear me, Conscript Fathers. Plebs are hungry and idle in the streets, for they have no labor. Where is their work? Slaves, in and outside of Rome, do it all. We Romans used to be proud farmers, owners of land worked by *our* hands, farmed by *our* skills, and planted to produce *our* crops. Now we turn to latifundia, farms owned by wealthy men in this very Senate. Men who have never even touched a plow, never trod in the mud, or even plucked a pear from a tree."

Marcus pointed a finger toward empty seats, his imaginary audience.

"*Your* latifundia, operated by slaves, gains you immense riches, yet is done so guardedly, preventing your humiliation. Until we offer common people a sustainable workload again, plebs will continue loitering in the streets, stealing from us, and becoming criminals. They starve now and will go on starving."

Marcus swelled with pride. Rhesus was smiling and nodding. Perhaps Grandfather Orator's spirit really was here.

"My plea, Senators, is to give ear, not only to plebs, but to tribunes. Their concerned, grieved voices go unheeded by your greed. Stop pressing forward with your own agendas. Lend an ear to what they advise. Rome may conquer and continue to swell, her borders broadening with additional lands. However, her capital will remain mired in graffiti and filthy conditions until you listen to the representatives your people choose. Let me close by asking you: When will citizens once more have reason to believe in the governing body created to lead them? When will you treat plebs like your own—the beloved Romans they are?"

As he finished, Rhesus pounded his staff on the marble stair nearest him, nodding in appreciation. "And that, my dear Antonius, is how passion will win others to your cause. Learn to use it. It can be as powerful as a gladius."

Marcus pondered Rhesus's last statement. Words as cutting and powerful as a blade? He'd need more convincing there.

Despite all he was learning, Marcus still benefited most from afternoons with Eumenius at the gymnasium.

The young Greek had been training a big-boned bay for the horse trader with whom he worked. It was a much larger, muscled horse than Marcus had ever seen. Eumenius rode over and dismounted, offering his friend a chance to try the animal for himself.

Swinging up, Marcus commented, "Most of my countrymen don't enjoy riding. I've never understood that."

"Your legions place trust in men," Eumenius pointed out, "not their horses. If Alexander had no strong, swift horses at Gaugamela, he would never have become 'the Great.'"

Marcus nodded in agreement. "Well, I'm different from other Romans. I happen to love riding." Spurring the bay into a jog, he kept his legs beneath him, dispersing his weight solidly in a vertical line.

"Ride like you walk, legs well under you." He could still hear Lupus's grating voice shouting in his memory. He had despised the man, yet the Bastard had taught him well.

"Try his canter," Eumenius called.

Marcus urged the horse forward into the smoothest of all gaits. Like floating on a cloud, the beauty of riding a fine horse brought back memories of the last time he'd ridden like this.

Fadia was behind him, soft arms holding him firmly around the middle. Recalling her clinging to him, her breath on his neck, Marcus pulled up short. Sick at heart, he trotted the bay back to Eumenius after just one lap around the field.

Perplexed, Eumenius asked, "Does he not please you?"

Marcus struggled for composure and shook his head. "Not today," he answered, sorrow straining his voice. As he dismounted, a thickness in his throat made it impossible to swallow grief or comment further. Pacing away briskly, he felt Eumenius's probing stare at his back.

The pain of losing her always hit without warning, and his guilt tormented him. Would life ever be worth living without her?

CHAPTER XXII

JULIA ANTONIA IN ROME TO HER SON MARCUS
Antonius in Athens:

Recently, I attended the wedding of Atia to Lucius Marcius Philippus. Do you remember when her husband, Gaius Octavius, died in Nola? It was near the time when Pompeius and Julia Caesaris married. Atia will be happy, I think. That boy of hers, little Octavian, is still delicate. He'll need guidance from a stepfather.

Concerning Hybrida's offer of Antonia, she would not be my first choice for you. However, I'm pleased you're planning on marriage with a respectable woman of status. I barely know this niece of mine who will be my daughter. How wrong of me, paying her so little attention.

Now let me inform you of the political scene since it centers on our cousin. Caesar is accused of starting an illegal war—one not sanctioned by the Senate. So he is surrounded by Gauls on one side and *a critical Senate on the other. I fear he has a long struggle ahead.*

Rest easy knowing that we are safe. We sacrifice for your well-being, health, and safety.

Marcus had a second chance at riding the big bay. The horse pranced beneath him, responding beautifully to leg cues.

Eumenius was working a large horse sale today at his employer's estate. Kyros the horse trader was known throughout Attica as a fair seller of fine stock. While his friend was busy preparing for clients, Marcus enjoyed the usage of Kyros's spacious training arena.

He barely thought of cantering before the bay responded. Marcus allowed the animal its head. As one with his mount, he sped into a swifter gallop, leaning forward in perfect balance. After several laps, he slowed to a halt, staring at the side of the arena.

Kyros, with Eumenius at his side, was leading a Roman officer to where Marcus was riding. In full armor, the fellow was obviously someone of note. His gleaming cuirass—the breastplate of high command—shimmered in the hot Athenian sun. Nestled in the crook of his arm was a plumed helmet. Behind him filed an impressive entourage of fellow officers.

Pleased to see some of his own countrymen, Marcus cantered over to the low wall surrounding the riding arena. Kyros was talking to Eumenius in Greek. While they spoke, Marcus sensed the Roman commander's scrutiny. With his full beard and Greek dress, it occurred to him that the Roman probably thought he was Athenian.

Spending over a year in Greece had prompted Marcus to dressing similarly to people around him. There was no reason to cut his hair; he'd grown it longer, tying it back neatly. In his continued state of mourning, his beard still remained. It was his reminder of loss.

Marcus addressed the commander as an equal. "Salve, citizen."

Eyebrow cocked, the Roman studied him in surprise. "Salve to you," he replied.

Marcus smiled, swinging his leg over the bay's rump to dismount. "Pardon, sir, but despite my appearance, I'm not Greek." One of the other officers edged up to his commander protectively, hand on the hilt of his gladius.

With a slight lift of his hand, the commander countered. "It's quite all right, Canidius. We may be in the presence of a highborn Roman, costumed as a Greek. Would I be correct?" he asked Marcus.

Marcus grinned. "Yes, sir."

"Which noble family is honored with such a gifted horseman in its gens?"

"The Antonii, sir. I am Marcus Antonius."

"Marcus Antonius. We've not met, have we?"

"I think not, sir."

"I've heard your name..."

"I'm afraid my reputation in Rome is tarnished at present." There was no point lying. Marcus knew he was many things. A hypocrite was not one of them.

"I recall your grandfather, of course. Orator, yes?"

Marcus nodded.

"He was a great Roman," the older man said. "My own father fought under his command when he defeated the Cilicians. That means your father was Creticus, correct?"

"I'm afraid so."

His finger wagged back and forth at Marcus, scolding, "Never be ashamed of your father, boy!"

Marcus shrugged. "I hardly remember him." Desiring to change subjects, he asked, "May I ask your name, sir?"

"Aulus Gabinius, Proconsul Provinciae to Syria."

Gods above! Marcus was passing niceties with the new governor of Syria, and a former consul? "It's a great honor, sir." He extended his hand, and Gabinius responded by grasping it in friendship.

"Actually, the honor is mine. I tell you, I've never seen any Roman ride like you."

"Gratias, sir."

"What are you doing in Athens?"

"Well, I hope to go home soon. I'm studying—rhetoric, military tactics..."

"And how to hide your nationality under Greek costume?" Gabinius joked with a grin.

Marcus laughed. "I love Hellenic culture, sir."

"How old are you?"

"Twenty-four years."

"Have you experience with a gladius?"

"In training, yes. My cousin Caesar hired an ex-cent—"

"Gaius Julius—*Caesar*? Gods infernal, you're Caesar's kinsman?"

"I am."

Gabinius licked dry lips, pondering a moment. "What are your plans when you return to Rome?"

Marcus scratched his head, sighing. "Actually, I'm to be married."

"Married?" Gabinius exploded with throaty laughter, several officers joining in. "Well, do you need Aulus Gabinius to rescue you from the mires of matrimony? I shall, if you desire."

Marcus raised a brow, puzzled. "How do you mean, sir?"

Gabinius turned toward his staff officer again. "Canidius, have I any social obligations tonight?"

The slender officer leaned toward Gabinius discreetly, giving an almost imperceptible nod at Kyros and Eumenius, who were still conversing about horses for sale. Softly, he said, "Sir, you were to dine with the horse trader and some other merchants hoping to profit from equipping our army."

Gabinius nodded his head slowly, looking thoughtful. "Ah, well. Canidius, I'll trust you to seal that business. Convey my regrets and host them yourself, along with others of our staff." He nodded at Marcus, smiling again and showing yellowish teeth. "I've some things to discuss with Antonius here. My boy, we're docked at Piraeus, about six miles out. Come to my galley tonight at sundown. We'll dine together, just the two of us. I may have an offer for you."

Marcus closed his eyes, trying to relax in the barber's chair. He'd mourn Fadia in his heart now. She would have wanted the best for him. He was certain of that. Gabinius was a man of power, and one he wanted to impress. So once the beard was gone, he ordered his hair cut in the short republican style.

Marcus rented a horse and rode the distance to Piraeus, arriving where the harbor suburb of Athens had once stood. Though the port city had slowly been rebuilding, only poor cottages dotted the rocky shoreline, where little was left of the bustling complex Sulla had burned decades before.

A series of wooden piers, built hastily to accommodate bigger ships in this post-Sullan era, jutted out into deeper waters. It was here that Gabinius's flagship and his larger vessels were docked. More rested at anchor farther out.

Horses purchased by the proconsul stood hobbled on the flats and hillsides, grazing on sparse growth. Marcus estimated nearly one-hundred. Of one thing he was certain—Gabinius was forming a cavalry.

His gaze shifted back to the galleys, and he rode to the dock and dismounted. After tying his horse, he walked between the ships, their sleek, graceful forms awing him. Each was uniform and powerful, adorned with decorative bronze rams, the deadly weapons of ship-to-ship warfare. Neatly tucked and stored, each sail was tightly bound to its mast. The largest of the fleet bore a bronze eagle standard, posted on the prow.

Gabinius's flagship.

"I'm afraid I've no proper triclinium, Antonius," the proconsul jested in apology as Marcus arrived. "Since we've no couches, we'll have to dine like good Republican women, sitting in chairs!"

Marcus laughed, the two of them clasping hands again. "Please, no apologies. Your invitation honors me."

A beautifully painted slave boy served them, porting a krater of wine imprinted with reliefs of Dionysian rituals. Referring to the dispenser, Gabinius remarked, "You seem appreciative of Greek culture, so this krater's artistry should interest you. An antique, it was crafted in Magna Graecia, in our own lands. My son gave it to me upon my appointment."

"It'll remind you of home while abroad," Marcus remarked approvingly. "As for my own admiration of Greece, you're correct. If I weren't Roman, I'd be most comfortable being Greek." He flashed a smile as the slave filled his cup.

Gabinius indicated a boy busy serving them wine. "That one was my wife's surprise, purchased as my galley servant. She named him Triton, and I daresay he's brought me good luck. We had calm seas all the way from Brundisium."

Eagerly taking a sip of wine, Marcus sighed in delight. Of savory Italian grape, it was a taste of home. Almost a year had passed since he'd enjoyed wine from Italia. But no getting drunk tonight. He wasn't among friends, but with a powerful man of senatorial rank. "How long will you stay in Athens?" he inquired.

Triton began serving steamed shellfish.

"We sail by week's end. I wish to reach Antioch, rest my men there, and then visit Damascus and a few other cities requiring tours by land."

"Then I'll sacrifice for you, to ensure another safe voyage."

"That's most generous."

Gabinius downed the rest of his wine, reaching for some boiled quail eggs. Triton offered Marcus sautéed eels, a dish he'd never liked. However, being polite, he felt obligated to try a few.

Gabinius explained, "The Senate has authorized me to clean up disturbances in Syria and Judea. There have been insurrectionists troubling provincials there since Pompeius left. Scaurus, the proconsul before me, did a less than satisfactory job, so the Senate recalled him. Pompeius and Clodius appointed me specifically to smoke out the troublemakers."

"Do you know who they are?"

"I sent men ahead as scouts to organize reports. A few messages reached Rome before I left. The Hasmoneans down in Judea stir up trouble—along with those damned Parthians. The Senate gave me the fleet and one legion. Another awaits that Scaurus trained and left behind. Problem is Syria covers enormous territory. I need horse simply to cover distance. I tell you, under my command, disorder will end."

Marcus tentatively dipped some bread into the eel sauce. "I don't envy you traveling inland down there," he said. "I've read a little about Syria. Lots of hot, desert country. You may as well be in Egypt."

"True," Gabinius agreed. "And I may well be in Egypt before my tenure in the East ends. King Ptolemy Auletes is reportedly having trouble with insurrections himself." He shook his head. "That Egyptian line may be coming to a nasty close. All his whelps are troublemakers. They fight one another as readily as rutting crocodiles."

Triton brought out another platter stacked high with sliced lamb in a rich cream sauce. Marcus pushed his eel to one side, replacing it with an ample serving of the newest course. "Hopefully, I'll make it to the East someday," he said.

Gabinius wiped his fingers on a moist towel. "Antonius, let me help you. I can't tell you how much your riding impressed me today. There's never been a Roman as confident in a saddle."

"You flatter me."

"I'm sure I do not." Gabinius was a brusque man, somewhat unrefined, reminding Marcus of a shrewder form of Uncle Hybrida. Short, barrel-chested, with thinning, grizzled hair, he was probably a little older than his uncle.

Triton stepped forward, politely offering Marcus more roasted lamb. He waved the boy away, carefully selecting words. "I greatly appreciate your kindness, but what can you do for me when you're leaving so soon for Syria?"

"As you know, Roman cavalries are typically comprised of foreigners. I've never much liked that fact, but here it is; Romans typically aren't horsemen. So in the heat of battle, generals risk using auxiliary horse units, when those foreigners could be the first to defect or bolt when things go awry. That's unsettling since I'll rely so heavily on cavalry, especially in such a vast region as Syria. I may have savage fighting ahead with rebels. They will be overzealous, not caring how they die. I'd prefer a Roman keeping my auxiliary cavalry loyal. Today, when I saw you, I knew I'd found my man."

Nearly choking on a stuffed olive, Marcus wiped his mouth with the back of his hand. "You want *me* to command your auxiliary cavalry?"

"Yes."

Astounded, Marcus reminded him, "I have no previous military experience, sir."

"You'd join us in a private capacity, of course. For glory only."

Marcus's heart fell. What good would ever come to him if he couldn't secure a military commission? Mars, be faithful—now was the time to try. "Proconsul, though I may be inexperienced, I'm no fool. I'd expect a commission and nothing less."

"Antonius, you're Creticus's son—and Lentulus Sura's stepson."

Face flushing with anger, Marcus still remained composed. "You just told me today not to be ashamed of my father, and I am *not* my father. You also said your grandfather served mine. And as for the Catilina affair, I assure you my family has received punishment enough for their affiliation with Lentulus Sura. You may have heard I have a poor reputation. Some senators probably turn their noses the other way at mention of my name. But I have honor, and my Grandfather's victory and triumph is more than your family has to show for itself."

The proconsul tilted his head back, looking down at his guest. "And I have other officers to consider," he snapped abruptly, bristling at Marcus's words. Reaching for more meat, Gabinius spilled sauce on the table and snapped his fingers impatiently at Triton. "I can't possibly commission an inexperienced cavalry officer, overlooking my own staff. They're all loyal men, expecting me to promote from within. Unfortunately, none of them knows horses. I'd think under your present circumstances, you'd appreciate an opportunity to make a name for yourself while serving Rome as well."

"You said you'd never seen anyone ride quite like me," Marcus challenged. Leaning back in his chair and smugly crossing his arms, he added, "Though you've not yet seen me fight, I assure you, you've never seen anyone handle a sword like me either."

Gabinius remained silent. Marcus got up slowly, lowering his voice and steadying himself. He wanted this position, but he would not lower himself to serving his country outside official status. Only hired mercenaries and desperate men did that. "Aulus Gabinius, if you offer me a commission, I'll be honored to serve Rome under your command. Otherwise, I regret I'll not be joining you. For not receiving rank for my services would be unacceptable."

Gabinius remained silent. He simply reached for his wine cup and took a sip, smacking his lips and ignoring Marcus as though he were already gone.

The gamble lost, Marcus nodded in stiff courtesy. "May the gods protect you on your journey, Proconsul." With that, he exited Gabinius's quarters, his heart heavy with disappointment.

Cool evening breezes from the sea stirred Marcus's hair. His horse plodded up the road leading back to Athens. Disheartened at how things had turned, he let the animal pick its own slow pace.

If only Gabinius had offered him a commission and given him a chance. Another opportunity was gone.

Depression's suffocating darkness crashed back in full force. Suddenly, Fadia's death felt keen and new. Every failure, from his father's poor judgment on to Lentulus's treason and finally extending to Uncle Hybrida's recall, seemed magnified and overwhelming.

Just ahead, some travelers were sitting around a fire next to the ruins of the Long Wall. Someone must have told a joke, for they were all laughing. As he passed their jollity, Marcus decided to stop at the first tavern he could find. Sadly, the wine wouldn't be as full and heady as Gabinius's. But when his only objective was to get completely drunk, it didn't really matter.

Suddenly, his horse lifted its ears and head. Whinnying, the animal blew and flared its nostrils. Marcus halted. Behind him, he heard hoofbeats. Someone was riding hard and fast. Since he wasn't in a hurry, he turned his horse to the side of the road. Whoever it was could gallop on past. Something had to be awfully urgent to push a horse that fast in the dark.

When the rider was even with Marcus, he pulled up quickly. "I'm looking for Marcus Antonius," he declared.

"I am he."

"I'm a courier from Aulus Gabinius, Proconsul Provinciae of Syria. I've a message for you."

The courier handed over a small scroll cannister.

Marcus's heart raced as he popped the lid. He left the courier standing in the road and backtracked a short distance to borrow light from the travelers' fire. They were welcoming, and he sidled in, unrolling the message:

Aulus Gabinius, Proconsul Provinciae of Syria, to Marcus Antonius:

I hereby offer you full commission in my legion as Cavalry Commander of my auxiliary units. My courier awaits your answer. Report directly to me within three days' time for orders.

Marcus reread the scroll four times, hardly believing his eyes. The blackest of nights morphed into victorious dawn.

He had a command.

CHAPTER XXIII

THIS WEEK'S ASSIGNMENT WAS AS AN ESCORT.

Marcus glanced over at his riding companion curiously. Archelaus of Pontus was a bastard son of Mithridates, former King of Pontus. He was also Pompeius's appointed high priest of a small Eastern nation called Comana.

Richly dressed, he and his colorfully attired compatriots wore brilliant silks and dazzling Eastern jewelry. Intelligent and well-spoken, the prince was near Marcus's own age, with a thick beard, neatly oiled and trimmed.

Just yesterday, a contingent of Gabinius's infantry, training only miles from Antioch's walls, had halted Archelaus's impressive procession. Comprised of dignitaries and honor guard, they were a wealthy lot. Harmless as they appeared, however, Gabinius wanted to know their intent. The Mithridatic dynasty had formerly been at war with Rome. Though things had settled in recent years, some Pontic people still held contempt for Romans.

Gabinius interviewed Archelaus personally. Satisfied that he was harmless, he ordered Marcus to escort him south under light cavalry guard. Apparently, the entourage was headed to Egypt for a wedding.

They'd been traveling most of the day when Archelaus suddenly spoke up in perfect Latin. "Commander?"

Marcus smiled at him in mild surprise. "You speak Latin?"

"Having lived around Romans all my life, I've learned your language."

Marcus nodded, smiling approvingly.

"Will there be a pleasant place to camp outside Ashkelon?" the prince asked.

"I confess I don't really know, having only arrived in Syria a little over a month ago myself. I'll be happy to inquire."

For a while, they continued in silence. Then Archelaus asked, "Do you know your proconsul well, Commander?"

Marcus shrugged. "Not personally. Why?"

Archelaus gazed toward the fields of farmland through which they were passing. "He was hesitant to let me pass through Syria."

Marcus shrugged. "He had just cause. Your company was traveling through his province bearing arms. I'm sure that because of your father, the King—"

Archelaus laughed derisively. "We mostly carry ceremonial weapons to distinguish my station. Besides, would you travel unarmed with such riches? We bear gifts for a royal bride."

"So I've heard. Who's getting married?"

The prince hesitated before answering. "A daughter of Ptolemy Auletes."

"Then shouldn't we be heading to a port? Sailing to Alexandria would be much easier."

"Perhaps. Many have warned me against taking the Way of the Sea."

"I hear it's harsh country," Marcus agreed.

"Whatever route we decide upon, I'll never travel through Syria again, so long as Gabinius governs," he said bitterly. "I have little respect for him."

"Why do you say that? He can be gruff, but—"

"He's a thief," Archelaus snapped. "I hope the Senate recalls him and that he'll suffer shame."

Marcus barked a short laugh. "Really? How much did he finagle you for?"

"Over fifteen talents."

Gods! So that was how Gabinius intended to finance projects and keep provincials loyal. And he'd probably skim some off the top for himself.

"I'm sorry for your misfortune and losses," Marcus said, shaking his head. Subtlety wasn't one of Gabinius's strong points, to be sure.

By the time they reached Ashkelon, the young Pontic noble had feasted Marcus twice.

It was more than pleasant befriending someone nearer his own status and sharing conversation and laughter. Since leaving Athens, he'd had little social interaction with anyone, really. Marcus had persuaded the proconsul into hiring Eumenius to oversee the horses' health and upkeep. However, because of Marcus's position of command, their relationship had taken a more professional turn of late.

As of now, he had no camaraderie amongst his own peers. When Gabinius introduced him as cavalry commander, nobody was overly friendly. Officers in the proconsul's company were all wondering how someone without any experience, and sporting a poor reputation, had won out over them.

Resentment was something Marcus Antonius had rarely encountered.

He felt his colleagues' aversion, so Marcus watched his back. There was no use fighting for acceptance. It would have to come with time. Respect had to be earned.

Fine. He'd earn it.

A day or so after Marcus returned from Ashkelon, Gabinius summoned a consilium—a meeting to discuss a troublesome revolt that was brewing. He requested Marcus give a full report on the situation.

As he was about to enter the ornate Seleucid dining hall where the meeting would take place, he overheard part of a conversation concerning him.

"—do you think of this Antonius?" someone was asking.

It sounded like Sextus Siscuria, another staff officer.

"Antonius?" The responder laughed. "He's nothing but an inexperienced upstart whose father sold Rome to pirates!"

That was Publius Servilius Isuaricus, an officer who had made his dislike for Marcus clear since the beginning.

Keeping calm and knowing that, for now, any payback had to wait, Marcus entered the hall.

Inside the large space, small folding chairs had replaced dining couches on an open terrace. Abundant natural light filtered in through brightly tiled colonnades. Triton, Gabinius's boy, had hung a large leather map of Syria high on a wall.

The other officers had already seated themselves. Not caring for their company after the short exchange he'd just overheard, Marcus simply strolled to the other side of the room and stood against the wall.

Then Gabinius entered and the consilium began.

With pursed lips, the proconsul stood, studying the map. Finally, he reached for a pilum leaning against a bench. Angling the sharp spear tip upward, he moved it south along jagged coastlines all the way to a large X delineating Jerusalem. "So many challenges," he mused. "Syria is such a recent addition to our lands; it's loosely compiled. Regrettably, troubles of unrest already boil to our south, where most of the population is Judean. I've asked Antonius to explain the particulars."

Every eye in the room rested upon Marcus. As he stepped forward, his pulse raced with the task of proving himself worthy of his assignment. "Today our greatest threat involves members of the Hasmonean dynasty," he began. "It's a buzzing hornet's nest of irreligious Jews, who have dominated this area for the past hundred years. They're an astounding cast of characters. First, there's Hyrcanus. He's currently high priest down in Jerusalem."

Sitting down not far from Marcus, Gabinius added hastily, "Pompeius selected him for that office before leaving."

Marcus nodded, continuing, "Yes. In fact, one of the reasons Pompeius chose Hyrcanus was because he wasn't as ruthless as the rest of the family. King Antipater of Judea convinced Pompeius to appoint him because the king could better control him on behalf of Rome in Pompeius's absence."

"So who's planning to revolt?" asked Canidius, his steely gray eyes fixing into a frown.

"One of his kinsman," Marcus replied. "You see, when Pompeius left Syria, he took Hyrcanus's brother Aristobulus and his son Antigonus prisoner with him to Rome. Pompeius decided it would be wisest not to leave them here because Aristobulus would kill Hyrcanus off. The two of them are still in Rome. But what Pompeius *didn't* consider was Aristobulus's second son, Alexander. Unfortunately, he stayed behind. And he's our troublemaker. He's angry because Pompeius didn't appoint his Tata. Now Hyrcanus's sons will inherit the priesthood."

"Meaning we'll be sending troops south," Siscuria said.

Marcus nodded. "But first someone has to go locate Alexander."

Publius Servilius Isuaricus was scowling. Marcus glared his way, wanting to bloody his face.

Gabinius intervened, "I see discontent on your face, Servilius. Speak up. Share your unease."

"Sir, you ask for trouble sending men farther south. Let those savages fight their own battles. I propose we only secure Roman lands that Pompeius held firmly. If the Hasmonean scum venture northeast toward us here, only then should we act."

Marcus ground his teeth. The fool didn't see the obvious. Shaking his head, he explained. "Servilius, you see our border extending only to Byblos or so. However, our proconsul and others in the Senate support the original borders Pompeius delineated. That means defending the south."

Servilius scoffed. "But why bother with lands so far away when we barely have enough manpower to cover the area we occupy here?"

Gabinius nodded toward Canidius, allowing him the floor. Of them all, he seemed the least antagonistic where Marcus was concerned. "I must agree with Antonius," he said. "Pompeius's conquest of Syria was only four years ago. It's so recent there aren't any distinguished borders yet—aside from what Pompeius first dictated to the Senate. Naturally, the Senate would want those maintained. Therefore it's men such as us—"

"Men such as ourselves who wind up spilling our own blood," Servilius argued hotly. "Men like us, dying far from Rome and fighting other petty kings' useless battles. We should stay here in Antioch and nurture trade. Creating a stable Syria is far more important than worrying about where its borders should be." That said, Servilius leaned back in his chair, crossing his arms and scowling petulantly.

Marcus cocked an eyebrow at him. There sat a young man without any sense of boldness or adventure. Servilius was nothing more than a spineless senator's brat. He and Uncle Lucius would make fine bedfellows.

Sextus Siscuria, the swarthy, wolf-faced officer, spoke up. "We all know you prefer dealing with merchants, Servilius. You like feeling cool coin in your palms. However, what we need to live with is where the proconsul wants Syria's borders to remain. Then we must make it so." Looking at Gabinius, he asked, "Do you want your borders clear down in Nabataea?"

Gabinius replied, nodding, "I want to secure these lands. By maintaining Pompeius's original conquests, I assure the Republic that these new territories will remain ours. Even ones only partially subjugated, which means those to the south." Arising, he eyed the map and strolled next to Marcus, studying his domain.

Marcus crossed to a table, picking up a scroll and brandishing it. "This message is from Hyrcanus to our proconsul, warning that Alexander is raising an army. In it, he pleads for our intervention."

Silence descended. Marcus eyed the men. Everyone was hashing out their own thoughts on the matter.

Gabinius paced slowly before the map, thinking out loud. "If Pompeius's influence stretched that far south, then certainly Aulus Gabinius's must also."

Siscuria sighed. "Then Antonius is right. We need to send scouts down to determine where Alexander's army is."

"Indeed," murmured Gabinius.

Marcus tossed the scroll neatly to Servilius to read for himself. His voice dropped low in volume, and he leaned in close to the irritating officer. "If we have a full-scale revolt brewing to the south, we must act immediately. Revolts interfere with trade, *Servilius.*"

That tidbit of logic caused the young officer's upper lip to twitch, his eyes glinting with anger at being singled out.

Gabinius stood up straighter, thinking aloud. "I'll show these rebels a thing or two about Roman governance. If Pompeius meant Hyrcanus to reign over that region, I'll enforce it. Little pup Alexander needs to be sent back into the desert, tail between his legs."

"Who will serve as the scout?" inquired Canidius.

"Antonius will take the cavalry south. He'll gather intelligence and find Alexander's army, which is probably hiding somewhere in the Nabataean desert. He'll send me details of any suspicious activity suggesting revolt. Once we have Alexander's location, we march."

"When do I leave, sir?" Marcus asked.

"In three days."

After sailing the horses and men as far as Tyre, Marcus's company moved down the coastline.

Syria was a lovely, fertile land. Arid, gentle plains along the coast were beautiful and bountiful. Temperate breezes brought in the balmy smell of sea air as farmers worked their fields. Bountiful pastures of grain undulated in a rippling dance of plenty. It was peaceful, pastoral, pleasant.

Despite the idyllic setting, unfriendly receptions became more and more frequent the farther south they traveled. Judeans living in the region made their dislike for Romans very clear, turning their backs at their approach. Several times they became distressed and even confrontational when the legionaries needed water. It had to do with some sort of religious concern. They believed the Romans to be "unclean."

Marcus didn't know much about Jews and decided it was best to give their villages a wide berth. There were enough wells for watering horses and men on the outskirts of communities. No sense in stirring up angry bees.

Five days into their trek, an advance guard returned, riding hard.

"Large party about a mile ahead, sir."

"Armed?" Marcus asked warily.

"Not heavily, but their numbers are larger than an average caravan. Their weapons are mostly fancy-looking—not weaponry for active duty."

"How many?"

"Close to a hundred."

This description sounded familiar. "Go back toward them with about twenty riders. And I want you very obviously armed. If these travelers are peaceful, find out their intentions and who they are."

In less than an hour's time, a dust cloud rose ahead of the front line as the scout's party returned. Waving his men on by, he rode straight up to Marcus.

"It's a large group, but not hostile," he assured. "The leader's called Archelaus. Claims to be from Pontus and is off to be married."

Brows knit together, Marcus chewed his lip. The first part of the report confirmed his suspicions of who the travelers were. But the second part..."You say *Archelaus* is the one getting married?"

"That's what he said, sir."

Marcus's eyes widened. That was news.

The scout added, "They're pitching camp now. He even invited you to dinner."

Since he'd not had opportunity to include Eumenius in much lately, Marcus asked his Greek friend to join him for the evening. They took a small detachment of cavalrymen. Upon their arrival at Archelaus's encampment, the prince appeared, dressed in costly silks.

"Greetings, Romans!" he cried. To nearby slaves, he snapped, "Hurry, see to their horses—they're thirsty, no doubt."

Marcus dismounted. He was ever amazed at Easterners. Archelaus wore more rings than fingers, each golden and studded with precious stones. A bejeweled silk diadem crowned his head. In the East, such ornaments signified royalty.

"I greet you in the name of Aulus Gabinius, Proconsul of Syria," Marcus announced amiably, removing his helmet.

Archelaus's eyes twinkled. "Antonius, welcome! Come inside my tent."

This prince had entertainment and dining down to an art form. Male and female slaves scurried about, each bearing trays heaped with succulent fruit. Reclining on decadent embroidered cushions, Marcus eyed a young slave girl delicately removing his sandals and washing dust from his feet. Just across from where he lay, a painted boy brought forth a golden cup of wine, encrusted with cabochons of emeralds. The youth bowed deeply after serving Marcus, then backed away.

"You host us richly. We Roman soldiers are unaccustomed to such sumptuous surroundings."

"I regret it's only a tent. Someday you must join me in Alexandria, for then I'll fete you with honor befitting a king."

Marcus studied his host. "Yes, it seems you withheld something important from Gabinius. I was told *you're* the bridegroom." He took a sip of wine, watching for his host's response.

Archelaus paused, nervous hesitation in his reply. "Berenice, Queen of Egypt, has honored me by accepting my offer."

"*Queen* of Egypt?" Eumenius exclaimed from where he lay on the end of the couch.

Marcus sensed something amiss. "I'm no expert on Egyptian affairs, Archelaus, but did King Ptolemy die? I was unaware of a reigning queen."

Sweat glistened on Archelaus's brow in the flickering lamplight. "There has been...unrest in Egypt, Roman friend." He wasted no time changing the subject, taking a gulp of wine. "Tell me. How fares your proconsul?"

"He's quite well." But now Marcus had little interest in Gabinius. Obviously, Archelaus didn't want Roman interference with his Egyptian plans. Well, if Marcus handled the situation well, he could learn more about this intriguing prince and Archelaus could help him seek out the rebels.

Marcus said, "I'm looking for a certain Alexander, son of Aristobulus. He's of the Hasmonean line—a well-known family in these parts."

Archelaus tilted his head back, stroking his chin thoughtfully. "Not a name I've heard," he replied, shaking his head.

It seemed an honest answer. Damn. Well, at least his wine was excellent.

The prince still seemed apprehensive. Did he fear that Gabinius would learn about his upcoming marriage? "You have yet to sail to Alexandria," Marcus pointed out. "I thought you'd be in a hurry to leave Syria after losing your purse to Gabinius."

Archelaus responded, "My getting to Egypt must be handled... carefully."

"And why's that?"

A painted boy scurried over to mix more wine as musicians started playing. Slaves were serving dinner.

"Friend, things in Egypt have been most unstable. Hopefully, my arrival will help settle things, for certainly the Alexandrians desire peace." He smiled brilliantly. "Besides, everyone loves a wedding."

"Tell me more of this unrest."

"My bride's father, Ptolemy Auletes, quit his kingdom. He was such a poor ruler that his own people forced him into exile. Berenice, his eldest surviving daughter, took the throne in his stead."

"Eldest *surviving* daughter?" Marcus repeated.

"I thought the eldest daughter's name was Tryphaena," Eumenius interjected.

Archelaus's face flushed red with nervousness. "Berenice's staff has...ensured that Tryphaena will not trouble her again."

Marcus put his cup down, staring at Archelaus. "Just what's that supposed to mean?"

"Berenice had her murdered," Eumenius answered bluntly. "Antonius, right before leaving Athens, I heard Berenice was supposed to marry another prince, but she disliked his looks, so she had him killed. We Greeks hear all the messy sewage coming out of Alexandria."

"So is she dead—this Tryphaena or whatever her name is?" Marcus pressed, gaining more interest in the topic.

Archelaus swallowed his wine. "Yes. In families of rulers such as the Ptolemies, these things happen."

Eumenius persisted. "Ptolemy Auletes has more children, doesn't he? I thought he finally had a son?"

"Two, actually," Archelaus concurred. "Two little Ptolemies. The youngest barely walks of yet."

"And two other girls, are there not?" Eumenius pressed. "The third and fourth princesses?"

"Yes. The third has always been her father's favorite," Archelaus confirmed.

Marcus laughed, swigging a mouthful of wine. "Those younger ones better look out for your bride. And from what my friend here says, perhaps you should look out for her too. Let's hope your finely chiseled features please her."

"*Cleopatra!*" Eumenius burst out.

"What?" Marcus asked.

"Her name—the third girl is Cleopatra, and the youngest is Arsinoe."

"So where's the king now?" Marcus asked.

"Word is he went to Rome to ask for support from your people," Archelaus said. "The Alexandrians are content now that he's gone."

That explained the delicate travel arrangements. Archelaus was probably worried about running into King Ptolemy's agents or Roman mercenaries. Marcus smiled, wagging his finger toward his host. "You'd best hope Rome has no interest in interfering. It seems to me you're marrying into mayhem."

Archelaus smiled. "No illegitimate son of my father ever had a better prospect of marriage. Think on it, Antonius. I'll be the wealthiest man in the world. Egypt is made of gold and grain."

Marcus held up his cup for more wine, grinning and shaking his head. He liked Archelaus. And he had to ask himself if he was really any different from this opportunistic prince. "Have you seen her?" he asked.

"Berenice? No," Archelaus admitted. Leaning in, whispering so only Marcus could hear, he added, "Some say she's too tall."

Marcus barked a laugh, observing his men. They were more than content, reveling in the atmosphere. Their host's wines were excellent, and they feasted on roasted rabbit, fowl, and smoked fish. Slave girls were dancing now, and two syrinx players softened their melodies to something sultry, the strains growing lazy and seductive.

Picking at a piece of fish, Marcus mentioned, "I, too, will marry upon my return to Rome."

"Have you met your intended?" Archelaus asked.

"Yes. She's my cousin, and from what I recall, also too tall."

By now, the music was luring every man in the room into a heady trance. One girl began pulling off her costume, tossing pieces to Eumenius, her hips swaying temptingly. The cavalrymen began to cheer.

Marcus knew how easily he could fall prey to this. But not tonight. Too much was at stake with this mission. He had to return to camp and organize scouting efforts. They'd head inland come morning.

Duty called, and he wrenched himself away from the pleasure.

"Archelaus, I need your help. I'm seeking a rebel rising up against Hyrcanus, high priest in Jerusalem. I've reason to believe this Alexander has raised an army and intends on attacking him. Upon leaving here, I'll be hunting down information from villages toward the Arabian border. As you proceed toward Pelusium, send word if you hear or see anything suspicious."

"I'll do my best to help you. However, we're headed toward the coast. Berenice is sending ships from her own fleet to safely bring us into Alexandria. We'll head south from here, to a safe place she's designated. It's too dangerous for us to sail. Fortune-seekers and even King Ptolemy's supporters could be trolling waters off the Egyptian coast."

Marcus nodded in response. Archelaus trusted him, telling him that.

"Strike a bargain with me, Antonius," the prince offered, smiling. "I'll listen for whisperings of revolt if you in turn promise my journey will be unhindered. If I encounter anything suspicious, I'll send a rider to locate you. I give you my word in friendship." Archelaus extended his hand.

Marcus tilted his head back to look him over. "Agreed, Prince of Pontus," he said, clasping the offered hand.

"Now that we're in agreement, eat, drink, and enjoy my dancers. Since we marry soon, let's indulge in Dionysian delights while we may."

Eumenius was already embracing several girls. Though terribly tempted, Marcus reined in his usual hunger for sex, consumed with the task at hand. This was an important assignment. He had to succeed.

In his memory, he still heard Caesar's warning words of finality. Failure was not an option.

The next morning, Marcus gathered his riders. Some straddled camels, dressed in native attire. He stood before them, filled with stubborn determination. "Infiltrate every village. Go to their temples, visit their brothels, worship their God; do whatever you must to blend in. Find out anything you can about Alexander. If what Hyrcanus wrote to Gabinius is true, someone, somewhere is bound to know something."

Once they were gone, Marcus led the rest of his cavalry east toward the Salt Sea and Nabataea. It was rugged wilderness country. As they passed through the desert, they saw the ancient foundations of Jericho, a long-forsaken stronghold. Due south from there, craggy mountains formed a gaping jawline against the sky, whose blues matched the briny depths of the sea's waters below.

Most of the men spurned the area, superstitious and fearful of the Hades-inspired landscapes they traversed. Marcus, however, found the region fascinating. While hunting at dusk with one of his men, he spied a leopard gracefully slinking away, disappearing beyond a rocky outcrop. For several days now, they'd spotted gazelles. Some of the men tried their luck at spearing one, but they were far too swift to bring down.

In just over a week's time, Marcus's undercover riders began rejoining the rest of the detachment.

One man had visited a village stripped of grain by armed brigands on horseback. None of the villagers dared interfere since the riders were armed.

Another had encountered a caravan of cloth merchants. Questioning them, he'd learned an army unit of several thousand had marched past their camp in stealth. They were only visible by a full moon.

A third rider had traveled due north of the Salt Sea. He'd learned of several masons in a village, commandeered to reinforce an already established fortress in the area. Damned Hasmoneans had even taken their wives and children hostage until they finished the job.

Then came a messenger from Archelaus of Pontus. Only two days after dining with the Romans, his caravan had intercepted a detachment of armed men heading northeast from the coast. They guarded large grain supplies and water casks. Archelaus had extended a dining invitation to them, to no avail. Turning him down brusquely, the mysterious travelers kept moving, cool and secretive. Archelaus promised to have them followed.

Now came the hardest part of Marcus's mission—locating Alexander's army, all the while keeping his men concealed and safe.

CHAPTER XXIV

NABATAEA.

Mountainous, sometimes wildly beautiful and full of flowering fields. On other days, terrain was impossible to traverse. Parts of the rugged landscape were simply impassable on horseback, and the cavalry was forced to turn about and find a better route. Marcus's map proved to be full of errors. He wished he had a trustworthy native guide.

But he'd damned well succeed!

And succeed he did.

Finally, he found visual evidence of an army. One morning an advance guard discovered deep ruts in the sand. A very heavy cart with thick wooden wheels had been by—in the middle of an inhospitable wasteland—with no villages for miles. Later that same day, one of the men discovered hoofprints well off the beaten track. Out here, in the middle of nowhere, there could be no other explanation for wagons and horsemen.

Alexander's phantom army was near. Everyone sensed it. Now they had to find them.

Nights in the desert were cold enough to freeze blood. Marcus would never have believed it if someone had told him a man could freeze to death in southern Syria, but here they were. Everybody wrapped up in their cloaks and saddle blankets. Even bandages from the medical supplies became warm wraps for sandaled feet. Marcus ordered a couple of worn carpets they'd ported along for a bit of comfort stripped apart. Those became extra blankets. For four nights in a row, he arose to find a thin layer of ice in the water casks.

Perhaps the saddest thing was that he couldn't permit any fires. That would reveal their location to anyone for miles around.

Then, two days after spying the cart tracks, they pitched camp near some towering cliffs. Most of the men were enjoying rations when a panicked sentry galloped to Marcus's tent at top speed. "Commander, desert demons are coming!"

Marcus hurried outside. Everyone was in uproar, and he saw why. A gigantic, boiling brown cloud bore down on them. Every tent began to tug at its pegs as the wind began to whip and kick up dust.

Keeping his head, he shouted, "Pull the tents close and get the horses and supply wagons inside! Bring in any water you can find."

For two full days, the sandstorm raged. Each man blindfolded his mount, reducing the horses' panic throughout the ordeal. There would be no cavalry without the horses.

Hunkered down in flapping, ripping tents, everyone munched uncooked grain and beans. To preserve water, their only drink was gritty posca, the vinegar-wine of the Roman legions. There was no place to relieve themselves except in pots, which they did to avoid venturing outside in the stinging blast. By the end of the ordeal, everybody smelled like horseshit.

Once the storm passed, Marcus walked around the encampment, deciding to stay put for the time being. Their camp now had a perfect camouflage in sand. Barren, rocky hills flanked them on each side. And perhaps best of all, there was a small spring only a mile or so away, shaded beneath a tall rock face. This could be their base while they combed the area seeking Alexander.

One of the hardest things about command was keeping morale up. Marcus wasn't sure how long it would take for Gabinius to arrive, but he figured several weeks. He decided he'd send a man back to Judea to intercept the legion. It wouldn't be too hard for a rider to locate five thousand men on the main road.

In the meantime, every cavalryman spent time riding details, searching for the ghost army. In small detachments, riders left at dawn every morning on a constant quest for the enemy. Anyone staying behind was on a rotating sentry duty and work detail. Whether it was feeding horses, hauling in water every few days, or digging trenches around camp, everyone worked.

Mostly, men complained about the cold and not having any fires since it made cooking impossible. But for now, meals of dry grain and posca-soaked beans continued. It was better than being discovered by a disgruntled rebel army.

Fifteen days later, Marcus paced slowly, staring down at a beaten swath of footprints on the ground. He shook his head in disbelief. The army that had left this trail was enormous. Alexander showed alarming strength. For two weeks, evidence of his movement had been more and more frequent. They were probably practicing maneuvers and drilling. Still, there was no sign of an encampment.

From behind Marcus, Eumenius's horse stamped.

This was the farthest afield he had ridden into the desert without reinforcements. Disguised in native Syrian robes, his only visible Roman attribute was his gladius, strapped about his shoulder and hanging on his right. He sensed in his gut that Alexander was very near.

"I want to ride just a little farther," Marcus said. "They can't be far. If we find their encampment, we can observe them." He paced back to his horse.

Intensely focused on finding his prey, he was edgy. The horses were hot and tired, and it was unwise for just the two of them to be alone this far out. The phantoms could be around the next bend or over a rise in such deceptive landscape. Marcus warned his own men against doing this sort of thing. Yet here he was.

Eumenius reached out, grabbing Marcus's forearm, pointing up ahead. "There—"

A large dust cloud rose high above the next rise, yet there was no wind. Next came the thunder of hooves. A large group of riders was traveling fast on the other side of the hill.

"Ares," Eumenius whispered in panic. "It sounds like an entire cavalry."

They acted at the same time, whirling their horses about and spurring hard. Side by side, they barreled toward camp.

"Eumenius!"

The Greek looked over at Marcus.

"Split up!" Marcus shouted. "We can't risk leading them back. Ride in the opposite direction a while, then see where you stand. I'll do the same. Return when you're able."

Marcus sharply reined off the other way. Balanced low over his horse's head, he rode hard, occasionally glancing over his shoulder.

White lather flecked Marcus's horse down both sides of its sweating neck and flanks. He switched directions again, heading back to camp. Once he finally saw their camouflaged tents, he halted abruptly. He couldn't believe it.

Another detachment had moved in right next to theirs. Dumbfounded, he cursed himself for leaving in the first place.

Who was this?

He breathed easier when he saw that, beyond the mystery camp, his unit's eagle standard was still visible. In the new camp, soldiers moved about, stopping and pointing at him. They were not Roman, but they did not attempt to halt him.

Past the strangers now, he entered the safety of his own defenses. His men were casually involved in mundane tasks. Some groomed their horses; others were heading back to their tents from the latrines. One group of cavalrymen stood outside their tent examining a horse's foot. Several shouted greetings and waved.

Marcus jogged his horse toward his tent.

Two sentries stood at the entrance, but sitting cross-legged in front were two Syrians.

Marcus swung down, handing his reins to the waiting sentry. Loaded with questions, he ripped the turban from his head and peeled out of his foreign costume.

Both strangers rose to meet him. "Commander Marcus Antonius?" said the shorter one in thickly accented Greek. Smiling pleasantly, he extended a hand in greeting.

Under the circumstances, Marcus's response bordered on hostile. "Who in Dis Pater's dark name are you, and why are you camping on top of us?"

The short, stocky one stepped forward again, providing both answers. "Commander, we were sent to reinforce you. I felt it safest to locate my men as close to yours as possible."

The other chimed in, "King Antipater sent us, upon request of Gabinius. You were well hidden—difficult to locate. Fortunately, your scout on the main road gave excellent directions."

Marcus stared them down, trying to take it all in. "You're from Jerusalem, then?"

The smaller, kindly looking one spoke again, "I am Malichus of Jerusalem. This is my brother in arms, Pitholaus. We bring greetings from King Antipater and Proconsul Gabinius—"

"Where is Gabinius?"

"Probably a half day's journey behind us."

Pitholaus added, "He moved quickly after hearing from you. Alexander's army is near."

"*Damn* near," Marcus spat. "I nearly ran into them." Chewing his lip, he turned to the sentry still holding his horse. When Eumenius returns, inform me. Send refreshment to my tent, enough for my guests and myself." Marcus turned back to the Judeans. "Pardon my rudeness. I've ridden hard today. Come inside. I'll offer what comfort we have."

Marcus ate sparingly as he listened to his guests' thickly accented and poorly spoken Greek. Something more bothered him.

By the end of the evening, Eumenius still hadn't returned.

Marcus sent riders out until dark, and again early the next morning, searching.

The Greek was gone.

Just before dawn, a scout in a search party eased Marcus's sense of loss. Alexander's phantoms had materialized.

Concealed in a low valley, dunes and rubble from some ancient ruins hid them from view. If the scout's estimate was accurate, Alexander's army was larger than Marcus would have guessed. Around ten thousand infantry and over a thousand cavalry.

Since Gabinius wasn't far, Marcus decided to break camp and head toward the legion. Antipater's Judean infantry accompanied his horsemen but made progress slow. After descending onto a flat plain, everyone became lethargic in the increasing heat. Early summer had arrived.

About two hours into their journey, Malichus rode up. "Someone is following us."

"Probably one of my scouts."

Malichus shook his head. "He's not Roman."

Marcus stared at him, then twisted around in his saddle, craning his neck. Dust from the men and horses hid everything to the rear. "What did he look like?"

Malichus shrugged. "A wanderer. Someone lost—a shepherd, perhaps?"

"Fimbria!" Marcus hailed a trusted cavalryman. "Ride back behind the Judean column. Someone's on foot back there. See who it is."

Saluting crisply, the young soldier disappeared into the dust at full gallop. Within a half hour, he returned, a second man astride behind him.

Marcus rejoiced. Stripped of his armor and weapons, and wearing only his Syrian garb, was Eumenius.

Marcus dismounted and embraced him. The Greek was exhausted, dark rings under his eyes.

"Are you all right?"

Eumenius nodded wearily.

"Can you ride?" Marcus asked.

Eumenius nodded again. He was terribly dehydrated. Moments later, someone brought up a spare horse.

Marcus uncorked his waterskin. "Easy," he warned. "Drink slowly."

Eumenius's only response was taking short gulps, one after the other. He heaved a sigh of relief. Slowly, he began his story in a raspy voice. "They took me prisoner." He drank more water.

"And?"

"They asked if I fought for Rome. They were preparing to break camp and argued over what to do with me. One, a scholarly man, spoke Greek. Turns out he was spying for Archelaus. I tell you, he saved my life. Many there urged Alexander to kill me, but Archelaus's man advised against it. He reminded Alexander that his war isn't against Rome, but against Hyrcanus. So Alexander ordered me blindfolded, and they rode me into the desert and released me."

Marcus shook his head. "It was foolhardy of me, taking us out so far. I'm indebted to Archelaus for his part in returning you. Hopefully, I may someday return his kindness."

Soon, distant figures materialized on the horizon, resembling a wavering mirage. As Marcus's company got closer, the image stopped undulating. The sight of the legion sent a charge of excitement amongst the men. For Marcus, it was a huge relief, returning among his countrymen. The legion was in fighting array, helmets gleaming, shields up, standards high.

A single rider approached. Marcus called a halt, cantering out alone to meet the proconsul.

"Salve, Antonius."

"Salve, sir."

"What have you to report?"

"After weeks of searching, it was only today that we found

Alexander. He was well hidden. We call them 'the Phantoms.' They are masters when it comes to sneaking around. I've had a reliable report that they're on the move now."

"Any idea of their destination?" Gabinius asked.

"None."

Removing his helmet, the proconsul wiped his sweating face. More horses arrived at Marcus's back; the two Judean commanders were riding in.

Lowering his voice, Marcus murmured privately, "Sir, be wary. If my men were close to getting numbers right, we'll need every man to take them. Alexander has quite an army."

"What are his numbers?"

"Around ten thousand infantry, accompanied by fifteen hundred cavalry. A few scouts said less, but if we think high, we'll be relieved if numbers are lower."

Gabinius whistled, shaking his head. "That pits two men against every one of ours."

"If we stay in this area, chances are we'll intercept them. Is that your intent, sir?"

Gabinius nodded. "I'd be pleased to engage and end this nonsense."

Marcus noticed familiar faces as Canidius and Servilius trotted up to Gabinius's side. There was one more piece of news Marcus felt obligated to share. "One more thing, sir—I ran into Prince Archelaus."

"Ah, really? You needn't bring him to my attention," Gabinius replied, waving the subject off. "Remember, I interrogated him before sending him south with you. He's of no concern."

"His plans may interest you—"

"My only interest lies in an army somewhere beyond these hills."

Well, Gabinius could never justly accuse Marcus Antonius of withholding information. Archelaus had proved loyal to his word. Marcus wouldn't raise the matter again.

Gabinius smiled tightly at Canidius and Servilius. "Antonius completed his first mission admirably. It seems I chose the right man." With that, he rode off, followed by Malichus and Pitholaus.

Marcus watched him ride away in exasperation. Those words certainly wouldn't ingratiate him to his peers, especially Servilius. Bracing himself, he saluted his fellow officers. "Salve, Canidius," he said, smiling.

"Salve, to you," Canidius answered.

Servilius simply showed Marcus his back, turning his horse abruptly and cantering into the ranks. Canidius gave a curt nod, at least acknowledging Marcus, then cantered off too.

For half a watch, Gabinius kept the legion in tight formation, awaiting Alexander to show himself, join in battle, or yield. At last, they could a see long string of riders and infantry against the sky on a distant ridge. The legion marched forward, but after a short pursuit, Gabinius halted. The fully armed Romans were fading in the sun.

"Damn. Antonius, send out riders and have him followed. I don't want to lose them, but nor do I favor pushing my infantry into heat exhaustion. They'll turn and fight eventually."

As luck would have it, Marcus shared a tent with Servilius and Canidius.

Several times already he'd nearly bloodied Servilius's mouth, but he reined himself in. Servilius's unpleasantness was only a burr under his saddle. Marcus commanded horse here.

Still, yesterday Marcus's horse had come up lame. As he'd examined his animal's foot, Servilius rode by, remarking loudly, "Not to worry, Antonius can always ride a stinking camel!"

Both Judeans and Romans within earshot had laughed at the ill-humored jest. But deciding to keep a sense of fun, Marcus let the barb go, even grabbing a passing camel by its bridle, acting as though he'd mount up. Everyone cheered, successfully turning Servilius's attempted humiliation into a personal triumph.

Tonight, he accepted an invitation to join Malichus and Pitholaus in their tent for drinking and gaming. Time with the Judeans meant less time with Servilius, so he accepted. It turned out to be worth it. After only several hours, Marcus's purse contained a fistful of silver. And their wine was more than passable.

Later, strolling back to his tent, he saw lamplight inside and heard low voices. What poison was Servilius serving up tonight?

It was Canidius he heard first. "Decent enough, for foreigners. He dislikes the quiet one who never smiles but says, 'Give them three or four cups of wine, and they become your fast friends!'"

Servilius snorted. "If Antonius is drinking, he'd befriend the King of Parthia. He's such an ass."

"I like him," Canidius admitted. "He's honest, tells you the way he sees something up front, and gets the job done. None of us likes admitting weaknesses, but he deserved the cavalry. Gabinius was right." He sniggered, before adding, "Why, just today you complained how sore you were from the saddle. Imagine riding through this desert searching for Alexander the way he did."

"Go ahead—enjoy his company. You wanted to wager on whether we fight tomorrow, but I say let's put silver down on whether he's drunk when he comes back tonight. I'd have a sure win."

Canidius conceded. "I grant you he drinks, but never around Gabinius. Whenever on duty or expected to command, he's sober."

"He's altogether inexperienced—not even blooded," Servilius spat in disgust.

Marcus chose that moment to lift the tent flap. Both men swiveled their heads toward him. Letting a pregnant pause pass before entering, Marcus glared at Servilius. Lifting his gladius off his shoulder, he unpinned his cloak, draping it across his cot.

The silence in the tent was palpable.

Before relaxing and lying down, he drew his gladius, placing it just under his arm. If Servilius tried something while he slept, he'd find Marcus in no mood for mischief.

"Sleep well, Antonius," Canidius offered. Marcus heard him shuffling about in his cot, dropping some dice on the ground. One lamp still burned—nearest Servilius, who was rustling through a leather satchel of scrolls.

An uneasy peace ensued until Servilius shattered it. "Canidius, want to know what I am reading?"

"What?"

"A treatise by Cicero entitled 'Ignoble Romans Causing the Republic Dishonor.' My father sent it for my pleasure."

Marcus sighed at mention of Cicero's name.

"Well, stop reading and go to sleep," Canidius grumbled. "We may have a battle to fight tomorrow."

Servilius ignored him. "In this treatise, Cicero lists 'ignoble Romans' by name. Guess who's nearest the top."

Clenching his teeth, Marcus felt himself stiffen, anticipating what was coming.

In a singsong voice, Servilius crowed, "He writes, 'The Senate proclaims Praetor Marcus Antonius *Creticus* as a traitor to the Republic. After a humiliating defeat against the pirates, he then made a pact with them. He's a fine example of an ignoble Roman given power because the Senate thought him too *inept* to use *or* abuse it.'" Servilius sniggered, pausing for effect before finding voice again. "You know, Canidius, if that had been me, if I were that stupid to have done such a thing, I would have spilled my blood the way real Romans should. What a coward not to do so."

Marcus heard Servilius toss the scroll down on the end of his cot, content. How much more of this vicious cock would he have to endure? Mars, he'd had enough!

In one lithe movement, he swung his legs over the side of his cot, rising and casting a towering shadow over where Servilius sat, smiling arrogantly.

"Going out to take a piss, Antonius?" he asked.

"Say that again," Marcus whispered.

"What?" Servilius chortled. "That you need to go out and piss?"

"No, what you said before that. I want to be certain I heard you right."

Canidius rolled over to watch.

Marcus took his time, picking up the scroll, scanning it in the dim light of Servilius's lamp. Gods, that Cicero was one egotistical—

"Let me see, what did I say?" Servilius pretended to ponder. "Oh, now I remember! Something about an 'inept coward.' Was that it?"

"Yes, that was it."

"I was commenting on what a coward your father was," Servilius spat, standing up to face him.

Marcus nodded, smiling brightly. "Indeed. That's exactly what I thought you said." Gods, was this going to feel good.

Marcus's fist shot out like a bolt from Jupiter, punching Servilius square in the nose. Careening backward, the officer landed flat on his back, clear through the tent flap, head protruding outside.

Canidius scrambled up, staring openmouthed, stunned at how fast it had happened. He smiled broadly, clapping Marcus on the back. "That should do it."

Still holding the Cicero work limply in his left hand, Marcus said, "Come to think of it, I do need to go out and take a shit. This scroll should work as well as a sponge."

Ten to fifteen miles southwest of Jerusalem, Marcus and his cavalry waited atop a steep escarpment. Spread across the basin below was Alexander's multitude. From his vantage point, they resembled toy armies he played with as a boy. Arranged in deep ranks, bearing shields, swords, and pikes, their numbers were impressive.

Facing them was the might of Rome.

A flurry of activity began. Gabinius was moving troops onto his front line, each legionary falling into rank. Mesmerized, Marcus watched over five thousand men moving in perfect rhythm, shields ready, pressing forward in merciless cadence. Armed with pila, gladii, and shields, they'd be first to engage, backed by auxiliary archers.

Marcus scanned the morning sky above. Already, the sun was relentless. Trickles of sweat eased down his spine under his cuirass. His temples drummed under his bronze helmet, in sync with thousands of tramping feet far below. Jeers from the Hasmoneans quickened his beating heart, a cacophonous roar in the narrowing breach. Droves of Roman pila and arrows suddenly arced skyward, thinning enemy ranks with death falling from above.

Marcus shouted back to Malichus, "Let's get into position."

The older man rode forward. He studied Marcus's face with steely eyes. "Your lip is bleeding, Antonius."

Marcus lifted one hand to his mouth, hastily wiping blood away. Damn.

Malichus whispered, "You'll do well, Roman. No man's a soldier without fear as his friend."

By the time they descended onto the plain to form up, Marcus had to yell over the noise and confusion. Screams, banging, metal on metal, all punctuated with piercingly bright sounds of tubicines blasting orders on their trumpets.

So this was war.

Once the legionaries broke the enemy ranks, Marcus's orders were to pursue the fleeing Hasmoneans. They were to show no mercy. Just as Rhesus used to say, Gabinius warned him not to allow his horsemen to ride out too deep into the fray.

Impatiently awaiting the Hasmoneans to cave, Marcus studied the Roman front. He'd heard of exchangeable ranks in legionary units, how they'd fight all day without tiring. At a centurion's whistle, they swapped places methodically, letting each man in front retreat to the back for rest, a comrade filing into his fighting position. Alexander's army would never outlast that, even if they held men in reserve. They had no such organized method of relief.

It was impossible to see due to rising dust. After waiting for what felt like too long, Marcus sent two horsemen into the cloud to observe the action. Frustrated, he chewed his bottom lip again, never taking his eyes from the all-encompassing grit.

Horses snorted and stamped, the animals as impatient as the men.

Time passed. Still no word from the riders.

What was happening? If the enemy retreated, and he simply couldn't see...*Then,* out of the dust bolted a rider. "Sir, a large

Hasmonean infantry unit just broke into retreat. They're running due west. If you ride steady from here to the north-northwest, you'll overtake them easily. Their front lines are crumbling."

Marcus would have to trust that Pitholaus was responding too, as he commanded the other flank. There was no way of knowing since he was so far away. They couldn't even see one another.

But it was time. *Now*—

Marcus's hand tightened on his javelin, lifting it for all to see and spurring his horse in front of the cavalry. "See that patch of scrub? That's your landmark. Go no farther than that, or they might overtake you," he repeated several times, cantering and shouting from one end of his line to the other. "Stay together, *work* together. Don't let me see any of you afraid of these curs. Now let's show everyone how a real cavalry rides!"

Their cheers were heartening, each man eager to fight. This was it—Marcus's first taste of combat.

His horse needed no encouragement; the line surged forward with animal instinct. As every mount fought for its head, the charge turned into a rumbling thunder of hooves and dust.

As he drew closer, he saw details of the Hasmoneans' armor and clothing. They were running for their lives in panic. Javelin raised and poised, he shouted for those riding nearest him to do the same. He held steady, then launched, each rider following suit. Dozens of missiles were airborne. As the volley descended, Hasmoneans dropped in their tracks.

Marcus drew his gladius, guiding his horse with his left hand. Legs tightly wrapped around the animal's flanks, he overtook one rebel. Before he could slay him, the fellow stumbled, dropping in front of another rider beside Marcus.

Trampled—a miserable death. Marcus heard the man cry out. He rode on. His horse dodged two javelin-pierced victims already down.

As he neared another Hasmonean, the man whirled about, standing his ground, slashing out with a curved blade.

It never made its mark. Marcus leaned sideways in his saddle, gripping one of its horns with his left leg. His gladius parried the blow, then followed through, cutting the Hasmonean down like wheat. He didn't need to stab; the impetus of his horse did the job for him.

The rebel fell.

Marcus rode on.

He drove forward, slamming into another sword-wielding Hasmonean. This pitiful victim had no chance to fight, stumbling and falling instead. Marcus leaned sideways, stabbing. A shriek emanated from the soldier whose life he extinguished. The longer he rode the more mechanical his actions became, sticking men like pigs in a slaughter pen. Deadly as ravenous birds of prey, the cavalry fanned the field.

Yet another man whirled about to fight. Marcus reined in, circling tight, forcing the rebel to follow in dizzying close range. With a swift slash, he lopped the man's head off. It happened so quickly it would've been painless. Then there were cries from behind, and he looked back.

Surrounded, Malichus was desperate. Six Hasmoneans were intent on bringing him down. Mars, they were nearly fighting each other for the chance to kill him—a fellow Judean they considered traitorous.

"Away from him!" Marcus bellowed in Latin, using speed to scatter them. Reining savagely, he jerked his mount in tight, forcing the men on Malichus's left to retreat. Then on his shield arm, two were trying to get the better of him. Cold fear pricked his heart. It was much harder to fend them off on that side. This time, Malichus reacted, killing both of Marcus's aggressors in consecutive slashes with his great curved blade.

Seeing their comrades perish, the rest fled.

Marcus blinked at Malichus, breathless. They'd saved one another's lives.

The Judean grinned with yellowish teeth like an apparition from the Underworld, spattered with blood and dirt. Helmet lost, his hair hung limp and stringy, soaked in sweat. An open slash on one cheek drained blood down his neck. He raised his curved blade in salute, nodding at Marcus.

Strange how Marcus's mind had a million thoughts flitting through it.

How long had they been fighting?

Why did his hand feel sticky? He glanced down to see his entire lower arm drenched in blood. Whose was it?

Visibility was still difficult, the air thick with dust. Eyes smarting with grit, he strained to see beyond the unsettled sand.

Horsemen were still heading into the distance, and he came to his senses, shouting for a tubicen to call them back. The trumpet player sounded several calls. They responded, returning one by one. Some hissed curses at enemies still escaping.

As they reassembled, carnage revealed itself in the settling dust. Pleas for death, grown men weeping. How it pained Marcus to see cavalrymen from his own auxiliary lying still, smeared with blood.

Nearby, writhing in anguish, one still lived.

Marcus drew near, swinging off his mount. The boy was weeping in agony. Lifting a hand toward him feebly, he pleaded, "Finish this, sir—I beg you..."

It was Timaeus, Marcus's youngest rider and a gifted Macedonian horseman. He had suffered a deep gash on his head, and Marcus saw his exposed skull through the blood. Sadly, the real deathblow was much lower, in his gut. A broken Hasmonean sword arced through his abdomen.

"Please," Timaeus sobbed.

Marcus retreated to his horse, jerking a skin off his saddle. That morning he'd filled it with water and posca in case he took an injury himself. Surely, it would ease Timaeus's pain.

He knelt, offering the youth his skin. Carefully tilting his bloodied head back, liquid drizzled into his mouth.

Malichus knelt next to him, wordless and watchful.

Some of the posca spilled onto Timaeus's injured scalp. The young soldier moaned, wincing in pain.

"Do it," whispered Malichus. He grasped Marcus's hand. With a grip like iron, he guided it firmly to the hilt of his gladius, nodding stern encouragement. "Send him to Sheol swiftly, as he asks, or he'll suffer needlessly on his journey there."

Marcus looked at the Judean in horror. Breathing raggedly, he drew his weapon from its scabbard. Timaeus swallowed hard before closing his eyes, lips mouthing an inaudible prayer in Greek. Pale, accepting death, his body shook.

Marcus Antonius steeled himself, grasping the cavalryman's chin and tilting it up to expose his neck. Voice quivering, he whispered, "No more pain."

He sliced deep, ending Timaeus's suffering, his fading life ceasing with a soft gurgle.

Eyes closing momentarily, Marcus exhaled a long sigh, then pushed himself up with his bloody sword. Twenty or so of his men sat on their mounts, observing solemnly.

Immersed in grief and shock, he walked away from them, not stopping until he was alone on the plain. There, he stood in the relentless Judean heat, weeping silent tears for one of his own.

CHAPTER XXV

IN THE JUDEAN DESERT OUTSIDE JERUSALEM STOOD AN OLD fortress called Alexandrium. It was a veritable ruin. That is until Alexander the Hasmonean led his defeated army there and built reinforcements. He moved so quickly Gabinius barely knew his whereabouts before Alexander had restored walls and prepared for a siege.

Located on a lofty knoll, it was the thickness of the stone walls as much as the height that made it impenetrable. Once Gabinius issued orders for his men to surround Alexandrium, Marcus and the others were at a loss as to how to proceed. Without proper siege equipment, they had little choice but to starve the rebels out and await their next move.

A month into the operation, a sentry interrupted Marcus and Canidius in the praetorium tent where they were poring over supply lists. "They're firing at us!" he cried. "Six men are down."

Marcus leaped up, grabbing a shield and bolting outside, Canidius at his heels. One hand shielding his eyes from the sun, he immediately saw the trouble. "Up there." He pointed at archers high on the walls. "Siege ladders—now!" They were the only useful resource they'd been able to build.

This opportunity couldn't slip away. Rarely did the cowards show themselves.

Marcus watched impatiently.

The men worked in unison, hauling the ladders and hoisting them against the walls. At first, the rebels tried shoving them off their battlements, but once the Romans put weight onto them, grappling hooks held fast.

"Testudo!" Marcus shouted, backing away from another volley of arrows raining down. Damn, those archers up there were dangerous. He watched as his men created the classic "tortoise maneuver," shields above them, roundabout.

In formation, legionaries surrounded each ladder's base, allowing soldiers to ascend one at a time while providing a shell of protection for those awaiting their turn. Unfortunately, the men climbing up were ideal targets. Most strapped their shields onto their backs. It was safer, but slowed progress.

Marcus saw several rebels have a good laugh, using their feet to push one hapless legionary to his death. The shield's weight on his back pitched him backward.

"Canidius, keep them moving," Marcus ordered, jogging off toward the nearest testudo formation.

"Where are you going?" Canidius called, bewildered.

"Up that wall."

Shield out front, Marcus felt a thud. He'd taken an arrow. Joining in the frenzied clump of legionaries, he called, "All right, boys, I'm going up, and all of you are following." Under the shell of shields, it was hot and stank of sweat.

Marcus peered up between the shields. He didn't want to feel unbalanced, like the soldier who'd just died before his eyes, so he decided to discard his shield. He'd be an easy target, but someone had to get up there. If he moved fast enough, he'd make a tougher mark.

After some slaps on the back and words of encouragement, he began his ascent. Quickly, one rung at a time, shoulders heaving, he looked straight up. An arrow whizzed by his ear. He kept climbing. "Follow me!" he yelled, hoping the men below would obey. "Come on!"

Finally, he felt tremors from other climbers beneath him.

From his perspective, looking straight up, it was impossible to tell whether an enemy rebel awaited him. For several dicey moments, Marcus held on with only his left hand, using his right to draw his gladius. Now how to climb with it? Awkwardly, he put the blade between his teeth, just beneath the hilt, grimacing. It was heavy, but he only had a few rungs to go.

Somewhere below, he heard Canidius shouting for more ladders. In his peripheral vision, another one dropped into place to his right.

There was a whooshing of arrows up top and to the left. Those archers were very near. Up two more rungs, he snatched his blade from his teeth. Then he sprang with as much leverage from his legs as he had, punching his gladius forward. He managed to stab the archer closest to him. Another was on his right but was busy firing and slow to respond. Marcus nimbly turned and stabbed him too, the man's face registering wide-eyed disbelief. Now he was on top.

Before any more rebels could reach him, he glanced down the ladder. "Hurry—I need help up here!"

As he desperately fought two more rebels joining up to attack him hand-to-hand, more Hasmoneans barreled up the ramparts with torches and buckets of boiling oil. Marcus's heart quickened in fear. Romans were heading up the ladders now in droves. Men he'd personally ordered to climb up here. He was so busy fending off attackers there was little he could do to warn them.

Soon he heard them screaming. Next came the sickening thuds of bodies falling and the smell of burning flesh and hair. Some legionaries were luckier, their suffering cut short. They smacked against Alexandrium's stone walls as they fell, brained on impact.

Absorbed in swordplay, Marcus wished for a shield again. Gods! He was still the only Roman on top.

"Fall back!" he shouted to men climbing up behind him. They couldn't compete against oil and fire. Things were turning very quickly. On nearly every ladder except the one he defended, there was screaming, smoke, and flames.

Another rebel charged him with a shield.

Marcus needed that shield to stay alive. Hurling himself at the Hasmonean, he punched his gladius straight at the man's throat, his hand awash with blood. Deftly tearing the shield away from the dying, he glanced around, backing toward the edge of the wall.

Shit! He hadn't climbed all the way up just to have to go back down.

Two other attackers came barreling his way, and he didn't have time to think. Shield in front, he defended himself until he saw a hole, taking one of them down. He was still fighting when someone called behind him.

"Commander!"

Breathless, he couldn't disengage. Yet another was hurrying to join the rebel he was still fighting.

"Commander, step back. We'll guide your feet."

Canidius had sent men back up to rescue him.

Marcus stood at the edge of the wall, soldiers' hands grasping at his ankles. Frantic, he used his shield to punch and shatter one of his attackers' skulls.

Taking the second big risk of the day, he stepped backward into thin air, a legionary guiding his foot down onto the rung of the ladder. Off balance, his clumsiness was perfectly timed as the second Hasmonean hurtled forward, swinging his sword. The rebel's slash missed Marcus, but his momentum tumbled him straight over the wall. Marcus let his men support him until he located the rungs of the ladder and righted himself, sheathing his gladius, then he hurled the rebel's shield away.

Down he descended, quickly as possible, to cheers from legionaries below.

But Marcus was angry. Romans had died, painfully burned, scalded, or falling from Alexandrium's ramparts. They died following his orders. There was nothing to celebrate.

Still, Marcus became a hero.

Gabinius returned a week after the wall-scaling incident, hearing gallant tales of Marcus Antonius's heroism and courage. As the first man to scale the enemy's walls, he was awarded a golden Corona Vallaris in front of the entire assembly. While legionaries beat their swords on their shields in thunderous approval, the proconsul tied the thin braided gold band around Marcus's head.

Foolhardy and brash he was, but he'd made a real name for himself. He only wished he could erase the tragic memories of scalded legionaries falling from Alexandrium's battlements.

After the ceremony, Gabinius shared wine with Marcus in the praetorium. "Don't cease your efforts," he said. "I cannot afford squandering resources in this wasteland. I've too many important undertakings elsewhere. I'm hoping my improvements and building projects will help develop better relations with the natives. It's worked in other provinces. Given baths, proper theaters, and fora, they'll settle."

Marcus took note that Gabinius avoided discussing one of his current headaches: publicani. They were Syrian nationals responsible for collecting and meting out taxes for Rome. They hated him now, and had good reason. Gabinius had taken over tax collection himself, bolstering his own accounts for his projects. Usually loyal to Rome, some were so outraged they offered Alexander aid. For several months, Gabinius hunted them down and executed those he captured. Faced with more threats of revolt, he finally softened, cutting taxes. For now, the native population remained in a subdued calm. That is—natives besides Alexander.

"Let's hope these rebels concede to defeat soon," Marcus commented. "Otherwise, we could have a long, frustrating campaign ahead. We'd be playing cat and mouse a long while."

Gabinius snorted. "Yes, and right now the mouse's hole is here at Alexandrium."

"I'm hoping Alexander will soon see the futility in resisting. Especially since his own mother has."

It was true.

Alexander's mother had surprised everyone by showing up and pleading mercy for her son. Gabinius had ordered her to write Alexander a request for surrender. It was promptly delivered via an archer on an arrow shaft. Unfortunately, nothing had come of it.

"Continue the siege," Gabinius commanded. "Tomorrow I'm returning to Antioch and other pressing tasks."

No sooner had he spoken when a sentry poked his head into the tent. "Proconsul, a message was just shot out to us."

Anxious to hear any new development, Marcus had no intention of leaving unless Gabinius ordered him out. It was his lucky day. The proconsul read the message aloud:

Alexander to Gabinius,

Upon request of my mother, I'll surrender Alexandrium into your hands, provided I have your word that my men and my own person receive safe passage into Nabataea to forage what life we may find for ourselves.

Marcus's jaw dropped, and he immediately voiced his outrage, "Absolutely *not*! He deserves no leniency."

Gabinius stared at the message, eyebrow cocked. "Wars are costly, Antonius. Someday you'll understand that. If the man agrees to live quietly, it would end an expensive operation."

Stunned, Marcus exclaimed, "But we can't trust him. He shed Roman blood and even his own people's blood. Put an end to him. Call for the construction of a battering ram, and we'd have him in days."

Gabinius stared out the tent's entrance, lost in thought.

Desperate to plead his case, Marcus added, "Letting him go sends the wrong message, especially to those wounded while scaling those walls."

To Marcus's chagrin, Gabinius thought otherwise. He terminated the siege, letting Alexander go, unscathed, along with his men.

Morale was at an all-time low.

Marcus would never forget the day Alexander's men exited the fortress. Understandably enraged, Roman legionaries required restraint. Several tried to break through to kill Hasmoneans passing through the fortress gates, straight to freedom. Centurions had to intervene, preventing violence from breaking out. Nor was it easy afterward. After its inhabitants were safely away, discontented cohorts had to destroy Alexandrium. There was no profit in it—no pillaging or justice. It was just wrong.

Marcus was genuinely glad to be away from Gabinius for the time being.

Safely away from the rubble of Alexandrium, he, Servilius, and Siscuria relaxed, naked and damp, under a canopy of palms. They were on their way to Jerusalem, and here was a delightful, green, grassy oasis near the West Faria River. It was worth the stop. Legionaries were bathing, and men's laughter carried on the breeze.

"I still can't believe he did it," Servilius growled. "Men gave their lives to be rid of Alexander. Ho, when the Senate hears about this, they'll recall him. Wait and see."

Siscuria had recently arrived from Antioch, relieving Canidius, who returned there. Arriving late in the siege, and stoutly loyal to Gabinius, he refrained from comment. He seemed unsure what to make of the mess. "What do you think, Antonius?" he deferred.

Lately, Servilius seemed to enjoy pointing out Gabinius's flaws even more than Marcus's. Marcus had remained silent on the subject, though he harbored a strong opinion. Maybe it was time to voice it. "I think it would've been wiser making a few rebels angry about Alexander's death," he admitted. "Gabinius wasted time and effort pursuing someone he merely set free in the end." There. He'd said it. And for once, he and Servilius agreed on something.

"What of Gabinius?" Siscuria persisted. "Is Servilius right? Will Rome recall him?"

Marcus trod carefully. "Siscuria, an enormous amount of wealth and effort raised that siege. We fought some heated skirmishes and, in the end, reduced Alexandrium to rubble. But what did we gain? Our men received no plunder. Instead, they escorted the enemy out like slaves surrounding a lady's litter." He shook his head in disappointment. "Men pay dearly for disappointing the Senate, you know. They wind up losing dignitas and coin—or an entire province. Usually, all three. Gabinius fought this one with a dull blade. If this is how he governs, he won't last. Now once and for all, let's end the topic. There's no use puking it up repeatedly."

Marcus sat upright, lacing on his caligae. Snatching his tunic and gladius, he ambled off to inspect siege equipment.

He'd earned respect now. It no longer mattered whether Servilius liked him, for the others did. Yes, he was young, less experienced than they, but ever since Alexandrium, Marcus Antonius had become Gabinius's accepted second south of Antioch. And, even more importantly, legionaries loved him.

He'd often make suggestions to Gabinius with positive results. Even Alexandrium produced at least one profitable gain. Gabinius had finally agreed to build catapults and a battering ram. Next time there was a siege, they'd be ready.

Well-constructed and sturdy, the war machinery was untouched as a virgin. Marcus slapped the ram's iron head with his palm. Legionaries walked by, calling out greetings. Marcus acknowledged them, then leaned over to inspect the conveyance's wheels. Dismayed, he barked at the first soldier he saw, naked and dripping from bathing. "Dress yourself and grease these wheels. We can't afford new equipment breaking down."

"Yes, Commander," came the reply.

He was still studying the ram when he heard a familiar voice. "Commander."

It was a cavalryman called Tyrannio.

"Salve. What do you think of our new ally?" Marcus asked, proudly nodding toward the ram. "Our next siege will be easier, agreed?"

"Yes, sir. Sir, I thought you would want to know, Eumenius is ill."

Marcus frowned, turning to Tyrannio. "How so?"

"Two days past, while hammering tack, he took a nail through his hand. It turned septic. The physician's given him rest and excused him from duties."

Marcus shook his head in bafflement. The longer he commanded, the more every bizarre twist of fate keeping men healthy or ill, wounded or dead, mystified him. "Good. See that he rests and keep me informed."

Tyrannio saluted. "Yes, sir."

His mood turned dismal. Marcus watched Tyrannio walk away. Gabinius's senselessness, his friend injured—what else could go wrong?

Everything changed.

Aristobulus, Alexander's father, held captive in Rome by Pompeius, escaped. Having a stronger claim for his brother's priesthood than his son, he hastened back to Judea. With him came Alexander's brother, Antigonus.

Aristobulus was a shrewd man. He rallied not only Hasmoneans but devoutly religious Jews who despised King Antipater and Hyrcanus.

Until now, Gabinius had been unconcerned about the orthodox, conservative population. But Aristobulus's return changed everything. Here was a mature leader. Commanding, utterly ruthless, he was politically savvy. Devout Judeans flocked to his cause under a guise of piety to their God.

While Marcus led a weary legion into Jerusalem following Alexander's release, Aristobulus arrived at the ruins of Alexandrium with newly gathered rebels and immediately began building new fortifications.

Once Gabinius learned of it, he was livid. That a damnable, self-proclaimed despot escaped Rome, under the considerable noses of senatorial aristocrats? This only furthered his province's havoc. He ordered Marcus, Siscuria, and Servilius to turn around— straight back to Alexandrium.

But upon their return, Aristobulus and his forces had vanished. Forewarned of the Romans' approach, their retreat left little evidence of activity. Only fouled wells and the beginnings of masonry walls betrayed insurgent activity.

Forced to ration the little water they had left, Marcus led a frustrated, dust-covered Roman legion back across the desert toward Jerusalem—for the third time.

About ten miles outside Alexandrium, he spied Siscuria's advance guard ahead. They'd rounded up a large group of Judeans, who knelt in the dust, hands bound.

Marcus trotted his horse to where Siscuria waited.

The lupine-faced officer grinned brightly. "Chisels and picks. Looks to me like a bunch of stonemasons. And they're quite thirsty too."

Marcus scanned the group. "Who speaks for you?" he demanded.

Siscuria nodded toward an older man with a scraggly, graying beard. "That one knows some Greek."

Fimbria hauled the weary Hebrew up, shoving him in front of Marcus's horse.

"Who are you?" Marcus demanded in Greek.

"Nahshon, son of Jeziel," the man answered, staring straight ahead. His Greek was barely comprehendible, and the others probably spoke nothing but Aramaic.

"What are you doing with those tools? Ah, trowels too," Marcus observed. "Rebuilt any walls lately?"

Silence.

"And no water? You Judeans should know better, taking a hike in the desert without bringing something to drink." Marcus was in a foul temper, weary from pursuing an enemy that kept vanishing.

Nahshon glared back defiantly. Fimbria whacked him from behind with the butt of his javelin.

The Judean staggered, catching his breath. "Aristobulus promised us freedom from Rome if we helped rebuild Alexandrium and win him the priesthood. But his spies reported that you were returning, so he fouled the water. He and his army fled, leaving us nothing to drink."

Marcus shook his head. "Following a leader who strands you in the middle of a desert with no water." He chewed his lip. Aristobulus was probably only a day or two ahead since these pitiful wretches were thirsty but still hearty. "Where's Aristobulus now?"

Nahshon said nothing. Marcus nodded at Fimbria, who came forward, pressing his javelin's point against the Judean's throat. Still no answer.

Losing his temper, Marcus changed tactics. "Ah, well. Since you're so slow of tongue, we'll crucify some of your friends. Maybe then you'll recall some more Greek."

Nahshon's head jerked up. Eyes panicky, he stuttered, "A ha-half day's ride."

"How many men does he have?"

"Eight thousand, perhaps."

"Eight thousand?" Servilius fumed, riding up. "How'd he get so many men?"

Siscuria silenced Servilius with a hard look, shaking his head. But he was right to be concerned. Those numbers were exceedingly high for just recruiting men in villages along the way.

"Someone joined him," Marcus declared, directing his bitterness to the bedraggled Jew. "Someone with a substantial army."

Nahshon just stared at the ground, remaining silent.

"Very well, Fimbria, ride back and tell the engineering unit to start hauling out timbers."

Fimbria obeyed, turning to go when Siscuria stopped him, all eyes back on Nahshon.

The aging patriarch gazed upward, hatred in his eyes. "Pitholaus of Jerusalem joined him with over four thousand," he spat.

Pitholaus?

Marcus's jaw dropped as the betrayal sank in. Pitholaus had ridden to his aid in Nabataea, along with Malichus. He'd even commanded the other cavalry wing outside Jerusalem. Mars, he hoped Malichus wasn't involved.

"Where are they going?" he demanded. "And remember, I'm hot, thirsty, and irritated. Evade my questions again and my man here will scourge the skin off your back like peeling a pear."

Nahshon whispered hoarsely, "Machaerus."

Machaerus. Another desert fort, larger than Alexandrium.

Thinking aloud, Marcus turned to Siscuria and Servilius, switching to Latin. "If Gabinius doesn't know Pitholaus is a traitor, Aristobulus could easily return and put Jerusalem under siege. Without us, it wouldn't have enough defenders. We should return to Jerusalem. Gabinius needs to know about this."

Gabinius's decision was that they take Machaerus. Marcus just hoped that was where Aristobulus had really gone. Scouts rode ahead to assure the rebel was indeed there. He wanted no ugly surprises.

Then, while on the march, misfortune hit hard. Tyrannio galloped up from his position in the cavalry unit with troubling news for Marcus.

"Sir, Eumenius fainted off his horse. We've put him in one of the mule carts."

Marcus left command to Siscuria and rode back with the cavalryman to see to his friend's care.

Eumenius had never been as pale. His head bounced against some sacks of sand inside the small wagon. Beneath a soiled bandage, his injured hand oozed fluid. Through the wrappings, its grotesque swelling was obvious. Even the rest of his arm farther up was turning an unnatural dark color.

"I want a medic to ride in the cart with him until we stop for the day," Marcus ordered.

That evening, he left the praetorium and walked through a veritable legionary tent forest toward the cavalry unit. Tyrannio had sent word that Eumenius's condition was steadily deteriorating.

The legion's chief physician had been with him for hours. Marcus feared for his friend. From the sound of it, Eumenius wasn't far from paying the Ferryman.

The cavalry unit's encampment was a good walk away. A camp of over five thousand men and camp followers covered considerable space. Soldiers huddling together at a cooking fire called out greetings as he passed. One man offered him rations. It warmed Marcus, their faces lighting up at his presence.

Upon his arrival, Tyrannio stepped outside. His face was dark. "Commander."

"Is the physician still here?"

"Yes. The infection is terrible. Eumenius's spirit wanders."

As soon as he entered, Marcus set his teeth at the strong, sickly odor.

"His flesh rots," Icilius, the physician, explained. "When such sickness enters a man's blood, little can be done."

Tyrannio dragged his own cot over, and Marcus sat down.

Eumenius looked dreadful. His color had gone gray. Though open, his eyes were sunken and glassy.

"Antonius?" he whispered, so low that Marcus barely heard.

"Yes, I'm here."

Eumenius smiled weakly through cracked lips. "All this because I was clumsy with a hammer." He closed his eyes, then suddenly jerked back to consciousness. "Don't let him take my arm," he mumbled.

Marcus looked at Icilius inquiringly.

The physician shrugged. "His arm is poisoned. Infection may already be in the rest of him. We won't know unless we remove it."

Merciful gods.

Eumenius weakly shook his head back and forth where he lay. "I won't be a freak." He whispered. "I won't be an invalid."

Marcus swallowed, responding calmly, "Many men have lived through amputation, Eumenius. You wouldn't be the first. It may be the only way to save your life."

Eumenius shook his head stubbornly. "No. I'll live whole or not at all."

Close to Eumenius's side, Icilius lifted a stained coverlet off the wounded hand. Marcus grimaced at what he saw. Unbandaged, it was as glossy as a ripe melon—turning black. Icilius took a scalpel from his kit, firmly slicing into Eumenius's flesh across a rotten area that was splitting from severe inflammation. Yellowish pus and runny blood oozed from miniscule cracks in the bloated skin. At the point of incision, Icilius squeezed from both sides, pressing it out like paste.

Disgusted, Marcus focused on his poor friend. He was sweating, teeth chattering.

"Commander," Icilius said, compelling Marcus to look at the wound again. "See these punctures—here and here? I lanced him twice since his fall. My incisions aren't healing. If he refuses amputation, there's nothing more to be done."

"You have no slaves," Eumenius murmured to Marcus.

Confused at the odd change of subjects, Marcus answered, "Slaves? No. Only at home, friend." It seemed Eumenius's mind was going. *Slaves?*

"Help me..."

"Anything," Marcus assured him.

"There's part of me you don't know. A dark story..."

"We all have one."

"But I broke Roman law."

Marcus frowned, listening more intently.

"I have a boy who is a slave."

"A boy?" Marcus repeated, perplexed.

Eumenius nodded, pausing between phrases to pant in shallow breaths. "Legally, I'm a slave. I belonged to a wealthy landlord on the island of Paros. I loved a slave girl in his household. When she bore my child, my master, Dracon, only allowed the babe to live if I swore never to touch her again. He wanted her for himself."

"So you killed him?" Marcus guessed at the answer before it came.

A tear coursed down the side of Eumenius's nose. "When she refused him, he raped and strangled her. So yes, I murdered him."

327

ANTONIUS ~ SON OF ROME

Marcus wondered whether to believe him. Beyond hope now, Eumenius might be babbling foolishness. For a slave to murder his owner for any reason was a heinous, unforgivable crime, punishable only by death.

"I stole my baby boy and some coin from Dracon," Eumenius explained. "We fled on the first ship off the island. For a while, I wandered the streets of Athens, doing odd jobs to buy milk for my son. But he was growing thin and sickly. I was afraid he'd die. Kyros offered to pay me for assisting in his horse trade. And he had a slave woman who nursed my boy. When I came with you here to Syria, I left my son with Kyros."

Marcus stared at him. It seemed so unbelievable.

Suddenly, Eumenius grabbed Marcus's wrist with surprising strength. "*Find* him," he begged. "Find my Eros. Send for him, I beg you. I want him to see more of the world."

"Eros?" Marcus repeated softly.

"Please—a rising military officer like you needs slaves. You'd treat him well, I know it."

Marcus didn't know what to say. Surely, this "Eros" was but a child.

Eumenius moaned in pain, tears running freely now. "At least I'll die with a clean spirit. There are horrors some men take with them in death. But not me."

Marcus studied Eumenius. His last sentence struck a troubling chord of truth.

Eumenius knew nothing of his gambling debts, of Fadia, and the men he'd killed in the Subura. Slave or not, this man was steadfast and good. Because of him, he'd met Gabinius. Eumenius was part of Marcus's fate, their lives interwoven for a purpose. If he really did have a son, Marcus couldn't refuse him.

Gently, he placed a hand on Eumenius's head. "Rest for now. I promise that if your son is with Kyros, I'll retrieve him and care for him. He'll be my personal slave."

Eumenius heaved a long sigh. His features relaxed. "You're a great man, Antonius. Now I can rest." In sheer relief, he closed his eyes.

Moving his hand to Eumenius's head, Marcus sighed. Hot as a brazier in winter. An irksome fly buzzed as Icilius rubbed sulfur salve on the dying man's ruined hand, adding to the stench. There was nothing more to do here. Killing enemies of Rome was something Marcus did without thinking. But when it came to seeing his own suffer...

Standing slowly, he gestured to Icilius, drawing him away from Eumenius's cot. "If he's in great misery, give him something to gently hasten his end. When the time comes, I'll bury him myself."

Marcus left the reeking tent. Oh, what he'd give to have Fadia's comforting embrace right now. But this was his new normal: life without her. There were moments—thank the gods they were few—in which his heart bled as though she had died only yesterday.

Tonight was one of those times.

Before the tent's entrance, he pulled his cloak closer for warmth. He studied the heavens, breathing in clean, fresh air. Marcus loved the night sky. There were few things as peaceful and lovely as twinkling stars. The firmament was so constant and unchanging in comparison to the unexpected and often harsh realities of military life.

He often wondered if Fadia was up there. Sometimes it felt as though she was very near. He had trouble believing that the Underworld was so dark and unforgiving. It seemed more just for a human spirit to soar upward, becoming one with the stars.

That's where Fadia was. He was sure of it.

CHAPTER XXVI
55 BC

COMMANDER MARCUS ANTONIUS TO PITHOLAUS
of Jerusalem:
You are a traitor to Rome. If captured, you face
crucifixion. Think on this: laying down arms spares
the blood of your countrymen. Convince Aristobulus
or his son to surrender.

Pitholaus of Jerusalem to Commander Marcus
Antonius:
Malichus may tolerate Romans, but no longer will
I stand by and accept the rule of unclean Gentiles.
My men are pleased to shed Roman blood. Prepare
for battle.

The Romans were prepared for a siege, not for a sudden

confrontation with Aristobulus and Antigonus outside Machaerus. The rolling, rocky landscape concealed the Hasmonean army until the legion crested a rise. Marcus barely had time enough to organize his front lines before Aristobulus attacked.

Yet there was one fortunate factor aiding the Romans. Clearly, Aristobulus had put his army together hurriedly, without much training. They had quantity, not quality.

As the fighting wore down, Marcus stopped his exhausted horse. He let his reins rest on his animal's neck and reached behind his saddle to pull out some posca. Wineskin to his lips, he drank several mouthfuls, then deftly loosened his helmet's strap beneath his chin.

That's when it happened. Two Hasmoneans came out of nowhere and attacked on his shield side, spooking his horse and nearly throwing him to the ground. One of the bastards managed to hang on to his saddle girth, about to stab his horse and bring it down. Marcus dropped the wineskin, cursing. His helmet clanked to the ground, and he snatched his reins. The second attacker grabbed at his shield, immobilizing it. Unable to use it to either offensively strike out or defend himself, it was useless.

His life was over. One moment of weakness, wanting a drink, and that was it.

With one arm still sheathed in the shield that his enemy was clutching, his other hand was busy with the reins. Terrified, his horse squealed in panic, rearing. There was no way Marcus could fight them off—except with his left leg. He kicked out as hard as he could, and the man trying to knife his horse missed. Marcus's leg took the blow instead.

Strange. It didn't really hurt at first. It just felt like a swift kick in the calf.

If the Hasmoneans had come out of nowhere, the three legionaries who saved Marcus's life materialized like ghosts. They took the two Hasmoneans from behind, stabbing them repeatedly.

Gaius Naevius, Marcus Ahala, and Manius Brocchus. These three men saved Marcus Antonius's life that day. He'd see them rewarded and would never forget their names.

In the frenzied fight, the Hasmoneans tore through a full cohort, exacting heavier Roman casualties than usual. But legionary discipline prevailed. With so many of their numbers dead on the field, Aristobulus and his men fled back to their fort—Machaerus.

But Marcus had his battering ram now, and tomorrow the cat would eat the mouse.

Throat sore at every swallow from shouting, his eyes burned from the blazing desert. Looking down, he winced at the nasty open gash on his left calf. Blood drenched his lower leg, staining his horse where his leg hung limply. Dark droplets dripped off his boot, slick and soaking the leather soles.

Siscuria cantered up, halting even with him. "Worst part of war, this is. I just ordered lads to start carrying wounded to the ox carts. As for them," he tilted his head toward some dead Hasmoneans, "the birds'll pick 'em clean in two days." Looking up, he laughed harshly. "See—they're already here."

Marcus silently gazed up. Vultures were making lazy loops overhead.

Siscuria wrapped his reins around one horn of his saddle, stretching around with his arms until his back popped. "Servilius is supervising entrenchment a half mile from here."

"Gratias." Marcus acknowledged, shifting uncomfortably. His leg pulsed in pain. "How many lost?"

"Near eight hundred, probably. But don't you worry, Antonius. We took at least four thousand. Tyrannio and your cavalry chased a good thousand of them the opposite direction from Machaerus. And guess who was leading their retreat? Our man Alexander!"

Marcus widened his eyes a little at that, despite his injury. "Really? That should leave around three thousand to man the fortress."

"I guess so." Siscuria barked a laugh, reaching over and clapping

Marcus firmly on the back. "We did well, I think. And once Gabinius sees that leg, he'll give you another corona for valor."

Marcus ignored him. "I want cavalry posted on all sides of Machaerus tonight. None of those bastards are getting out this time. And delegate cohorts to move among the fallen. Kill any rebels still alive. Our men may have plundering rights. However, if anyone finds Pitholaus of Jerusalem, send him directly to me."

"Will do. Camp's over there, beyond that rise," Siscuria directed with a nod. "And look after that leg. I want to hear what happened later."

Steering his weary horse away, Marcus plodded in the direction Siscuria indicated. Hopefully, tomorrow would bring an end to this annoying game of chase.

Roman camps were always set up the same, two long avenues crisscrossing at the commander's tent, known as the praetorium. Marcus always fortified his camps, regardless of how long his men remained in one place.

Legionaries hailed him as his horse passed the trenches they were digging. Fimbria was driving a final stake into the praetorium when he arrived. Marcus dismounted, landing painfully on his bloody left leg. He leaned into his horse, gasping, eyes squeezed shut.

"You're wounded, sir," Fimbria observed, hastening over, concern in his eyes.

"One got me pretty deep in the leg."

"Shall I find Icilius? We can't let it fester."

Fimbria was probably thinking of Eumenius. During yesterday's march, they'd stopped just long enough to bury the Greek.

Marcus shook his head. "Give me a little time, then anyone will do." Icilius's staff would be busy enough this night.

Fimbria always left an amphora inside the tent containing cheap wine that Marcus, Siscuria, and Servilius shared. Once gone, posca was their only option, so they used it sparingly, despite its low quality.

Marcus eased back onto his cot, propping up his injured leg. Then he reached under his cot, fishing for his cup. Unstopping the amphora, he plunged his cup in until it overflowed. Delirium would be sweet relief. He didn't even bother adding water. Instead, he licked at the wine sloshing over the lip. No point wasting any. With a deep breath, he moved his bloody extremity closer and clenched his teeth. With a slight tilt to the cup, out poured half the wine, drizzling over his lower leg. It flowed into the laceration, then down, soaking into his cot. Eyes squeezed shut, Marcus groaned, pressing his face against his knee in agony.

As the pain subsided, he leaned back again, stretching out and plumping his cloak beneath his head like a cushion. He lifted the wine cup to his lips, swallowing the remainder. After that, he twisted over to dip the cup into the amphora for more.

This went on for some time until he ceased counting cups. Hazy warmth dimmed his mind. He dozed for a time, then came to with a start.

The tent flap had snapped open, and a tall shadow cast over him. "Next time wear greaves," snapped Servilius.

"Tried them once," Marcus muttered. "Didn't like them."

"Fool, not arming yourself adequately will result in losing more than a leg out there."

Marcus's head swam. A few more and he'd be ready for the seamstress to start sewing.

He stared at his leg. It burned with searing pain. A bright red stain had colored the end of his cot crimson. Once more he reached back, his cup sloshing into the amphora.

"Io, Bacchus! Leaving any for us?" Servilius challenged as Marcus drank.

Before the final dregs, he replied, "Depends on how fast I get drunk from it."

Servilius just stood there, staring down at him. Gods, the man was exasperating.

"Go find someone to come sew me up, would you?" Marcus suggested. "Unless you want to do it yourself? You'd probably enjoy causing me pain."

Servilius glowered down at him. "You're one sick bastard, Antonius."

At least he left for a while. When he did return, it was with a youth who wore a bloodstained tunic and carried a basket of twine and bone needles.

Damn. This was bound to feel nice. The boy passed one of his instruments through a lamp's flame several times.

Mind fuzzy with drink, Marcus noticed it was dark outside. When the needle first pierced his flesh, he cried out. All the while, idiot Servilius sat on the cot across from him, watching the show.

"Here," Marcus hissed. "Make yourself useful and fill my cup."

Servilius glared at him, incensed at another order.

"Sorry," he belched from his toes. "I've no poison for you to put in it." Laughing at his own joke, he swallowed what Servilius gave him after only four long swigs, screwing up his face at the sour, undiluted relief. After another pierce of the needle, he complained, "What are you using down there, boy, a tent peg? Easy, I'm not a piece of meat."

This time the youth glanced up. "Sorry, sir."

More dips of the needle. In his drunken state, Marcus considered how much pain Fadia had endured before she died. Their final words together had been so quiet, so calm. She'd been so brave. Gods, how he missed her.

"Ever been married, Servilius?" Drunk and in fiery pain, Marcus babbled. "I married a freedwoman, and I loved her." He felt dizzy and light—drifting. Sweat beaded on his forehead. "I really did. I loved her so..." His cup thudded to the ground.

The boy got up, wiping bloody hands on his soiled tunic. Marcus closed his eyes in relief.

"Servilius, Siscuria—whoever you are—wake me. Wake me before dawn. We take Machaerus tomorrow. It'll be ours."

Speech slurred, his body and spirit relaxed onto the cot in a welcome, wine-induced torpor.

Commander Marcus Antonius to Aristobulus:
Surrender Machaerus and you'll save the lives of
many. Hand over the traitor Pitholaus and I will see
to your honorable treatment.

Boom.

Centurions were counting rhythmically in unison until the next strike. Like a fine group of percussionists entertaining at a feast, it all happened on cue.

Boom.

There was no need for Marcus to count with them anymore. The next strike would sound, sure as honey filled a hive. He watched his legionaries bearing the mighty hammer, moving forward in cadence. Relentlessly, the ram struck the reinforced portal, and another cloud of dust arose.

Boom.

Sitting still as possible on his mount, Marcus kept a firm rein on his horse and patted its neck. With each impact, it quivered with a start.

Boom.

"How's the leg, Antonius?" queried Siscuria, riding up with Servilius.

Marcus wiped sweat from his forehead, his jaw set in stubborn determination. Truthfully, he had a fever. "Well enough to carry me over that wall."

Servilius shook his head. "Your foolhardy, reckless nature will turn you to ash."

Marcus glared at him from under his helmet. Too bad he wasn't within punching distance.

Boom.

All three horses started.

"I'll not die today," he assured them both, "because I intend to give that dog Pitholaus an appropriate greeting."

"I'm with you." Siscuria pledged with a nod.

Marcus shook his head. "Gratias, but I need you commanding cavalry. See that the perimeters are secure once we get in. Kill any of them making a run for it."

Boom.

"What about me?" Servilius asked.

Marcus cocked his head, staring at him in dislike. "Oh, best to keep you here where you're safe. That way you and Gabinius can see that each of the prisoners go to slave markets for the highest prices. That should please your economic sensibility."

Boom—crash!

Before Servilius could retort, more cracking split the silence. Stonework around the heavy wooden entry crumbled and fell with a sonorous rumble. As chunks settled, gritty dust ascended, clouding everyone's view.

Next, the doorway collapsed, and Machaerus was open.

Marcus blinked his eyes to moisten them. He'd have to wait to sound an advance. Too much detritus was still settling, and legionaries nearest the fortress were choking and gagging on the gray cloud billowing toward them. Centurions were ordering everyone to use rags and mask their faces. In the meantime, Siscuria took off with the cavalry, securing points around the fortress to prevent anyone from escape.

It seemed like eons, but Marcus was finally able to begin entry. Swinging off his horse and drawing his gladius, he stepped into the cloud of grit at the infantry's head. Shield in front and slightly forward, he kept his blade at a ready position to stab if a Judean blocked his path. Men around him grumbled in confusion and anxiety, everyone's visibility limited in the dust.

"Look to your footing and watch out in front," he shouted, climbing over rubble. Marcus searched through the dust for anything moving. Hawking sandy grit out of his mouth, he heard yelling just ahead.

Someone was rallying the remnant of Hasmoneans, urging their numbers forward, toward the incoming Romans. They pounded their shields with swords, but the only Roman response was the steady sound of men scrambling through the littered opening without stopping. Turning toward those behind him, Marcus yelled encouragement, "Who wants this revolt over?"

The response was a cacophonous roar of voices, drowning out the Hasmoneans. They kept moving forward, kicking and shoving stones out of the way. Marcus was the first man in, and he stood tall atop the remains of the ramparts. Four cohorts poured in at his back. He waved them through.

Two mounted men caught his eye. In brilliantly colored garb, the older one rode a handsome white horse. Marcus's best guess was that he was Aristobulus. Next to him was a younger man of powerful build carrying a richly plumed helmet under one arm. Antigonus, Alexander's brother? Both wore polished bronze armor, surrounded by an honor guard of at least a hundred.

Both sides came together in a rush. It was only a matter of time before Rome conquered. Marcus hated the victory's cost, though. Eight hundred sacrificed yesterday for today's success.

He watched closely as the bastion of fighting Judeans in front retreated. The young man holding his helmet turned his horse, spurring toward the stronghold in Machaerus's courtyard. He obviously preferred to save himself. The one Marcus assumed was Aristobulus remained where he was atop the white steed. His honor guard started fighting the first cohorts to reach them.

Men darted everywhere. Romans were entering the broken portal like locusts onto ripe fields. They were eager for blood, eager to end this chase once and for all.

When defeat seemed imminent, Aristobulus finally swung off

his horse. He slapped it on its rump, and the animal cantered off. Then he disappeared into Machaerus's hall.

Within minutes, Marcus joined the centurions of the legion's Second Cohort. The soldiers diligently pried and muscled the iron-clad doors leading to the palace gate. It gave way with a resonant scrape. Marcus pushed through, limping slightly on his wounded leg and flanked by legionaries.

As the Romans entered the scene, one Judean officer panicked, shaking his head and muttering to himself. He raised an angry fist to the heavens, then, drawing his sword, pressed it against a wall, hilt first, and pushed himself into the point. Marcus watched him sink slowly. Red smeared the wall all the way to the floor. For several seconds, the suicide held sway, nobody saying a word.

Outside, however, things intensified, individual voices yelling in Latin, "Secure the entrances!"

"How many are there?"

"Can't tell—run around the side. We've got the front!"

There was much tramping in the corridors behind where Marcus stood. Sounds of nail-shod feet echoed as a second wave of Romans entered the hall from the other direction, pila pointed threateningly at Hasmoneans.

Marcus stood proudly, shifting his injured calf only slightly. He ignored the fact that his bandage was red with fresh blood. Gladius drawn, his eyes landed upon a solitary figure in the back of the chamber.

Pitholaus, the traitor.

Aristobulus was Gabinius's main target, but for Marcus Antonius, Pitholaus was who he wanted. There were many things Marcus could forgive. Treachery was not one of them.

"Pitholaus of Jerusalem," Marcus called out in perfect Greek. "Pleasant seeing you again. No need hiding behind your comrades. Last time we were face-to-face, we were allies, you and I." He spat on the floor.

Pitholaus stood his ground, face still as stone.

Marcus grinned, beckoning to him with his free hand. "Come

here. We were once brothers in arms, were we not? We shared wine while playing dice and even ate together in my tent, sleeping in the same camp. How much silver did I win from you the night I bought you a whore? Hmmm?" It was difficult making the last phrase sound cordial. But Marcus pulled it off nicely, he thought.

Aristobulus smiled graciously, stepping forward from where he stood near Antigonus. "You fought well, Roman. I'm sure Pitholaus desires to greet you—respectfully, as you deserve."

Pitholaus sheathed his sword in disgust, glaring at Aristobulus. But he stepped out from behind the other Judean officers and slowly walked toward Marcus.

Marcus stood with his feet slightly apart in a statuesque stance. Extending his left hand, he offered it in a friendly gesture.

Pitholaus came forward, and they clasped hands. "Antonius," he muttered quietly.

Marcus's grip closed like a vice, holding Pitholaus firmly in place. "Pitholaus of Jerusalem, I never demand anything from my soldiers that I'm unwilling to give. And the foremost thing I require is *loyalty*."

Fear flashed across Pitholaus's face as he tried to pull away. Marcus clutched his wrist securely, unmoving, preventing escape. "Do you really think we Romans tolerate betrayal?" he asked in a dangerous, soft voice. "Do you take us for idiots?"

"No, I take you for foul, unclean sons of bitches," Pitholaus spat.

Marcus raised his strong voice, and it resonated in the hall. "Let me tell you something, Pitholaus of Jerusalem. I think it's better being a loyal son of a bitch than to die a traitor. At least I'll rest with honor in the end."

So quickly did he gut Pitholaus with his gladius that everyone stood frozen—stunned. There was a sudden outpouring of blood, then Pitholaus sank to his knees, eyes wide in astonishment. Both his hands clutched at the wound, and he made a withering cry.

Swiftly, Marcus withdrew his weapon and released the Judean, who slumped sideways onto the decorative floor tiles. The stain on the stone floor grew larger, seeping its way into the cracks of masonry.

Marcus wiped his blade neatly on Pitholaus's still form. Then with a hiss, he sheathed it back into its scabbard. "You're all prisoners of the Senate and people of Rome," he stated to the silent, stunned bystanders. "Your fates will be decided by Proconsul Gabinius upon reaching Jerusalem."

Pain shot through his leg as he pivoted about. He clenched his teeth, willing himself not to limp, and walked away from the captive Judeans and two dead men—one of them a traitor righteously killed.

"Wait until you hear this." Siscuria slid in next to Marcus at the table, away from other legionaries, plopping down a bowl of porridge.

Marcus eyed him, his left leg propped on a bench. It had been well over a month, and it was healing slowly, always looking and feeling angriest after heavy usage. Sweaty and hot, he'd just returned from morning cavalry drills and was nursing watered wine. Siscuria leaned in, avoiding the curiosity of nearby legionaries. "King Ptolemy Auletes of Egypt arrived here in Jerusalem last night under Roman guard and private escort. He traveled light, nothing fancy. Wants to avoid causing a stir or letting people in Egypt know he's next door. Anyway, Servilius overheard him talking to Gabinius. Ptolemy wants military assistance to win his throne back."

Marcus whistled, causing other men to look their way again.

Siscuria leaned in closer, glancing about, whispering low. "And he's willing to pay. Servilius said Ptolemy offered Gabinius *ten thousand* talents."

"If he accepts without senatorial decree, he'd definitely face recall. What do you think? Will he do it?"

Siscuria shrugged, dipping bread into his porridge. "Servilius said Antipater's feasting the king and Gabinius tonight. Can you much blame him if he's tempted? Ten thousand talents. It ought to be illegal being that rich."

Marcus spoke his thoughts aloud. "Being recalled wouldn't even matter. Exiled with that much coin, he could live like Midas, and it would scarcely matter where." There was an uneasy silence before Marcus queried, "Would you support it, Siscuria?" He awaited Siscuria's answer, trifling with puffy scar tissue forming on his wounded leg.

Siscuria grunted, shaking his head. "I want nothing of the sort. I serve in *Syria*. Gabinius does too, if he keeps his senses."

Marcus smiled in satisfaction. He stretched his leg out farther, leaning back against the wall. Siscuria absently knocked a beetle off the table before it could crawl into his bowl.

"How would one go about taking Alexandria?" Marcus wondered. "It's a port city—approachable by sea. But if you had a land army pushing through from the east..." He paused, narrowing his eyes, his voice dropping to a whisper, "Mars above, you'd be virtually unstoppable."

"A *land* army? From the East?" Siscuria scoffed. "Are you mad, Antonius? You'd have to take the Way of the Sea. Not even caravan drivers favor that route. Put it out of your mind. It's barely autumn. You'd never survive."

Marcus smiled to himself. His sense of adventure and opportunity was already spinning a scheme.

CHAPTER XXVII

JULIA ANTONIA IN ROME TO HER SON
Commander Marcus Antonius, under command of
Aulus Gabinius, Proconsul Provinciae in Syria:

Dearest Marcus, I sacrifice daily for your health
and safety. Surely, you must be away from Antioch,
as I've heard nothing from you in over a year. I pray
my letters reach you.

Rome recently hosted a foreign guest: King
Ptolemy of Egypt. He mingled with the most
influential, of course. Pompeius Magnus, Marcus
Crassus, and the like. Aurelia and I were at Pompeius's
new theater one night seeing a play when he arrived
with his retinue. Oh, what a gaudy display of riches.
His slaves wore enough gold to have been kings
themselves. Sitting surrounded by bodyguards, his
presence caused such a fuss it was more entertaining
watching him than the comedy.

Our cousin Caesar is the subject of every Senate
meeting and dinner party. He crossed the Rhine,

building a long bridge over it. Recently, I heard he intends to cross over into Britannia, subduing savage tribes there.

Hybrida's trial ended. The Senate declared him guilty of corruption in Macedonia. They're exiling him to some remote island in Greece. Poor Antonia is devastated. I've taken her into our domus to live.

Iophon has taken over Syrianus's duties. I allow the old man to greet guests and attend me at parties. He's still capable of those sorts of things.

Take care in all you do, my son. I awake each morning with you on my heart, closing my eyes at night with you still resting there.

Write soon, I beg you.

Commander Marcus Antonius in Jerusalem to Julia Antonia in Rome:

If you are well, I am well. I've not been in Antioch for over a year. Recent duties have left very little opportunity to write personal correspondence. I don't know when I shall return home. Many things here remain unsettled.

If Aurelia writes to Caesar, implore her to mention my continued interest in serving him.

I pray the gods keep you and our domus safe and in good health.

Marcus climbed the stairs leading to Gabinius's quarters in Antipater's Jerusalem palace. It wasn't grandiose like Antioch's Seleucid bastion. Instead, it possessed simple patriarchal dignity.

Evidently, Antipater loved all things green. Hosts of fruit trees greeted guests upon entering. Everywhere, ivy choked ancient columns and wound its way up staircases. The gardens sent a pang of homesickness through Marcus's core.

He looked up, sensing another's presence. Gabinius stood in the doorway of his study, waiting. "Welcome, Antonius. How's the leg?"

"Improving, sir."

Gabinius clasped his hand, smacking him hard on the back and leading the way into his study. "So—I suppose you heard. Ptolemy is here, asking for help."

"That's in part why I requested to see you, yes."

"Then we must chat. Sit down."

The proconsul pulled a cord, and Marcus heard a faint chime in the next room. Moments later, the boy Triton materialized with an assortment of refreshments: fruit, boiled eggs, and two cups of bright red pomegranate juice.

"Not your favorite wine, but drink up. I'm told it's good for the body," Gabinius invited heartily.

Marcus took a sip. It had a tangy flavor. "Sir, one reason I asked to see you is to request use of a courier for a personal need."

"For what, exactly?"

"Eumenius recently died and left property to me."

"Property? Really? Where?"

Marcus chose his words carefully. "Kyros the horse trader, in Athens, has a slave in his possession. The boy was bequeathed to me."

"As long as it's not a woman. For that, visit a brothel."

"He's not for sex."

"Then consider it done. We may need more horses from Kyros anyway, and he was fair as any man to deal with. I'll dispatch a message for you tomorrow via courier."

"Gratias, sir."

Gabinius clapped his hands together, rubbing them in excited relish. "Now—I need your help." Leaning back in his chair, he placed his empty cup back on the tray. "As everyone in the palace already knows, Ptolemy wants me to reinstate him onto the Egyptian throne."

"That would be rewarding, no doubt."

"Siscuria candidly urged I not entangle myself in Egyptian affairs. He wants no part of it. Servilius voiced his opinion shortly after overhearing the initial conversation between the king and me. You can well imagine how he felt."

Marcus grinned, lifting his cup again to drink.

"If Canidius were here," Gabinius continued, "he might show interest, but only if you did. He's a follower, that one. You, however, are different from them all. Only you own the nerve and mettle to undertake such a venture. Will you help me?"

"Sounds exciting. But what would my compensation be?"

Gabinius pursed his lips, avoiding eye contact as well as an answer. He gazed toward the window. "You'd gain high favor with the King of Egypt."

Marcus smiled slightly. "Ah, that would be most advantageous if I ever wanted to visit the pyramids. Come, sir. From what I've heard, King Ptolemy's unable to manage his own family, much less his country. I say this assuming you've no senatorial nod for this undertaking. You could lose your position here without official sanction." Before Gabinius could reply, Marcus quickly queried, "What exactly did King Ptolemy promise in return for such a demanding task?"

The proconsul narrowed his eyes, and Marcus sensed his displeasure. The old man usually favored him, but who knew how far that sentiment extended? There were traits of Gabinius's character that Marcus had come to dislike. His not wanting to dirty his hands on the battlefield was at the top of the list.

"Damn Servilius," Gabinius muttered. "He told you."

"He told me nothing." Siscuria did.

The proconsul sighed, drumming his fingers in an annoying rhythm before stopping abruptly. "Ptolemy will pay me ten thousand talents for taking Alexandria," he disclosed, speaking in a hushed tone. Sighing, he walked to the front of his desk and leaned against it. "If successful, he could be generous in rewarding a commanding officer of mine as well. However, what you say is true. It'll be a difficult move to defend in the Senate. In fact, it'll be the greatest gamble of my career."

"So I take it you'd want me as your second?" Marcus asked, rising and thoughtfully strolling around the room. It was spacious, attached to a corner terrace with large, open windows on two of the four walls. Idly walking its perimeters, he caressed a stone windowsill overlooking Jerusalem's Horse Gate.

"Second-in-command, yes," answered the proconsul.

Well, there would be a price to pay if Gabinius wanted his help putting Ptolemy's royal ass back on the throne. Marcus deserved a share in the reward. And he wanted Gabinius to unleash him from his side and recommend him to Caesar. All of this *before* becoming embroiled in a senatorial recall.

Gabinius interrupted his reverie. "It's a generous offer I extend, Antonius. Very generous. Remember, if it weren't for me, you'd probably still be with some old, impotent philosopher in Athens, reading Plato."

"And were it not for me," Marcus shot back evenly, "you'd have no cavalry disciplined enough to run down Alexander's rebels. Pitholaus's cunning would have led to your possible downfall, and you'd be short two prisoners by the name of Aristobulus and Antigonus. Proconsul Gabinius, I've shown you my loyalty. Now I ask for something in return."

Gabinius growled testily, "I commissioned you, against my better judgment in lieu of your sordid past. I overlooked other fine men, casting favor upon you more than once and rewarding you with military honors in front of an entire legion. How dare you insinuate I'm indebted to you?"

"You're the proconsul," Marcus pressed, softening his voice. "You can order any of your officers wherever you want. But once you enter Egypt, you overstep provincial boundaries. You risk dishonor, opening yourself to recall, so you need someone who *wants* this job—a risk taker. You *need* me. Understand you wouldn't be the only one jeopardizing everything in this undertaking. I've presented myself as an outstanding soldier in your service. By joining you in

Egypt, I place my own career in peril. For me to act as your second-in-command, I want my fair share."

Gabinius was silent, tensely grasping the arms of his chair. Losing no momentum, Marcus made his demands. "I want two thousand talents of your ten."

Gabinius inhaled sharply, parting his mouth to protest.

Marcus hurried on. "That's not even a third. And I want a letter written by you to my cousin in Gaul, commending me for bravery, excellence in command, et cetera, et cetera. Lastly, release me from my commission to you once we successfully reinstate the king. These demands must be agreed upon for me to serve in this capacity."

Gabinius stared at him coldly. "You demand too much, Antonius."

Marcus snorted, shaking his head and crossing his arms. "No. The King of Egypt asks for too much."

Gabinius set his jaw, and for a very, very long moment, said nothing. "All right," he finally muttered, walking back behind his desk again.

The response was so brief Marcus could scarcely believe his ears. "You agree—to *all* of it?"

"Yes. However, you shan't receive your cut of the ten thousand, my letter to Caesar, or your termination of service until *after* we succeed. If your part in this venture is unsuccessful or if we fail, you'll remain bound to me and my fate. Tonight we'll dine with King Antipater and his distinguished guests. I suggest you spend the rest of this afternoon researching how best to enter Egypt. This evening will be strategic planning. You're not to reveal our sharing of the ten thousand. That shall remain in confidence." Gabinius extended his arm. "Do we understand one another?"

Marcus reached out, clasping Gabinius's hand firmly. "You have my word, sir."

Marcus reclined on an ornate couch, dressed in a clean red military tunic. Mostly, he kept his own counsel, observing the distinguished guests and getting a feel for each man with whom he dined.

To his left was a well-groomed Roman in his thirties, the banker Gaius Rabirius Postumus. One could almost smell gold on him. He was well-known by everyone in Rome. Orphaned as a babe, Rabirius's wealthy financier uncle had adopted him. Now rich as Crassus from international monetary systems, he had assumed his uncle's place as Rome's premier usurer.

When Ptolemy of Egypt entered Rome seeking assistance to reclaim his throne, he sought someone to stand for his wealth while in the city. Immediately recommended to the Rabirii, Rabirius the Younger attached himself to the king, traveling with him to Syria. He struck Marcus as a quiet man of expensive taste, intent on keeping his affairs in strict order.

Next, Marcus's eyes rested on King Antipater of Judea, reclining across from him on a separate couch. Dressed simply for a man acting the role of an Eastern monarch, the Judean wore a long silk tunic belted by a braided girdle of bright green dyed leather. Antipater kept himself fit, by the look of him. His only other display of affluence was his beringed hands. He had graying hair, parted in the middle and plaited elegantly. He reminded Marcus of statues he'd seen in Antioch.

King Ptolemy, called Auletes, King of Egypt, was altogether different. Short and rotund, he bore himself effeminately. Wearing a thick jeweled diadem around his receding hairline did nothing to disguise his baldness. Layers of bright blue silk shimmered and rustled whenever he moved. Whoever styled his robes had stitched tiny gold and silver beads here and there. A tasseled belt boasted not only similar baubles, but hollow gold-and-silver bells with minute clappers, producing sweet, tinkling musical sounds whenever he moved.

Marcus listened patiently as the two monarchs discussed topics ranging from prices of dye-producing shellfish off the Cyprian coast to the best cure for flatulence. They chatted about long-dead Hebrew monarchs practicing bigamy but avoided Roman policy completely.

One thing was clear: Gabinius, Rabirius, and Marcus Antonius were all here for one reason alone—to be used.

After dinner, five ebony-skinned slaves bore away the last morsels. Marcus found the fresh seafood from Joppa too outlandish in its presentation. It didn't appeal to his stripped, unadorned soldier's palate. Legionary living had altered his tastes. Antipater made sure to include eels, Gabinius's favorite, along with strange mollusks in a sweet honey sauce. Marcus ate sparingly, instead savoring the fine wines. He only wished he could drink his fill.

Gabinius clicked his fingers for Triton to refill his own cup, catching the attention of everyone in the room. Clearing his throat, he announced, "I invited Commander Marcus Antonius to join us this night. He'll serve as my second in our endeavor."

Antipater inclined his head deeply in Marcus's direction. Smiling slightly, he responded with a curt nod.

Ptolemy, however, scrutinized Marcus, eyeing him dubiously. "What experience has this young man had in battle?" he asked in a whiny voice.

Gabinius glanced Marcus's way and inclined his head, prompting him to answer. "I recently took Machaerus on behalf of the proconsul, Majesty."

Ptolemy sniffed, reaching for another serving of eels.

Pressing on, he added, "Gabinius awarded me honors at Alexandrium, and I spent time in the desert, investigating the revolt of Alexander the Hasmonean. I provided Gabinius the intelligence needed to proceed with military action against him."

Ptolemy sipped his wine, licking puffy lips. He never even met Marcus's eyes.

"I think you'll find Antonius an excellent choice," Antipater interjected graciously. "Why, he's served here in Jerusalem for over a year now. I feel as though I trust him personally."

Marcus raised his eyebrows, stunned. He and Antipater had never even seen one another. Ah, well—at least he was providing positive input.

Gabinius added quickly, "Young Antonius is a fine officer, loved and respected by his men. I couldn't present a finer man to assist you back to your throne, glorious Majesty."

Marcus reached for a leather map, placing it on the table in front of King Ptolemy. Unrolling it, he held it up, so each man could see. "The proconsul requested I put together a strategy for you—Your Majesties this evening. It was brought to my attention, that the path to Pelusium, the Way of the Sea, is troublesome almost any time of year."

"Indeed," Ptolemy agreed. "Summer may be gone, but one must still deal with residual heat and high dunes. Temperatures can still cause men to faint, for it's still hot in the desert. In the delta, there may still be standing water, leftover from last winter's floods. If so, beware of deadly vipers and hippos posing threats. Such conditions strike fear into men and can mire riders to the point of exhaustion and death."

Marcus heard him out patiently, then continued, "The king's daughter, Berenice, controls a sizeable fleet. That might make a sea approach difficult. In my opinion, it would be wisest for me to move ahead of Gabinius through the desert. Occupants of Pelusium will be forced to give way once we take their port and country roundabout. They'd be forced to confront us or surrender in short order to avoid starvation or thirst. They'll have no choice. Such a siege wouldn't even require war machines, which, I'm certain His Majesty knows, would be unwieldy in such traveling conditions."

"What sort of force do you propose taking?" Gabinius inquired.

Marcus smiled with pride. "I want my auxiliary cavalry, sir. They know me, they trust me, and they would weather the difficulties."

Gabinius nodded. "Of course. And I intend to leave behind a healthy number of legionaries here as well. Not to do so would be an invitation to Parthian invaders. Or, just as bothersome, another revolt from Alexander, who I'm certain is still out in the desert, waiting for the right opportunity."

"Let me help," Antipater offered in grand gesture. "I consider it a blessing to help my neighbor King Ptolemy. I shall provide monetary assistance, weapons, grain, and for young Antonius, a cavalry detachment under my own commander Malichus. He is a man Antonius both knows and trusts."

Marcus stiffened but said nothing. Indeed, he knew Malichus, but no longer did he trust him. He'd been close friends with the traitor Pitholaus.

Gabinius seized the Judean monarch's offer. "Rural Judeans in smaller villages despise us Romans. It would greatly help if Malichus secured passes to the southwest. Any men you can send ahead to keep peace with locals will make Antonius's task easier. Here's what we will do. Antonius goes before us to take Pelusium. Meanwhile, King Ptolemy, Rabirius, and I head north to my fleet."

"When I hit Raphia, I'll send word to you," Marcus offered.

Gabinius nodded assent. "Good. That'll be our signal to sail for Pelusium with reinforcements. Once Antonius holds that city, he can indicate when we're safe to dock. Then we'll come ashore, join his force, and approach Alexandria together via land. King Ptolemy's people will welcome their true ruler."

"A reasonable plan," voiced Antipater.

"I think not," Ptolemy said irritably, waving a beringed hand at Antipater in dismissal. "Proconsul, would you have the King of Egypt enter his land on a Roman warship, in hiding, arriving after the battle for his border is fought? Is he a coward?"

"Majesty," Gabinius groveled, "I thought only of your safety. I would never think you a coward."

"It's well you do not. You'll meet me at Pelusium, Proconsul, for I'll accompany Antonius."

Marcus met the king's eyes for the first time. Lined with thick kohl, they were puffy with insomnia or drink. A red-veined, hook nose jutted from his face, vulture-like. The man was downright unhealthy. Could he even make it to Pelusium? What a fine mess it would be if he up and died while returning to Egypt.

Ptolemy smiled wistfully. "To think I'll be back in Alexandria with my sons."

Marcus saw tears in his eyes.

"And I pray my little Lotus Flower is safe," he continued,

directing his words to Antipater. "I left so quickly under cover of night; I couldn't see to her safety. If Berenice has harmed Lotus, her death will be tortuous misery."

Abruptly, the Egyptian ruler rolled off his dining couch and padded out of the room, overcome by emotion.

Antipater leaned in toward the three Romans, offering an excuse for his guest's sudden exit. "'Lotus' is his favorite child. Her real name is Cleopatra. He claims she speaks six or seven different languages—and is barely fourteen. What an extraordinary child she must be."

Marcus barely listened. He was staring at the map, his fingers tracing the path from Jerusalem to Pelusium: the gateway of Egypt.

CHAPTER XXVIII

ACCURSED HEAT.

Undulating mirages and exhausted horses were only a few of its manifestations. It sucked life out of men, placing them at Apollo's mercy as they traversed the vast, empty space.

Marcus sent Gabinius the promised dispatch upon arrival in Raphia. His original goal was to arrive in Pelusium in just over a week's time. But now, experiencing the merciless, arid stretches of unending desert, he doubted that was possible.

And the damned king took four times as long as Marcus's cavalry to do anything. Ptolemy's entourage was mostly camels. He himself preferred traveling by veiled litter. His baggage wagons were ponderously heavy, and none of his party was accustomed to military discipline on a march. Granted, camels were excellent for desert travel. However, time was a concept of which the king simply wasn't conscious.

It wasn't until they were past Raphia that Marcus realized he had never truly seen a desert. Judea's wilderness and the far reaches of Nabataea were nothing compared to what lay before him now.

This was desert. Open, limitless, unending wasteland, composed of sand, grit, and illusions.

Astride his horse, he watched the column pass, reading misery in each man's face. He tried issuing words of encouragement, but his own throat was so dry the intended message failed.

Marcus made use of half the night and the mildest part of daylight, breaking camp before dawn daily. His gravest concern was the horses. By noon each day, they struggled, heads down, and blowing hard. Fifty miles or so out of Raphia, the first animal went down.

After that, Marcus started respecting King Ptolemy's camels a lot more.

They kept going.

As promised, Antipater sent Malichus and a small cavalry to strengthen his own. The Judean made good on assurances that passes to the south were safe. No rebels or zealots hid in ambush. However, due to Pitholaus's betrayal, Marcus simply couldn't trust him as before. He kept his forces to the rear of the train. Better to be wary than sorry. Perhaps in time he could test Malichus's loyalty in some way.

The next village was tiny Rhinocolura, comprised of poor, ramshackle huts. Villagers hid in their hovels, terrified of the well-armed Romans. Marcus sent Fimbria and one of Ptolemy's servants who spoke the local language to explain that their mission was peaceful. After that, the men crowded around the village well.

Marcus warned them not to drink too much too quickly. "It can prove fatal," he cautioned sternly. However, today his words of advice didn't deter Fortuna's ill humor.

He knew trouble was afoot when Stentor, oldest and most seasoned of his cavalrymen, rode in hard, kicking up dust, his horse flecked with foam. Nobody pushed their horse above a walk this time of day. Something was wrong.

"Commander, the king's servants were talking about a lake nearby, and some of our men overheard. Four of them went in search of it for water."

"Didn't they know there was water here?"

"They complained it would take too long to get their share. Even now, they're there, watering their horses."

Marcus was no longer hot from the sun, but with anger. "Change horses, Stentor. Fimbria, ride back with him. Order them all back and inform them they face disciplinary action."

That's when the accompanying physician overheard and approached Marcus worriedly. "Commander, they might die if they drink from a desert lake. Many are filled with poisonous minerals and oils, unfit for man or beast."

"Then you go too. Maybe you can help."

By late afternoon, Marcus was sitting on his cot, rubbing olive oil onto his sun-scorched forearms and face. Using a bowl of cool water from the village, he moistened a cloth, wiping it carefully around his eyes and nose.

"Requesting permission to enter, sir." It was Stentor.

"Come."

"We found them. One man is already dead. Fortunately, only he drank from the lake. We brought his body back with us. The others let their horses drink, so those animals are dead too. The other three men didn't drink, claiming the water looked foul."

"The water looked foul?" Marcus mimicked angrily. "Idiots! I should make them walk to Egypt." Sighing, he puffed his cheeks out, shaking his head. "Where are they now?"

"With Fimbria, outside. They expect punishment."

"As they should. Assemble the men. I want this business done so everyone can rest before riding again tomorrow. Go get Tyrannio and Fimbria. You three will administer thirty-nine heavy lashes by rod to each man. Give them only two cups of water apiece tonight as additional punishment. Tomorrow morning, they may drink their fill, but *only* under supervision of the physician. Then they'll walk behind the column all day. That'll teach them to risk lives. I'll speak to the rest."

"Yes, sir."

Marcus ducked out of the tent, followed by Stentor. Fimbria

saluted smartly, his abrupt movement causing the perpetrators to lift their heads. As he passed, Marcus shot them a dark look, heading to where his men would assemble. Once tubicines sounded, it didn't take long. He signaled for his horse, mounting so everyone could see.

"Before you go to your tents, observe the punishment these men receive. Today they left their positions, riding elsewhere to seek water. Because of their stupidity, one man lies dead. He drank from a poisonous lake. Three horses also lie dead. Can you not see there are dangers in this land? That's even more reason to stay together."

Behind him, the three men knelt, and their punishment commenced. Marcus turned his horse about, watching. He hated this, but reminded himself that holding command meant enforcing strict conduct within a unit. Everyone was silent as the slapping of rods raised fresh wounds on bare flesh.

Once it was over, he addressed the soldiers a final time. "Next time we approach water, hold back, be patient, and every man will receive his fair share. Foolhardiness will get us killed out here. I, for one, want to reach Alexandria alive so I'll have the chance to bathe and visit a brothel or two. Don't any of you wish to join me?"

There was loud, boisterous cheering at that remark.

Marcus rode over to the punished men and spoke quietly to Fimbria. "Have the physician salve their stripes. Tyrannio, take a small detachment a mile or so out and cremate that poor bastard." He held out a denarius. "Here, this is for the Ferryman. Afterward, get some sleep—all of you."

That night Marcus's nightmares returned. They always visited whenever he was nervous or under duress.

Now awake, he drank three cups of posca to calm himself. Inside his tent, he noticed shadows from flickering firelight outside. Since there was no wood in the middle of the desert, Marcus hadn't allowed his men to waste spare wood for kindling. Curious, he smacked his tent flap aside and stepped into the night. Two sentries guarding the entrance snapped to attention, saluting. Giving them both a slight nod, he gazed upward. Hosts of stars glimmered in the clear desert sky. Balmy air and gentle, dry breezes ruffled his hair. Out under this peaceful space, it was so hard to believe he'd lost a man today.

Following the glow of the welcoming firelight, he slowed his steps, hearing something foreign and lovely. It was the soft, low tone of a flute playing a tender, ethereal phrase. As Marcus came around the back corner of his tent, he beheld King Ptolemy rocking slightly to the sound of his own music. The monarch sat before the dancing flames.

Only he would have enough firewood for such a luxury out here, next to nowhere.

Marcus always ordered his tent pitched next to that of the king, though Ptolemy kept to himself. Attendants stood at the entrance to the royal tent. Brightly dyed and ornate, it bore bizarre little pictures of men with animal heads. The strange script resembled some sort of code.

The king ended his melody, and Marcus clapped, walking forward out of the darkness, startling Ptolemy. His armed bodyguards materialized from both sides of his tent. Marcus ignored them. "Gratias, Majesty." He joined the king within the glow of the firelight.

Ptolemy nodded graciously, looking a little befuddled at the sudden appearance of this late-night visitor. Waving the guard away, he motioned for a servant. "Attend to my guest." Immediately, a figure came forth, offering Marcus a deep, cushioned chair.

He sat down, sinking into plush comfort. "Please play some more. It's been a long while since I enjoyed entertainment. And to see royalty perform—this is a first for me."

Ptolemy balked, narrowing swollen, kohl-lined eyes and staring hard at Marcus in distrust. Finally, he inhaled deeply, expanding his broad girth wider, and played a haunting melody.

Marcus closed his eyes, only opening them minutes later when the king stopped playing. Ptolemy was staring at him, and another servant materialized to offer him wine.

Accepting the cup, he asked, "Have I been impolite? If so, forgive me. I've no experience with kings."

"No," Ptolemy replied. "Actually, you honor me. Never has a Roman requested I play or appreciated it. I played for Pompeius when he visited my court. He said nothing about my music, and his men seemed ill at ease during my performance. Then one night while in Rome, I hosted a dinner party. Very important dignitaries attended. When I played for them, they laughed while I performed. It was appallingly rude."

Marcus smiled, nodding. "Men of my country aren't schooled in the arts of music or dance," he explained. "We're trained in warfare and oratory skills for use on the battlefield or in the Senate. Oh, we get a little mathematics, literature, and history. But nothing finer than that."

"A pity," Ptolemy murmured with one of his sniffs. "With educations like that, no wonder your people are so inclined to stealing and pillaging the lands of others."

Marcus bristled at the comment. "Careful, Romans are risking their lives and careers to reinstate you."

Ptolemy stared at Marcus wordlessly. Presently he lifted his instrument and played again. Marcus leaned back in the chair, gazing up at the night sky. He was weary, but this was a rare pleasure.

A shooting star shot through the cloudless black, and he smiled wistfully. Mother used to say shooting stars portended something important. He hoped this one predicted a safe, swift victory at Pelusium. What an odd fate, being in the middle of a desert, hearing the King of Egypt perform. Marcus chuckled lightly at his circumstances, shaking his head.

The music ended abruptly.

"Do you join your countrymen now, mocking me?" Ptolemy demanded sharply.

"No. I'm laughing at myself. Do play on. I'm enjoying this, really. It's calming." He drank deeply, draining the cup. A slave brought him another. Good music, good wine ...

"Lotus always says my music soothes her spirit," Ptolemy said, smiling. "When she was very little, I would play, putting her to sleep with sounds of my flute."

Marcus yawned. "She's right. You have a gift."

Ptolemy nodded, eyes distant and watery with emotion. Lifting the alabaster flute, he played again. Its melancholy tone pierced the night. Sighing, Marcus leaned back, relaxing into the chair's soft cushions.

He awoke to music too—a sonorous blast of a bucina, the large, round horn used to awaken camp. It jerked him into consciousness. Disoriented and stiff, Marcus found himself alone beside the fire's dying embers.

Several days later, as the journey continued, the road abruptly disappeared, having been covered by sand in either a seasonal flood or sandstorm.

Marcus ordered the men onto camels, making the change himself as an example. Though despising their crude noises and foul smell, they had better footing over rolling dunes. They also managed heavier loads, grain for men and horses, waterskins, and even armor.

The poor horses were pathetic, struggling their way through the deep and uneven drifts. Two more died.

Marcus cast caution to the wind, allowing his men to strip to their tunics. Several had fainted in recent days due to the weight and heat of their armor. He prayed to Mars they wouldn't run into hostile soldiers while traveling nearly naked. Yet the alternative was risking sunstroke. That wasn't much help in a fight either.

As the heat of the day wore on, Marcus found himself riding a camel next to King Ptolemy.

"Egypt is preserved because of her deserts and isolation," the king explained, waving a beringed hand over the landscape. Together, they'd ridden up the tallest dune in sight, and it was tough going even for camels. Several times Marcus caught his breath, the animal foundering. Now on top, his burning eyes took in desolate wasteland in every direction.

Pointing due north, Ptolemy said, "The sea awaits. Sometime

in the next two days, the weather will change. We'll smell salt and feel the air stir."

That was hard to visualize, sitting on a camel in an ocean of sand. But if their geography was correct, the king spoke truth.

"I'll be greatly relieved to see water again," Marcus replied. "Even if I can't drink it."

Over the next day and a half, another horse died, leaving no more spares. Marcus nearly cried with joy when he spied a white bird flying high above.

A seagull—a damned beautiful seagull!

As Ptolemy had foretold, the feel of the air changed, gulls becoming frequent company. Humidity settled in, and so did the Etesian winds. Late that night, after rubbing his skin with the last of his olive oil, Marcus slept with the tent flap wide open, pleasant breezes caressing his blistered flesh and cracked lips.

At the final encampment before Pelusium, he granted his men an extra day of rest. He also sent scouts ahead to determine their distance from the fortress.

Marcus received them personally upon their return.

"The path is so muddy men and animals will sink to their bellies. And the mosquitoes—we covered ourselves in mud to keep them off."

"We must take care, sir," another warned. "There was ample evidence of hippos, though we saw none."

Marcus stepped closer to one of them, picking away dried mud on the man's cheek. As black as tar, he let it crumble between two fingers. Grinning broadly, a crafty idea took hold in his mind.

Marcus scoffed at King Ptolemy's excuse for not joining in the battle.

He complained of illness, wanting to await the battle's outcome in camp until his health improved. Unsurprised at his cowardice, Marcus pressed forward with his plan.

The time to test Malichus had come. He entered the Judean's

tent unannounced, bearing a bundle of traditional Eastern garb. Malichus stared at the neatly folded clothing. When Marcus told him his intent, the Judean looked stunned.

Where once they'd saved one another's lives and enjoyed open camaraderie, nothing but unspoken avoidance had prevailed between them on this journey to Egypt. Once clear of the passes and threats of ambush, Marcus had kept Malichus's small cavalry to the rear. They followed King Ptolemy's dusty baggage train.

Malichus bore the indignity and never complained. Marcus simply wouldn't risk any disaster in this undertaking.

The Judean officer rose to his feet, exclaiming incredulously, "I command King Antipater's finest forces. Yet you order me and my best horsemen to strip ourselves of armor and honor to ride into Pelusium on camels dressed as merchants?"

"Yes. Once there, you'll enter the city as though you're traders."

"And do what?"

"Locate your men around their water supply, then visit their garrison commander. Offer him terms of unconditional surrender. If he refuses or apprehends you, your men will poison their water sources. Should it be needed, our physician has prepared an unforgettable vintage for Pelusium's occupants."

Malichus shook his head sadly.

"Go on," Marcus insisted, offering Malichus the bundle. "Put these on. Let me have a look at you."

Unhappily, the Judean removed his armor, reaching for the layered robes one at a time. Marcus waited patiently, not bothering to comment until Malichus wrapped the final swath of material about his head.

"You look exquisitely native," Marcus declared in complimentary appraisal, sitting down on Malichus's cot.

"Wouldn't you prefer the added strength of my riders, Antonius? They once served you well outside Jerusalem."

"You can help more from within Pelusium this time. Anyway, you'll select only twenty of your men. Most will remain here with me."

"I see. When will you attack?"

Smiling, Marcus stepped forward, clapping him on the back. "We'll await nightfall and move in the dark, smeared with mud to avoid detection. Black as tar we'll be, taking the dock and surrounding village before anyone's slave adds oil to late-night lamps! Play your part well, and they'll have to surrender or risk their water being fouled."

"Where will you camp?" Malichus asked uncertainly.

"Near the docks, in the village outside the walls."

The Judean knitted his brows in consternation.

Marcus snorted in reply. "Stop acting like a woman, Malichus. We'll be easy to find." He stage-whispered the rest, winking. "We'll be the ones in the Roman helmets. The rest of your men will be safe; have no worries. If you can't find them, look for men in armor *without* Roman helmets!"

Malichus didn't warm to the humor. Jaw set, he cocked an eyebrow and reasoned, "Sieges can last forever. It could be days, weeks before we can escape, if we must resort to poison and siege."

"Take plenty of water with you and bury it. But I tell you, it'll be easy. They'll give in if their water's at risk. Do you think Egypt's poor, living way out here, isolated as they are, have any desire to take on well-armed Romans? Pelusium may have been a grand outpost in the past, but from what our scouts say—"

"Antonius, why did you choose me for this task?"

"Honor follows danger." Marcus shrugged.

"You could send another whose loyalty you don't esteem as much as mine. Or do you no longer value that as highly?"

Sighing, Marcus studied him. "Ah, well. You back me into a wall." Pausing only a moment, he continued, "You're concerned you've lost my trust? Well, your fellow citizen and friend Pitholaus betrayed me. So what am I to think? You were close to him, were you not? So far you've given me no reason to doubt you. But trust is fragile. And this scar on my leg from Machaerus gave me doubts about trusting Judeans. There it is."

Malichus said nothing.

Marcus stood up, stretching his scarred leg and flinching as the muscle cramped. "Serve me well and perhaps our friendship will be closer to what it once was. Of course, if you were thinking of betraying me and my men, being inside Pelusium is the ideal place for you. You'll be ensnared inside with our enemies."

The Judean stared at him remorsefully, Marcus smiling pleasantly in return. "My, but you look like a real merchant traveler from the East. May the God of your fathers grant you wisdom in this endeavor, friend." Changing his tone, he added, "And once this is all over, won't it be wonderful to share a cup together again?"

And over it was.

Not a single man drew a blade in the taking of Pelusium, whose leaders surrendered without need for poison. Malichus approached the city leaders as planned. He persuaded them to turn the city back over to Ptolemy. By that time, Marcus's troops had arrived, stealthily entering the garrison by use of rope ladders.

Pelusium's inhabitants surrendered immediately. Marcus received assurances of loyalty and appreciation for spared lives. Short on rations, the garrison had received no supplies from Alexandria, as in past years. Nobody seemed certain of whether the oversight was poor management of the frontier or lack of grain.

Now Marcus knew that attention would focus on the march's next phase: Alexandria.

There would be talk about Princess Berenice and the man Marcus assumed was now her husband—Archelaus of Pontus. As good a friend as he'd proven to be, neither Archelaus or Berenice had endeared themselves to Pelusium's garrison.

By noon the next day, King Ptolemy arrived outside Pelusium's earthen walls. Marcus, Malichus, and their cohort of men filed out in welcome. An excited crowd of villagers had gathered, watching the rich caravan. Women ululated and children darted in front of adults, everyone eager to know if their king was truly here.

Ptolemy made a great show of prostrating himself on his hands and knees before the fortress gates. The rest of his escort followed suit, every head lower than the king's.

Lips pressed to the hot sand, Ptolemy kissed the ancient earth. An attendant hurried forth, wiping excess sand from his mouth. Another offered him cool honeyed wine. Four painted boys surrounded their king on every side, holding aloft a billowing cotton canopy for shade.

Marcus stepped forward to greet Ptolemy, smiling. "Pelusium is taken, Majesty. Egypt is restored to you."

With his usual sniffing sound, Ptolemy raised a hand in friendly gesture to the onlookers, his sardonic laughter and acerbic words a complete contradiction to his facial expression. "Commander, I'll only call my lands restored when I'm on my throne and that bitch of a daughter Berenice is prostrate. I'll have my foot upon her exposed neck."

Marcus raised his eyebrows at the king's words, then ignored them. He let his full voice ring out for the people to hear, "Welcome, Majesty, welcome home!" It was Marcus's first attempt at playing the people. He needed their complete support to continue the takeover without bloodshed.

Still waving and acknowledging the throng, Ptolemy hissed, "I am not home. Alexandria is my home."

What a fool. No wonder his people didn't want him. Marcus stepped closer, speaking softly in the king's ear. "Your people are inside the fortress awaiting you. Don't disappoint them."

Ptolemy stared hard at him. "What do you mean by that?"

Marcus had pretty much decided he'd kissed Ptolemy's fat buttocks for the last time. Becoming impatient, he replied, "I meant what I said. Pelusium's soldiers have promised loyalty, and as we speak are on bended knee, waiting to receive you."

Ptolemy coughed, spitting phlegm onto the ground. "Execute them."

Marcus dropped his jaw, staring at the king in shock. "I will not!"

At that, Ptolemy snarled so vehemently his spittle sprayed Marcus in the face. "I am King of Egypt! You are in Egypt! Kill them all! They occupied a fortress denying me aid, giving allegiance to my usurper. Kill them!"

Marcus stubbornly held his ground, eyes snapping. "No. You may be Egypt's king, but I command the forces placing you back on your throne—at least until the proconsul arrives. Pelusium surrendered without endangering lives. Therefore I'll not put them to the sword, nor will I allow you to."

His heart raced, knowing he was gambling on whatever influence Ptolemy held over Gabinius.

The king's fleshy face was becoming red and he was sweating profusely. "Proconsul Gabinius shall hear of your refusal to comply with my will in this matter."

Unfazed, Marcus shrugged. "As I once said, I know nothing of pleasing kings. However, I do know men inside this fort spared lives of soldiers on both sides by giving up peaceably." Fat little coward. Why not make him really mad? Gesturing to the villagers, Marcus raised his voice again, striding in front of Ptolemy before the Egyptians. "Look at these people gathering here," he announced loudly, so the Egyptians heard. "They see you've returned, Ptolemy of Egypt. Men inside the fortress await your mercy. Your countrymen submit peacefully. Shouldn't they receive mercy from such a forgiving master?"

As if on cue, the crowd erupted into a chorus of cheers. Gods, this was fun! By the time Marcus was done, the people would want him on the throne of Egypt instead of Ptolemy. And by Jupiter, he'd probably do a finer job.

Ptolemy sniffed again, glancing nervously at the growing swarm of cheering subjects. To keep those smiles, clemency was now his only option. He smiled tightly, masking his anger.

The king raised his right hand to greet the Egyptians. In his high-pitched, nasal voice, he said, "Lead me to the fortress, Commander. I'll sojourn within these walls, once more at home, in my land—my Egypt."

As he passed by Marcus, his right eye twitched in fury.

Winning this round, Marcus Antonius followed King Ptolemy Neos Dionysus Auletes into the fortress, passing the garrison soldiers cowering in the dust.

Interesting—no joyful cries welcomed the king. Instead, the revelation struck Marcus that Ptolemy was more captive than the men inside Pelusium. And by his own desperate design.

Assured that the garrison's men were safe, Marcus encamped his men outside Pelusium's walls, along the coast, where Etesian breezes kept mosquitoes at bay. Today he'd been victorious in three battles: taking Pelusium, proving Malichus's trust, and forcing Ptolemy's hand.

Not bad for one day's work.

CHAPTER XXIX

BY EARLY EVENING, GABINIUS'S SHIPS WERE IN SIGHT. Marcus hurried to Pelusium's small dock, flanked by some of his men.

One, two, three flaming arrows arced through the darkening sky like shooting stars. Soon Marcus was welcoming Gabinius and the financier Rabirius to shore. "Proconsul, welcome to Egypt." He saluted, crisply.

"Salve, Commander. Is the area secure?"

"Yes, sir."

Marcus guided his guests through the village outside the fort, heading to his makeshift praetorium.

"How long was the siege?" Gabinius asked, briskly tramping at Marcus's side.

"Barely a night, sir."

Gabinius raised his eyebrows, impressed. "Then fatalities were few?"

"None at all."

Once inside his tent, Marcus poured posca into three cups, apologizing, "I'm afraid our drink is only standard soldier's fare."

Gabinius accepted his portion readily, but Rabirius shook his head, waving the cup away with his hand.

"How was the desert crossing?" Gabinius inquired.

"We lost one man foolish enough to drink some bad water from a putrid lake. Ten—no, eleven horses dead. The Arab stock did best. They're lighter and bred to survive in these conditions."

Gabinius helped himself to a seat, Marcus pulling out a folding chair for Rabirius, who was battling seasickness.

"No real difficulties getting to Pelusium through the marshes?"

"We crossed those at night, smeared in mud. Nobody saw us. It worked, and the mud kept mosquitoes at bay. Poor horses struggled, though. Kept sinking up to their bellies."

"Mosquitoes?" Rabirius glanced about, his face ashen.

"They live around the marshes," Marcus alleviated his concern. "They're not so bad here with the coastal breezes."

This adventure was clearly not to Rabirius's elevated tastes. He was whiter than a newly laundered toga.

Gabinius sipped from his cup. "Whose idea was the mud?"

"My scouts wore some back to camp one day. I thought it an excellent way to close in on the enemy unawares. Much can be said about surprise as an offensive tactic."

"So true. How is Ptolemy faring?"

"Angry with me. He wanted to kill everyone in the garrison. But they surrendered. Those men trusted me and were compliant to every order. They want no trouble, acknowledging him as king again."

Rabirius's eyes were wide. "He wanted to kill them all?"

Laughing dryly, Gabinius said, "Rabirius, welcome to the East. These exotic despots mind Roman manners when in Rome, posing like kittens with cream. In their own lands, they're quite different. The cats have claws." To Marcus, he stated bluntly, "You can forget being in his good graces anymore."

"Ho," Marcus responded. "A little mercy and generosity might gain him some respect. The commander of Pelusium is Greek, but the common soldiers all hail from Upper Egypt—brown as broth. I've noticed plenty of prejudice between Greeks and true Egyptians."

"Yes, well, the king and his forebears have done little to rectify intolerance between Egyptians and Hellenes. Let's just hope it causes us no trouble. It serves none of us if Ptolemy is booted out of Egypt once we leave," Gabinius reminded.

"He's been inside the fortress since we arrived. Hates sleeping in tents." They all laughed. "I ordered Malichus and his men to set guards on him. The Egyptians may be compliant, but the garrison didn't cheer his return, despite their oaths. Nor did I want Ptolemy harming Pelusium's soldiers behind my back."

"Sound judgment," Gabinius concurred before changing topics. "Antonius, inform your men we'll leave in three days for Alexandria. No sense staying holed up here. I could go by sea, taking the port and splitting our forces, but their navy remains an unknown risk. We'll take them more assuredly by land. Has Berenice threatened force?"

"No word of resistance yet. I sent scouts west two days back, once we took the dock and village. It may be a while before they return."

Gabinius nodded. "Having fun playing general?"

Marcus smiled. "Yes, sir. I hope I've performed adequately."

"Anyone capable of taking a garrison without violence has performed admirably."

"Gratias. Might I suggest leaving Malichus and a handful of his cavalry here in Pelusium to hold it?"

Rabirius frowned at that. "The Judean? Can we trust him? Gabinius, Pelusium must remain loyal, or this country's borders will be unsafe and unstable for trade. You know how essential that will be—"

"Yes, yes, Rabirius," Gabinius replied testily.

Marcus saw through them like glass. They couldn't suck the Alexandrians dry without adequate commerce. "I, too, was skeptical of his loyalty at first," Marcus offered. "But I tested him. He's steadfast. Besides, we'll have most of his men with us."

"Very well, we'll rely on your judgment," Gabinius said.

Rabirius stood abruptly, wavering on unsteady legs. "Antonius, where are our accommodations? Sea travel has sapped me."

"King Ptolemy has invited you both to join him inside the fort."

"Then with all respect, I'll retire."

"Do you need a physician?" Marcus offered.

Rabirius shook his head. "Rest and dry land is all I need."

Once Rabirius parted, Gabinius declared, "Ah, before I forget, I've a delivery for you." Gabinius called for Triton, loitering in the shadows. "Fetch that little piece of baggage arriving for Antonius."

The slave was gone for some time, and Gabinius finished his posca, discussing new cavalry stock. When young Triton finally returned, he held the arm of a small boy around ten years old. "The boy, Dominus."

"Here's the property you sent for. Kyros sent him promptly. I'll leave him with you." Gabinius arose from the cot. "By Neptunus, it's good to be back on dry land!"

When he was gone, Marcus studied the small boy standing alone and barefoot before him. In a stained and worn tunic, he scratched his head like a dog.

Lice. Excellent.

Marcus said in Greek, "Tell me your name, boy."

"Eros," he replied softly.

Did he know his father was dead? He studied Eros's face, searching for Eumenius in the gentle blue eyes. He had straight black hair that needed shearing. His skin was clear, olive-toned. Small but alert.

"Did Kyros the horse trader tell you about your father?"

Eros looked down at his feet sadly. "Yes."

Marcus narrowed his eyes. "He was a good man."

Eros still stared at the floor.

Tilting the boy's chin up, Marcus instructed kindly but firmly, "Always respond when spoken to. It will need to be 'yes, Dominus' to me."

Eros nodded. "Yes, Dominus." He wriggled one grubby toe in the sand, drawing loops.

"Your father was a fine horseman." No response. "I was his commanding officer in the cavalry."

At that, Eros froze, looking up at him, eyes wide. "You're Marcus Antonius?"

Marcus smiled. "That's me."

"Kyros said I'd be your slave now."

Marcus nodded. "It was your father's wish."

"Will I go to war with you?" Eros asked, eyes round as agate marbles.

"Perhaps," Marcus answered with a frown. "First, we must do something about your name."

"Why, Dominus?"

"Because I dislike it. I don't want a slave named after the god of love-making. Bacchus would better suit me," he exclaimed with a grin.

Eros shook his head stubbornly. "I answer to no other name, Dominus. Eros is who I am—my name at birth. My Mamma's name was Aphrodite."

"How original," Marcus snorted, sitting down on his cot.

Eros continued, "When I was born, our master named me Eros because I was her son."

"Of course."

"He killed her."

"I know."

"He was a very bad man. Father took me from him, hiding me so I would never have to go back."

"So your father really was a slave?"

"Yes, Dominus."

"Eros." Marcus sighed with distaste, shaking his head. "We'll see. I'll try to get used to it." He scrutinized the boy. "We must find you some shoes."

"I could make some, Dominus," Eros said. Clearly, he wanted to please.

Marcus jerked the side lacings of his cuirass loose. The breastplate was starting to show a lot of wear. "Make some? You know how to make shoes?"

Eros shrugged. "No, Dominus. I never made any before, but I would try. I could learn."

Marcus reassured him, suppressing a smile. "I'll find you shoes, boy. Now here are my expectations: You're to serve me. You'll learn to shave me daily and wash my feet after a march. My armor needs frequent polishing, same for my helmet. And when we get to Alexandria, I'll need a new cloak. Mine's getting old and looks too common. Once in the city, I'll give you coin and you'll find something suitable for an officer."

He stopped, suddenly realizing the boy had no idea what he was saying. He was tired and had rambled back into Latin, losing Eros completely. Switching to Greek again, Marcus added, "You must learn to speak, read, and write Latin, becoming a proper Roman slave. Someday I should like you to write correspondence and attend me at dinners, meetings—"

Eros gazed up at him in wonder, his mouth hanging open. "Are you a general, Dominus?"

Marcus shook his head. "Not yet, no."

"You look like one, Dominus."

Marcus smiled again, unable to disguise his amusement. Eumenius was right. Eros was a good boy. Motioning him closer, he couldn't help but recall Vindelicus's devotion. Dear, faithful Vindelicus. How could another be as good and devoted as he? Especially when the "other" was so small in comparison to what the towering Gaul once was?

"Will you be loyal?" Marcus asked.

Never was there a child with such deep, wondering eyes. Eros nodded solemnly. "Always, Dominus."

"Good." Marcus arose. "One of my men will bring in a pallet, and you can sleep at the foot of my cot. In the morning, we'll get your hair cut. When we leave for Alexandria, I'll arrange for you to ride a camel in the king's party."

Eros beamed. "A real camel?" he exclaimed.

"Yes. Tomorrow, when it's light, you'll see we're surrounded by desert."

"Where's Alexandria?"

"It's the greatest city in Egypt, still a good distance from here. King Ptolemy lives there in his palace. We're supposed to put him back on his throne."

"Do I get to see the king, Dominus?"

Marcus rolled his eyes. "Maybe, but try not to be too disappointed. I'll place you among his servants. You'll be safer there."

"Yes, Dominus."

"You must stay out of the way and out of mischief."

"Yes, Dominus."

"Yes, Dominus, yes, Dominus," Marcus mimicked and laughed. "You'll do very well, Eros. Very well indeed."

A single rider barreled toward them on the flat.

Marcus halted the column, everyone watching. At breakneck speed, the returning scout pulled up, his horse covered with lather and quivering in exhaustion.

"Water!" Marcus ordered. "What news?"

The soldier pointed back, gasping. "Some ten to fifteen miles back—armed men with royal insignia. They chased us—firing arrows."

"The other scouts?"

"Dead, sir."

At that moment, Marcus learned that one could have a chill in the middle of the Egyptian desert.

Three hours later, the hot Egyptian sun perched on the edge of the horizon, a hovering golden disk.

Eros carried a platter of food over to where Marcus and Gabinius sat on canvas stools. Poring over a leather map, the proconsul commented, "Let's hope it's a small detachment. If they delay us here for more than a day or two, we could die of thirst before reaching Alexandria."

"Certainly they were Berenice's scouts."

"Then they're expecting us—and have an army."

"Maybe they'll send a dispatch offering terms," Marcus mused hopefully.

"Hmmm, possibly. It's more likely they'll outnumber us. But in Egypt, any men recruited locally would be ordinary citizens, not knowing a fig how to fight."

Marcus nodded wearily in agreement. "I'm unconcerned about numbers. Like in Syria—quantity, not quality."

Eros set the platter of food on a third stool between them.

Gabinius smiled, reaching for a bowl of steaming beans. Spooning in a mouthful, he said, "I tell you, I look forward to visiting Alexandria. It's the one place I've always wanted to see. Before leaving Rome, I was at a dinner party and Pompeius Magnus had just returned from the East. He told us all about it. Do you know one can view Alexander the Great lying in state? His tomb displays him like trophy. Apparently, the Egyptians mummified him. He's in pristine condition."

Marcus raised his eyebrows at that. A dead man in perfect shape? "Poor man. I'd never want strangers staring at me lying dead. Doesn't seem respectful."

"You know how Egyptians are—into strange art and customs when it comes to death."

Eros returned from the tent carrying a water basin and towel. Kneeling, he unlaced Marcus's caligae, lifting his foot out to wash it.

"There are other places I'd prefer visiting," Marcus said with a knowing grin.

"Ah!" Gabinius laughed. "I've heard Alexandria is the place for that too."

Marcus snorted. "There was a brothel back at Pelusium, but the women had fleas. When I saw one of those girls scratching like a mangy dog, I turned on my heel."

"Wait until you're on a long campaign. You'll settle for anything female on two legs." Gabinius chuckled knowingly, swigging his posca.

Their merriment was short-lived as rapid hoofbeats approached.

One of Fimbria's riders galloped up to the tent at a dead run. Marcus and Gabinius stopped eating and arose simultaneously. Eros glanced back over his shoulder, hands still in the basin with Marcus's right foot.

"Sir, a detachment of enemy cavalry and war chariots is heading our direction."

"From where?"

"Due north, sir."

"How many?"

"Difficult to tell. Perhaps a hundred. Maybe more."

"Shit!" Marcus whirled about, nearly tripping on Eros, who was hastily relacing his boot. He shouted at the sentry, who was still mounted, "Call the men to arms! Assemble in battle formation with shields at the ready on the north end of camp!"

Plagued by skirmishes, it was the longest of nights. Enemy archers used fire, panic ensuing when tents were set ablaze. Marcus ordered them all broken down, preventing further destruction. Legionaries rolled empty supply carts to the perimeters, just inside the trenches. In total darkness, there was no determining numbers of enemy charioteers. Clashes occurred on all sides of camp. Marcus praised Mars that entrenchments and carts kept the enemy at bay. Several veered too close to the legionaries' freshly dug ditches. Their horses screamed as they capsized.

By sunrise, they had disappeared back into the desert, leaving nearly fifty Romans badly injured and twenty-nine dead. Back on the march, Marcus ordered Ptolemy and his attendants to the rear. He surrounded them with his best cavalrymen. Gabinius's legionaries led the way, setting the pace. It was slower going, but broad legionary shields could withstand a charge if it came to that.

Damned king wouldn't die under Marcus Antonius's watch!

By midmorning, the Nile's Bolbitinos branch came into view. Fortunately, it was narrow and shallow this year. It should have been the last hurdle between Ptolemy and Alexandria. But now it was clear—an army also stood in their path.

Two hours later, more riders appeared on the horizon. Holding their ground, they fired bolts and missiles. Marcus ordered his front lines into testudo formation. By the time the enemy scattered, the legion's configuration resembled a hedgehog. Hundreds of enemy arrows jutted from the shell of shields.

Small attacks continued all day. That night Marcus joined Gabinius under the royal canopy. He hadn't been in Ptolemy's presence since refusing to execute the soldiers at Pelusium. With pillows stuffed under his paunchy little ass, Marcus couldn't tell if he wore more silk or hostility.

"May we expect more attacks this evening?" Ptolemy inquired tersely, running fingers across a gold chain at his neck.

"It's likely, Majesty," Marcus admitted. "They're trying to tire us before meeting in decisive battle sometime tomorrow or the next day."

"Oh, it'll be tomorrow, I assure you. No Ptolemy wants pitched battle too close to Alexandria. Trade's interrupted, and people get restless and riot."

Marcus saw Rabirius and Gabinius exchange anxious glances. The king drawled on, "Alexandrians are a fickle lot."

"Would they parley, do you think?" Gabinius inquired.

"Never," Ptolemy spat.

"I think we should tender the option," Rabirius reasoned. "If they turn us down, we'll have at least tried. If they accept, so much the better."

"They'll never accept defeat," the king insisted. "Berenice knows what'll happen once I reenter the city. She knows her days are numbered."

"Would she actually lead the attack?" Gabinius asked.

"Possibly. She's always been an unseemly daughter, and Alexandrians consider her mannish. Then again, that illegitimate Pontic filth she married may take command. If he's not a coward."

"Archelaus," Marcus murmured.

Ptolemy shot him a glance. "How would you know Archelaus?" he demanded, his eyes narrowing.

Marcus answered carefully, "We met in Syria." Telling the king any more than that would only invite trouble.

"Well, let me say this to you," Ptolemy stated curtly to Marcus and Gabinius, "when you capture Berenice and Archelaus, their fates are *mine* to determine."

With that, he arose, striding into another room of his spacious tent.

Gabinius moved to Marcus's side. "Just how long have you known Archelaus's intention was to wed Berenice?" he asked suspiciously.

Marcus met his cold gaze defiantly. "I tried telling you shortly before we fought Alexander outside Jerusalem. You waved it aside as trivial."

"Careful, Antonius. Mind your tone—and the king," Gabinius warned. "He hasn't any respect for your absurd code of honor. Make him angrier, and he'll readily have either of us murdered in our sleep."

"Well, then, he'd be a new breed of stupid. He needs us to defeat his usurpers," Marcus reminded him.

Back in his tent, he took a long draw on some posca. Disgusted at putting on polite airs in front the king, he was even more annoyed at Gabinius. He constantly coddled the monarch. Marcus had no intention of compromising dignitas the way Gabinius did.

Never.

Commander Marcus Antonius on behalf of Aulus Gabinius, Proconsul Provinciae of Syria, to Archelaus of Pontus and Berenice of Egypt:

We offer you the peaceful option of surrender. There is no reason for others to die when defeat is only days away. Respond to this message favorably and I'll grant you both honorable burial. On that, I give my word.

Queen Berenice of Egypt, Lady of the Two Lands, beloved of Serapis, Hera, and Hathor, Daughter of Artemis, to Marcus Antonius:

I would sooner bed my own father the flute player than receive burial at the hands of Roman whoresons!

King Archelaus of Egypt to Commander Marcus Antonius:

I regret we must fight, as you're allied with the former king. So I must refuse your offer, my friend. I have sent my wife the Queen back to Alexandria. I plead mercy on her behalf if Ares favors you.

CHAPTER XXX

IF ONLY IT WAS JUST BLOOD AND DEATH THAT MADE soldiering hard.

Marcus was conflicted. He'd do his duty, but he was deeply troubled at having to face Archelaus on a battlefield. Here was a man with whom he'd broken bread, one who'd aided him—a trustworthy friend. Archelaus had gambled in marrying Berenice. Now he'd probably lose everything.

According to scouts, the Alexandrians had cavalry, chariots, and heavy infantry. Archelaus would want to break Roman lines early on. Marcus persuaded Gabinius to use a maneuver Rhesus had once taught in his lessons: the wedge.

However, Marcus used it differently. Instead of one large triangle, he arrayed his entire line with smaller wedges. From a bird's view, it resembled the jagged teeth of a crocodile. As Marcus rode back and forth inspecting it, he heard centurions shouting reminders to infantry and auxiliaries.

"Aim for the horses!"

"If a driver infiltrates, close ranks and kill him."

"Hold your positions. Allow this line to break, and you'll face punishment and humiliation."

Everything started when Alexandrian archers shot a volley of arrows.

Defensively, legionaries lifted their shields. Once the torrential rain of arrows ended, the Romans readied their pila, holding back until ordered to fire. From Marcus's perspective, it was unnerving to watch. He sat astride his horse, far to the enemy's right flank, with his cavalry.

Alexandrian chariots were charging now. Horses screamed in agony as barrages of pila soared and hit them deep in the shoulders or chest. Maimed animals dropped and writhed. If their horses were down, the drivers were helpless. Stranded charioteers scrambled from underneath wreckage. A few managed to infiltrate the wedge formation, but legionaries closed the trap, as ordered. Every victim vanished in the fray.

At the sound of tubicines, Antipater's Judean archers let fly torrents of arrows. Legionaries hefted their shields, marching forward in machine-like cadence toward the enemy. Marcus heard tramping, nail-shod caligae drumming over hard, dry earth. Dust clouds rose.

Before he initiated the cavalry, every man on the battlefield had to be engaged. Infantry in outer ranks threw another volley of pila. Any Alexandrian in range fell like cut barley. Then the Roman center advanced unhindered. Legionaries joining the fight roared, opposing sides converging in sudden chaos. Marcus heard centurions blowing their bone whistles, relieving soldiers in front.

He awaited one more change in the lines. It seemed decades before the whistle sounded again. As the legionaries switched, the Alexandrian left flank suddenly surged like an incoming tide. Gods! They were maneuvering into a pincer formation, even before the Roman cavalry was engaged.

Marcus reminded himself that the Alexandrian infantry would never outflank the Romans because his cavalry would outmaneuver them first.

It was time.

Lifting his javelin, he shook it wildly, screaming at the top of his lungs, his cavalry responding in explosive chorus behind him. Galloping at top speed, he and his auxiliaries bypassed the Alexandrian right flank, behind the enemy.

The Alexandrian rear guard whirled about, suddenly faced with Roman horse. Unprepared and outflanked, they panicked, deserting their positions. Shouting in confusion, they found no escape, running into the backs of their own infantry.

"Now!" Marcus yelled, drawing back his javelin.

His cavalrymen followed suit, spraying the air with spears, seeking indiscriminate death. Alexandrians dropped everywhere, javelins in their backs. Others still ran, chased down by horsemen. Marcus's own pilum landed so hard in the back of a fleeing man the spearhead pierced the infantryman behind him.

Marcus whooped loudly—two instead of one!

Encircled and ensnared, the Alexandrian army was in its death throes.

Javelins spent, the Roman cavalry began hand-to-hand combat. At first, fighting was difficult because of the press. Panicked men from both sides banged against Marcus's legs as he fought. He used his shield mostly as a weapon, cracking skulls and shoving it into charging infantry. In such tight surroundings, his horse could barely move. It was a long while before the dense pack thinned and he could see more clearly what was happening around him.

Some Alexandrians in this rear guard wore exquisite armor. They were obviously nobles from the royal court. Marcus smiled grimly. Rich, palace-born cocks, thinking they'd be safe in the rear ranks. Though well-trained, they lacked the stamina and discipline found in career soldiers. Costly gilt trappings couldn't save them now.

As brash as he was feeling, Marcus still eyed each Alexandrian noble carefully. He half expected to meet Archelaus but prayed he wouldn't.

Covered in sweat and blood, Marcus's head throbbed beneath his helmet. Temples pulsing, his eyes scanned the field. Using his shielded left arm again and again, he punched, knocking enemies off balance, crushing limbs with its edges.

When Tyrannio came under attack from two nobles, Marcus spurred forward. Knocking into one of their mounts from behind, the Alexandrian toppled from his frightened horse. After that, it was easy spearing and trampling him. Tyrannio dispatched the other.

Immediately after came the sweet, sweet sound of a centurion's whistle not far off. Craning his neck, Marcus saw breaks in the enemy lines. Legionaries were near.

"Forward—push farther into their rear guard!" he screamed over the din.

Breathlessly slapping his exhausted horse on its rump, he led the cavalry on. Another whistle sounded, followed by calls from tubicines.

Marcus glanced about, anxiously searching for the incoming legionaries. Muscles in his right arm were tense, and his left shoulder cramped from wielding his shield so offensively.

Finally—there they were. A break in the fighting revealed helmets belonging to Roman infantry.

Now his riders could pursue remaining enemies retreating on foot. In this heat, few could run far. Already, carrion birds gathered in lazy circles above. Hundreds of men lay scattered in the sand, staining it red.

Stentor rode up close. Placing a hand on Marcus's arm, he pointed to a lone unhorsed Alexandrian.

Bedecked in ornate armor, he was obviously highborn. Silence fell at his approach. A deep wound in his thigh had blood coursing from it. Marcus could see him wrestling with pain as he walked. He carried a bloody sword aloft, the blade resting flat on the palms of his hands.

It was an offering.

Marcus's auxiliary cavalrymen rode in tight, surrounding him. Stentor swiftly dismounted, pointing his gladius at the man's neck.

Marcus shook his head. "Pull back."

Stentor stepped away, sheathing his weapon.

Standing straight, his wound bleeding out, the Alexandrian met Marcus's eyes.

"Take the sword, Stentor," Marcus ordered.

Stentor obeyed, holding it up so Marcus could see it. It was a magnificent blade.

In melodious, flowing Greek, the Alexandrian introduced himself, "I am Melanthius of Alexandria, once friend to King Archelaus of Egypt. My king is dead, may he live eternal. I killed him myself to save the rest of our army. I surrender to prevent further bloodletting. To whom do I offer his sword?"

"Marcus Antonius, second-in-command to Proconsul Aulus Gabinius."

"You fought cleverly, Roman."

Marcus glared at him. "Treacherous filth. You killed your own king? Where is he?"

"I won't allow his body to be desecrated," Melanthius declared defiantly. "I only did what was necessary for my brothers-in-arms."

"And I'd never humiliate a man so betrayed," Marcus replied. "I'll bury him with honor. He was my friend."

Melanthius's eyes widened in surprise. He blinked in bewilderment.

In the middle of the Egyptian desert, there was little with which to build a funeral pyre.

A few legionaries located a damaged Alexandrian supply cart. At Marcus's order, they swiftly emptied it of contents and placed Archelaus's body on top. Underneath, the soldiers stacked the brittle remains of wicker and wood from Egyptian chariots.

In his tent, cleansing himself before the rites, Marcus received a messenger from King Ptolemy. Under a black beaded wig, the fellow's eyes were lined with kohl.

Ptolemy's message was brief:

King Ptolemy Neos Dionysus to Marcus Antonius:
I demand the remains of Archelaus, the Pontic
bastard. So says Pharaoh of Upper and Lower Egypt,
the land that you, Roman, merely visit.

Marcus smiled tightly, tossing the scroll back at the messenger.

"Tell King Ptolemy that unless he wants to get his rotund ass kicked out of Egypt again, he should start treating people respectfully. He can start with Archelaus. Should he care to join us for the funeral, we could use a good flute player to honor the dead." That said, Marcus stood up and marched out of his tent, grinning at the look on the messenger's womanish face.

Outside, the setting sun was a grand orange ball.

Legionary soldiers formed groups with Marcus's cavalry to watch Archelaus's burial.

All the men had plundered from fallen Alexandrians. One cavalryman responsible for bringing Archelaus's body from the battlefield had confiscated his magnificent purple cloak. Prodded by his comrades, he stepped forward, presenting it to Marcus.

"I took this from him, sir. Now I give it to you."

Marcus gratefully placed a hand on the legionary's shoulder in thanks. He moved before his men and raised his voice, holding Archelaus's cloak high for all to see. "Brothers, fallen enemies who fight bravely deserve respect."

Marcus lithely climbed atop the cart, using the rich cloak to reverently cover his head. "Archelaus of Pontus was son to a king. He lived richly, but when he found my cavalry in the Arabian desert, he welcomed us with hospitality. That day he became my friend. Little did I know we'd someday have to fight each other. Now our warring is over. Archelaus, I send you to the gods with my own hands."

After several moments of silence, Marcus lifted the purple cloak off his head. Solemnly, he draped it over Archelaus's still form. Stentor, the grizzled old cavalryman, climbed up, liberally pouring oil over the entire cart. Its excess spilled underneath to the fragmented chariots.

Marcus waited until he finished, then leaped down. A sentry offered him a torch, which he tossed on top of the cart. There was a hiss and a swoosh, and the fire was ignited. Marcus backed away, joining his men. Together, they all watched the flames stretch toward the heavens.

Marcus stayed until the cart and its contents burned down to glowing coals. At dawn, he'd see the ashes gathered.

While proceeding back toward camp with Stentor, Tyrannio, and some of the legionaries, he noticed a huge multitude in the waning light. They were under some of Ptolemy's guards and sitting in their armor. Looking them over, he saw hopeless, battle-weary faces. These were men who would never see their city again.

Pulling up, he motioned for Stentor. "How many are there?"

"Nearly a thousand, I think, sir."

"Need I inquire about their fates?"

"He's executing them all at dawn."

"Damn king." Marcus's heart was heavy. Melanthius had killed Archelaus to spare these men's lives. How sickening to hear of their imminent execution. "I'll speak on their behalf. At the very least, he should sell them for good coin. Maybe he'll listen if I convince him that their sales would add gold to his hoard." He set his jaw, letting his horse plod on. If Ptolemy had any wisdom, he'd set them free so they'd follow him.

A single voice from the condemned men caught him off guard, calling out in Greek, "Hail, Marcus Antonius! We Alexandrians salute you!"

Marcus reined in, looking at Stentor, astonished.

The older man answered before he could ask. "They know about Archelaus's honorable treatment. They saw the cremation from here."

Nodding, Marcus spurred his horse again, slowly riding on. But more voices cried out as he passed.

"You are welcome in Egypt, Antonius!"

"Bring Egypt hope!" one cried in broken Latin.

"Antonius, we Alexandrians honor you!"

Then the prisoners suddenly rose as one, waving and shouting in roaring chorus.

"Hail, Antonius! Hail, Antonius!"

It was overwhelming. Marcus swallowed hard, hearing the voices of men who'd all die at sunrise. In his heart, he knew his pleas to Ptolemy on their behalf would fall on deaf ears.

Emotion burned his eyes, but he lifted his hand, acknowledging them, then tapped his cuirass over his heart. Not even the Corona Vallaris compared to this.

Alexandria.

Marcus gazed upward as he rode beneath the massive Canopic Gate of Egypt's capital. Built of solid red granite, glistening flecks in the stone flickered in the sun.

Ptolemy triumphantly processed into his city as a returning monarch, aided by Roman might. Surrounded by buildings, the legion's marching resonated into a militant thunder.

This part of Egypt was flat. So much so, the road through town appeared long and infinite. Marcus was stunned at how wide open, spacious, and level everything was. And Alexandria pulsed with life. People crowded on both sides of the road, watching Gabinius's troops parade by.

Broader than Roman roads, the Canopic Way had two vast lanes allowing heavy traffic to flow efficiently. In the middle were decorative water cisterns for thirsty animals. A long caravan of merchants paused at one, their camels drinking deeply.

To the west, where the Canopic Way intersected a smaller but no less splendid avenue, was a gilt marker identifying the Street of the Soma. Marcus craned his neck toward the left, eyeing a curious-looking hill in the shape of a cone. It was the highest point visible, and paths wove their way to the top. Crowning it was a golden statue of Pan, merrily playing his instrument. It was a fanciful place.

Gabinius noticed it too. Marcus overheard Ptolemy tell him, "It's the Paneum."

Mouth agape, Marcus barely knew where to look next. Jupiter! Every official building was hewn of polished marble or red granite. Even the streets were expensive—paved in similar stone and full of sparkling crystals. So unlike Rome, composed of obscene graffiti, rough-hewn red brick structures, and malodorous gutters running through narrow streets.

Another feast for the eyes was the tasteful blending of culture and styles.

Larger columned buildings boasted Greek design. Colonnaded entrances with elegant facades reminded Marcus of Athens. However, as they left the Jewish quarter, shops on side streets were completely different, adorned with symbols like the ones on Ptolemy's tent. Statuary outside these establishments consisted of Egyptian deities, human in form from neck down but bearing heads of jackals, hawks, even cats and crocodiles. Vibrantly painted, some were even gold.

Why, this roadway could hold at least thirty, maybe forty men abreast. It was three times the width, or more, of the Via Sacra. Alexandria was awesome—positively breathtaking.

People perched atop monuments, crowding the streets, watching the legion pass. Citizens shoved one another, jostling for better views. Marcus heard them chattering mixed opinions about Romans entering their city. He recognized Greek, but many other languages were comingled.

His heart skipped a beat when he suddenly heard people chanting his name in unison.

"Antonius, Antonius, Antonius!"

Marcus swallowed hard. What were they doing?

"Your noble reputation for mercy precedes you," Gabinius berated heatedly from where he rode to Marcus's right. "They should be welcoming their king, not you. Do something about it!"

Do what? Marcus set his jaw, face flushing. He turned in his saddle, barking an order to Stentor, who rode behind him. "Take some infantry and line both sides of the road. Order these people to stop shouting my name and tell them to shout for Ptolemy."

Stentor grinned. "Can they help having good taste, sir?"

Marcus made a wry face. "*Now,* Stentor."

Cheers for Marcus eventually ceased, though no cries sounded for the king.

A short time later, Gabinius abruptly raised his hand, calling a halt. Mounted on a white horse and flanked by bodyguards, Ptolemy rode across the street to a distinguished Greek building. Like a temple, the foundation was raised, but had a curious entrance. Stairs ascended into an open space on top. The area's sweeping capaciousness above was void of a cella, a typical temple vault. Surrounded by magnificent columns, it was taller than any other nearby building. Marcus scanned the massive walls. Scribed into the entablature, was a Greek inscription in gold:

> *To the almighty god and king, Alexander, son of Philip, father of nations, savior of Greece, conqueror of the world. Here, may the founder of this city rest in glory.*

One of Ptolemy's painted boys rushed to the king's horse, holding its head. The king dismounted and turned to Gabinius, extending his hand in invitation. In his high-pitched, nasal voice, he announced, "Proconsul Aulus Gabinius, let us honor the god who founded this City—Alexander the Great!"

Gabinius was all smiles, swinging off his horse to ascend the Soma's heights with Ptolemy. Once on top, the two men disappeared, invisible from Marcus's vantage point.

He waited outside with the rest of the legion, sweltering in the noonday sun. Head pounding from the heat, he jerked his helmet off, careless of decorum. Snatching a waterskin off his saddle, he took several swigs. Then he promptly ordered the rest of the legionaries at ease so they could do the same.

It seemed a second lifetime passed before Gabinius and the king reemerged from the tomb. Arm in arm, one would have thought they were the best of friends.

Once they remounted, the procession resumed. Ptolemy headed south, down a smaller street. Here, legionaries narrowed their columns due to the tighter passage. Turning east once more, they reentered the royal quarter and returned to the Street of the Soma, traveling north.

Here, the road was deceptive, appearing to end at the sea. But instead it took off over the water, supported by jetties and heavy stonework. It was a slender yet impressive causeway leading to the most favored of the royal palace complexes. Stone sphinxes rested on well-manicured gravel plots along the way. Each creature possessed a unique human face, representing various Ptolemaic rulers.

As he rode, Marcus beheld the royal harbor to his left, sheltered within a square quay. Open water sparkled to his right. He squinted; the pavement was blinding in the afternoon sun. Now they passed the towering Lochias promontory, built of stone. It served as a high lookout over the harbor. Beyond that, high gates enclosed the palace grounds.

Out here, surrounded by the water, Etesian winds eased the sun's heat, billowing from the northwest. Turning his face into them, Marcus smiled, seeing the fabled Pharos lighthouse rising as if from the sea.

Gabinius stopped abruptly, Marcus coming up even with him.

"Antonius, I'll wait here with the king and his contingent until you secure all premises of the palace. Arrest and hold everyone you encounter until His Majesty has opportunity to question and release whomever he pleases. If Berenice knows what's good for her, she already lies dead. If she lives, take her prisoner as well. Her father longs for vengeance."

Marcus responded with a crisp salute. Followed by a century of infantry and some favored cavalrymen, he cantered through the deserted guard-gates of royal Egypt—straight into the palace of the Ptolemies.

It only took a quarter of a watch before the palace complex was secure.

There was no fighting or opposition. Palace guards had fled for their lives. As Marcus and his men combed the corridors, they discovered bodies of ill-fated slaves who had chosen suicide. How well they knew their king. He'd put them to the sword just for being alive under Berenice's rule.

Then Marcus and his infantrymen entered the Great Hall.

Berenice of Egypt sat on the great Horus throne in her royal robes. Stiffly, she clutched the crook and flail, Egypt's iconic symbols of royal power. Her statement was bold, if not hopeless.

Marcus walked straight up to where she sat.

Archelaus's informants had been correct. She was tall, especially for being Ptolemy's progeny. She shared only one inherited trait with her father—a hook nose. And unfortunately for Berenice, it filled her face. The usurper queen's only real loveliness was exquisite skin.

Poor girl. That Tata of hers would make her death dark and dreadful.

"Salve, Lady," Marcus announced. "I am Commander Marcus Antonius, second-in-command—"

"Where is my father?" she interrupted, her tone imperious and cold.

"He's outside, waiting until the palace is secure. And now it is. I'm to send word letting him know it's safe to enter." Marcus hesitated but then drew his pugio, offering it to her. "If you have a use for this, I'll ask my men to leave, and we'll allow you privacy." It would piss off Ptolemy and Gabinius like the Furies that he'd given her a chance at dignity, but it would be a better death than whatever her father had in mind.

Berenice shook her head ever so slightly. "No. I won't die by a Roman blade." Her eyes filled with tears. Troubled, she stared past him at one of the walls.

Marcus saw fear on her face. Surely, her gods would have mercy on her. Ptolemy would not.

"I must ask you to relinquish the throne," Marcus stated.

Holding herself erect and proud, Berenice rose. Silently, she walked down the stairs of the raised dais and wandered out into the middle of the huge hall, as though lost.

Marcus returned to the massive doorway to send two messages. The first was to Gabinius and Ptolemy.

The second was to Tyrannio and Stentor.

Once the enormous doors heaved shut, Marcus stepped back to watch. It took four of his men on each side, pushing hard, to close them. Gods, tortoiseshell veneer over bronze—extraordinary! There was a large oculus in the ceiling above the throne, letting sunlight stream in. Other than that, the place was dim. Giant gold-and-silver lamp stands sat near the walls. The place probably blazed when lit up at night.

Marcus turned his attention back to Berenice.

She had wandered into the darker part of the Great Hall, pacing about. Even in the gloom, light from the oculus caught glints of spun gold in her queenly robes. Sensing his stare, she glared back sullenly.

Marcus turned away and he strolled about too, examining the wealth of Egypt to kill time. The walls dazzled him. In gold leaf over marble, they retold the life of Alexander the Great. Finally, he climbed up the granite stairs to Egypt's Horus throne, awestruck by its workmanship. He'd heard of Horus while in Pelusium. He was the hawk-headed god and son to Osiris and Isis, two of the main players in the Egyptian pantheon.

Made of solid gold, the thing had to be heavy. Crafted into Horus's two wings, the tips touched in the back. Lapis lazuli, mother-of-pearl, turquoise, coral—Marcus had never in his life seen handiwork as magnificent as this. And it was probably ancient. Only the gods knew how many kings had used it.

Mesmerized, he tentatively reached out to caress one arm of the throne.

"Don't touch that!"

At Berenice's sharp outburst, he froze, eyebrows raised in surprise. She had crossed the room toward him. He descended the stairs to meet her. "Lady, now that you're willing to speak—"

"I'm not *willing* to speak to you, Roman," she sneered. "But nor am I willing to see royal Egypt's relics defiled by your greedy touch."

Marcus sighed. He paced back to the entry, speaking softly to one of his men, "Go see if it's here."

The cavalrymen heaved open only one of the heavy doors this time, the soldier disappearing outside.

Time passed, Marcus silently watching over his charge.

Finally, the cavalryman returned bearing a large leather satchel. He heaved it over to Marcus and saluted, returning to his post at the door.

Marcus ported the weighty bag over to one of the dining tables, placing it gently on top. It clunked within its hide sheath. Returning again to the other side of the room, he leaned against the wall in silence. It was but a matter of time.

Sure enough, Berenice's curiosity finally won out. She stepped to the table and loosened the satchel's leather ties. The sack sagged around its contents. Inside was a hefty pottery urn.

"What's this?" she demanded grimly. Most likely she already knew.

"The remains of your husband, Archelaus," Marcus answered gently. "I don't know how you would have honored him. I did the best I could." The fired clay was course. A simple egg-and-dart design encircled the mouth, sealed with thick wax. It wasn't at all ornate, but it served the purpose.

Berenice ran her forefinger around the rim. "We had no deep love for one another, he and I," she whispered, probably more to herself than Marcus. "But he was a good man—very brave. He always treated me well and would have been a far better king than Father. Oh, Archelaus, I want your rest undisturbed." Looking over at Marcus, she asked, "Why did you do this?"

"Because he was my friend."

Stunned, she slowly walked over to where he was. Her features softened, and her large eyes filled with emotion. Hands trembling, she removed her heavy gold earrings, shaped like sun-discs. "I see you're a kind man. Therefore I beg you to help me." She held out the earrings. "Take these and go to the western necropolis. Place his urn in a niche someplace where his ashes will rest—away from my raging father. These earrings will be enough to pay for a fine feast. I don't wish to die knowing his spirit wanders without peace."

Marcus nodded. Accepting the earrings, he dropped them into a small leather purse attached to his cuirass.

Berenice paused. "Thank you, Roman."

Marcus nodded again, silent. What words of comfort could he offer a woman who would soon die at the hands of her own father?

CHAPTER XXXI

TO MARCUS ANTONIUS, CAVALRY COMMANDER:
Ptolemy XII Neos Dionysus commands you
to attend a banquet commemorating his return to
Alexandria. You are to dine with friends of the king.
A chamberlain will show you to your place.

Another troupe of musicians and dancers made an energetic, choreographed entrance into the Great Hall. Naked Nubian slaves hauled open huge tortoiseshell doors. Each course of the meal was cause for a new round of entertainment. It was incredible!

Marcus sat surrounded by wealthy Alexandrian courtiers and merchants, each dripping with intricate gold jewelry. As the only foreigner at his table, he mostly listened to everyone else. There was no need to talk. Just being here was enough.

Soft, silk couches surrounded tables laden with delicacies. Even the slaves wore brilliant blue silk. Of different nationalities, he noted that none were homely. In fact, they were all youthful. Each young man was muscled and hearty looking, each female lithe and shapely.

Gabinius and Rabirius were both invited to join Ptolemy on his raised dining couch not far from the Horus throne. However, Marcus's seat was below with courtiers. He was unsurprised, having annoyed both Ptolemy and Gabinius. The king had not received his people's acclaim earlier that day; a serious blow to royal pride. They had chosen to honor a Roman commander instead.

Gabinius was still upset that Marcus hadn't followed Ptolemy's wishes regarding Archelaus.

Marcus's argument was simple. He'd honored a single man with a funeral; one slain by his own army to preserve lives. Ptolemy had slaughtered all of those lives needlessly.

The king hated him, and Gabinius's constant attempts at pleasing the monarch had become tiresome. Marcus concluded that if Ptolemy lifted his gown asking Gabinius to kiss his fat white ass, the proconsul would do it smiling. Gods, he'd anoint it with perfume and give it a nice pat!

Happier without their company, Marcus Antonius was content, drinking delicious wine and eyeing desirable slave women. Did it really matter what Ptolemy thought of him? He'd followed Gabinius's orders to the hilt. Their mission was successful, and Marcus was ready to claim his earnings.

Oh, the stories he'd tell his brothers when he returned to Rome.

His mind returned to the present as dancers near him began performing an erotic routine. Aroused and fascinated, he was annoyed at first when a sudden commotion near the hall's entrance interrupted the performance. Alexandrian courtiers nearest him rose in a furor of interest, chatting excitely in Greek.

"Are you sure? I assumed Berenice killed her."

"No, she was hidden away—someplace in the city."

"How can that be? Someone would've recognized her."

"I heard she went to Rome with her father."

"Look for yourself—there she is."

Intrigued, Marcus rose too, looking the same direction as the other men. There was a flurry of activity near the doors of the hall.

A petite young girl, lost somewhere between adolescence and womanhood, strode self-assuredly toward the royal dining dais. She was richly clothed in a Greek-style chiton of deep blue silk, a gold chain studded with carnelians on her breast. A diadem of pearls crowned her tightly bound knot of lustrous dark hair. As though on a mission, her bearing reminded him of Aurelia—striking, despite her tender age.

Ptolemy stood abruptly, the enormous hall falling silent.

She stopped directly at the foot of the stairs, prostrating herself onto the floor. Craning his neck to see around other courtiers, Marcus saw her bejeweled forehead touching the polished mosaics. In the East, such obeisance was the ultimate show of humility. Ptolemy scurried forward, shoving serving slaves out of his way. Hastily, he descended the stairs. Reaching the place where she lay, he crouched down and gently took her hand.

"Lotus Flower, arise. We're both safe now."

She lifted her head, meeting his eyes. In one fluid motion, graceful as a hind, she arose. Ptolemy followed clumsily. Shedding royal restraint, father and daughter embraced. Nobody stirred, the two royals holding one another. Marcus heard the king sobbing softly in genuine relief.

The girl was first to pull away. "Father, I'm your servant. What would you have of me?"

"Merely to see you again."

He took her hand and lifted it high. Through tears, he addressed everyone. "I left a girl-child in Egypt. Today I return to find a woman. Behold your Princess Cleopatra Philopater, Fame of her Father, who will be queen."

Every courtier around Marcus immediately fell prostrate, foreheads touching the floor, as did everyone else in the room—excluding the three Roman guests, that is.

Marcus had no intention of kneeling, but it was terribly awkward.

The princess surveyed her side of the room proudly, hesitating when she saw Gabinius and Rabirius up on the dais.

Removing her hand from the king's, she said loudly and clearly, "Father, the common people already recite stories of your victory. I heard of your leniency to Egyptian soldiers at Pelusium and of the honorable burial the Roman Commander Antonius gave to Archelaus."

Marcus flushed, staring down at his feet. For some ridiculous reason, he couldn't stop his heart from hammering.

Cleopatra moved toward the bottom of the dais, gesturing to Gabinius and Rabirius. "Introduce me to this man the people love for his mercy."

Ptolemy motioned for his two Roman guests to come down. "Daughter, I present to you the Proconsul of Syria, Aulus Gabinius, and the illustrious financier of Rome, Gaius Rabirius Postumus, now serving us as Royal Treasurer."

Cleopatra tilted her head back, smiling and studying them. Sizing them both up in no time, she commented loudly, "Ah, Father, what honor the people shall have for Rabirius. No doubt they'll line up to open their purses to him!"

The hall tittered with laughter.

To Gabinius, she nodded graciously, extending her hand, which he accepted eagerly. "Proconsul, what an honor to meet a man I never knew existed."

Ha! Marcus snorted to himself. Gabinius's eyes widened briefly, as though someone had delivered a well-placed punch in his gut. What wit this girl possessed.

Turning back to her father, Cleopatra said, "I'm disappointed Antonius is not here to receive my gratitude for his part in your restoration. I trust he's been rewarded and honored."

Marcus's palms were moist with sweat. He was relieved to be on the other side of the hall. He swore under his breath, astounded that an adolescent girl was manipulating everyone in sight, himself included.

She turned, scanning the crowd, and spied him. It took only

several heartbeats for her to stride over to where he stood. Ptolemy, Gabinius, and Rabirius followed in tow, albeit unwillingly.

"Father, Romans never make it their practice to bow to Eastern rulers, do they?" she asked knowingly. "Then surely this man among humble merchants is the one I seek. He alone is left standing in the hall."

Face-to-face with one another, Marcus met Cleopatra's eyes. Wide-set and almond-shaped, they were brown with flecks of green and gold, highlighted by kohl. Her cosmetics were tasteful, unlike those of her father. They enhanced her maturity, making her appear as adult as anyone else in the room. She was not overly beautiful, but elegant, tasteful. She held an exotic appeal he couldn't deny. Despite her youthfulness, she possessed a sophisticated allure he'd never encountered before. Everything about her pleased his senses: her spicy perfume, the tilt of her head, the tinkling sound of her jewelry. Even her lilting voice was distinct and lovely.

Ptolemy spoke hoarsely behind her, not attempting to disguise irritation, "Yes, Daughter, you've found Marcus Antonius."

She ignored his displeasure. "We're in your debt, Commander," she declared. Reaching out, she took his hand, squeezing it sincerely. "I thank you for returning my father to Egypt. I thank you with my whole heart."

Her hand still held his, her touch stirred him. Somehow Marcus found his tongue, muttering the first thing coming to mind. "I did only what duty required, Princess."

Cleopatra released his hand, smiling brilliantly, eyes sparkling. She glanced back at her father. He was glaring down his long, hooked nose at Marcus with hate, sniffing, as usual.

Cleopatra laughed teasingly. "Please, Father, command the people to rise. Their knees must be numb by now!"

Rabirius laughed aloud at her lighthearted humor. Ptolemy fumbled for words, stammering and grandly motioning with his arms, "Get up, all of you—rise and enjoy the feast."

Alexandrians around Marcus arose, bowing their heads

respectfully to him. A few clapped him on the back with words of praise. One called a slave to pour him more wine.

Marcus barely noticed their homage.

For the rest of the night, he found himself stealing fleeting looks toward the royal dais more often than was appropriate. It was the pleasant yet imposing nature of her presence that consumed him, an encounter he was unsure if he desired again or feared.

Five frustrating days passed.

Marcus expected a summons from Gabinius to complete their terms. While waiting to hear from the proconsul and receive his due, he kept a detailed account of what had happened since arriving in Alexandria.

On day one, the Alexandrians had cheered him, Gabinius and Ptolemy had scorned him, and Cleopatra had honored him.

On day two, he laid Archelaus's ashes to rest in Alexandria's famous necropolis. Then, at Gabinius's side, he witnessed Berenice's decapitation. What a bloody, sorry affair. Marcus despised the contemptable king he'd restored.

On days three and four, with no word from the proconsul, he journeyed east along the coast, escaping to Canopus, Alexandria's suburb of pleasure. There he drank himself into oblivion and romped with six prostitutes at tempting brothels in the district.

On day five, he returned to Cape Lochias, vexed to discover that Gabinius still had not sent for him.

Fine, if he received no summons by tomorrow, Gabinius would see him, like it or not.

Day six arrived. Still no word.

Marcus bathed, put on a clean military tunic, and Eros pinned a fibula onto his handsome new cloak. Marching straight into the king's reception hall, he confronted Ptolemy's chamberlain, a curt, cool, unfriendly sort.

"I'm here to see Proconsul Aulus Gabinius."

"The proconsul is being entertained by the king."

"Really? Where is the king entertaining him?"

"His Majesty shares literary discourse with Gabinius in the Great Library."

"Literary discourse, eh? How helpful you are," Marcus muttered to the eunuch, irritated.

He found the king, Gabinius, and Rabirius in the throes of deep, tedious literary discussion, led by thirteen white-haired Hellenes, all reminding him of Rhesus.

They were in the Great Library's odeon, a small performance hall intimate enough for private readings, presentations, and small concerts. At present, the king's large retinue had crowded the place. Marcus settled onto a seat toward the back, rudely propping his feet onto a marble bench in front of him.

He listened for a good portion of an hour. Two of the thirteen old farts debated Aristotle's premises on whether poetry and rhetoric were related or different arts altogether. Finally, Ptolemy stood abruptly to leave, stopping everything. As he swept out, his entire entourage, including Gabinius and Rabirius, followed.

Marcus popped up too, shouldering his way through the crowd of perfumed attendants. "Sir—Proconsul!" he called within a stone's throw from Gabinius, who was nearing a long string of litters.

Gabinius turned his head, annoyance fleeting across his face. "Antonius. Is there something amiss?"

"No, other than I hope to leave by week's end."

"Leave?"

"Yes. Per our agreement, remember? I must acquire my honorable release, your letter to my cousin—"

"Ah, a private matter."

Marcus gestured at the shaded colonnade behind him. "Everyone's leaving; there's plenty of privacy right here."

"Not today. I attend the king."

Why was he hedging? Was it that he no longer wanted to pay up? Or was it that he and Rabirius didn't have the coin yet?

"Pardon me, of course," Marcus said, unable to prevent sarcasm.

"I'm only a cavalry commander, after all. Mission accomplished, I'm no longer much use. Can we not finish our business, part amicably, and move on in our careers?"

"Tomorrow—tomorrow I'll send for you."

Marcus clenched his fists, trying to remain calm. "Have I your *word* on that, sir?"

"Watch your tone, soldier," Gabinius spat. Showing Marcus his back, he climbed into the waiting litter.

When Marcus finally received a summons, a legionary led him into an impressive suite of rooms.

The proconsul stood at a marble table poring over a Syrian map. Several slaves attended him, moving large feathered fans in unison. Their labors resulted in soft, steady breezes passing through the open space.

"Antonius," Gabinius muttered, not bothering to look up.

"Salve, sir." When the proconsul didn't respond immediately, he asked, "Trouble in Syria again?"

"Damned Alexander, I shouldn't have let the man go."

Marcus smirked in agreement. But alas, it was no longer his concern.

Gabinius continued, "He's emerged with yet another army, demanding his father and brother be released. Canidius has been desperate, trying to hold things together. I'm leaving early tomorrow."

"I wish you success and a safe voyage."

Gabinius faced him at last with a sigh. "Come, Antonius. Change your mind. Come back with me. The cavalry won't be the same without you. You alone made them what they are." When Marcus said nothing, he said, "Ah. You want to join Caesar in Gaul, don't you?"

"Upon your recommendation, yes."

Gabinius retreated to another low table where two scrolls lay in cases. "Here you are, then." He offered Marcus the canisters. "Hopefully, they'll meet your approval."

Marcus uncapped the first:

> *I, Aulus Gabinius, honorably release Commander Marcus Antonius from military service as chief cavalry officer. Having fulfilled his commission admirably, I recommend him for future service if called upon by the Senate and people of Rome.*

After rolling up the first scroll, Marcus opened the second, reading:

> *Aulus Gabinius, Proconsul Provinciae of Syria, to Gaius Julius Caesar, Proconsul Provinciae of Gallia Comata:*
>
> *For the past three years or so, your kinsman Marcus Antonius has been under my command. He single-handedly built my cavalry unit into the capable fighting machine it is today. I decorated him for courage in battle, awarding him commendations on more than one occasion. He is a successful officer, winning the respect of his men and the rest of my staff. I recommend him to you for his courage and dedication.*

Marcus nodded approvingly. "Gratias, sir. There's only one more thing I require, then."

Gabinius poured wine into a rich-looking gold cup. He took several long swallows before speaking. "Antonius, I don't have your two thousand yet. Once Rabirius's taxes take effect, we should have the sum. I'm sorry, but it'll take some time. You'll have a promissory note until then."

Marcus ground his teeth. He was afraid of this. "Proconsul, you have great influence over King Ptolemy. Why not ask him for two thousand in advance? Certainly, the king of such a wealthy nation—"

Gabinius had the nerve to laugh. "Have you any idea how much that man hates you? You never heed his commands—"

"I heed yours!" Marcus raised his voice slightly, regaining control only after a fierce glance from Gabinius. "You were my superior, not him," he emphasized.

Refilling his cup, Gabinius wagged a finger at him. "An unwise move on your part. A prudent man would consider both of us important figures to respect and obey. Your actions at Pelusium and at Archelaus's death hardened Ptolemy against you. Expect no assistance from him."

"He'd never need to know the coin was for me. You could find a way if you had mind to."

Gabinius took a long swallow of wine, smacking his lips. "If I had mind to, as you say." He shrugged. "You served me well. Your service is over. As you said yesterday, 'Can we not finish our business, part amicably, and move on in our careers?'"

Marcus shook his head, stoking his fury. "Then I'll stand here watching while you write that promissory note."

Gabinius lost patience at that, slamming the wine cup on the marble table, burgundy liquid sloshing out and staining the leather map. An effeminate slave fanning next to the wall jumped involuntarily. "No, you won't, damn you! You'll receive it when I'm ready to give it to you."

Frozen in anger, Marcus watched Gabinius stalk out, leaving him alone.

The pleasant Etesian winds breathed through a window from the west. Marcus chewed his lip. His emotions had manifested themselves mightily on the leather scroll canisters. Gripping them like talons in his rage, permanent claw-like impressions scarred the leather.

"In three days, go to the Temple of Isis at noon. There, you'll receive your reward."

Those were Eros's exact words. The boy had placed Gabinius's promissory note on Marcus's cot. What a relief to finally have it. But why the Temple of Isis? And why two messages, one written and the other given orally to his slave?

It was strange. Isis was a woman's goddess, no? Why would Rabirius choose her temple as a meeting place? Was paying Marcus such an issue that he and Gabinius were nervous someone would find out about it?

Well, there was little sense trying to figure those two out.

As far as Marcus Antonius was concerned, it was a splendid day to become two thousand talents richer. With refreshing breezes blowing in from the sea, Marcus dressed lightly. Wearing only a military tunic and caligae, he buckled on his pugio. He intended to enjoy the weather and walk the distance to the Temple of Isis.

Though Auletes spent most of his time in the royal quarters on Cape Lochias, other palace buildings from earlier years in the dynasty lined streets west of the Brucheum, which was Alexandria's Greek District. From there, Marcus passed a stately theatre and busy marketplace. Pleasant smells of cinnamon and pepper blended with grilled meats and fresh breads.

Beyond that stood the impressive Posidium, dedicated to the temperamental sea god. To its south was a smaller Egyptian-looking building; its stout pylons rising like fortress walls. This was the Isis Temple.

Marcus walked beneath the pylons, heading to the stairs. On the way, he passed an impressive gilt litter with attendants dressed in fine silks. A muscular, bronze-skinned man, taller than he, leaned quietly against one of the pylons not far away.

There was welcoming shade inside the temple's cool interior. As Marcus entered, he coughed. Clouds of incense from a recent sacrifice overwhelmed his senses.

He continued through the second and third gateways leading toward the holy of holies, which contained an effigy of Egypt's mother goddess. A stern, elderly priestess prevented anyone entering, privy only to those of the royal household. Marcus curiously studied the stone image beneath two burning lamp stands.

Isis smiled down, looking serene. Her sculpture looked ancient in origin. The womanly representation wore a plaited wig topped with a curious throne-shaped crown. Her gown was ankle-length and fit tightly, with no sleeves save for snug straps over both shoulders. Stepping forward on her left foot, she seemed to be approaching him.

Lit only by high window slats toward the building's ceiling, the place was dim and mysterious. A chill crept up Marcus's spine.

Suddenly, a man's booming voice sounded from behind, "Commander Marcus Antonius?"

Nearly levitating out of his sandals, Marcus whirled about, sizing the stranger up, one hand on his pugio. It was the man from outside. His coal-black hair was bound back tightly with gold twine. Built powerfully, a sword hung from his side.

"Who asks?" Marcus demanded, eyeing the weapon.

The imposing giant bowed his head in a curious, reverent way. "One greater than I."

Marcus chewed his lip, glancing about. Nobody else was around. The priestess had gone. Who was this? Rabirius's bodyguard? He'd probably need one, wrestling coin from the Alexandrians. Certainly, he'd never bring the entire sum of two thousand talents of gold here through a city this size. Marcus was expecting either another written guarantee or advance payment.

"Follow me," the dark stranger beckoned. Crossing to a side exit, he opened a small access door probably used for temple staff. There, he awaited Marcus, who was naturally mistrustful and hesitant.

The stranger assured him, "Please, Commander. Your reward awaits you in the temple garden."

"Really?" Marcus replied, not budging. "Too heavy to haul up the stairs, is it?"

The bodyguard cocked his head, baffled. "Heavy? No, light, well-made, and strong. The finest metalsmith in Alexandria worked it."

What? Marcus stared at him, at a total loss. "Finest metalsmith?"

With one hand planted firmly on his pugio's hilt, he followed.

Blinding daylight burst forth at the short corridor's end. Beyond were lush gardens overlooking the harbor. Why, it was a verdant paradise. Sucking in air, Marcus almost tasted green. Soon he'd be home, spending entire afternoons in the peristyle court, lying under the fruit trees.

Lost in his reverie, he heard his name again.

"Commander Antonius."

When he whirled about, he stood facing not Rabirius, but Princess Cleopatra.

Dressed in emerald-green silk, she smiled pleasantly, a large bundle at her feet.

Marcus stood dumb as an ox. Cleopatra was absolutely the last person he expected to encounter today.

The princess's bodyguard walked forward obediently, kneeling before his mistress.

"Commander, it has become clear to me that you had the foremost role in bringing my father home. Therefore I wish to reward you. It was a most dangerous task, but you were successful. His safe return is a deed for which I can never adequately thank you. In preserving his life, you have preserved mine. Apollodorus, please."

On cue, the bodyguard untied the parcel at her feet. A muscled bronze cuirass decorated with a lion's head sat gleaming in the shade-dappled sunlight. Atop each shoulder perched a Roman eagle, wings spread. Indeed, it was most impressive. The last thing Marcus wanted to be was ungrateful. However, he was expecting two thousand talents, not a piece of armor.

"I hope it pleases you," she said. "Your slave thought it would. He's a lively little thing and most impressed that you're related to Heracles. That's why I chose the theme of the Nemean lion. He said you would be pleased with a new cuirass and that you needed one."

Marcus recognized the familiar symbolism crafted into the breastplate and hastily responded. "It is—it's magnificent. Many thanks, Princess."

She bowed her head, earrings ringing softly.

Several silent moments passed, turning into awkwardness. This girl had been generous. Could she help it if her father and Gabinius were selfish, greedy asses? Oh gods, he had to say something...

But Cleopatra spoke first, "Something is wrong. You're disappointed in the workmanship, perhaps? I warned Leosthanes not to make the eagles disproportionately large. Do they overshadow the lion?"

She moved over next to him, critically viewing the finished product.

Marcus faced her, feeling horrible and embarrassed at the misunderstanding. "Please, *please* forgive me. Your gift is exceptional. I'm ashamed, no—*embarrassed*..."

"There is something amiss, then?"

"There is, but not with your gift," he assured her. "I'll wear this with much pride." He decided it was best to be honest with her. Sighing, he began, "A few days ago, I received a promissory note in regards to payment I was expecting, that's all. When my slave, Eros, gave me the message to meet someone here, I thought..."

"Ah, you came for gold, not bronze." She nodded in agreement. "That would be disappointing."

Marcus shook his head. "Truly, I appreciate this. It's most generous, and I feel inept, having to explain myself." He ended, the sudden silence uncomfortable again. Casting about for something more to say, he managed, "This is a pleasant place, this garden. It reminds me of home."

"How much?" she asked, pointedly directing him back to the issue.

The frankness of her question surprised him. "A hefty sum. Two thousand talents."

Cleopatra tilted her head back, studying him. "Marcus Antonius, forgive my prying, but was that amount supposed to be payment for restoring a king to his throne?"

"Yes," he admitted. "It was the sum agreed upon." Gods, she was perceptive!

She walked toward a fruit tree, her manicured fingers lightly caressing the natural grooves in the bark. "Now I understand. Either

Father or Gabinius promised the said amount. While you're waiting, Rabirius is squeezing it out of the people. Father's playing difficult, refusing to pay out of his own purse, and Gabinius is unable to give you anything. Am I correct?"

Immortal gods! She was more than perceptive. She was a female Caesar! "That pretty much explains it, yes." He waved the subject off. "No matter. I still leave a richer man." A partial lie, but she needn't know all his troubles: Fadia gone forever, Callias awaiting him. "Over these past three—four years, I know what I am now. And that, at least, is a comfort and reward of sorts." He stopped, running one hand through his hair. Why was he telling her all this?

Cleopatra came to his aid, changing subjects smoothly. "You mentioned these gardens. They are beautiful. Someday, when I'm queen, I'm going to build here. It's peaceful near the harbor, is it not? A perfect place for another temple, I think."

"For which god?"

"I'm not sure. Isis is my patroness, but I think I'll wait and determine who to honor once my reign begins. All monarchs have building projects. There will be much to do. Egypt will flourish because I'll honor her traditional gods."

"I see. Will it look Egyptian, like this temple?"

Cleopatra smiled, the sight of her dimples warming him. "No, a composite of styles, I think. A little Greek, a little Egyptian..."

"Like the rest of the city, then?"

"Yes. Structures should blend with their surroundings, acquiring a semblance of harmony."

"For an Egyptian, that's a very Greek concept."

"But I am Greek. Remember that my ancestors come from Alexander's line. That's how our city got its name."

"I like Alexandria. Clean, beautiful, cool breezes."

"I would probably think Rome's climate too cold."

"Sometimes in the winter, yes."

Momentarily, she dropped her guard. Pure, girlish curiosity bled through. "Does it ever snow? I've never seen snow."

Marcus leaned back against a tree, watching her and liking very much what he saw. "You should visit and find out."

Demurely, she fondled the pearls at her throat. "I'll do that, Commander. Someday I'll surprise you and visit Rome."

Marcus was surprising himself. He hadn't enjoyed conversation with a woman this much since—

"Yet now I must apologize," she said, interrupting his thought.

"For what? You've just given me an incomparable gift."

"My father is not always wise in his judgment or financial dealings. If I had access to his gold, I would pay you myself."

"Please, don't—"

"No. Listen to me," she insisted. "You've rendered to me the greatest possible service, placing him back on the throne. I'll never forget what you've done. It wasn't the proconsul's name hailed in the streets. It was yours. The people knew their true hero."

Unbelievably, she reached out, placing her hand on his. Marcus froze.

"My gift today seems paltry in place of what is owed you," she said. "Again, you must accept my deepest apologies, Commander."

"Of course."

"Now I must go," she said, removing her hand from his. "Father thinks I've come here to sacrifice. He's most watchful over me." Before leaving, she paused. "Antonius, you're a rising officer amid Rome's ranks. I need the skills and courage of men who may be mere officers today but will be tomorrow's consuls and kings. Might I depend on you to be a champion for Egypt, protecting her independence?"

Stunned once again at her directness, Marcus pondered an answer, crossing in front of her to the shade's edge, and looking out to sea. A small skiff unfurled a sail, skimming calm waters in the harbor with effortless grace.

"Princess, I've no power in the Senate. But if I ever come to that point in my life, I'll try to maintain Egypt as a friend and ally."

She gave him the brightest of smiles, tilting her head to one side, studying him. "Then let us hope our friendship is long-lasting. I will pray this cuirass always protects you against enemies intending harm."

She hesitated, glancing back, her smile and dimples both girlish and desirable. Politely inclining her head, she left through the corridor, traces of lotus oil lingering in the air.

Marcus stood where she left him. Etesian winds tousled his hair and carried away the last of her scent. Venus! Now he hardly wished to go. He wanted to follow her, to stay in her company, share her laughter.

But there were wars to fight in other lands.

Far, far against the Great Sea's horizon was even more blue in the beyond. And even past that. Marcus believed his next destination was Gallia Comata—Long-Haired Gaul. There, upon more battlefields, he'd need to prove himself worthy of higher command. He'd earned Gabinius's trust. Now he'd have to earn Caesar's.

Marcus picked up his new cuirass. The Nemean lion glared at him with blazing eyes, its mouth open in a savage roar. He'd wear it home to Rome. He'd wear it proudly in battles to come. Oh, there were many things of which Marcus was uncertain, but he was sure his battles were not over.

There would be wars ahead. And he would be victorious.

AUTHOR'S NOTES

THERE ARE SO MANY PEOPLE TO WHOM I OWE THANKS, but naturally, a few names stand out. First and foremost, my love and heartfelt thanks to my husband, Carlton. He has endured fifteen years of living with Marcus Antonius *and* me. Historical Editorial's founding editor, Jennifer Quinlin is incredible. Jenny, thank you for putting up with endless emails, long phone calls, and my adverbs. Your cover design nearly made me cry—for all the right reasons! Tamian Wood and Beyond Design International helped develop a charming map of the Roman Forum, complete with umbrella pines, no less! Bestselling author Margaret George has been a dear friend. She has been an inspiration, giving sound suggestions and encouragement. Silvia Prosperi's guide services, *A Friend in Rome*, helped me access archaeological sites that are closed to the public. Her help in getting me into these amazing treasures helped me to vividly visualize Marcus's Rome. Gordana Mourouzi has shown me important sites for my upcoming books and also assisted with fine-tuning Marcus's search for a tutor in first-century BC Athens, informing me about the "ecclesia" and the Theater of Dionysius. During my time in Egypt, Salwa Abdel Meguid was my phenomenal guide in Alexandria. Thank you for being bold and traveling with me, my friend! Also, I cannot forget my generous colleague Stephanie Harman. Her gift of photography has added a final elegant polish to this book.

Ever since I was a sophomore in high school and first read Shakespeare's *Julius Caesar*, I've wanted to write on late Republican Rome. For years, I never thought I had the life experiences or knowledge to make this dream a reality. I selected Marc Antony's life because he was controversial, had an exciting military career, and was full of human foibles. In short, a delightful character to portray!

One of the craziest things one encounters when writing on the Roman period is the dilemma of *names*. Romans weren't very imaginative, using identical familial names again and again. Multiple children in a household often had the exact same praenomen (first name), and there are only around seventeen known praenomina. It must have been *beyond* confusing! I have done my best to skirt around repetitive names of different characters, and occasionally that meant leaving someone's son or family member out completely. I felt it was better to omit than to confuse. Desirous that this book reflect the realities of the Roman world, mindset, and customs, I chose to use Marc Antony's Roman name: Marcus Antonius.

A great deal of *Son of Rome* takes place in Rome itself—and much of it is within the four walls of the domus Antonii. Nobody knows exactly where Marcus's home was, though we do know he lived on the Palatine in his early years. In fact, the only domus location of which we can be certain is that of the Hortensius family, which later became the domus Augustus. Any other character's home location on the Palatine was purely my own invention. (See map.)

When visualizing late Republican Rome, one must really strip down today's extant buildings to imagine what the city looked like. Very few buildings from the first century BC remain. The Tullianum prison (now called the Mamertine) still exists, but not in the building form it did during Marcus's lifetime. The only entrance accessible to visitors today is through the Church of San Giuseppe dei Falegnami. The "hole" through which Lentulus once descended is usually the only access for visitors, who don't use ladders anymore, but stairs. Lentulus's name can still be read on the list of doomed prisoners who faced their grisly fates within.

The Tabularium was begun under Sulla's leadership. Though long considered to be a public records building, modern scholars still argue its designated purpose. Clearly, because of its location on/around the Capitolium, it was an important building both politically and spiritually for the Romans. For my story, I chose it as the location for Fadia's manumission. However, manumissions may have taken place in other locations, as there were various methods for freeing slaves. Visiting the Tabularium is a *must* if you go to Rome, and it's now actually a part of the Capitoline Museum. It's one of the best places to take a picture of the length of the Forum Romanum—and indeed, it is most likely one of the few places in Rome where someone can walk down the exact corridors that Marcus, Cicero, and Caesar once trod.

Only one ancient city is more difficult than Rome to visualize in its early state: Alexandria, Egypt. So much of "Alex" still needs to be excavated, but due to modern-era buildings, much of the ancient city remains buried and uncharted. Due to several earthquakes and a tsunami in antiquity, most of the places that Marcus would have been associated with are now underwater. The Great Harbor has been the focus of several underwater archaeological expeditions over the past several decades. Fortunately, that has at least allowed for the mapping of the ancient city's coastline, versus the existing one.

One naturally wonders what Marcus's early relationship with Caesar was like. I confess that I used the stereotypical extended Italian family as a model! Marcus and Caesar were "distant" cousins, but it appears that their blood-bond was still influential. And Plutarch's mention of Caesar's support in sending Marcus to Athens early in his career bolsters this. Coming from a Southern family, I was quite close to some of my own extended cousins, so using such a relationship between Marcus and Caesar in my story is quite plausible, I think.

In his *Philippics*, Cicero made much of a possible homosexual scandal between Marcus Antonius and Curio. Plutarch's account acknowledges Marcus's "shady" dealings with him, but doesn't blatantly expose the nature of their relationship as homosexual. Whether this was another of Cicero's attempts to simply heap more coals over Marcus's head is unknown. However, there is no other mention of Marcus Antonius ever having a male lover during the remainder of his life.

Again, it's from Cicero where we also hear of Fadia. Yet aside from the mention of her name and that of her father, we know little about her. Whether she actually gave Marcus children, as Cicero stated in his *Philippics*, is unknown. If so, he claimed they were all dead by the time Caesar was assassinated in 44 BC. Her status as a slave within the domus Antonii is certainly possible but has no historical origin.

Since we know so little about Marcus Antonius's early life, I naturally resourced historical events we do know about that occurred during this time span. Hopefully, it helped weave a more "complete" story of his possible activities. Several sources were especially helpful: Eleanor Goltz Huzar's scholarly *Mark Antony: A Biography* (1978), but especially Patricia Southern's *Mark Antony: A Life* (2005). Southern's work really aided me in understanding the bleak, unforgiving world in which Marcus and his family lived. *Josephus: The Complete Works* was my main source for Marcus's early career regarding his service under Gabinius's command.

One thing is clear: Marcus Antonius's formative years were filled with violence, political strife, and civil conflict. Life in late Republican Rome was not easy, even for a young man of noble birth, such as he was. By filling in the gaps of his tempestuous early years, it becomes easier to comprehend the sort of man he came to be later in life.

Be on the lookout for Brook Allen's forthcoming novel,

SECOND IN COMMAND

the next book in the *Antonius* trilogy.

CPSIA information can be obtained
at www.ICGtesting.com
Printed in the USA
FFHW021655180319
51126445-56572FF